THE

LAST

SUMMER

I

LIVED

KATHY WINSLOWER

DEDICATION

*For those who have loved, lost, and found their
way back to themselves—this story is for you.*

CONTENTS

CHAPTER 1: THE LAST ARRIVAL

The black SUV coasted slowly down the winding driveway of the Hampton estate, the gravel crunching rhythmically beneath its tires. Caleb Morgan sat in the backseat, staring out of the window with an expression of hollow sadness. The sun, setting in a golden blaze, painted the landscape in warm hues, but to Caleb, it felt like a cruel reminder of the emptiness he carried inside.

He glanced down at the urn in his lap, its dark surface reflecting the sun's last rays like a dull mirror. Inside it was Milo's ashes, his faithful dog who had been more than just a pet—Milo had been Caleb's silent confidant, his anchor in a world that often felt unsteady. Now, that anchor was gone, and the void left behind was enormous, a chasm Caleb wasn't sure he'd ever be able to bridge.

The city lights of New York had faded in the rearview mirror, and with them, the relentless pace and harsh reality of his life had slipped away. The transition from the bustling streets of the city to the serene, sprawling countryside of the Hamptons was stark. Caleb felt as if he were moving from one world to another, each mile making the loss of Milo feel more profound.

He looked out at the rolling fields and distant forests, the colors blending into a tranquil tapestry of greens and golds. The scenery was meant to be soothing, a balm for his raw emotions, but all Caleb could think about was how different everything was now. The quiet beauty of the countryside did little to calm the storm raging inside him.

In the front seat, his parents sat in their own bubble of strained silence. His father, Senator Thomas Morgan, had his eyes fixed on the road, his jaw set in a tight line of concentration. Caleb could feel the weight of unspoken words and unresolved issues between them. Their relationship had always been distant, marked by expectations and disappointment, but Milo's death had deepened the rift.

Next to Thomas, Evelyn Morgan sat with her hands clasped tightly in her lap, her gaze occasionally drifting towards Caleb through the rearview mirror. Her eyes, though warm, were clouded with concern and an almost helpless worry. Evelyn had always tried to protect Caleb, but she had been unable to shield him from this grief. She was caught in a delicate balance— trying to be a mother who understood but also feeling helpless in the face of Caleb's overwhelming sorrow.

The SUV continued its journey, each turn in the road revealing new aspects of the sprawling estate that awaited them. Caleb could see the outline of the mansion in the distance, its grandeur a stark contrast to the simplicity of the life he had left behind in New York. The estate, with its manicured lawns and distant ocean views, seemed to stand as a testament to the life his family had built—one that Caleb felt increasingly disconnected from.

As the car approached the estate's entrance, Caleb closed his eyes for a moment, trying to shut out the flood of emotions threatening to overwhelm him. He thought of Milo's loyal eyes, the way his tail wagged so eagerly every time Caleb walked through the door. He thought about how that simple, unwavering companionship had been taken from him, leaving behind a gaping hole.

When Caleb finally opened his eyes, the car had come to a halt, and the sprawling grandeur of the estate stretched out before him. The sun was casting its golden light over everything, but Caleb couldn't shake the heaviness that pressed on his shoulders, the weight of the urn in his lap only adding to his burden. This summer was supposed to be a chance for family healing, but it felt more like a battlefield of unresolved pain and expectations he wasn't sure he could meet.

And as the vehicle came to a stop, Caleb's father, Senator Thomas Morgan, stepped out with his usual air of practiced composure. His impeccably tailored suit and the gleaming watch on his wrist seemed to contrast sharply with Caleb's own sense of disarray, a reflection of the turmoil he'd been feeling since Milo's death. Thomas's face was a mask of detachment, his eyes scanning the estate with a cold, almost indifferent appreciation. It was as if he were gearing up for another day in the world of politics rather than bracing himself for the emotional storm brewing within their family.

On the other side of the car, Evelyn Morgan, Caleb's mother, stepped out with a softer demeanor. Her eyes softened as they took in the grand estate, a place that was meant to be a haven of sorts. Yet, to Caleb, it felt like a gilded cage, where the memories of Milo were overshadowed by the relentless expectations his parents had always placed on him.

The air was filled with the mingling scents of saltwater and sun-warmed sand, a subtle hint of cedar drifting from the towering trees that lined the estate. Caleb could hear the distant crash of waves against the shore, their rhythmic pounding a bittersweet reminder of the simpler times he'd shared with Milo. As he stepped out of the SUV, he felt the sun's warmth on his face. It was a warmth that felt almost mocking, a stark contrast to the cold, aching void inside him.

The estate loomed before him, a grand structure with whitewashed walls and sweeping ocean views that were meant to inspire tranquility. Instead, it felt like a backdrop to his grief, a place where every corner and every vista only highlighted what he had lost and what he was expected to endure. Caleb took a deep breath, trying to steady himself as he prepared to face the summer that lay ahead, knowing that this season of family togetherness was as much about confronting old wounds as it was about finding any semblance of peace.

Mr. Hayes stood at the entrance of the estate, his presence a calming fixture amid the grandeur of the mansion. His gray hair was neatly combed, and there was a quiet wisdom in his eyes, born from years of witnessing the ebb and flow of the Morgan family's lives.

"Welcome back, Senator, Mrs. Morgan," Mr. Hayes greeted with a voice that was both warm and steady. "And you too, Master Caleb."

Caleb's response was a nod, his throat tightening as he struggled to keep his composure. "Thank you, Mr. Hayes," he managed to say, his voice wavering slightly. His grip on the urn tightened, the weight of it a constant reminder of the loss that seemed to shadow him wherever he went.

Senator Thomas Morgan observed his son with a mix of detachment and unspoken frustration. He had always prided himself on his discipline and control, qualities that had brought him success in politics but had done little to bridge the growing divide between him and Caleb. The Senator's own battle with alcohol had cast a long, silent shadow over their relationship— a chasm he hoped this summer might somehow bridge, though he wasn't sure where to begin.

Evelyn Morgan stood beside her husband, her expression a blend of concern and resignation. She watched Caleb, her heart aching at the sight of her son's struggle. Her attempts to nurture and protect him often felt like a balancing act, caught between her desire to shield him from pain and her need to hold the family together.

The estate, with its sprawling lawns and stately architecture, felt like a stage set for a drama that Caleb had never fully wanted to be a part of. As he looked around, he could almost hear the echoes of past summers, where family gatherings had been filled with laughter and love. Now, the same spaces seemed to hold only shadows of what had been, and the promise of a summer that was supposed to heal felt more like a reminder of everything that had gone wrong.

Mr. Hayes's gaze lingered on Caleb, a silent acknowledgment of the young man's internal battles. The caretaker had seen the strain in the Morgan family before—seen how they tried to mask their struggles with polished smiles and carefully crafted appearances.

He knew that healing wasn't as simple as a change of scenery or a few well-placed words. It required something deeper, something more elusive.

As Caleb stepped past Mr. Hayes and into the estate, he could feel the weight of the urn in his hands, a tangible representation of his grief. Each step he took seemed to echo with the unspoken conflicts and unresolved emotions that had been building for years. He hoped that this summer would bring some form of resolution, but as he glanced at his father's stern face and his mother's anxious eyes, he wasn't sure how—or if—things could ever be the same again.

As Caleb stepped inside, the cool air of the house hit him like a sudden embrace. It was a welcome contrast to the sweltering heat outside but also a stark reminder of the contrast between the serenity of the surroundings and the chaos within him. The aroma of polished wood and fresh flowers lingered, a cruel reminder of the perfect image his family was desperate to uphold. The walls, adorned with family portraits and picturesque landscapes, felt foreign to Caleb, who was too wrapped up in his grief to appreciate their beauty.

He glanced over at his parents. His father, Senator Thomas Morgan, maintained his usual facade of composed elegance, while his mother, Evelyn, tried to mask her own worry behind a forced smile. Both were wrapped in the trappings of their privileged lives, unable to see the emotional chasm growing between them and their son. Caleb's gaze then shifted to Mr. Hayes, the estate's caretaker, whose quiet presence offered the only genuine solace he felt.

Caleb knew this summer would be a turning point. It was a chance to confront not just the grief of losing Milo but also the chasms that had widened within his family. The high expectations his parents had for him, the unspoken tensions, and the overwhelming weight of their collective pain all seemed to converge in this one season. He felt as though he were standing on the precipice of a major shift, unsure if he was ready to face the changes that were bound to come.

Thomas followed Caleb and Evelyn inside the house, glancing around at the meticulously kept gardens and the impressive grandeur of the estate. The contrast between the serene beauty of the surroundings and the storm brewing within his family was almost jarring. His mind buzzed with thoughts of political commitments and deadlines, a world that felt increasingly distant from the personal turmoil Caleb was facing.

Evelyn, her heart heavy with a mix of worry and helplessness, watched her son. She had always been the one to mend wounds and offer comfort, but now, it seemed like her constant hovering had only pushed

Caleb further away. She understood that Caleb's grief was deep, but the tangled dynamics of their family left her struggling to find the right way to reach him.

She placed a gentle hand on Caleb's shoulder, trying to convey a sense of warmth and support. "Let's get settled in," she said softly, her voice trembling with quiet concern. Evelyn's own sorrow was intertwined with a deep sense of helplessness; she wanted to make things right, to mend the rift between them, but it felt like she was fighting against an unyielding current.

As they moved further into the house, the grand halls and elegant decor seemed almost to mock their inner struggles. The estate, with its polished surfaces and grand rooms, was meant to be a refuge, but it now felt like a stage for their unresolved pain. Evelyn longed to turn back time, to ease Caleb's heartache and restore their fractured family, but the path forward seemed obscured by the shadows of past mistakes and unspoken fears.

Thomas, his face a mask of stoic determination, struggled to reconcile his professional responsibilities with the personal crisis unfolding before him. The estate, with all its opulence, felt increasingly like a prison, its walls a stark reminder of the emotional distance that had grown between him and his son. He wished he could find a way to bridge the gap, to reach out to Caleb in a way that mattered, but the weight of his own regrets and failures felt like a barrier he couldn't overcome.

Evelyn's touch lingered on Caleb's shoulder, a small gesture that carried all the love and concern she felt. She watched him with a mixture of hope and despair, praying that this summer would offer them a chance to heal and reconnect. In the quiet moments that followed, the house seemed to hold its breath, waiting for the next chapter in their lives to unfold.

The old Mr. Hayes moved quietly through the house, retrieving the luggage from the car and carrying it into the grand foyer. The estate, though beautiful, seemed to loom over him, heavy with unspoken tensions. Once the bags were appropriately stashed away inside the bedrooms, he made his way to the kitchen, the aroma of simmering spices and fresh herbs greeted him—a comforting contrast to the storm of emotions brewing among the Morgans.

Evelyn Morgan stood in the kitchen, the rhythmic chopping of vegetables providing a soothing counterpoint to the whirlwind of emotions inside her. The room was filled with the warm aroma of garlic and onions sautéing in olive oil, mingling with the faint scent of fresh herbs from the garden. She moved with a practiced grace, peeling carrots and dicing potatoes, her mind preoccupied with thoughts of her son and the strained family dynamics that had brought them to this estate.

Mr. Hayes entered the kitchen, his steps soft on the tiled floor. He glanced around at the neatly arranged countertops and the gleaming appliances, taking in the homey yet elegant atmosphere Evelyn had created. "Everything looks wonderful, Mrs. Morgan," he said, his voice carrying a note of genuine admiration. "The kitchen is always my favorite part of the house. It's where the real magic happens."

Evelyn smiled faintly, her eyes not quite meeting his. "Thank you, Mr. Hayes. It's nice to hear that. I've always believed that food has a way of bringing people together, even when everything else seems to be falling apart."

Mr. Hayes nodded, his gaze lingering on the bubbling pot of stew on the stove. "It's true. This estate might be grand, but it's the little things that make it a home. The gardens, the kitchen… they all tell a story of comfort and care."

Evelyn stirred the stew, the rich aroma of chicken and vegetables filling the room. She added a sprig of rosemary and a pinch of salt, savoring the simple act of cooking. "This estate has been in my husband's family for generations," she said softly, her voice tinged with nostalgia. "We used to spend every summer here when

Caleb was younger. It was a place of laughter and joy. I had hoped it would be a refuge for us now, but it feels more like a reminder of what we've lost."

Mr. Hayes placed a hand on the counter, his eyes reflecting a quiet understanding. "Sometimes, places carry more than just memories—they carry the weight of our hopes and regrets. This estate has seen many seasons, and it's always had a way of holding on to the past, even as life moves forward."

Evelyn's eyes grew distant as she glanced out the window, where the sun was setting over the manicured lawns and the distant ocean. The sky was a canvas of oranges and pinks, a beautiful yet poignant backdrop to the evening. "Caleb's been having a hard time adjusting," she admitted, her voice barely above a whisper. "He's been distant, and I can't help but feel like I've failed him somehow."

Mr. Hayes gave her a reassuring smile. "It's not easy, dealing with a teenager. But sometimes, it's the simple things—like a warm meal and a quiet conversation— that help bridge those gaps."

Evelyn nodded, feeling a flicker of hope amidst her worry. With a deep breath, she looked around the kitchen, feeling a mixture of sadness and hope. She hoped that this meal, this simple act of sharing food and conversation, might be the first step toward healing the rifts within her family.

She turned towards Mr. Hayes, offering a weary smile. "Mr. Hayes," she said softly. "I hope you're not too tired to help me set the table."

"Not at all, Mrs. Morgan," he replied, his voice steady and warm.

Together, they set the table in the dining room, the clink of porcelain and silverware filling the silence between them. Evelyn glanced occasionally at Mr. Hayes, grateful for the quiet support he provided.

The table was adorned with crisp white linen, gleaming silverware, and flickering candles that cast a soft, comforting glow. The sight of it was a small consolation, a reminder that even in the midst of turmoil, there was still room for warmth and connection.

As she placed the final dish on the table, she glanced at Mr. Hayes, who was quietly arranging the glasses. "Thank you for your help tonight. It means a lot to have you here."

Mr. Hayes nodded, his gaze kind. "It's my pleasure, Mrs. Morgan."

It wasn't long before sunset when the Morgans gathered around the dining table. The flickering candlelight added a gentle glow to the evening, though it did little to dispel the heaviness that seemed to hang in the air.

As they sat down to dinner, the warm glow of the candles cast a gentle light over the table, flickering softly against the backdrop of their summer retreat. The aroma of Evelyn's cooking filled the room—her famous roasted chicken and fresh vegetables, the kind of comforting meal that promised solace and familiarity.

Thomas Morgan, ever the politician even in these rare moments of family togetherness, had just picked up his fork when his phone buzzed insistently on the table. He glanced at the screen and saw his campaign manager's name flashing in bold letters. With a sigh, Thomas excused himself from the table and stepped away, his voice low but firm as he spoke into the phone.

"I need you to make sure everything's under control," he said, his tone leaving no room for argument. "I'm with my family for the summer. No distractions, no interruptions. This is important to me."

As he hung up, he glanced back toward the dining room, catching a glimpse of Evelyn's hopeful eyes. She sat there, her expression a mixture of pride and concern, silently cheering for the small victory of having her husband home, even if only for a short time.

Returning to the table, Thomas plastered on a smile and took his seat. He looked around, trying to focus on the positive. "Evelyn, this meal is incredible," he said, his voice warm and genuine. "You've outdone yourself."

Evelyn's face lit up with a soft smile, her eyes sparkling with gratitude. "Thank you, Thomas. I'm glad you like it."

Caleb, sitting at the end of the table, fiddled with his food absentmindedly. He pushed the vegetables around his plate, his expression far from impressed. The forced cheerfulness in his father's voice seemed to make the gap between them even wider. Caleb felt the emptiness of the house, the grandeur of the estate, and the hollowness of their family dinners more acutely in that moment.

Thomas's gaze flickered to his son, and he noticed Caleb's lack of enthusiasm. His heart ached with the realization that no amount of praise or effort could bridge the gap that had formed between them. Still, he tried to maintain the pretense of normalcy, hoping that the summer might somehow mend the wounds that felt too deep to heal.

As they continued to eat in strained silence, the warmth of the meal and the beauty of the setting seemed to clash with the underlying tension in the room. The summer ahead held the promise of change, but for now, it felt like a delicate facade, with each family member grappling with their own struggles and unspoken words.

In the dim light, surrounded by the scents of home and the remnants of a family dinner, the Morgans were left to face their own silent battles, hoping for a chance to rediscover what they had lost and to find solace in the simple act of being together.

Thomas Morgan, his face a mask of practiced composure, cleared his throat as he stood to make a toast. His voice was steady but lacked warmth. "I'd like to propose a toast," he began, holding up his glass. "To new beginnings and the hope that this summer will bring us closer together."

Caleb, sitting at the far end of the table, felt a tightness in his chest. He had been struggling to keep his emotions in check all evening, but the weight of his grief was becoming unbearable. As his father's words hung in the air, Caleb felt a tear escape down his cheek. He tried to blink it away, but it was no use.

He stood abruptly, his chair scraping against the floor, and without a word, he excused himself from the table. The room fell silent, the Morgans' gazes lingering on the empty chair he had just left behind. Evelyn's eyes were filled with concern, but she said nothing, sensing that this was something Caleb needed to face alone.

Caleb retreated to his bedroom, the familiar surroundings of the Hamptons estate offering him no comfort. He closed the door behind him and sat down heavily on the edge of his bed. The room was dark, save for the soft glow of his phone screen as he pulled up pictures and videos of Milo. Each image was a reminder of the loyalty and love he had lost, each video a snapshot of better times.

He let the tears flow freely, his shoulders shaking with the weight of his sorrow. His resentment toward his father, who seemed so distant and out of touch with his pain, was a bitter undercurrent to his grief. Caleb felt a deep-seated anger that his father's attempts at normalcy and new beginnings felt so hollow in the face of his loss.

He clutched his phone, looking at a video of Milo's playful antics and he couldn't help but feel that the warm, sunny Hamptons was a world apart from the reality of his heartache. The room, with its soft furnishings and distant ocean view, seemed to mock his misery. Yet, amidst the tears and frustration, there was a glimmer of hope—a faint belief that perhaps, in the coming days, there might be a chance for understanding and healing, even if it seemed like a distant dream.

CHAPTER 2: THE LAST GOODBYE

The nightmare always began the same way. It was a rainy night, the kind of rain that slashed through the darkness, making everything slick and dangerous. Caleb stood at the front door, calling Milo's name, but his dog's frantic barking was already fading into the distance. Panic surged through him as he sprinted out into the storm, the cold rain pelting his skin, soaking through his clothes.

"Milo!" Caleb screamed, his voice lost in the roar of the downpour. He could barely see a few feet in front of him, but he caught a glimpse of Milo, a dark blur against the wet pavement, darting into the street.

Time seemed to slow as headlights appeared, the bright beams cutting through the rain. Caleb's heart leapt into his throat as he watched, helpless, as Milo ran directly into the car's path. There was a sickening thud, and then everything went silent.

Caleb jolted awake, his heart pounding in his chest, the remnants of his nightmare clinging to his mind. He could still see Milo, his beloved dog, lifeless on the wet pavement, the image seared into his memory. Sweat soaked his sheets, and his breathing came in ragged gasps.

The Hamptons' summer home, usually a place of solace, felt like a prison.

His bedroom was a mix of old memories and new pain. The walls were lined with shelves of books he'd loved as a child, their spines worn from the countless nights of reading under the covers. A framed photograph of him and Milo sat on his bedside table, taken on a sunny day at the park, both of them smiling, oblivious to the heartbreak that would come.

Caleb's bed, with its familiar quilt, had always been a comfort, but now it felt suffocating. Posters of his favorite bands from his teenage years adorned the walls, and a model airplane, a gift from his father, hung from the ceiling. Each item was a reminder of the boy he used to be, the boy who had dreamed of adventure and freedom, not the young man weighed down by grief and expectations.

The storm outside mirrored Caleb's inner turmoil. Dark clouds loomed overhead, and the wind howled through the trees, rattling the windows. Rain lashed against the panes, a relentless reminder of his grief and isolation. He sat up in bed, wiping the sweat from his forehead, and tried to steady his racing thoughts.

He pushed the covers off and swung his legs over the side of the bed, his feet hitting the cold floor. The room was dark, the only light coming from the faint glow of his alarm clock. He stood up and walked to the window, pressing his forehead against the cool glass. Outside, the storm had passed, leaving the world fresh and glistening under the early morning light.

Caleb's heart ached with a grief that seemed to have no end. Losing Milo had been like losing a part of himself. The dog had been his confidant, his companion, the one constant in a world that often felt overwhelming. Now, without Milo, the void was immense.

Downstairs, Evelyn stood by the kitchen window, her gaze fixed on the stormy sky outside. The rain hammered against the panes with a relentless rhythm, mirroring the turmoil inside her heart. She couldn't shake the worry gnawing at her, the concern for Caleb who seemed to be struggling more with every passing day. The shadows of grief from Milo's death loomed large, and the weight of her husband's expectations only seemed to deepen Caleb's pain. Evelyn knew her son needed more than just time; he needed understanding, compassion, and a space to grieve without the constant pressure to be strong.

She sighed softly, her breath fogging up the glass as she turned away from the storm. At the stove, she focused on the comforting sizzle of bacon in the pan. The smell of it filled the kitchen, a simple but sincere gesture of care. She hoped that the warmth and aroma of a home-cooked meal might offer Caleb some small measure of comfort, a fleeting escape from the heaviness he carried.

In the dining room, Thomas Morgan sat alone, his thoughts swirling with the weight of the day. The storm outside seemed to echo the storm within him. He glanced at the family photos on the wall—images of happier times, of a younger Caleb with a bright smile and Milo at his side. Each picture was a reminder of the bond that had frayed and the expectations that had become burdens.

Thomas's mind wandered to the countless hours he'd spent trying to make sense of his own life. The pressure of his political career, the constant juggling of public image and personal disappointment—it all seemed to converge into a single, overwhelming reality. His relationship with Caleb had always been strained, clouded by his own struggles with alcohol and the emotional distance he maintained as a shield. He wished he could find a way to bridge that gap, but he wasn't sure how.

He ran a hand through his hair, feeling the sting of regret for the missed opportunities and the hurt he'd caused. His attempts at forming a toast for new beginnings felt hollow, his heart heavy with the knowledge that words alone couldn't mend the rifts within his family. He wanted to offer Caleb a sense of renewal, but it seemed like an impossible task when his own actions had contributed so much to the pain.

When Evelyn returned to the dining room, she could see the strain in Thomas's posture, the tightness in his shoulders. She approached him with a gentle touch on his arm. "Breakfast is almost ready," she said softly, her voice filled with a mix of hope and resignation. "Let's try to make today a little better, for Caleb's sake."

Thomas looked at her, his eyes reflecting a weary resolve. "I want to help," he said quietly, "but I'm not sure where to start. I know I've made things harder."

Evelyn nodded, her own eyes welling with unshed tears. "We're all doing our best, even if it doesn't always seem like enough. We need to be patient with Caleb and with each other. This summer might not fix everything, but it's a chance to start over."

Upstairs, Caleb lay wide awake in bed, staring at the ceiling as the early morning light filtered through the curtains. The remnants of the nightmare clung to him like a second skin, the images of Milo's final moments replaying in his mind with an unsettling clarity. The storm brewing outside mirrored the turmoil inside him—dark clouds gathered on the horizon, and the distant rumble of thunder seemed to echo his own internal storm.

As the wind picked up, rattling the windowpanes and sending occasional raindrops splattering against the glass, Caleb's thoughts churned with a mixture of frustration and sorrow. He felt trapped in a suffocating void, where the normal rhythms of life had been replaced by an oppressive grief that refused to lift. The storm outside seemed to be a physical manifestation of his emotional state—a tempest that grew more intense with each passing moment.

He rolled onto his side, trying to find a more comfortable position, but the weight of the night's dreams pressed heavily on him. The flashes of lightning illuminated the room intermittently, casting fleeting shadows that danced across the walls, like specters of his past haunting him. Each crack of thunder felt like a jolt through his very core, a reminder of the thunderous void left by Milo's absence.

With a sigh, Caleb reached for his phone on the bedside table. His hands were cold and clammy as he unlocked the screen, hoping to find some distraction from the turmoil within. But the sight of his social media feed only deepened his sense of isolation. His friends' posts from exotic locales and carefree adventures felt like a stark contrast to his own stagnant, grief-stricken reality. Each image was a painful reminder of the life he was missing out on, and the storm outside seemed to add to the sense of being cut off from the world.

Caleb's finger hovered over the search bar as he impulsively typed "How to end your life." The instant he pressed search, his screen was bombarded with an overwhelming array of crisis resources—hotline numbers, chatlines, and ads for mental health services. The sheer volume of responses was disorienting, a torrent of lifelines that seemed both distant and unreachable.

As he scrolled through the options, tears welled up in his eyes. The storm outside intensified, the wind howling and the rain pounding against the windows, as if nature itself was crying with him. Caleb felt a mix of despair and confusion, unable to decide what to do next. The sight of the emergency contact numbers felt like a cruel joke—an endless list of possibilities that seemed both too distant and too close to grasp.

He tossed the phone aside, the soft thud barely audible over the roar of the storm. Caleb pulled the covers up to his chin, trying to find some comfort in their warmth, but the storm raged on outside and within him. He lay there, listening to the relentless drumming of the rain and the rumbling thunder, feeling more isolated than ever. But a gentle knock on his bedroom door pulled him from his thoughts.

"Caleb, sweetheart, breakfast is ready," his mother called softly from the hallway.

He sighed, sitting up and running a hand through his tousled hair. "Coming, Mom."

Slipping into a pair of flannel pajama pants and a faded t-shirt, Caleb made his way downstairs. The house was quiet, save for the soft hum of the rain against the windows. The scent of bacon and eggs wafted through the air, mingling with the aroma of fresh coffee, but it did little to lift his spirits.

In the dining room, his parents were already seated at the table, both dressed in their own comfortable pajamas. His father, Senator Thomas Morgan, wore a navy blue robe over striped pajamas, looking more relaxed than usual. His mother, Evelyn, was in a floral nightgown with a cozy cardigan, her hair pulled back in a loose ponytail. Their good spirits seemed almost at odds with the gray, stormy morning.

"Morning, Caleb," his father greeted him with a rare smile. "Sleep well?"

Caleb nodded, forcing a smile. "Yeah, fine."

"Have a seat, darling," Evelyn said, gesturing to the spot beside her. "I made your favorite—bacon and eggs."

Caleb sat down, mechanically reaching for the food. The warmth and familiarity of his mother's cooking was comforting, but it couldn't chase away the heaviness in his heart. He picked at his plate, barely noticing the flavors.

The bacon, crispy and golden, was more than just food; it was a symbol of Evelyn's love, her desire to offer comfort in the midst of their struggles. The storm outside continued to rage, but within the walls of their home, there was a flicker of warmth and a quiet promise of healing, however slow and uncertain it might be.

Thomas glanced out the window, frowning at the downpour. "Looks like the beach is off the table for today," he said, trying to keep his tone light. "Maybe we can stay in and enjoy some family time instead."

Evelyn placed a reassuring hand on her husband's arm. "We'll make the most of it. We can play some board games or watch a movie. It'll be nice to just relax together."

Caleb nodded absently, pushing his food around his plate. The idea of spending the day indoors, surrounded by the ghosts of his memories, felt suffocating. He excused himself from the table, mumbling something about needing some fresh air, and wandered through the mansion, each room echoing with reminders of his past.

Each room was filled with memories of happier times. The grand hallways echoed with the laughter of his childhood, the days when Milo would chase him through the house, his loyal companion always by his side. He could almost hear Milo's paws skittering on the polished floors, see the blur of his tail wagging furiously as they played their endless games of fetch.

Caleb's footsteps echoed softly in the quiet mansion, the familiar creak of the floorboards underfoot bringing a bittersweet comfort. He paused in front of a large window, gazing out at the rain-soaked garden. The vibrant flowers and meticulously trimmed hedges seemed to mock his mood, a stark contrast to the storm brewing inside him.

As he walked, Caleb felt the weight of his secret pressing down on him. It was more than just the loss of Milo that haunted him—it was the expectations of his father, the constant pressure to live up to the Morgan name, and the deep, dark thoughts that had been consuming him. His father, Senator Thomas Morgan, was a man of discipline and control, traits that had served him well in politics but had created a chasm between him and Caleb. The senator's disappointment was palpable, a constant reminder that Caleb wasn't living up to the family legacy.

Mr. Hayes, the estate's caretaker, noticed Caleb's melancholia as he wandered through the mansion. The kind old man approached him with a warm smile, hoping to lift his spirits. "Morning, Master Caleb," he said kindly, his voice a soothing balm to Caleb's troubled mind. "I was thinking of doing some work in the garden house today. Care to join me?"

Caleb forced a smile, appreciating the gesture but feeling too numb to respond with genuine enthusiasm. "Maybe later," he replied, his voice barely above a whisper. The weight of his sorrow made it hard to muster any real interest in anything.

Mr. Hayes nodded understandingly, his eyes filled with quiet sympathy. "Alright, Master Caleb. The garden will be there whenever you're ready."

Caleb watched the old man walk away, his heart heavy with gratitude and sadness. He wished he could find solace in the simple tasks of gardening, but the fog of grief clouded his mind, making it hard to focus on anything but the pain.

He wandered into the sunroom, where the soft patter of rain against the glass created a melancholic symphony. The room, usually a place of solace, now felt like a cage, trapping him with his grief and guilt. He sank into a chair, burying his face in his hands.

The expectations of his father, the constant pressure to excel, and the deep, dark thoughts that had been consuming him for months now seemed unbearable. He felt like he was drowning, unable to break free from the currents pulling him under. The loss of Milo had been the breaking point, the final straw that shattered his fragile hold on hope.

Caleb's heart ached with the weight of his secret. It was more than just the grief of losing Milo—it was the fear of disappointing his father, the dread of never being enough. The storm outside mirrored the turmoil inside him, a relentless downpour that blurred the lines between past and present, joy and sorrow.

As he sat there, the memories of happier times felt like a cruel joke, a reminder of what he had lost and what he could never reclaim. The laughter that once filled the halls was now a haunting echo, a ghost of a life that seemed impossibly distant.

Caleb knew he couldn't keep running from his pain, but he didn't know how to face it, either. The weight of his father's expectations, the crushing pressure to live up to the Morgan name, and the dark thoughts that threatened to consume him left him feeling hopeless and alone.

The rain still drummed against the windows, creating a

soothing yet melancholic melody. Caleb sank into a chair, his gaze fixed on the raindrops trickling down the glass. The rhythmic pattern was almost hypnotic, a fleeting comfort amidst the storm of emotions within him. Yet, despite the calm exterior, he couldn't shake the feeling of being watched.

Every so often, Caleb caught glimpses of a red haired girl—just a fleeting shadow at the edge of his vision. Her presence was elusive, like a ghost drifting through the mansion. Intrigued and slightly unnerved, he found himself rising from the chair, curiosity pulling him forward. He wandered through the familiar halls, following the phantom trace of the mysterious girl.

Each room he entered was empty, yet he felt her presence just beyond his reach. He saw her reflection in mirrors, a silhouette in the corner of his eye, but whenever he turned, she was gone. It was as if she was playing a game, leading him on a chase through the house.

As he moved through the mansion, memories of his childhood intertwined with the present. He passed by the old family portraits, the grand piano his mother used to play, and the cozy reading nook where he had spent countless hours with Milo by his side. Each step stirred a mix of nostalgia and sorrow, the weight of his grief pressing heavier on his heart.

Caleb brushed off the sightings as his mind playing tricks on him, a desperate attempt to distract him from the pain. The house, filled with memories and shadows, seemed to amplify his loneliness. He wondered if the girl was a figment of his imagination, a manifestation of his need for connection, or if she was real, another soul lost in the labyrinth of this grand, yet hollow, home.

He returned to his bedroom, sinking back into a chair with a heavy sigh. The rain continued its steady rhythm, a lullaby for his troubled heart. He closed his eyes, trying to find solace in the sound, but the image of the girl lingered in his mind, her presence both comforting and unsettling.

In the quiet of his room, with the rain tapping a steady rhythm against the window, Caleb sat at his desk. The soft glow of the desk lamp illuminated the paper before him, stark white against the dark wood. His mind was a storm of thoughts and emotions, each one vying for release, each one begging to be heard. He picked up his pen, the cool metal a grounding weight in his hand, and took a deep breath.

The first words were the hardest, but once they were down, the rest seemed to flow like a dam breaking. The ink bled into the paper, capturing his pain, his frustration, and the emotions he had kept buried for so long.

Dear Mom and Dad,

I don't really know where to start. There's so much I've been keeping inside, things I should have told you a long time ago. But I didn't know how. I guess I still don't. Writing this letter is probably the hardest thing I've ever done, and that's saying a lot because it feels like everything has been hard for a long time now. I know you both expect a lot from me. I'm a Morgan, after all. But the truth is, I don't feel like I belong in this family, in this life. Every day, I feel like I'm drowning under the weight of who I'm supposed to be. Dad, you've always talked about strength, about living up to the name, but I'm not sure I know what that means anymore. I've tried so hard to be the son you want me to be, but I keep falling short. And every time I do, it's like a piece of me breaks off and disappears.

You probably don't know this, but Milo was my best friend. He was the only one who ever really understood me, the only one I could talk to without feeling judged or inadequate. Losing him…it's like I lost the only part of myself that made any sense. I know he was just a dog, but to me, he was so much more. He was my anchor, and without him, I've been drifting, lost at sea.

I'm not writing this letter to blame you or make you feel bad. I just need you to understand that I'm not okay. I'm not as strong as you think I am. And the truth is, I'm tired, so very tired of pretending. I'm tired of trying to live up to a name that feels more like a curse than a blessing.

I've been carrying a secret, something I should have told you a long time ago, but I was too scared. Scared of disappointing you, of not being good enough. But I can't keep it inside any longer. It's eating me up, making it hard to breathe. I don't even know who I am anymore, and I'm not sure I want to find out.

This summer, I've made a decision. I can't keep living like this. I can't keep pretending that everything is fine when it's not. I don't know what's going to happen next, but I needed to write this letter, needed you to know the truth.

Please don't be angry with me. I never meant to hurt anyone. I just...I just want the pain to stop.

With love,
Caleb

Tears welled in Caleb's eyes, blurring the words as he finished the letter. He carefully folded the paper, his hands trembling slightly, and slipped it into an envelope. The act of sealing it felt final, like closing a door he would never walk through again.

He placed the envelope on his desk, staring at it for a long moment. The finality of his decision hung in the air, heavy with sorrow and resignation. In some small way, writing the letter had brought him a sense of calm, a release of some of the pressure he'd been carrying for so long. But it also left him with an emptiness, a void that he wasn't sure how to fill.

The storm outside raged on, each raindrop a testament to the turmoil within him. Caleb sat there, listening to the rain, feeling the weight of his decision settle over him like a shroud.

As the rain continued to pour, a soft knock sounded at his door. Evelyn peeked in, her eyes filled with concern. "Caleb, come on downstairs," she said gently, her voice a soothing balm. "Let's watch a movie."

Caleb nodded, forcing a smile. "I'll be down in a minute, Mom."

She lingered for a moment, as if sensing the heaviness in the room, before closing the door softly behind her.

Alone again, Caleb took a deep breath, trying to steady himself. This summer, he had decided, would be his last.

CHAPTER 3: THE LAST DAY

At the crack of dawn, Caleb moved inside the quiet mansion like a ghost through the corridors. His heart was heavy, and his steps were deliberate as he carried the urn containing Milo's ashes. Each step felt like a solemn beat of a drum, echoing in the empty house.

Caleb made his way to the cliffs, the world outside still draped in the soft blanket of morning fog. The ocean roared beneath him, its waves crashing against the rocks with a relentless rhythm. He reached the edge, the wind tugging at his clothes as if urging him to reconsider. Caleb held the urn close, his fingers trembling as he prepared to scatter Milo's ashes into the churning sea.

Taking a deep breath, Caleb began to speak, his voice breaking the stillness of the morning. "Milo, you were more than just a dog to me. You were there for me when no one else was."

Tears streamed down his face as he continued. "I'm sorry I couldn't save you that night. I wish I could have done more. But I hope you know how much I miss you every single day."

With a final, trembling breath, Caleb opened the urn and let the ashes drift out into the wind. They swirled and danced in the air, carried away by the breeze, before slowly settling into the sea below. Caleb watched as the urn, now empty, slipped from his grasp and tumbled down the cliffs, shattering against the rocks with a final, definitive crash.

As he stood there, the wind whipping through his hair and the sound of the ocean filling his ears, Caleb felt a strange sense of peace. The act of letting go, of saying goodbye to his beloved Milo, felt like the end.

The sun had barely risen, casting a golden glow over the beach, yet Caleb felt engulfed in darkness. His heart ached with an unbearable mix of sorrow and resignation. He was about to take a final step into the abyss when he heard the sound of footsteps behind him—light, almost hesitant.

Lila stood at a distance, her red hair bright against the backdrop of the ocean. Freckles dotted her sun-kissed skin, and her eyes, sharp and blue, held a mixture of determination and concern. She had been up before dawn to go surfing, and had noticed someone standing on the edge of the cliff. Her heart raced as she realized the gravity of the situation.

Without hesitation, Lila sprinted toward the young

man, her bare feet pounding against the rocky ground. "Stop!" she called out, her voice carried by the wind.

Caleb barely registered her presence, his mind clouded by despair. But her urgency pierced through his haze.

Before he could react, Lila reached him, grabbing his arm with surprising strength. "No!" she shouted, her voice a lifeline in the storm of his thoughts. "You don't have to do this!"

Caleb, startled by her grip, lost his balance. Both of them tumbled over the edge, plunging into the cold, unforgiving sea below. They miraculously avoided the jagged rocks, but the impact with the water was brutal. The waves crashed around them, pulling them under.

Caleb struggled against the waves, panic setting in. "I can't swim!" he gasped, the fear in his voice palpable.

Lila knew there was no time to waste. She reached out, her fingers brushing against Caleb's as she fought to keep them both afloat. With a strength born of desperation, she pulled him toward the shore, guiding him back toward the safety of the sand.

They collapsed on the beach, the distant roar of the waves now a comforting sound rather than a threat. Lila knelt beside an unconscious Caleb, her hands shaking as she began chest compressions. Her breath mingled with his in a desperate bid to keep him alive. Her determination was fierce, her movements precise and urgent.

As she pressed down on his chest, she muttered under her breath, "If you die on me, I swear I'll make you go to jail for this." The absurdity of the thought brought a bitter smile to her lips, but all she could think about was keeping him alive.

Caleb's eyes fluttered open, the harsh reality of his near leap sinking in as he gasped for air. He looked up to see a red-haired girl with a freckled face, her expression a mixture of relief and exhaustion. For a moment, their eyes locked, and an unspoken connection formed—a bridge over the chasm of Caleb's despair.

"You're okay," she said softly, her voice trembling with emotion. "You're going to be okay."

Caleb stared at her, the realization of what had just happened slowly sinking in. The despair that had gripped him moments ago began to fade, replaced by a flicker of hope. In that moment, he understood that he wasn't alone—that someone cared enough to save him from the brink.

"Why...?" Caleb managed, his voice hoarse, "Why did you...?"

"Because you're not alone," the girl said softly, her eyes filled with a rare mix of empathy and defiance. She offered him a tentative smile, one that spoke of understanding and resilience. "Sometimes, we all need someone to remind us of that."

Caleb watched as she pulled out her phone, her fingers trembling slightly as she started to dial 911. Panic surged through him. "Wait!" he blurted out. "It was an accident. I wasn't trying to..."

Her eyes narrowed slightly, skepticism evident. "You sure about that?"

Caleb nodded vigorously, his mind racing. He couldn't let this turn into a scandal, not with his father's re-election campaign just months away. "Yeah, I just... got caught in the wind. Please, don't call anyone. My dad... he can't deal with this right now."

She hesitated, then slowly lowered her phone. "Alright. But you need to talk to someone about this. Promise me."

"Promise," Caleb said, relief washing over him. He tried to gather his thoughts, his emotions a tangled mess of confusion and gratitude. "Thank you."

She offered a small, wry smile. "So, you nearly drowned, huh? Not the best way to start the day."

Caleb chuckled weakly, appreciating the attempt at comic relief. "Yeah, I wouldn't recommend it."

They stood in silence for a moment, the tension easing slightly. Caleb couldn't shake the feeling of having crossed paths with her before. There was something familiar about her, something he couldn't quite place. "Who are you?" he asked, curiosity piqued.

She shrugged, her eyes twinkling with a hint of mischief. "Just a surfer."

Caleb raised an eyebrow. "You don't look like any surfer I've ever met."

"And you don't look like someone who can swim," she shot back playfully.

He grinned, enjoying the conversation. "How about you teach me, then?"

"Nah!" she said, shaking her head, a smile tugging at her lips. "I've got better things to do."

With that, she turned and walked away, her footsteps light on the sand, leaving Caleb standing there with a bemused smile on his face. He watched her go, her red hair catching the rays of the rising sun, and a sense of wonder and curiosity stirred within him. Who was she?

And why did she feel so familiar, like a distant memory he couldn't quite place?

Caleb glanced around, the sprawling Hamptons estate looming in the distance, its grandeur now feeling more like a prison than a home. The red-haired girl's presence was like a revelation, a reminder that even in the darkest moments, there could be light and hope. It was as if she had walked into his life just when he needed a sign, something to hold onto.

As he stood there, the storm clouds that had been gathering all day began to dissipate, revealing patches of a clear sky. The sight of the sun breaking through the clouds felt symbolic, a quiet promise of better days ahead. Caleb took a deep breath, the salty ocean air filling his lungs, and looked toward the horizon. The waves lapped gently at the shore, the rhythm steady and reassuring, much like the beat of his heart.

But then, almost as if the sky had other plans, a soft drizzle began to fall, the raindrops cold against his skin. Most people would have run for cover, but Caleb stood his ground, rooted to the spot. He felt the rain falling on him, soaking through his clothes, but instead of feeling the discomfort he might have expected, he felt something else—a strange, almost electric sense of release.

He tilted his head back, letting the rain wash over his

face, and for the first time in what felt like forever, he let go. He let go of the anger, the sadness, the weight of expectations that had been pressing down on him for so long. With each drop that hit him, he felt the burden on his shoulders lighten just a little bit more.

The rain fell harder, the sky opening up above him, and Caleb laughed—a sound that surprised even him. It was a moment of catharsis, a release of everything he'd been holding in. The rain mingled with his tears, though he wasn't sure if they were tears of sorrow or something else entirely. Maybe it was both.

After a couple of minutes of rain shower, Caleb walked back toward the mansion. Each step felt lighter, as if the rain had washed away a small part of his grief. The weight of his struggles remained, but there was a strange sense of renewal within him—a faint glimmer of hope kindled by the unexpected kindness of a stranger who seemed to understand more than he initially realized.

When Caleb returned, he quietly avoided his parents and managed to slip inside his room. He noticed he was drenched, and sand clung to his clothes in places where the sun didn't shine. For the first time in a long while, he laughed—a genuine, unguarded laugh that echoed in the room and surprised even himself. It was a fleeting moment of joy, but it felt like a small victory.

Sitting on the edge of his bed, Caleb glanced around his room. It was filled with reminders of his childhood—old toys, books, and photos that now seemed like relics from another life. He felt a bittersweet pang of nostalgia, mixed with the renewed sense of hope he had felt on the beach. He wasn't sure what the future held, but for the first time in a long time, he felt a spark of something he hadn't dared to feel in months—possibility.

Downstairs, his parents were likely discussing plans for the day or debating about the weather, but Caleb felt a world away from their conversations. He knew the road ahead wouldn't be easy, and the weight of his secret and the expectations of his father still pressed heavily on him. Yet, as he lay back on his bed, the image of the red-haired girl and the clear horizon stayed with him, a reminder that even in the darkest times, there was always a chance for light to break through.

Caleb closed his eyes, the sound of the ocean waves crashing against the shore outside his window. He allowed himself to drift, feeling a sense of peace he hadn't known in a long time. There was still so much to face, but for now, he let the hope of new beginnings lull him into a restful sleep.

Out in the ocean, Lila's surfboard cut through the morning waves with practiced ease. The salt spray on her skin felt like a comforting embrace, but her mind was elsewhere. She couldn't stop thinking about the boy whom she had saved earlier that day.

Caleb Morgan. He didn't seem like the typical rich kid. There was something in his eyes—something dark and melancholic.

She shivered as the memory of him standing on the edge of that cliff flashed through her mind. Was it really an accident, or had he intended jump? The thought sent chills down her spine, making her lose focus. A sudden wave caught her off guard, and she slipped from her surfboard, tumbling into the ocean.

Surfacing with a gasp, she shook off the fear. It was time to head back. She paddled to shore, packed up her surfboard, and started the walk back to her bike, the weight of her thoughts pressing heavily on her.

Lila entered through the back door of the Morgan estate. The house was abuzz with preparations for the evening's party. She slipped quietly into the servant's cottage where she lived with her father. But the small space was empty; he must have been busy with the party arrangements too.

Sighing, Lila reminded herself of why she was here. High school would be over soon, and she needed to save as much money as possible for college. It wasn't an ideal job, but it was a means to an end. She took a quick shower, the hot water washing away the salt and sand, then dressed in her server's uniform. The black and white attire felt like a costume, a stark contrast to her usual carefree self, but she had no choice. Beggars can't be choosers, right?

The Morgans' summer parties were legendary in the Hamptons. This was the first one in years, ever since Senator Thomas Morgan had fully immersed himself in politics. The grand hall buzzed with laughter and clinking glasses as the guests mingled. Dressed in designer clothes, dripping with jewelry, and exuding an air of effortless sophistication, they epitomized the high society of the Hamptons.

Thomas and Evelyn Morgan moved gracefully through the crowd, their practiced smiles masking the underlying tension. They engaged in polite conversation, discussing stock markets and vacation homes in the South of France.

"The market's up again," one guest said, adjusting his cufflinks. "Just invested in a new tech startup. It's the next big thing, I tell you."

Another guest, a woman draped in pearls, laughed

lightly. "Oh, I must tell my husband. He's been looking for a new venture ever since we got back from the Riviera."

Meanwhile, Lila moved through the crowd, serving drinks with a practiced smile. She kept her eyes down, blending into the background. Overhearing snippets of conversation, she couldn't help but marvel at the extravagance of their lives, so different from her own.

"Did you see the new yacht the Stevensons bought?" one guest whispered to another. "Absolutely massive!"

"Yes, and they're throwing a party on it next weekend. It'll be the event of the season."

Lila chuckled inwardly at the absurdity of it all. Just then, her phone buzzed. She glanced at it to see a text from her boyfriend, Logan.

"Party tonight. You coming?"

She ignored the text and returned to work, her mind a whirl of thoughts. As she passed by the grand foyer, she caught a glimpse of Caleb Morgan. He was dressed in a sharp suit, yet there was an air of detachment about him, as if he were adrift in a sea of expectations and responsibilities. Lila felt a pang of empathy. Maybe they had more in common than she thought.

Lila, too, carried her own burdens. The daughter of Mr. Hayes, the Morgan's Hampton house caretaker, she navigated a world of privilege and disparity. She attended the local public school, a stark contrast to the elite institutions Caleb had been accustomed to. Her boyfriend, Logan, was a rugged Hampton native, grounded and straightforward, but sometimes oblivious to the subtleties of her world.

She moved around serving the guests their drinks, Lila couldn't help but notice the stark contrasts between her life and that of the Morgans. While they lived in a world of opulence, her life was defined by hard work and modest means. She knew the mansion's ins and outs, every corner and crevice, yet it never felt like home. It was merely a place where her father worked, and she helped out when needed.

But outside on the patio, a young man, clearly drunk, started bothering Lila. "Hey, gorgeous, why don't you take a break and join me for a drink?" he slurred, grabbing her arm.

Lila pulled her arm back, trying to maintain her composure. "I'm working," she said firmly, her voice steady despite the annoyance simmering beneath.

The young man leaned closer, his breath reeking of alcohol. "Come on, just one drink. What's the harm?"

Lila's tray wobbled precariously, and drinks spilled everywhere. From a distance, Caleb saw what was happening and instinctively moved to help. But before he could intervene, Lila slapped the drunk man's hand away with surprising force.

"Why don't you go get something to eat?" she said sharply, her voice carrying a firm authority that left the man visibly embarrassed. He stumbled away, muttering under his breath.

Caleb watched the scene unfold, impressed by the red-headed waitress. He wished he could be more like her—strong, assertive, unafraid to stand up for herself.

Mr. Hayes, quickly arrived to help Lila with the spilled drinks. "What happened here?" he asked, concern etched in his features.

Lila pretended to be flustered, her hands shaking slightly as she picked up the broken glass. "Oh, it's nothing, Daddy. My hands just slipped."

"Here," Caleb stepped forward, offering a hand. "Let me give you a hand," he said, bending to pick up the shards of glass scattered across the floor.

Mr. Hayes smiled warmly. "Thank you, Master Caleb. Lila, you remember him, don't you?"

Suddenly Mr. Hayes excused himself and headed to the kitchen where he was needed. But a rush of memories came flooding back to Caleb. He remembered a younger version of himself and Lila, running around the mansion with Milo, their laughter echoing through the grand hallways. They had played countless games together, their bond forged in the innocence of childhood.

Caleb's eyes widened in recognition. So it was Lila, the same surfer who had saved his life that morning. He extended his hand to her, a friendly smile on his lips. "It's nice to officially meet you, Lila."

Lila looked at his hand, then back at his face, her expression cool and guarded. "I know who you are," she said bluntly, ignoring his outstretched hand.

Caleb's smile faltered slightly, but he quickly recovered, understanding that their shared past did not guarantee an immediate connection. "It's been a long time," he said softly, hoping to bridge the gap between them.

Lila nodded, her eyes softening just a fraction. "Yes, it has."

They continued to clean up the mess together, and Caleb couldn't help but marvel at how much things had changed since their childhood days. The mansion, once a place of laughter and carefree adventures, now felt like a battleground of unresolved emotions and unspoken words. Yet, in Lila's presence, he felt a glimmer of hope, a possibility that this summer might bring more than just heartache.

But Caleb's thoughts drifted back to Milo and the void his loyal companion had left behind. The weight of his grief was a constant presence, but in that moment, standing beside Lila, he felt a flicker of something he hadn't felt in a long time—a sense of connection, of not being entirely alone.

Lila finished gathering the last of the broken glass and looked up at Caleb, her eyes searching his. "You okay?" she asked, her voice gentler now, a hint of concern breaking through her tough exterior.

Caleb nodded, swallowing the lump in his throat. "Yeah," he said quietly. "I think I will be. So you're not exactly a fan of parties, are you?"

"Not really," Lila replied, her tone lightening slightly. "I've just seen enough of these parties to last a lifetime."

Caleb laughed. "Well, that makes two of us. So, any tips on how to survive?"

Lila smiled for the first time, a genuine smile that lit up her face. "Stick with me, and you might just make it."

Caleb felt a strange sense of relief. Maybe this summer wouldn't be so bad after all.

CHAPTER 4: THE LAST MEMORY

The party had started winding down, and the guests were dispersing into the night, leaving behind a trail of laughter and music that still echoed softly in the air. Caleb watched his parents, Thomas and Evelyn Morgan, busily saying their goodbyes to the last of the guests, their smiles polished and practiced. The estate, with its grandiosity and formality, seemed even more imposing in the dim light, a stark contrast to the carefree atmosphere that had prevailed just hours earlier.

On the fringes of the gathering, Lila stood quietly, her eyes scanning the crowd for her father. The estate's grand hall was filled with laughter and chatter, but she felt like an outsider, more a waitress than a guest. She had always felt out of place at these events, her role more defined by service than by belonging. The air was thick with the scent of expensive cologne and aged wine, the atmosphere stiff and formal, a far cry from the freedom she craved.

As her gaze swept the room once more, Lila realized her father was nowhere to be found. A small pang of worry settled in her chest. It wasn't like him to disappear without letting her know. She decided to slip away and check on him, the thought of the beach bonfire calling to her, a tempting escape from the gilded confines of the estate.

She made her way through the back corridors, the sound of her footsteps muffled by the thick carpet. The estate's grandeur faded as she approached the servants' quarters, where she and her father lived. The old cottage on the estate grounds was a stark contrast to the main house, its charm lying in its simplicity. The walls were weathered, the paint peeling in places, but it was home—a place where she and her father had shared countless memories, both good and bittersweet.

Pushing open the creaky door, Lila found her father sitting in his favorite chair, nursing his knee. His face was etched with lines of age and weariness, but his eyes still held the same warmth she had always known.

"Dad," she said softly, stepping into the room. "I've been looking for you."

Mr. Hayes looked up, a small smile playing on his lips. "I needed a break from all that formality," he replied, his tone light but with a hint of exhaustion. "Besides, this old knee isn't what it used to be."

Lila frowned, her concern deepening. "You need to rest, Dad. You shouldn't be pushing yourself like this."

He chuckled softly, waving off her worry. "I'm not

young anymore, Lila. No more parties for me. But you, you should be out there, having fun."

She knelt beside him, her hand resting gently on his knee. "You're all I care about, Dad. If you're hurting, I'm not going anywhere."

Mr. Hayes reached out, brushing a stray lock of hair from her face. "I'm fine, sweetheart. Just a little ache. You've done enough for me today. Go on, enjoy yourself. The beach won't wait forever."

Lila hesitated, her heart torn between staying and the pull of the bonfire party. But she knew her father well—he wanted her to live her life, not be held back by his.

"Lila, you heading out?" Mr. Hayes asked, his voice gentle yet tinged with concern. He knew his daughter well enough to sense her restlessness and understood her need to break free from the constraints of the estate.

"Yeah, Dad. Logan's waiting for me at the bonfire," she replied as she moved to her small room. The familiar sight of the worn bedspread and the modest furniture brought her a sense of comfort. She unbuttoned the top of her waiter uniform, feeling the tension ease slightly as she slipped into a pair of shorts and a loose-fitting shirt. It was a simple change, but it made all the difference—a small act of reclaiming her own identity in a world that often dictated who she should be.

She returned to the small living room, grabbing her keys from the bowl on the counter. Before she left, she paused, looking back at her father, who was watching her.

"Be careful, Lila," he said softly.

"I will, Dad," she promised, leaning down to kiss his cheek. "I'll be back before you know it."

She made her way to the mansion kitchen to grab a quick bite before heading towards the path that led to the beach. Inside the busy kitchen, Lila ate a small sandwich and grabbed an unopened bottle of champagne, her thoughts drifting to Logan Bennet, her boyfriend. She remembered the first time she met him in school. He had this air of danger around him, a silent but palpable presence that made everyone wary. But for Lila, that made him perfect. He was a rebellion against the mundane, a way to navigate the harsh realities of high school without succumbing to them.

Lila slipped into the mansion's kitchen with the practiced ease of someone who had learned to move without being seen. The catering staff was busy packing up and cleaning, their conversations blending with the clatter of dishes and the hum of the industrial dishwasher. She maneuvered through the chaos, careful to stay out of their line of sight, her footsteps light on the polished tiles.

The kitchen was a flurry of activity, but Lila managed to find a quiet corner where she quickly ate a small sandwich, her thoughts far from the bustle around her. As she chewed, her eyes fell on an unopened bottle of champagne, its golden liquid sparkling in the dim light. Without hesitation, she grabbed it, tucking it under her arm as if it were a precious secret.

Her mind drifted to Logan Bennet, her boyfriend. He was the kind of guy who turned heads wherever he went, but not just because of his looks. There was an edge to him, a dangerous allure that made people keep their distance. But for Lila, that danger was part of his charm. He was her way of rebelling against the expectations that had always been placed on her, a beacon in the otherwise mundane world of high school.

She remembered the first time she met him, how he had stood out in a crowd, exuding a quiet confidence that made her heart race. There was something about Logan that made her feel alive, that made her believe she could navigate the harsh realities of life without losing herself.

But out on the patio, Caleb noticed Lila as she slipped out of the gates, a shadow in the night. He didn't approach her, though he wanted to. Throughout the party, their eyes had met more than once, but the unspoken rules of their worlds kept them apart. She hadn't dared to talk to him in front of his parents, and he understood why.

Caleb watched as she made her way toward the path that led to the beach, her figure gradually disappearing into the darkness. He knew where she was going, to the one place where she could find a semblance of peace, even if just for a little while. He envied her for that, for her ability to escape, to find solace in the simple things. For him, the weight of his life felt like chains, each link forged from the expectations and pressures that came with being a Morgan.

As he leaned against the patio railing, his thoughts spiraled back to a conversation he had overheard earlier that evening, a conversation that now echoed in his mind like a haunting refrain.

"I'm worried about Caleb," Evelyn's voice was soft, tinged with concern. "He barely spoke to any of the guests tonight. He seemed so...distant."

Thomas's response was curt, dismissive. "That's better than him making a scene. Silence is preferable if it means he's not doing anything stupid to ruin the Morgan name."

There was a pause, a heavy silence that spoke volumes.

"But don't you think he should be more involved, more engaged?" His mother's voice trembled slightly, as if she were afraid of pushing too hard. "He's so withdrawn, Thomas. It's like he's not even here."

"He's fine, Evelyn," his father replied, his tone firm, leaving no room for argument. "Caleb needs to learn that his role is to uphold our family's reputation, nothing more. As long as he doesn't embarrass us, I don't care if he's silent. He'll grow out of it."

Caleb felt a tightness in his chest as he heard his father's words, each one a heavy blow to the fragile sense of self he had been trying to hold on to. They didn't understand him, didn't see the weight of the world he was carrying on his young shoulders. To them, he was just another piece in the Morgan legacy, a tool to be molded and used.

Caleb closed his eyes, the memories settling over him like a shroud. The voices of his parents faded into the night, but the pain they caused lingered, a constant reminder of the distance between him and the world around him.

He looked out into the darkness where Lila had disappeared, wishing he could join her, wishing he could find the freedom she seemed to possess. But the chains of his life were too strong, too deeply rooted in the expectations that had been placed upon him since birth.

With a heavy sigh, Caleb turned away from the night, retreating into the mansion, where the walls were filled with memories he wished he could forget. But even as he walked away, a small part of him held on to the hope that maybe, just maybe, there was still a way out. A way to find himself, to break free from the weight of his past and the expectations that threatened to crush him.

He just didn't know how to take that first step.

Outside, Lila was walking the path that led to the beach, the cool night air filling her lungs. She could hear the distant sounds of the bonfire party, the laughter and music blending with the rhythmic crash of the waves. It was a world away from the estate, a place where she could let her guard down and just be herself.

As she walked, her thoughts drifted to Logan. He had been her anchor in the turbulent sea of high school, a constant amidst the chaos. He had a reputation that kept others at a distance, but to Lila, he was someone who understood her struggles. Their relationship was a refuge, a place where she could escape the expectations and find a semblance of peace.

The scent of saltwater mingled with the aroma of blooming flowers, and the distant sound of waves crashing against the shore created a rhythmic backdrop to her thoughts. The night sky was a canvas of stars, twinkling like tiny beacons of hope.

Lila's world was a blend of simplicity and complexity. Growing up as the caretaker's daughter amidst opulence had given her a unique perspective. The grandeur of the Hampton estate never ceased to amaze her, yet she remained grounded, thanks to her father, Mr. Hayes. His steadfast presence was a constant in her life, a source of unwavering love and support. Logan Bennett, her boyfriend, was another pillar. His adventurous spirit and unwavering support grounded her in ways she couldn't fully articulate.

As she neared the beach, the glow of the bonfire came into view. Logan stood there, his tall frame silhouetted against the flames. He greeted her with a warm smile, pulling her into a tight embrace.

"Hey, you," he murmured, his voice a soothing balm against the noise of the world. "How was the party?"

"Same old," Lila replied, rolling her eyes playfully. "But I'm glad to be here now."

The beach was alive with the laughter and chatter of their friends, the bonfire casting flickering shadows on their faces. The warmth of the flames contrasted with the cool evening breeze, creating a perfect summer night ambiance. Lila and Logan joined the circle, greeted by familiar faces.

There was Elara, with her dreams set on attending an Ivy League school. Next to her was Jacob, the star athlete, who had his sights on a sports scholarship. Juno and Kai , the inseparable duo, were planning a cross-country road trip after graduation. Each of them had their own dreams and aspirations, and the bonfire was a place where they could share and celebrate their hopes for the future.

"So, guys," Elara began, her voice filled with excitement, "Can you believe we only have one year left of high school? What are you all looking forward to the most?"

Jacob grinned, tossing a stick into the fire. "Winning the state championship, of course! And maybe getting a scholarship to USC. What about you, Elara?"

Elara's eyes sparkled with ambition. "Harvard, definitely. I've been dreaming about it since I was a kid."

Juno leaned into Kai, his eyes gleaming with

anticipation. "Our road trip! We've got the whole route planned out. It's going to be epic."

As the conversation flowed, Lila found herself lost in thought. She was happy for her friends and their dreams, but a nagging sense of uncertainty tugged at her. She turned to Logan, hoping to find solace in his familiar presence.

"And what about you, Logan?" Elara asked, her curiosity piqued. "Any big plans after graduation?"

Logan shrugged, a casual smile on his face. "I'm staying here, in the Hamptons. College is for losers. Why waste time and money when you can live the good life right here?"

Lila's heart sank at his words. She had always assumed they would face the future together, but it was clear their paths were diverging. She had dreams of going to college, of exploring the world beyond the Hamptons, and she couldn't imagine doing it without Logan by her side.

"Seriously, Logan?" Lila couldn't hide the disappointment in her voice. "You don't want to go to college at all?"

Logan chuckled, pulling her closer. "Why would I, Lila? We have everything we need right here. The beach, the parties, our friends. It's perfect."

Lila forced a smile, but her mind was racing. She loved Logan deeply, but his lack of ambition troubled her. She didn't want to spend her life in the same place, doing the same things, day after day. She craved adventure, growth, and new experiences. She wanted to make a difference in the world, and she feared that staying in the Hamptons would hold her back.

The bonfire continued to crackle, and the conversation shifted to lighter topics. But Lila's thoughts remained heavy, a whirlwind of emotions swirling within her. She glanced at Logan, his carefree demeanor a stark contrast to her inner turmoil.

Back at the house, Caleb couldn't stop thinking about Lila. There was something about her that captivated him, a lightness that seemed to pierce through his darkness. He wandered through the mansion, each step echoing with memories and regrets, the weight of his thoughts almost too much to bear. His mind was a whirlwind of emotions, a storm that seemed to have no end.

When he passed the back corridors, he saw her again, this time she was out in the center garden. The silver glow of the moonlight outlined her delicate features as she licked the ice cream off her bowl. But Caleb felt an inexplicable pull towards her, a desire to connect with someone who seemed so different yet so familiar.

"Lila," he called out, his voice hesitant yet hopeful.

She turned, a surprised smile on her face, her mouth full of ice cream. "Caleb? What are you doing out here?"

"I couldn't sleep," he admitted, his gaze dropping to the ground. "I keep thinking about... things."

Lila's eyes softened with understanding. She motioned for him to join her, "Come on, I'll fix you a bowl of mint chocolate chip ice cream. It's my favorite."

Caleb followed her inside, feeling a strange sense of comfort in her presence. As she scooped the ice cream into a second bowl, he couldn't help but notice the easy grace with which she moved, the way her laughter seemed to fill the cold kitchen with warmth.

"Here you go," she said, handing him the bowl with a smile. "Mint chocolate chip. The best there is."

Caleb took a tentative bite, the strong mint flavor almost making him wince. He hated mint, but he didn't have the heart to tell her. Instead, he forced a smile, hoping she wouldn't notice his discomfort. "Thanks, Lila. It's... great."

She laughed, the sound like music to his ears. "You don't like it, do you?"

Caught, Caleb chuckled and shook his head. "Not really. But it's the thought that counts, right?"

Lila smiled, her eyes twinkling with amusement. "I appreciate the effort. You don't have to pretend with me, Caleb."

They sat in comfortable silence for a moment, the moonlight casting a gentle glow over the garden. The world seemed to slow down, the chaos of his thoughts fading into the background.

"So," Lila began, breaking the silence, "what did you think of the party earlier? Quite the crowd, huh?"

Caleb sighed, thinking back to the pompous guests and their superficial conversations. "It was... overwhelming. Everyone seemed so perfect, so put together. I felt like I didn't belong."

Lila nodded, her expression thoughtful. "I get that. It's easy to feel out of place in a world that demands perfection. But you don't have to be perfect, Caleb. You just have to be you."

Her words struck a chord deep within him, resonating

with the part of him that longed for acceptance and understanding. He looked at her, really looked at her, and saw someone who seemed to understand his pain, his struggles, in a way no one else did.

"Thanks, Lila," he said quietly, his heart feeling a little lighter. "I needed to hear that."

She smiled, reaching out to squeeze his hand. "Anytime, Caleb. We all need someone to remind us that we're enough, just as we are."

As they sat there, sharing a moment of genuine connection, Caleb felt a flicker of hope. Maybe, just maybe, this summer wouldn't be as unbearable as he had feared.

"Lila," he began as he tried to break the ice, "so, do you live here?"

She laughed, a light, musical sound that made Caleb smile. "Sort of," she replied. "I help my dad take care of the place. Your parents don't mind as long as I don't break any of their antiques."

Caleb chuckled, appreciating her humor. "Well, that sounds like a pretty good deal."

"It is," she agreed, her eyes sparkling with amusement. "And it's a lot better than some alternatives, trust me."

He nodded, then looked at her more seriously. "So what about you? What's your life like?"

Lila sighed, a wistful look crossing her face as she remembered her conversation with Logan earlier. "I dream of going away to college. I want to see the world, meet new people, experience life outside of Hamptons."

Caleb felt a pang of envy at her determination and clear sense of purpose. "That sounds amazing," he said softly. "My life is pretty much set in stone. I'm supposed to pursue law and join my father in politics."

Lila looked at him with a mix of sympathy and curiosity. "But what do you want to do, Caleb?"

He was silent for a moment, the question hanging heavily in the air. He realized he didn't have an answer, and that frightened him more than anything. "I don't really know," he admitted, his voice barely above a whisper.

Lila reached out and placed a hand on his arm, offering a comforting touch. "It's okay not to know," she said gently. "Sometimes it takes a while to figure out what you really want."

Caleb looked at her, feeling a connection that went

beyond words. "Thanks, Lila. I appreciate that."

They sat in silence for a while, the sound of crickets filling the night air. Caleb felt a strange sense of peace, as if talking to Lila had lifted a part of the burden he carried.

For the first time in a long while, Caleb felt a glimmer of hope, a belief that maybe, just maybe, things could get better. And as he looked into Lila's eyes, he knew that he wasn't alone in his struggles. They were both searching for their place in the world, and in that search, they had found each other.

The next couple of days, Caleb found himself wandering the halls of the mansion, his thoughts often drifting back to Lila. Despite his aimless searching, he didn't see her around. Her absence left a feeling he couldn't quite explain, like a missing piece that gnawed at the edges of his consciousness. The mansion, with its grand rooms and echoing hallways, felt emptier without her presence, the silence more oppressive.

Late one night, unable to sleep, Caleb found himself in the kitchen. He moved absentmindedly, his mind lost in a swirl of memories and unspoken words. He opened the freezer and, without thinking, scooped himself a bowl of mint chocolate chip ice cream. The flavor, once so distasteful, now held a strange comfort, a reminder of their brief connection.

As he sat at the kitchen island, the house shrouded in quiet, he heard the soft click of the back door. He turned to see Lila walking in, her hair slightly damp from the night air, a look of surprise crossing her face as she saw him.

"Caleb? What are you doing up so late?" she asked, her voice breaking the stillness.

Caleb smiled sheepishly, holding up his spoon. "Couldn't sleep. Guess I was craving some mint chocolate chip ice cream."

Lila laughed softly, the sound warming the room. "You must really be desperate if you're eating that," she teased, her eyes sparkling.

He chuckled, the tension in his shoulders easing a bit. "Yeah, well, it's growing on me."

She walked over and leaned against the counter, her expression softening. "I'm sorry I've been scarce. I've been busy with work lately."

Caleb nodded, taking another bite of ice cream. "Where do you work?"

Lila smiled, her eyes taking on a faraway look. "Part

time jobs. It keeps me busy, but I love it."

"That sounds... nice," Caleb said, meaning it. "It must be fulfilling, being able to help people and stay busy."

"It is," she replied, her gaze meeting his. "But I also like being here. It's peaceful, a good place to think."

They fell into a comfortable silence, the only sound the occasional clink of Caleb's spoon against his bowl. Lila's presence was soothing, a balm to his restless spirit. He realized how much he had missed her these past few days, how her absence had amplified his loneliness.

"So how have you been, Caleb?" Lila asked gently, her concern evident.

Caleb sighed, setting his spoon down. "It's been tough. This place holds so many memories, and not all of them are good. It's hard to escape them."

Lila nodded, understanding in her eyes. "I get that. Sometimes the places meant to be our sanctuaries can feel like prisons."

He looked at her, seeing the sincerity in her gaze. "Yeah. I guess that's exactly how I feel."

She reached out and placed a hand on his arm, a simple

gesture that meant more than words could convey. "You're not alone, Caleb. We all have our struggles, but we don't have to face them by ourselves."

They sat there together, the night stretching on, two souls finding comfort in each other's company. Her words lingered in the air, a promise of companionship and understanding. Caleb felt a flicker of hope, a small light in the darkness of his mind. Maybe, just maybe, he could find solace in this unexpected friendship, and through it, begin to heal.

Suddenly Lila stood up, her form sure and steady. "Wanna see something cool?" she asked, a mischievous glint in her eyes.

Curiosity piqued, Caleb nodded. She led him through a series of winding paths and hidden doors, the estate revealing its secrets one by one. They finally arrived at a small, hidden room tucked away in a corner of the mansion. It was filled with old books, trinkets, and photographs—remnants of a past long gone.

"This was my secret hideout when I was a kid," Lila explained, her voice soft with nostalgia. "I used to come here whenever I needed to escape."

Caleb looked around, his heart aching with a mixture of longing and sadness. "It's amazing," he said quietly. "I had a place like this once, too. But it was with Milo."

Lila's eyes softened with understanding. "Milo… your dog, right?."

Caleb nodded, his throat tightening. "Yeah. He was more than a dog to me. He was my best friend. Losing him... it broke something inside me."

They sat in silence for a moment, the weight of Caleb's grief hanging heavy in the air. Lila reached out, her hand resting gently on his.

"I'm sorry, Caleb," she said softly as she thought about her own mother. "I know what it's like to lose something that means the world to you."

He looked at her, his eyes filled with a gratitude he couldn't quite express. "Thank you, Lila. It helps... talking about it."

In that hidden room, amidst the relics of the past, a connection began to form between them. It was fragile and new, but it held the promise of healing, of finding solace in shared pain. And as they sat together, the world outside seemed a little less dark, a little more hopeful.

CHAPTER 5: THE LAST WORD

Caleb and Lila's paths began to intertwine more frequently, their interactions slowly evolving into a budding friendship. Despite the vast differences in their worlds, there was something about Lila's grounded, hardworking nature that intrigued Caleb, drawing him away from his privileged yet stifling life. The days at the Hamptons estate seemed to blend into one another, but Lila's presence brought a new sense of purpose and curiosity into Caleb's routine.

One morning, Caleb found Lila tending to the gardens, her hands covered in soil as she hummed a tune under her breath. He watched her for a moment, admiring the way she moved with such ease and confidence.

"Good morning," he greeted, stepping closer.

Lila looked up, a smile lighting up her face. "Hey, Caleb. What brings you out here?"

"I was just... curious," he admitted, glancing around at the vibrant flowers and meticulously trimmed hedges. "I've never really worked in a garden before."

Lila raised an eyebrow, a mischievous glint in her eyes. "Really? Never had to get your hands dirty, huh?"

Caleb shrugged, a little embarrassed. "Not really. My parents always had someone to take care of things like this."

"Must be nice," she said, her tone light but with an undercurrent of something deeper. "But you know, there's something satisfying about working with your hands, seeing the results of your hard work."

"I bet I could do it if I wanted to," Caleb said, a hint of defensiveness in his voice.

Lila chuckled, wiping her hands on her jeans. "Is that a challenge? Because I'd love to see you try."

Caleb met her gaze, a determined look in his eyes. "Fine. What do you want me to do?"

A wicked smile spread across Lila's face. "Oh, I've got a few ideas. How about you join me at one of my summer jobs? We'll see if you can handle it."

Caleb nodded, feeling a mix of excitement and trepidation. "You're on."

The next day, Lila took Caleb to her job at a beachside restaurant. As they walked in, the scent of saltwater and fried food filled the air. The bustling atmosphere was a stark contrast to the quiet elegance of Caleb's usual surroundings.

"Alright, first things first," Lila said, handing Caleb an apron. "You're going to help with the breakfast rush."

Caleb fumbled with the apron, feeling out of place as he watched Lila move effortlessly between tables, taking orders and balancing trays. He tried to mimic her, but it quickly became clear that he was in over his head.

"Here, let me show you," Lila said, stepping in to help him carry a tray laden with plates. "You've got to balance it, like this."

Caleb nodded, trying to follow her instructions, but his hands were shaking, and he nearly dropped the tray. Lila laughed, not unkindly, and steadied him.

"Don't worry, you'll get the hang of it," she said, giving him an encouraging smile.

By midday, Caleb was exhausted. His arms ached, and he had developed a newfound respect for the hard work Lila did every day. But the day wasn't over yet. Lila had another job for him.

Next, they headed to the beach, where Lila worked as a lifeguard. The sun was high in the sky, and the sand was hot beneath their feet. Lila handed Caleb a whistle and pointed to a spot on the lifeguard stand.

"Think you can handle keeping an eye on things?" she asked, a teasing note in her voice.

Caleb nodded, determined not to back down. He climbed up the stand and took his position, feeling a little ridiculous but also a strange sense of pride. He spent the next few hours scanning the waves, watching as Lila expertly maneuvered through the water, rescuing amateur swimmers and ensuring everyone's safety.

By the time the sun began to set, Caleb was sunburnt and exhausted, but he had to admit, he felt accomplished. Lila joined him on the stand, handing him a bottle of water.

"How are you holding up?" she asked, her eyes twinkling with amusement.

"I think I'm about ready to collapse," Caleb admitted, taking a long drink. "But it was worth it."

Lila smiled, her expression softening. "I'm glad you came. You did good today, Caleb."

He looked at her, feeling a warmth spread through his chest that had nothing to do with the sun. "Thanks, Lila. I needed this. I needed to feel... something real."

Just when Caleb thought he might escape the day's trials, Lila turned to him with a mischievous grin that hinted at her next grand plan. "Alright, Caleb," she said, "today you're going to learn how to swim in the ocean."

Caleb's eyes widened, and he couldn't help but chuckle nervously. The memory of when he'd fallen in and Lila rescued him, still stung. "You know that was an accident, right?" he said, trying to deflect.

Lila's gaze was unwavering, her eyebrow arched in playful challenge. "Sure it was. But today, we're making sure you can handle the waves."

The beach had transformed into an arena of clumsy attempts and laughter. Caleb's first few tries at swimming were a comedy of errors, with him flailing and stumbling more than he actually swam. Each tumble into the water elicited peals of laughter from Lila, whose bright eyes sparkled with joy.

"Stop flailing like a drowning duck," she teased, her voice laced with amusement.

Caleb looked up, sputtering as he wiped water from his face. "Easy for you to say," he shot back, "You're practically a mermaid."

Lila grinned, splashing him playfully. "Well, maybe you should start practicing your mermaid skills then!"

By the end of the day, Caleb had managed to stay afloat with only a few accidental swallows of seawater. Lila beamed with pride, her infectious enthusiasm making even the smallest victories feel monumental.

As the sun began to set, Lila led Caleb to a spot where the waves gently hit the shore. She motioned for him to sit beside her on the sand, their wet clothes clinging uncomfortably but their spirits high.

"Look at that," Lila said, her voice softening. The horizon stretched out before them, a breathtaking blend of fiery hues melting into the calm sea. The sky's beauty seemed to reflect the very essence of tranquility, a stark contrast to the turmoil Caleb had been grappling with.

"It's amazing," Caleb said, his voice almost reverent. He glanced at Lila, seeing her in a new light, not just as the carefree girl who had dragged him into the ocean but as someone who saw beauty and hope in places he hadn't thought to look.

Lila smiled, her eyes locked on the horizon. "It is, isn't it? Sometimes we get so caught up in our own messes that we forget to look around and appreciate the little things."

Caleb nodded, feeling a warmth in his chest that had nothing to do with the setting sun. The pain and isolation that had been gnawing at him seemed to ease, if only for a moment. "Thanks, Lila," he said quietly. "For today, for everything."

Lila looked at him, her expression soft and genuine. "Anytime, Caleb. Sometimes, all we need is a reminder that things can get better. Even if it's just learning how to swim."

Finally, when they walked back to the mansion, dripping wet and tired but feeling lighter in spirit, Caleb realized that the warmth he felt wasn't just from the sun setting behind them. It was the beginning of something unexpected—a connection that might just help him navigate the turbulent waters of his own heart.

Meanwhile, a world away from them, Logan was grappling with his own set of frustrations. The summer stretched out before him, an endless expanse filled with the hum of car engines and the clatter of tools. The car workshop, inherited from his grandfather and now run by his mother, was both a haven and a prison.

Logan's frustration was palpable. He would stare at his

phone, willing Lila to respond to his texts and calls, only to be met with silence. The rumors about her and the tall boy at the beach, only fueled his anxiety. He didn't want to lose her, but the emotional distance between them felt insurmountable.

His mother, Martha, was a steady presence amid his growing discontent. She would chat with him while he worked, her voice a soothing counterpoint to his inner turmoil.

"Remember your grandfather's birthday?" Martha said one day, her voice tinged with nostalgia. "It's coming up next week. He would have been so proud to see you taking over the shop."

Logan glanced at her, his expression a mixture of determination and reluctance. "Yeah, I remember. I know it's important to carry on the family legacy. But... I just wish things were different."

Martha gave him a sympathetic smile. "I know it's tough. But you've got one more year of school left. Maybe you can figure things out with Lila before then."

Logan nodded, a heavy sigh escaping his lips. "I hope so. I just don't know how to make her see that I'm serious about us. I need this summer to matter."

The shop was more than just a business; it was a

symbol of a future that Logan felt increasingly trapped by. Every day spent working on cars was a day spent away from Lila and the dreams he harbored of a different life.

Yet, as the summer break wore on, Logan understood that he had to make a choice. He needed to reconcile his responsibilities with his desires, hoping that somehow, amidst the noise and grease, he would find a way to bridge the gap between his past and his future.

The final day of summer break dawned with a bittersweet glow. Caleb had been waiting for this moment all season, hoping for one last chance to see Lila. The beach, usually a place of solace, felt like an empty stage where he was waiting for a performance that might never come.

He arrived at the beach, the sand warm underfoot and the ocean stretching out like a vast, calming expanse. He found a seat under an umbrella, feeling a pang of disappointment when he didn't see Lila among the sunbathers and families dotting the shore. With a sigh, he sank into a beach chair, his mind heavy with the weight of his imminent departure. The salty breeze whispered through the air, and soon Caleb's eyes grew heavy. He drifted into a light sleep, lulled by the rhythmic sound of waves crashing against the shore.

A gentle nudge roused him from his slumber. Caleb blinked, his gaze focusing on the familiar, sunlit figure of Lila. She stood there, her face illuminated by the soft afternoon light, a mischievous smile playing on her lips.

"Hey, sleepyhead," she teased softly. "I didn't think you'd actually fall asleep out here."

Caleb stretched and smiled, feeling a rush of relief. "I was hoping I'd get to see you one last time before I left."

Lila's eyes sparkled with a mix of amusement and sadness. "I'm glad you did. I was a bit worried you might leave without saying goodbye."

He shook his head, his expression earnest. "I would never do that. Not after everything."

They sat together, the sun dipping low in the sky, casting a warm, golden glow over them as the day slowly melted into evening. Lila reached into a small cooler, pulling out a tub of her favorite mint chocolate chip ice cream. With a smile that didn't quite reach her eyes, she offered Caleb a scoop. He accepted it with a nod of gratitude, though his hesitation was clear—mint wasn't exactly his favorite.

"You know," Lila began, breaking the silence as Caleb

took a cautious bite, "this ice cream has always been my thing. My mom used to make it for me whenever I was feeling down. It was our little ritual."

Caleb forced a smile, determined to hide his distaste for the flavor. He didn't want to ruin the moment. "It's actually pretty good," he said, his voice soft. "Your mom must have been a great person."

Lila's smile faltered, her eyes clouding with a sadness that Caleb hadn't seen before. She looked down at the ice cream, her spoon idly stirring it around. "She was," Lila replied, her voice barely above a whisper. "But she passed away a few years ago. I was just a kid, really. I barely remember her."

The weight of her words hung between them, the air thick with unspoken grief. Caleb felt a pang of regret for bringing it up, but more than that, he felt a deep, aching sympathy for the girl sitting next to him. He hadn't known that part of her story, hadn't realized the depth of the loss she carried.

"I'm sorry, Lila," he said, his voice sincere. "I didn't know."

Lila shook her head, a small, bittersweet smile tugging at the corners of her mouth. "It's okay. I mean, it still hurts, but it's a different kind of hurt now. I've had time to live with it, to make peace with it, I guess." She paused, her gaze drifting to the horizon where the sun was beginning its descent. "But I still miss her. Every day."

They sat in silence for a moment, the only sound the gentle rustling of the trees and the distant hum of the cicadas. Caleb didn't know what to say, didn't know how to ease the pain he saw in her eyes. But he didn't have to. Lila turned to him, her smile returning, though it was laced with a trace of lingering sadness.

"You know, Caleb," she said, her voice lighter now, "this summer's been different. You've been the one keeping me on my toes, making me laugh when I didn't think I could. It's been... nice."

Caleb felt a warmth spread through his chest, not from the sun, but from her words. He hadn't realized just how much their time together had meant to her, or how much it had come to mean to him.

He looked at her, really looked at her, and in that moment, he understood just how much they had both been carrying—different burdens, but heavy all the same. And somehow, in the midst of all that, they had found a way to lighten each other's load, even if just a little.

"Thanks, Lila," he said, his voice filled with emotion he didn't quite know how to express. "You've been there for me too, more than you know."

They chatted about the summer's highlights, sharing memories and laughter. Lila spoke of an end of summer beach party, a lavish affair filled with the pomp and circumstance typical of the Hamptons social scene. Caleb could tell she was trying to lighten the mood, but he could also sense her own reluctance about the end of the summer.

"I guess it's true what they say," Lila said quietly, as they watched the sun dip closer to the horizon. "All good things have to come to an end."

Caleb nodded, feeling a lump form in his throat. "Yeah, it's hard to believe this summer is almost over. I'm not ready to leave."

As the day drew to a close, Lila handed Caleb a small, neatly wrapped gift. "Here, open it later," she said softly, her eyes filled with sincerity.

Caleb accepted the gift, feeling a mix of anticipation and dread. He watched as Lila walked away, the weight of their impending separation heavy in his heart. Alone now, Caleb unwrapped the small box to find a delicate shell necklace inside. The simple yet thoughtful gift spoke volumes, and Caleb's heart ached with the realization of what he was leaving behind.

He held the necklace gently, the shell catching the fading light. In that moment, he knew that his decision about leaving the Hamptons had become clear. The summer had changed him, and Lila's gift was a reminder of the transformative power of love and the painful beauty of goodbyes.

That evening, the Morgan family gathered for their last dinner together in the mansion. The kitchen was a comforting sanctuary, filled with the tantalizing aromas of a carefully prepared meal. Evelyn had outdone herself, serving roasted chicken with rosemary, buttery mashed potatoes, and crisp green beans. The table was adorned with elegant plates, and the soft clink of silverware provided a gentle soundtrack to the evening.

Caleb, for the first time in what felt like an eternity, was engaged in conversation. His once-distant gaze was now replaced by a thoughtful expression, and he spoke with a clarity and purpose that had been missing for months. His mother, Evelyn, watched him with a mixture of pride and relief, marveling at how much he had opened up over the summer.

"Mom, the mashed potatoes are amazing," Caleb said, a genuine smile touching his lips. It was a simple compliment, but it felt like a monumental shift from the silence that had previously characterized his interactions.

Evelyn beamed at him, her eyes glistening with unshed tears. "Thank you, Caleb. I'm glad you like them."

Thomas Morgan, ever the politician even at the dinner table, was eager to discuss his return to the campaign trail. He sliced into his chicken with practiced precision, his enthusiasm for his work evident in his voice. "I'm looking forward to getting back to New York. The campaign's heating up, and there's a lot to do. We've got big plans for the next few months."

Caleb nodded, though his mind was elsewhere. He took a deep breath, feeling a mix of apprehension and resolve. "Actually, Dad, I wanted to talk to you about something."

"Yes?" Thomas glanced up from his plate, raising an eyebrow. "Go ahead."

Caleb cleared his throat, gathering his thoughts. "I've been thinking a lot about my senior year. I want to stay here and finish it at the Hamptons public school."

Evelyn's face lit up with cautious hope. "Are you sure about this, Caleb? It's a big change."

Caleb met his mother's gaze, his eyes earnest. "Yes, Mom. I've thought about it a lot. I think it's what I need right now."

Thomas's expression hardened, his fork pausing mid-air. "This is absurd. You've got one year left before you start law school. Why disrupt everything now?"

Evelyn stepped in gently, her voice soothing. "Thomas, it's just one year. Maybe a change of environment will do him some good. He's shown so much progress this summer."

Thomas's frustration was palpable, but he tried to maintain his composure. "Caleb, this doesn't make sense. You're on a path, and it's a good one. Why would you throw that away?"

Caleb's voice wavered slightly, but he stood his ground. "It's not about throwing anything away. It's about finding a place where I can really figure out what I want. I've felt... different here. Like I've started to heal. I need this."

Evelyn reached out to touch Thomas's hand, her expression one of quiet determination. "Thomas, maybe it's time to let Caleb make his own decisions. He's been through a lot. If this is what he needs, we should support him."

Thomas sighed heavily, the weight of the decision evident in his tired eyes. After a long pause, he finally relented. "Fine. But only if you keep your grades up and stay out of trouble. I don't want this to be a setback."

Caleb's shoulders relaxed, a wave of relief washing over him. "Thank you, Dad. I promise I'll make it work."

The conversation shifted, the tension easing as Thomas returned to discussing his campaign and Evelyn spoke about the upcoming school year. Despite the heaviness of the evening, there was a newfound sense of understanding at the table. The summer had brought unexpected changes and revelations, and as they shared their final meal in the Hamptons, the Morgans found themselves on the brink of a new chapter.

Caleb looked around the dinner table, his heart full of mixed emotions. The mansion that had once felt like a gilded cage now seemed like a symbol of the possibility of change. As he took another bite of the delicious meal, he realized that this summer, though painful, had given him something invaluable: the courage to follow his own path and the support of his family, even if it came in unexpected ways.

But when he was back in his room, Caleb touched the shell necklace around his neck, a small but powerful reminder of Lila. Despite the challenges ahead, he felt a spark of hope. This summer had brought unexpected changes, and for the first time in a long while, he was ready to face them.

For Logan, it was another restless night as he paced back and forth in his bedroom, glancing at his phone every few seconds. The silence from Lila was deafening, and he could feel his frustration building. Her last text had been days ago, and the empty screen was starting to feel like a wall between them. Restless and determined, he grabbed his helmet and decided that the only way to win back her heart was through a romantic grand gesture.

The night air was cool as he roared down the empty streets on his motorcycle, the engine's growl matching the turbulence in his heart. The moon cast a silvery glow on the road ahead, guiding him toward the mansion grounds where Lila lived. As he approached the estate, he slowed down, the reality of what he was about to do hitting him. But Logan had always been fearless, and tonight would be no exception.

Parking his bike a safe distance away, he climbed over the tall fence, careful not to make too much noise. He made his way to the servants' cottage, the warm light inside contrasting sharply with the darkness of the night. Peering through the window, he saw Lila having dinner with her dad, Mr. Hayes. The sight of her brought a lump to his throat; she looked serene, at peace.

Gathering his courage, he knocked gently on the door. Mr. Hayes opened it, his kind eyes widening in surprise. "Logan? What are you doing here?"

"I need to talk to Lila," Logan replied, his voice steady. "Please."

Mr. Hayes glanced at his daughter, who had already risen from her seat. "Come in, son. Join us for dinner."

But Lila shook her head, walking over to Logan. "Dad, it's okay. We'll talk outside."

As they stepped into the cool night air, Logan turned to her, his heart pounding. "I miss you, Lila. Are you really going to ignore me forever?"

Lila sighed, her resolve weakening as she looked into his eyes. "Logan, I haven't been ignoring you on purpose."

Logan took a step closer, his voice softening. "I know. Your summer jobs kept you busy."

She looked away, her thoughts drifting to Caleb and the new friendship that had unexpectedly blossomed. "You should go," she said finally, her voice barely above a whisper. "I'll see you tomorrow at school,

Logan."

Logan's eyes searched hers for any sign of hope. "Is that a promise?"

"It's all I can give you right now," Lila replied, her voice tinged with sadness.

With a heavy heart, Logan nodded, accepting her words. He turned and began to climb back over the tall fence, the night seeming even darker now. As she watched him leave, memories of their time together flooded her mind. Logan had always been fearless, a quality that had once enchanted her. But now, as she thought of Caleb and the tender moments they had shared, she realized that fearlessness wasn't everything.

Inside the cottage, Mr. Hayes looked up as Lila re-entered, her face a mix of emotions. "You okay, sweetheart?" he asked gently.

Lila nodded, forcing a small smile. "Yeah, Dad. Just... a lot to think about."

He reached out, giving her hand a reassuring squeeze. "Take your time, Lila. The heart knows what it wants."

As she sat back down, the warmth of her father's presence enveloping her, Lila felt a sense of clarity. She didn't know what the future held, but she knew she had to follow her heart, wherever it might lead.

CHAPTER 6: THE LAST YEAR

In the morning, Caleb's parents left for New York, leaving him behind to start his school year in the Hamptons. The idea was to give him a fresh start, away from the constant pressures of his father's political life. But stepping into Hampton Public School for the first time was a jarring experience. The contrast between his exclusive private school and this new environment was stark.

He walked through the entrance, his backpack feeling heavier than usual as it slung over one shoulder. The first thing that struck him was the metal detector stationed just inside the door. Caleb stared at it, trying to make sense of this new addition to his school experience. It looked more like a security checkpoint at an airport than something meant for a school. The students were casually walking through it, as if it were just another part of their routine. Caleb, however, felt a pang of unease as he stepped through, the beeping of the detector and the bored glance of the security guard making him acutely aware of how out of place he felt.

Caleb walked through the front doors, his backpack slung over one shoulder, trying to ignore the nervous fluttering in his stomach. The halls were already buzzing with activity, students chatting and laughing, lockers slamming shut. He felt like an outsider in a world he didn't understand.

The other students seemed to move in a rhythm he couldn't quite grasp, their laughter and chatter like a foreign language. He found himself standing alone, trying to blend in but feeling more like an outsider than ever.

At the front office, he was greeted by Mrs. Cane, the principal. She was a petite woman with kind eyes and a welcoming smile, though there was a flicker of recognition in her gaze that made Caleb uneasy.

"Good morning, Caleb," she said warmly. "Welcome to Hampton Public. I hope you'll find our school to be a good fit for you."

"Thanks," Caleb mumbled, glancing around nervously. "I, uh, I appreciate it."

Mrs. Cane led him to her office, where they sat down to go over his paperwork and grades. She glanced at his transcripts, her eyes widening slightly. "Your grades are impressive, Caleb. It's clear you've worked hard."

Caleb shrugged, feeling a pang of discomfort. "Yeah, I guess so. My parents always expected a lot from me."

Mrs. Cane nodded, her expression sympathetic. "I

understand. Your father's a very influential man. But here, you can just be Caleb. No expectations, no pressures."

He looked at her, grateful for her understanding. "That's what I'm hoping for."

She smiled, leaning back in her chair. "I have to admit, I really support your father's work as a Senator. But don't worry, your secret is safe with me. No one here needs to know who you are unless you want them to."

Just as Caleb was beginning to feel overwhelmed, Mrs. Cane, continued with a reassuring smile. "So Caleb, I've assigned a student to show you around today," she said as she leaned forward to speak into the receiver, "Send in Ms. Hayes, please."

Caleb's heart skipped a beat as Lila walked in, her eyes widening in surprise when she saw him. Mrs. Cane noticed their reaction and smiled warmly. "Ms. Hayes is one of our top students, Caleb. I'm sure she'll help you settle in quickly."

Lila nodded, her surprise giving way to a professional demeanor. "Of course, Mrs. Cane. I'll make sure Caleb gets familiar with the school."

Once they were out of earshot of the principal, Lila turned to him, her voice a mix of curiosity and disbelief. "Caleb? What are you doing here?"

"I transferred," Caleb replied, trying to sound nonchalant. "Needed a change."

Lila narrowed her eyes, suspicion mingling with amusement. "Did you move schools because of me?"

Caleb chuckled, shaking his head. "No, it's not like that. But you did make this place seem a lot more appealing."

Lila laughed softly, her eyes softening. "Well, I'm glad you're here, Caleb. It's good to see a familiar face."

In truth, Lila had a significant influence on his decision. Her presence was a beacon of light in his dark world, and he craved that warmth more than he wanted to admit. The connection they shared, however brief, had given him a glimpse of something he hadn't felt in a long time—hope.

As they walked through the hallways, Lila pointed out various classrooms and important spots in the school. Caleb tried to focus on her words, but his thoughts kept drifting back to the night in the kitchen, the way she had made him feel understood and less alone.

"Honestly, what made you decide to transfer here?" Lila asked, genuinely curious.

Caleb shrugged, trying to downplay the turmoil inside him. "It was kind of a spur-of-the-moment thing. I just felt like I needed a fresh start, you know?"

Lila nodded, her eyes filled with empathy. "I get that. Sometimes, a change of scenery can make all the difference."

They walked in silence for a moment, the noise of students bustling around them fading into the background. Caleb felt a sense of peace being near her, a feeling he hadn't experienced in a long time.

"I'm really glad you're here, Caleb," Lila said softly. "It's nice to have a friend."

Caleb looked at her, his heart swelling with gratitude. "Thanks, Lila. That means a lot to me."

Lila explained the school hierarchy, the clubs, and the unspoken rules of the cafeteria. "Avoid the left side of the cafeteria during lunch. That's where the drama kids hang out, and they're... intense," she said, laughing.

Caleb smiled, feeling a bit more at ease. "Thanks for the tip."

The day passed in a blur of new faces and

endless introductions. Caleb tried to keep up, but his mind kept drifting back to Lila, to the way her presence seemed to make everything better. He realized that, despite the pain and the darkness, there was a part of him that was beginning to hope for something more.

During lunch, Lila led Caleb to their table, where he met Logan, her boyfriend. Logan's presence caught Caleb off guard; he hadn't known Lila was in a relationship. The realization stung, though he tried to hide it behind a polite smile.

"Hey, everyone, this is Caleb," Lila said, introducing him to her friends.

Logan's eyes narrowed slightly, a flicker of jealousy crossing his face. "Nice to meet you, Caleb," he said, though his tone lacked sincerity.

Caleb nodded, feeling a bit out of place. He sat down, trying to follow the conversation, but his mind kept drifting back to Lila and Logan. The dynamic between them was palpable, and it left Caleb feeling even more uncertain about his decision to stay.

"Caleb, this is Elara," Lila continued, gesturing to a girl with glasses and a stack of textbooks beside her.

Elara smiled warmly. "Nice to meet you, Caleb. So, what's your story?"

Caleb shrugged, trying to keep his tone light. "Just moved back here for the summer. Trying to figure things out, I guess."

Before Elara could respond, Jacob, the star athlete of the group, leaned back in his chair, a grin on his face. "Hey man, welcome to the group. I'm gunning for a sports scholarship this year. You into sports?"

Caleb hesitated, aware of the eyes on him. "Not really," he admitted, feeling a bit out of place. "I've never been much of an athlete."

The group laughed, but it wasn't unkind. "Caleb's more of a thinker," Lila said, her voice filled with a soft affection that didn't go unnoticed by Logan.

Lila introduced the last two members of the group, Juno and Kai. They were inseparable, constantly bouncing ideas off each other. "We're planning a cross-country road trip after graduation," Juno said, his eyes sparkling with excitement.

"Yeah," Kai added, "and before we leave, we've got this epic school prank in the works. It's going to be legendary."

Juno turned to Caleb, his expression mischievous. "Did you do any pranks at your last school?"

Caleb thought for a moment, trying to come up with something that wouldn't sound too lame. "Uh, yeah," he began, a small smile playing on his lips as he recalled a rather tame incident. "We once filled the principal's office with balloons. It was pretty funny watching him try to open the door."

The group laughed, and Caleb couldn't help but join in, relieved that they found it amusing even if it wasn't exactly legendary. For a brief moment, he felt like he was part of something, a sense of belonging that he hadn't felt in a long time.

But the moment was fleeting, as Logan's voice cut through the laughter, his tone carrying an edge that made Caleb's heart sink. "So, Caleb," Logan said, leaning forward slightly, "how do you know Lila?"

Caleb glanced at Lila, who gave him an encouraging smile. "Mr. Hayes, her dad, is the caretaker at my family's estate," he explained. "We met when I came back for the summer."

"Interesting," Logan replied, his tone still cool. "Lila's great, isn't she?"

"Yeah," Caleb said, meaning it more than Logan could understand. "She really is."

The words felt inadequate, but they were all he could

manage in the moment. As the conversation drifted to other topics, Caleb found himself retreating inward, his thoughts a jumble of conflicting emotions. He couldn't shake the feeling that he was on the outside looking in, caught in a world where he didn't quite belong.

The conversation shifted, the group reminiscing about their first day back at school and their plans as seniors. Juno and Kai talked animatedly about their prank, which involved a series of harmless but elaborate setups designed to surprise the entire school.

"We're thinking of starting with something small," Juno said, her hands gesturing excitedly.

"And then," Kai continued, "we'll escalate to something bigger."

The others laughed, contributing their ideas. Caleb found himself relaxing, enjoying the easy banter. Despite the initial awkwardness, the group's warmth was infectious.

But as he watched Lila laugh and talk with her friends, he couldn't help but feel a tug at his heart, a longing for something he couldn't quite name. In that moment, he knew that this summer would be more than just a time to figure things out. It would be a time of change, of decisions that would shape the course of his life in ways he couldn't yet imagine.

Caleb shared several classes with Lila, which made the school day more bearable. Her presence was a constant source of comfort and encouragement, and he found himself looking forward to the moments they spent together.

When the final bell rang, signaling the end of the school day, Lila walked him to the front entrance. "So, how was your first day?" she asked, a playful glint in her eyes.

"Not as bad as I thought it would be," Caleb admitted, a genuine smile tugging at his lips. "Thanks to you."

"Happy to help," she replied, nudging him lightly with her shoulder. "Now, how are you planning to get home?"

"I was just going to call an Uber," Caleb said, pulling out his phone.

Lila raised an eyebrow, a teasing smile spreading across her face. "Of course, you were. Typical rich boy. Come on, I'll show you how to use the public transportation system."

Caleb chuckled, pocketing his phone and following her. They walked to the nearby bus stop, and Lila patiently explained how the routes worked, which buses to take, and how to pay the fare. Caleb listened intently, appreciating her willingness to help him navigate this new aspect of his life.

As they boarded the bus, Lila continued to tease him about his fancy lifestyle. "You know, there's more to life than luxury cars and private drivers," she said with a wink.

Caleb laughed, shaking his head. "I guess I'm learning that now."

When they arrived back at the mansion, they headed to the kitchen for some post-school snacks. Mr. Hayes was already there, preparing dinner. The aroma of roasted chicken and fresh herbs filled the air, making Caleb's stomach growl in anticipation.

"Hey, Dad," Lila greeted warmly. "What's on the menu tonight?"

"Roasted chicken with vegetables," Mr. Hayes replied, smiling at them both. "Why don't you two have a seat and I'll bring out some snacks?"

As they sat at the kitchen table, Caleb glanced out the window, noticing the servant's cottage for the first time. "Is that where you live?" he asked Lila, nodding towards the small house.

"Yeah," Lila replied, following his gaze. "It's cozy. Not as grand as this place, but it's home."

Caleb felt a pang of guilt, realizing how different their lives were. "I'd love to see it sometime," he said softly.

Lila smiled, a hint of surprise in her eyes. "Sure, maybe one day."

Mr. Hayes brought out a plate of cookies and a pitcher of lemonade, setting them on the table with a gentle smile. "Enjoy, Master Caleb. Dinner will be ready soon."

Caleb nodded, the sweet aroma of freshly baked cookies filling the air, a small comfort in the midst of his emotional storm. Lila sat beside him, her presence soothing and warm, a stark contrast to the turmoil that churned inside him.

Mr. Hayes turned to his daughter, his eyes filled with a father's quiet pride. "Lila, could you tend to the roses in the garden while I prepare dinner?"

Lila smiled and stood up, brushing a stray lock of hair from her face. "Of course, Dad."

Caleb, sensing an opportunity to be close to her, stood up as well. "I can help," he offered, his voice tinged with eagerness.

Lila shook her head gently, her eyes meeting his with a kind firmness. "You've had enough of a first day back. Go cleanup for dinner. We'll catch up afterward."

Reluctantly, Caleb nodded and watched her walk towards the garden, her figure bathed in the golden light of the setting sun. He turned and made his way upstairs, the weight of the day pressing down on him.

In the Morgan estate's garden, Lila knelt beside the rose bushes, her hands deep in the soil as she tended to the flowers. She had always found solace here, amidst the vibrant colors and delicate scents, a place where she could escape the complexities of life and lose herself in the simple act of nurturing something beautiful. But today, her thoughts were elsewhere—on Caleb and the pain she saw in his eyes.

Caleb's struggles were evident, even if he tried to hide them. The way he moved, the shadows that darkened his gaze, spoke of a heart burdened with sorrow and secrets. Lila felt a pang of empathy, wanting to reach out and offer him comfort, yet knowing that healing took time and understanding.

She hadn't meant to get involved in his life, but there was something about him that touched her deeply. He was different from anyone she had ever met, and she felt an inexplicable connection to him. She knew her boyfriend Logan wouldn't understand, but she couldn't help the way she felt.

As she watered the roses, she thought about the moments she had shared with Caleb, the quiet conversations and the unspoken understanding that seemed to pass between them. She hoped he wouldn't let Logan's threats keep him away. There was so much more she wanted to know about him, so much more she wanted to share.

At school, Logan watched from a distance, his jealousy simmering beneath the surface. He saw how much time Lila was spending with Caleb, and it gnawed at him. The easy friendship they shared, the way Lila's eyes lit up when she was around Caleb—it all felt like a threat to his relationship with her.

And as the days went by, Logan's jealousy grew. He would watch from across the hallway as Lila and Caleb walked to class together, his fists clenching involuntarily. He couldn't understand why Caleb's presence bothered him so much, but he knew he didn't like the way things were changing.

Logan stormed down the hallway, his anger simmering just beneath the surface. Seeing Caleb around Lila stirred a storm of emotions within him—fear, jealousy, and a deep-seated insecurity he couldn't quite shake. He loved Lila fiercely, and the thought of someone else getting close to her was more than he could bear.

He paused for a moment, leaning against the wall, trying to collect himself. Why was he so threatened by Caleb? Was it because he saw in him something he couldn't offer Lila—a sense of understanding and shared pain? The thought gnawed at him, making his chest tighten with anxiety.

That was when Logan decided to finally confront Lila. He found her by her locker, when Caleb was nowhere in sight. "Hey, can we talk?" he asked, trying to keep his voice steady.

Lila looked up, sensing the tension in his voice. "Sure, Logan. What's up?"

"I just... I see that you're spending a lot of time with Caleb," he said, struggling to find the right words. "I mean, I get that he's new and all, but..."

Lila sighed, closing her locker and turning to face him. "Logan, Caleb's been through a lot. He needs a friend right now, and I'm just trying to be there for him."

"But what about us?" Logan asked, his frustration evident. "It feels like you're drifting away."

Lila's expression softened, and she reached out to touch his arm. "Logan, I'm not going anywhere. You're important to me. But Caleb needs me too. Can't you understand that?"

Logan looked into her eyes, seeing the sincerity in them. He sighed, the tension leaving his body. "Yeah, I guess I do. I'm sorry, Lila. I just... I don't want to lose you."

"You won't," Lila promised, giving him a reassuring smile. "I care about you, Logan. But Caleb's a part of my life now too. I hope you can accept that."

Logan nodded, though a part of him still felt uneasy. He knew he had to trust Lila, but the presence of Caleb continued to stir feelings of jealousy and insecurity. As he watched her walk away, he couldn't shake the fear that this new friendship might change everything.

It was one of those free period days, when Caleb found himself alone in the corridors, lost in his thoughts. The silence was interrupted by the sound of approaching footsteps, heavy and deliberate. Logan appeared at the end of the corridor, his expression dark and menacing.

"Caleb," Logan called out, his voice echoing off the marble walls.

Caleb turned to face him, his heart pounding. "Logan," he replied, trying to keep his voice steady.

Logan walked closer, his eyes filled with a mix of anger and jealousy. "I don't know what you're trying to do, but stay away from Lila," he warned, his voice low and threatening. "She's my girlfriend, and I don't need you complicating things."

Caleb met Logan's gaze, trying to stay calm. "I'm just trying to fit in, man. I'm not here to cause trouble."

Logan's eyes narrowed, his jaw clenching. "We'll see about that. But consider this your first and only warning. Stay away from her."

Caleb walked away from the encounter with Logan, his mind racing. He couldn't shake the feeling of unease that settled over him. Logan's warning had been clear, but there was something about Lila that drew him in, something he couldn't ignore. She was the light in his otherwise dark world, and he wasn't sure he could keep his distance.

CHAPTER 7: THE LAST MENACE

Caleb's phone buzzed on the nightstand as he was getting ready for school. He glanced at the screen and saw his mother's name. With a sigh, he answered, trying to muster some semblance of enthusiasm.

"Morning, Mom," he said, adjusting his plaid shirt in the mirror.

"Good morning, sweetheart," Evelyn replied, her voice warm yet tinged with concern. "Just wanted to check in on you. How's everything going at the new school?"

"It's fine," Caleb lied, forcing a smile. "Just the usual stuff."

Evelyn paused for a moment, as if weighing her words carefully. "And how are you holding up? Really?"

Caleb hesitated, the weight of his father's expectations and the recent loss of Milo pressing heavily on his shoulders. "I'm managing, Mom," he said softly. "How's Dad's campaign going?"

"Oh, you know how it is," she replied with a hint of weariness. "He's busy, always running from one event to another. He's rarely home these days."

Caleb's heart sank a little. "Maybe you could come stay at the Hamptons with me? It gets pretty lonely here."

Evelyn's eyes softened. "I wish I could, Caleb. But your father needs me here. This campaign is crucial, and he needs all the support he can get."

"I understand," Caleb said, his chest tightening. "I'll talk to you later, okay? I need to head out."

"Alright, love you," she said, blowing him a kiss through the screen.

"Love you too," Caleb replied, ending the call and taking a deep breath. He grabbed his backpack and headed out, steeling himself for another day.

Determined to avoid Lila and the questions he couldn't answer, Caleb left the house earlier than usual, catching the first bus to school. The ride was quiet, the morning stillness matching his somber mood. He stared out the window, lost in thought, the scenery blurring into a kaleidoscope of colors.

At school, he slipped into his first class, hoping to go unnoticed. But as the day wore on, it became increasingly difficult to avoid Lila. She had a way of finding him, her presence both comforting and unsettling.

During their shared English class, she slipped into the seat next to him, her eyes full of concern. "Caleb, is everything okay?"

He pretended to be busy reading the textbook, the words swimming before his eyes. "Just trying to catch up with the syllabus," he said, his voice strained, Logan's warning still fresh in his mind.

Lila wasn't convinced. "You've been acting different lately. If something's wrong, you can tell me."

Caleb forced a smile, though it didn't reach his eyes. "I appreciate it, Lila. But I'm fine, really."

"Okay," she sighed, her gaze lingering on him. "If you ever need to talk, I'm here. Don't forget that."

He nodded absently, grateful for her concern but unable to share the turmoil that churned inside him. As the class continued, he struggled to focus, his mind drifting back to the conversation with his mother and the heavy expectations that weighed him down.

Throughout the day, Caleb's thoughts kept returning to Lila. There was something about her that stirred a flicker of hope within him, a lightness that he desperately needed. But the darkness that enveloped his heart was hard to shake, and he wasn't sure he was ready to let anyone in, even someone as kind and understanding as Lila.

Despite maintaining a low profile, he could feel all eyes were on him, the whispers and the snickers. The privileged new kid, the rich boy who didn't belong.

In the hallways, students would shove past him, making snide comments under their breath. His locker was stuffed with grass and trash, a cruel prank that left him seething with frustration. But he remembered his promise to his father—no trouble. So, he swallowed his anger and cleaned up the mess in silence.

Lila noticed the change in Caleb, her concern growing with each passing day. She tried to protect him, standing up to the bullies whenever she could, but there was only so much she could do.

"Caleb, you don't have to deal with this," she said one day, her eyes full of empathy. "You should raise a complaint or something."

"I can handle it," he replied, though his resolve was wavering. "It's just a phase. It'll pass."

But it didn't pass. The pranks continued, each one more humiliating than the last. Caleb felt like he was drowning, each day a struggle to keep his head above water.

Meanwhile, Logan's jealousy simmered beneath the surface. He noticed the growing distance between him and Lila, and it fueled his anger. He took his frustration out in the gym, the punching bag bearing the brunt of his rage.

But it was Caleb who found Logan in the gym, his fists flying as he pounded the bag. Caleb approached, his anger bubbling to the surface.

"I know it's you," Caleb said, his voice steady but full of emotion. "You're the one sending those bullies after me."

Logan paused, his chest heaving, and turned to face Caleb. "What if I am? What are you gonna do about it?"

Caleb stepped closer, his eyes locked on Logan's. "I'm not going to give in. Especially not when it comes to Lila."

Logan's jaw tightened, but he didn't say anything. Caleb turned and walked away, his heart pounding in his chest. He had stood his ground, but he knew the battle was far from over.

In the bustling cafeteria, Caleb picked a corner table, hoping to go unnoticed. He pulled out a book, using it as a shield against the world around him. But his mind kept drifting back to his parents, their departure leaving a hollow ache in his chest. The weight of their expectations still lingered, a constant reminder of the life he was trying to escape.

Across the cafeteria, he saw a group of students laughing, their easy camaraderie a stark contrast to his solitude. He longed for that sense of belonging, but the walls he had built around himself seemed insurmountable. The thought of reaching out, of trying to connect, felt overwhelming.

As he flipped through the pages, he heard a sudden hush fall over the cafeteria. Caleb looked up just in time to see a tray of food descending towards him. The tray hit his head with a loud smack, spilling spaghetti and sauce all over him. Laughter erupted around him, the sound harsh and cruel.

"Logan! Logan! Logan!" the crowd chanted, and Caleb's stomach sank. Logan Bennet, Lila's boyfriend, stood on top of a table, fist-pumping the air, a triumphant grin on his face. Caleb's eyes locked with Lila's, who was sitting beside Logan, her face a mask of horror.

Caleb felt his face burn with embarrassment and anger.

He stood there, dripping with sauce, his fists clenched at his sides. The laughter around him seemed to echo in his ears, growing louder and more mocking with each passing second.

"What's going on here?" a stern voice cut through the noise, silencing the crowd. Principal Mrs. Cane stood at the entrance of the cafeteria, her eyes blazing with anger. "Logan Bennet and Caleb Morgan, my office. Now!"

The cafeteria fell silent, and Logan's smug expression faltered. Caleb wiped the sauce from his face, his heart pounding as he followed Mrs. Cane out of the cafeteria, Logan trailing behind him. The walk to the principal's office felt like a walk of shame, each step heavy with the weight of his humiliation.

In Mrs. Cane's office, the atmosphere was tense. Logan slouched in his chair, his confident demeanor replaced with a sullen glare. Caleb sat stiffly, his mind racing with a mix of anger and humiliation.

"Care to explain what happened?" Mrs. Cane's voice was calm but firm, her eyes sharp as they moved between the two boys.

"It was just a joke," Logan muttered, avoiding her gaze.

"A joke?" Caleb snapped, unable to keep the bitterness from his voice. "You call that a joke?"

Mrs. Cane raised a hand, silencing them. "Logan, this behavior is unacceptable. And Caleb, I understand you're upset, but raising your voice isn't going to help."

Caleb bit back his retort, feeling the sting of tears in his eyes. He looked down at his lap, trying to keep his emotions in check.

Mrs. Cane sighed, her expression softening slightly. "I expect better from both of you. Logan, you will apologize to Caleb, and I want to see a genuine effort to make amends. Caleb, if you need support, my door is always open. This school is a community, and we need to treat each other with respect."

Logan muttered a half-hearted apology, and Caleb nodded stiffly, not trusting himself to speak.

After Logan and Caleb left her office, Mrs. Cane sat back in her chair, her mind heavy with the weight of the day's events. The image of Caleb, humiliated and angry, was etched in her memory. She couldn't shake the feeling that she had failed him somehow, that she had let the cruelty of others go unchecked for too long.

She glanced at the clock, noting the afternoon hour.

Caleb's parents, the Morgans, were very busy people. She knew that calling them now would likely result in a brief, distracted conversation, one that wouldn't do justice to the gravity of the situation. But could she wait? Could she let another day pass without addressing the bullying that had taken root in her school?

Mrs. Cane sighed, rubbing her temples as she pondered her next move. She reached for the phone, hesitating as her hand hovered over the receiver. Caleb needed support, that much was clear. But involving his parents now, without proper context or a clear plan, might only add to his burden.

But Caleb's well-being was her top priority, and she couldn't ignore what had happened. Maybe, she reasoned, it would be best to wait for a better opportunity, a moment when she could speak to his parents in person and convey the depth of Caleb's struggles. She would need to tread carefully, to ensure that they understood the seriousness of the situation without making Caleb feel more isolated.

Meanwhile, as Caleb and Logan walked away from Mrs. Cane's office, the tension between them was palpable. Caleb's thoughts were a whirlwind of anger, humiliation, and sadness. Logan, on the other hand, seemed unrepentant, his swagger and cocky grin still firmly in place.

Caleb glanced over at Logan, a bitter taste in his mouth. How could someone be so cruel, so indifferent to the pain they caused? He clenched his fists, struggling to keep his emotions in check. He wouldn't give Logan the satisfaction of seeing him break.

Caleb stormed into the shower room in the gym, his face still burning with humiliation and anger. He quickly changed into a T-shirt and shorts, not caring that he was missing his Chemistry class. All he could think about was Logan and the way he had humiliated him in front of everyone. The warm water from the shower did little to wash away the sting of the food tray being dumped on his head, or the laughter that had followed.

Once he was dressed, he walked out of the locker room, only to find Lila waiting for him. Her presence startled him, and he immediately tried to sidestep her, his emotions still raw.

"Caleb, wait," Lila called out, her voice filled with concern. "I wanted to apologize for what Logan did. It was completely out of line."

Caleb paused, turning to face her. His eyes were filled with hurt and anger. "Why are you with him, Lila? He's a terrible person."

Lila's expression faltered. She had hoped her words would ease Caleb's pain, but now she felt like she was making things worse. "Logan can be a jerk sometimes, but he's not all bad. He just... has his moments."

Caleb shook his head, a bitter smile forming on his lips. "Moments? Lila, he humiliated me in front of the entire school. How many 'moments' does it take before you see him for who he really is?"

Lila took a step back, her eyes glistening with unshed tears. "I didn't mean to defend what he did. I'm just trying to understand why you—"

"Why me?" Caleb interrupted, his voice rising. "Because I'm the easy target, Lila. Because I don't fit in with the rest of you. And you standing there trying to apologize for him only makes it worse. Just stay away from me at school, okay?"

He turned and walked away, his heart pounding with a mix of anger and sorrow. He couldn't believe he had spoken to Lila like that, but the pain of Logan's betrayal was too much to bear. Lila watched him go, her heart breaking. She hadn't expected Caleb to react so strongly, but deep down, she knew he was right. Logan was mean, and his actions had crossed a line.

As Caleb walked through the quiet halls, his mind raced

with thoughts of the incident. He couldn't shake the feeling of betrayal, not just from Logan but from the laughter of his classmates. He found himself in the empty gym, the echo of his footsteps the only sound in the vast space.

Sitting down on the bleachers, Caleb tried to collect his thoughts. He knew he couldn't keep running from his problems, but confronting them seemed impossible. His father's expectations, the bullying, and the constant pressure to fit in were suffocating him.

Lila, on the other hand, stood frozen in the hallway, her mind replaying Caleb's words. She had always seen the good in people, even in Logan, but Caleb's pain was undeniable. She felt a pang of guilt for not standing up to Logan earlier, for not seeing how deeply his actions had hurt Caleb.

After school, Caleb retreated to his room, seeking solace in its familiar walls. The events of the day weighed heavily on him, each moment replaying in his mind like a relentless loop. The laughter, the humiliation, and the look of pity in Lila's eyes all haunted him. He lay on his bed, staring at the ceiling, his thoughts a tangled mess of anger and sadness.

As evening approached, Mr. Hayes knocked gently on Caleb's door before entering with a tray of sandwiches and soup. The old caretaker had always been a steady presence in Caleb's life, a source of wisdom and comfort.

"Rough day, huh?" Mr. Hayes said, his voice gentle and understanding.

"You could say that," Caleb replied, his gaze shifting to the garden outside, where the flowers swayed gently in the breeze.

Mr. Hayes set the tray down on Caleb's desk and pulled up a chair. "You want to talk about it?"

Caleb hesitated, then sighed. "It's just...kids at school. They're picking on me because I'm rich. They think I have it all, but they don't know anything about my life. I don't want to tell my parents because I promised I'd stay out of trouble."

Mr. Hayes nodded, his expression thoughtful. "You know, money can make people jealous, but it doesn't shield you from pain. It's okay to ask for help, Master Caleb. Even from your parents. They might understand more than you think."

Caleb shook his head. "My dad would just be disappointed. He expects me to be strong, to handle everything on my own. I can't let him down."

Mr. Hayes reached out and placed a reassuring hand on Caleb's shoulder. "It's not about letting anyone down. It's about being true to yourself."

Caleb picked up a sandwich, taking a bite. The familiar taste of the soup and the warmth of the meal began to ease some of the tension in his body. He hadn't realized how hungry he was until he started eating.

Mr. Hayes chuckled softly. "You know, you were quite the little menace when you were a kid. Always getting into trouble with Lila around the house."

Caleb looked at him, surprised. "Really? I don't remember much from back then. I always thought I was a good boy."

"Oh, you were a handful," Mr. Hayes said with a smile. "Fearless, always up for an adventure. You had a spark, Master Caleb. Still do."

Caleb felt a lump in his throat, Mr. Hayes' words stirring something deep within him. "I don't feel fearless anymore," he admitted, his voice barely above a whisper.

Mr. Hayes leaned in closer, his eyes filled with warmth and encouragement. "That spark's still in you, even if it's buried deep. Don't let these bullies snuff it out. Remember who you are, Master Caleb. Remember that kid who wasn't afraid of anything."

Caleb swallowed hard, feeling a mix of emotions. The caretaker's words were like a balm to his wounded spirit. For a moment, he allowed himself to believe that maybe, just maybe, he could find that spark again.

As Mr. Hayes stood to leave, he paused at the door. "If you ever need to talk, you know where to find me. I am rooting for you."

Caleb watched him go, a sense of gratitude washing over him. He finished his meal, feeling a bit better, the warmth of the food and Mr. Hayes' words giving him a small glimmer of hope. He knew the road ahead wouldn't be easy, but for the first time in a long while, he felt like he didn't have to face it alone.

CHAPTER 8: THE LAST CARD

The next couple of days were a blur of frustration and regret for Caleb. He couldn't stop replaying his outburst in his mind, the way his anger had flared uncontrollably in front of Lila. She had been nothing but kind to him, offering a glimmer of light in his otherwise dark world, and he had repaid her with anger and resentment. Determined to make things right, he spent the better part of the morning looking for her, hoping to apologize and start anew.

Lila seemed to have a knack for disappearing in the hallways of their high school, blending into the crowd effortlessly. Caleb wandered from one hallway to another, his eyes scanning for her familiar face. Finally, his search led him to their shared English class. There she was, seated by the window, her expression as cold as the winter wind. She barely glanced at him as he took his seat beside her, her body language screaming indifference.

Taking a deep breath, Caleb leaned over and whispered, "Lila, can we talk?"

She didn't respond at first, her eyes fixed on the book in front of her. After a moment, she sighed and turned to him, her gaze icy. "What do you want, Caleb?"

Her tone stung, but he couldn't blame her. "I wanted to apologize," he said earnestly. "I was out of line the other day. You didn't deserve any of that."

Lila's eyes softened just a fraction, but she didn't relent. "Why did you snap at me? I was just trying to help."

Caleb looked down at his hands, his fingers nervously twisting the hem of his shirt. "I don't know. I guess... I guess I'm just not used to people being kind to me. I've been dealing with a lot, and sometimes it all just... comes out wrong."

She studied him for a moment, her expression unreadable. "That's not an excuse to treat people like dirt, Caleb."

"I know," he admitted, his voice heavy with regret. "I'm really sorry, Lila. I'm trying to be better, I promise."

For a long moment, Lila didn't say anything. Caleb felt his heart sink, fearing that he had ruined any chance of a friendship with her. The classroom buzzed with the chatter of students settling in, and the teacher began to speak, drawing Caleb's attention away from Lila. He stole glances at her throughout the lesson, but she kept her eyes firmly on her notebook, scribbling down notes with a focused intensity.

When the bell finally rang, Caleb gathered his things, hoping to catch up with her. But Lila was quick to leave the room, slipping out the door before he could even stand up. He watched her retreating figure, feeling a pang of regret and frustration. He had to find a way to make things right.

The sun was high in the sky as the students filed out onto the field for gym class. Caleb's thoughts were still on Lila, his mind replaying their brief exchange over and over. The coach blew the whistle, signaling the start of the softball game. Caleb took his position in the outfield, trying to focus on the game, but his thoughts kept drifting back to her.

As the game progressed, it became clear that Lila's frustration was not limited to silence. She stepped up to the plate, her eyes narrowed in determination. When the ball was pitched, she swung with all her might, sending it soaring in Caleb's direction. He barely had time to react before the ball struck him hard in the ribs, knocking the wind out of him.

"Nice hit, Lila!" Logan shouted from the sidelines, his mocking laughter grating on Caleb's nerves.

Caleb winced, clutching his side as he tried to catch his breath. Logan sauntered over, a smug grin on his face.

"What's the matter, Morgan? Can't handle a little softball?"

Caleb glared at him, trying to hide the pain. "I'm fine," he muttered, straightening up.

Logan's grin widened. "Sure you are. Maybe you should stick to reading books in the cafeteria instead of playing with the big kids."

Ignoring Logan's taunts, Caleb focused on the game, determined to prove he wasn't going to be intimidated. But the sting of Lila's anger and Logan's words lingered, a constant reminder of how much he had messed up.

When lunch period rolled around, Caleb scanned the crowded cafeteria, his eyes landing on Lila and Logan. They were sitting together at a table, sharing a juice box and laughing about something. The sight made his heart ache, but it also spurred him into action. He couldn't let things stay this way.

With a deep breath, Caleb made his way over to their table. He could feel the eyes of other students on him, but he pushed the thought aside, focusing only on Lila.

"Lila, can we talk?" he asked, his voice steady despite the nervous flutter in his chest.

Logan rolled his eyes, clearly annoyed. "What do you want, Morgan?"

Caleb ignored him, keeping his gaze on Lila. She looked up at him, her expression unreadable. "Please," he said quietly.

Lila sighed and stood up, giving Logan a quick glance. "I'll be back in a minute," she said to him before turning to Caleb. "Okay, let's talk."

They walked to a quieter corner of the cafeteria, away from prying eyes and curious ears. Caleb took a deep breath, searching for the right words.

"Lila, I'm really sorry about everything. I didn't mean to hurt you," he began, his voice earnest. "I just... I don't know how to make things right, but I want to. Can we start over?"

Lila studied him for a moment, her expression a mix of hurt and determination. "Caleb, it's not just about what happened earlier. It's everything. You've been dealing with so much, and I get it, but you can't just shut people out and expect them to be okay with it."

Caleb nodded, feeling the weight of her words. "I know. I've been trying to handle everything on my own, but it's not working. I need to be better."

Lila's eyes searched his, looking for sincerity. After a long pause, she shook her head. "Caleb, it's not that simple. You hurt me, and now you have to live with the consequences of your actions. I can't just pretend everything is okay."

Caleb's heart sank, her words cutting deep. "I understand. I'm really sorry, Lila. I never wanted to hurt you."

Lila looked away, a tear escaping down her cheek. "I need time, Caleb. Maybe someday we can be friends again, but right now, I need space. You need to figure out your own stuff."

Caleb nodded, feeling a lump in his throat. "I get it. Thank you for being honest."

As she walked back to Logan's table, Caleb stood there, feeling the sting of her words. He knew he had a lot to work on and that forgiveness wouldn't come easily. The road to redemption was going to be a long one, and he had to face it alone.

The next day, Caleb sat in English class, his thoughts drifting far from the lecture. The laughter from the previous day's cafeteria incident echoed in his mind, a cruel reminder of his status at school. He glanced down at his test paper, purposely allowing himself to make mistakes. His once pristine grades began to slip, and he received a C on his latest test. It wasn't entirely untrue—his mind had been elsewhere lately.

After class, Caleb approached Principal Mrs. Cane's office, feeling a knot of anxiety in his stomach. He knocked softly on the door, and she called him in.

"Caleb, how can I help you today?" Mrs. Cane asked, her eyes kind but scrutinizing.

"I... I need some help with my English grades," Caleb began, his voice hesitant. "I was wondering if I could have a student buddy to help me improve. Specifically, I'd like Lila Hayes."

Mrs. Cane raised an eyebrow, sensing there was more to this request than just academics. "Lila Hayes, huh? Any particular reason?"

Caleb shifted uncomfortably. "She's really good, and I think she could help me understand better. Plus, I... I need to prove to myself that I can do better."

Mrs. Cane nodded thoughtfully. "Alright, Caleb. I'll talk to Lila and see if she's willing to help. You're lucky, you know. Lila is one of our top students."

Later that day, Lila was called into Mrs. Cane's office. She entered with a mixture of curiosity and apprehension, wondering what this unexpected summons was about.

"Hi, Mrs. Cane. You wanted to see me?" Lila asked, standing just inside the door.

"Yes, Lila. Have a seat," Mrs. Cane said, gesturing to the chair in front of her desk. "Caleb Morgan has requested a study buddy to help him improve his English grades. He specifically asked for you."

Lila's eyes widened in surprise. "Me? Why?"

Mrs. Cane smiled. "Because you're one of our best students, and he believes you can help him. Plus, you'd receive extra credit for your efforts. It could be beneficial for both of you."

Lila hesitated, thinking about the complexities this arrangement might bring. She glanced out the window, her thoughts racing. "Alright, I'll do it. But only because of the extra credit."

Mrs. Cane smiled, sensing Lila's reluctance but also her underlying kindness. "Thank you, Lila. I think this could be good for both of you."

Their study sessions began with an air of uncertainty, both Caleb and Lila unsure of how to navigate the new dynamic between them. They sat across from each other in the grand library of the Morgan estate, a room filled with towering shelves of books that had likely never been touched. The silence that hung between them was thick, laden with unspoken words and the weight of secrets they both carried.

Lila was the first to break the silence, her tone business-like as she opened her notebook. "Let's get started," she said, her eyes briefly meeting Caleb's before focusing on the task at hand.

Caleb nodded, feeling a swirl of relief mixed with anxiety. "Thanks for doing this, Lila. I know it's not exactly easy."

Lila sighed, flipping through the pages of the textbook. "Let's just focus on getting your grades up, okay? We'll take it one step at a time."

Their conversations at first were stilted and formal, sticking strictly to the literature assignments in front of them. Caleb struggled to concentrate, his mind more occupied with Lila's presence than with the words on the page. He caught himself sneaking glances at her, watching the way her brow furrowed in concentration or the way she absentmindedly twirled a strand of hair around her finger. He felt a strange mix of admiration and longing, feelings that he hadn't quite sorted out yet.

"Okay, so what do you think the theme of this passage is?" Lila asked, breaking him out of his thoughts.

Caleb blinked, realizing he hadn't been paying attention. "Uh... maybe it's about... I don't know, fate or something?" He knew it was a weak answer, but part of him hoped she'd see through his act and spend more time explaining it to him.

Lila gave him a skeptical look. "Come on, Caleb. You can do better than that. Look at the text. What's really going on here?"

He sighed, leaning closer to her as if the proximity would somehow help him understand better. "Honestly, Lila, I'm not sure I get it. Could you, uh, maybe go over it again?"

She raised an eyebrow but didn't protest. Instead, she launched into an explanation, her voice softening as she broke down the nuances of the passage. Caleb listened, not so much to the content, but to the sound of her voice—the gentle cadence that made even the most tedious subjects seem interesting.

As they continued, Caleb couldn't resist playing up his

confusion just a little, asking questions he already knew the answers to, pretending to be more lost than he really was. He wasn't proud of it, but he couldn't deny the small thrill he got from Lila's patient explanations, the way she leaned in a little closer, her frustration giving way to a sort of quiet determination to help him.

But as the days passed, the walls between them began to crumble, bit by bit. Their conversations, once strictly academic, started to veer into more personal territory. It was one afternoon, as they were working on an essay, that Caleb finally opened up, the weight of his thoughts too heavy to keep inside any longer.

"You ever feel like you're just… not enough?" Caleb's voice was quiet, his eyes fixed on the paper in front of him. "Like no matter what you do, you'll never be what they want?"

Lila nodded, her eyes filled with understanding. "I get that," she said softly. "My dad works for your family, and sometimes I feel like I'm just a part of the background. It's hard to navigate a world where you always feel like an outsider."

In those quiet corners of the library during lunch periods, they found solace in each other's company. The vastness of the estate's wealth and privilege seemed to fade away, leaving just two teenagers grappling with their own worlds of pain and expectation.

"I miss Milo so much," Caleb confided one rainy afternoon, the sound of raindrops tapping gently against the window. "He was the one constant in my life, like a friend who never judged me."

Lila reached out, placing a comforting hand on his arm. "I'm sorry, Caleb. Losing someone you love is never easy. But it's okay to grieve, and it's okay to remember him in your own way."

As they shared their stories, Caleb began to see a different side of Lila. She, too, carried her own burdens. The daughter of the Morgans' Hampton house caretaker, she navigated a world where privilege and income disparity were starkly contrasted. Her vulnerability was a revelation, a reminder that everyone had their own battles to fight.

"My dad does everything he can to make sure we're okay," Lila said, her voice tinged with both pride and sadness. "But sometimes it's hard not to feel resentful. Watching all this luxury around me, knowing it's not mine."

As they studied together, the tension between them slowly eased. Lila explained concepts with patience, and Caleb tried his best to keep up, his mind struggling to stay focused.

During a break, Caleb looked at her, his expression sincere. "Lila, I know I have a lot to make up for. Not just in grades, but in everything. I'm sorry for all the times I've been a jerk."

Lila glanced at him, her eyes softening slightly. "It's going to take more than words, Caleb. Actions speak louder."

"I know," Caleb replied, determination in his voice. "And I'm ready to prove it."

Their study sessions became a regular thing, and slowly, Caleb's grades began to improve. The walls he had built around himself started to crack, letting a glimmer of hope seep through.

In the midst of their growing connection, Logan noticed Lila's absence from his side and grew increasingly irritated. Seeing her with Caleb, spending more time together, made his blood boil. Logan had always thrived on attention and control, and the sight of Lila with someone else felt like a personal affront.

When Logan approached Caleb and Lila in the library, his face was twisted with anger. "Enjoying your little study sessions?" he sneered, his voice dripping with contempt.

Caleb tensed, ready for a confrontation, but Lila stepped between them, her expression calm and resolute. "Leave him alone, Logan. We're just studying."

Logan's eyes narrowed, a dangerous glint in them. "You think you can just take her away from me?" he spat, glaring at Caleb. "You have no idea what you're getting into."

Ignoring Lila's attempts to diffuse the situation, Logan leaned in closer to Caleb, his voice low and menacing. "You think this is bad? Just wait. I have a card up my sleeve that'll make your life a living hell."

As Logan stormed off, Caleb felt a mixture of anger and fear. The encounter left him shaken, but Lila's presence was a balm to his frayed nerves. She reached out, her touch gentle and reassuring. "Don't let him get to you," she said softly. "He's just trying to intimidate you."

Caleb nodded, appreciating her support. "Thanks, Lila. It means a lot."

That evening, Caleb sat alone in his room, the shadows growing longer as the day gave way to night. The unease Logan's words had stirred within him refused to fade, lingering like a dark cloud over his thoughts. He knew Logan was unpredictable, and the thought of what he might do next filled Caleb with dread. But as the quiet moments before sleep settled in, his mind drifted back to Lila—the kindness in her eyes, the way she believed in him when he couldn't even believe in himself. It was a small flicker of hope in an otherwise bleak world, and Caleb clung to it.

The soft chime of his phone broke the silence, and he glanced at the screen to see his father's name flashing. His heart tightened, and without hesitation, he silenced the call, letting it ring out into the void. He wasn't ready to talk to his father, not after what had happened. The wound was still too fresh, too raw. The terrible thing his father had done—a betrayal that cut deeper than any physical pain—was something Caleb couldn't forgive just yet.

Soon, the days passed quickly and Caleb found comfort in the study sessions he shared with Lila. Each session seemed to deepen their bond, an unexpected connection that brought light to the dark corners of his life. Lila was a force of strength and resilience, and through her, Caleb began to see the world differently. He realized that despite the wealth and privilege that surrounded him, true richness came not from material possessions, but from the connections he forged with others, from the love and understanding they shared.

When they sat across from each other, with their textbooks open between them, Caleb noticed the cute way that Lila's brow wrinkled. They were discussing Shakespeare, and he almost blurted out the right answer to a question she posed, catching himself just in time.

Lila paused, a small smile tugging at the corners of her lips. "You know, Caleb, I'm starting to think you're not as clueless about English as you're pretending to be."

Caleb chuckled, feeling a slight blush rise to his cheeks. "Maybe I'm just a quick learner," he teased, though he knew he'd been caught.

Lila laughed softly, her eyes sparkling with amusement. "Or maybe you've been faking it this whole time just to spend more time with me."

He shrugged, giving her a playful grin. "Can you blame me? You make studying Shakespeare actually bearable."

Their laughter echoed through the room, and for a moment, the heaviness in Caleb's heart lifted. There was something easy, something natural about being with Lila. It was as if she saw right through the walls he'd built around himself, understanding him in a way no one else did.

As their study sessions continued, they transformed into more than just lessons on literature. They became a sanctuary, a safe haven where both Caleb and Lila could confide in each other. They talked about their dreams, their fears, and the things that kept them awake at night. Caleb felt a sense of peace he hadn't known in years, a calm that settled over him whenever he was with her.

One rainy afternoon, they sat in the school library, books spread out before them. The soft patter of raindrops against the window created a cozy atmosphere.

"You know, you're not as bad at English as you think," Lila said with a small smile. "I think you're just distracted."

Caleb chuckled. "You might be right. There's a lot going on."

Lila's expression softened. "I get it. I know I've been hard on you, but... I'm glad we're doing this."

"Me too," Caleb replied, his voice sincere. "I'm sorry for how I acted. You didn't deserve that."

Lila nodded, her eyes meeting his. "It's okay. I think we're both dealing with a lot."

As they continued their study session, Caleb felt a sense of hope. He was starting to believe that maybe, just maybe, things could get better.

But Logan watched from a distance, his jealousy and anger simmering. He couldn't stand seeing Lila with Caleb, their connection growing stronger each day. It was time to put his plan into motion. He knew exactly what to do to make Caleb's life miserable. Logan's mind raced with possibilities, each one more devious than the last.

As he formulated his plan, he couldn't help but smirk. Caleb Morgan was about to learn what it meant to cross Logan Bennett. And in the process, he would make sure Lila saw Caleb for who he really was—or at least, who Logan wanted her to believe he was.

Back in the library, Caleb and Lila continued their study session, oblivious to the storm that was about to descend on their lives. The bond they were forming would soon be tested in ways neither of them could have anticipated, pushing them to their limits and forcing them to confront the true depths of their feelings for each other.

CHAPTER 9: THE LAST EXPOSÉ

Caleb had always known that his father's shadow was a large one, but it wasn't until now that he truly understood how suffocating it could be. The whispers began innocuously enough—a few students murmuring in the hallways, casting sidelong glances his way—but it wasn't long before the entire school knew. Caleb Morgan, the quiet, withdrawn boy who preferred to sit in the back of the classroom, was the son of Senator Thomas Morgan, one of the most powerful men in the country.

It all started one chilly morning as Caleb approached the school gates, his shoulders hunched against the cold. The usually peaceful entrance was now a chaotic scene, teeming with reporters and flashing cameras. They were clamoring for a statement, thrusting microphones toward him, their voices blending into an indistinct roar.

"Caleb! Caleb! Over here! What's it like being the son of Senator Morgan?"

"Caleb, do you have any comments on your father's latest bill?"

"Does the pressure of your father's position affect you at school?"

Caleb's stomach churned, and he quickened his pace, his heart pounding in his chest. The school security guards stationed at the entrance did their best to hold back the throng of reporters, but it was clear they were overwhelmed. Caleb finally pushed his way through, his face flushed with anxiety. He kept his head down as he made his way to his locker, trying to ignore the curious stares of his classmates.

Inside the principal's office, Mrs. Cane watched the scene unfold through the security monitors, a deep frown etched on her face. She turned to her secretary, her voice tight with concern. "This is getting out of hand. We need more security. I can't have these reporters harassing my students."

Later that day, Caleb found himself in the principal's office, summoned not for any wrongdoing of his own, but for his own protection.

"Caleb," Mrs. Cane said gently, gesturing for him to take a seat. "I want you to know that we're doing everything we can to keep the school safe and secure, but the media attention has made things difficult."

Caleb nodded, feeling the weight of his father's influence pressing down on him. "I didn't ask for this," he mumbled, his voice barely audible.

Mrs. Cane sighed, her expression softening. "I know

you didn't, and I'm sorry you're being dragged into the spotlight like this. I've spoken to your father about the situation, and we're working on a plan to handle the media. But in the meantime, I need you to be careful."

Outside the office, as Caleb made his way to class, he could hear the whispers that had once been soft and indistinct now growing louder and more pointed. The bullying, which had already been bad enough, intensified. No longer was he just the rich kid who didn't fit in—he was now the son of a public figure, a target for those who wanted to lash out at the system, or worse, make a name for themselves.

In the staff meeting that afternoon, Mrs. Cane addressed the situation with the school's budget committee, a group of stern-faced individuals who seemed more concerned with numbers than the well-being of the students.

"I'm requesting an increase in the security budget," Mrs. Cane said firmly. "We need to protect our students, especially with the recent media attention surrounding Caleb Morgan."

One of the committee members, a man with thinning hair and wire-rimmed glasses, glanced up from his notes, his expression skeptical. "Mrs. Cane, the budget is already stretched thin. We can't just allocate more funds every time a student faces challenges."

"This isn't just about a student facing challenges," Mrs. Cane countered, her frustration evident. "This is about ensuring the safety of all our students. The reporters are relentless, and the other students are picking up on the tension. It's creating a hostile environment."

Another committee member, a woman with a tight bun and an air of disapproval, shook her head. "We understand your concerns, but we simply don't have the resources. Perhaps if Senator Morgan were to make a donation, we could consider revisiting the budget."

Mrs. Cane bit back her retort, knowing that arguing further would be futile. "Thank you for your time," she said curtly, rising from her seat. As she left the meeting, she couldn't shake the feeling that the system was failing Caleb, that she was failing him.

The reporters were relentless, their questions invasive and unyielding, turning every moment of Caleb's day into a nightmare. They hounded him between classes, their flashing cameras capturing every uncomfortable expression, every flinch, while their shouted questions filled his every step with dread.

"Caleb, is it true your father's been hiding you away?"

"Is Senator Morgan ashamed of his son?"

Their accusations were cruel, each one more scandalous than the last. Caleb could feel the weight of their words pressing down on him, their voices echoing in his mind long after they had left. The whispers among his classmates grew louder, fueled by the headlines that painted him as the senator's hidden shame. It was a cruel twist of fate—he had come to this place to escape the pressures of his life, only to find himself under an even harsher spotlight.

Just as Caleb was surrounded by reporters near the school parking lot, their voices a chaotic blur of accusations and demands for a comment, a clear voice rang out over the noise.

"That's enough!" Lila's voice cut through the clamor, sharp and commanding. She pushed her way through the crowd, her eyes blazing with fierce determination. "Leave him alone!"

The reporters, momentarily stunned by her boldness, shifted their focus to the girl who had dared to interfere. One of them, a wiry man with a notepad and a cynical grin, quickly recovered and pointed his microphone toward her. "Are you Caleb's girlfriend? How long have you two been dating?"

Lila didn't flinch. "He's a high school kid, not a political pawn," she snapped, ignoring the question. "Why don't you go harass someone else?"

The crowd of reporters exchanged glances, their curiosity piqued by this unexpected twist. Another reporter, a woman with a camera slung over her shoulder, pressed further. "If you're not his girlfriend, then why are you defending him? Do you know something we don't?"

Before Lila could respond, Mrs. Cane, the school principal, stepped forward, her face set in a stern expression. "That's enough," she said, her voice leaving no room for argument. "You're trespassing on school property. If you don't leave immediately, I'll have no choice but to call the police."

The reporters hesitated, glancing at one another as if weighing their options. But Mrs. Cane's authority was unmistakable, and one by one, they began to disperse, their murmurs fading into the background as they retreated.

As the chaos subsided, Caleb and Lila managed to slip away, finding refuge in the relative quiet of the school's back entrance. Caleb leaned against the wall, his heart still racing from the ordeal. He looked at Lila, gratitude and embarrassment mingling on his face. "You didn't have to do that," he mumbled, feeling awkward under her determined gaze.

Lila softened, her eyes losing their fiery edge as she met his gaze. "I couldn't just stand there and do nothing," she said gently. "No one deserves to be treated like that, especially not you."

Caleb lowered his head, feeling a lump form in his throat. He had spent so long feeling isolated, as though no one could truly understand what he was going through. But here was Lila, standing by his side, defending him when he felt most vulnerable. It was a kindness he hadn't expected, one that touched something deep within him.

"Thank you," he whispered, the words barely audible.

"It's okay," Lila smiled, a warmth spreading through her. "You don't have to thank me, Caleb."

Caleb smiled faintly, appreciating her kindness more than he could express. For the first time in what felt like forever, Caleb allowed himself to believe that maybe he wasn't as alone as he thought.

But he knew that Lila standing up for him would have consequences, especially with Logan. Logan was furious when he found out, his anger simmering beneath the surface as he watched Lila and Caleb together. The strain in his relationship with Lila was growing, and it was all because of Caleb.

When Caleb's parents arrived in the Hamptons that evening, they were quick to pressure him to leave public school. His mother, Evelyn, was particularly insistent, her concern for his safety palpable. "You can't stay there, Caleb," she pleaded. "It's not safe, and with your father's campaign…we can't risk any more scandals."

Caleb knew the real reason behind their concern. It wasn't just about his safety—it was about the potential backlash against his father's re-election campaign. The last thing they needed was a scandal involving their son being bullied at a public school. But Caleb had his own reasons for wanting to stay, and he wasn't about to back down.

"I can handle it," he insisted, his voice steady despite the turmoil inside him. "Besides, this could actually help Dad's campaign. What other senator has their kid in public school? It'll make him look more relatable, more in touch with regular people."

His father, always the strategist, paused at Caleb's words, considering the potential advantages. But he wasn't convinced. "You don't need to prove anything, Caleb," he said firmly. "Your safety comes first."

Caleb took a deep breath, knowing he had to play his cards carefully. "I'll join your office as an intern after the school year," he promised, forcing himself to sound enthusiastic. "I want to help with the campaign, to learn from you."

Senator Morgan's eyes softened at his son's words, pride mingling with relief. This was what he had always wanted—Caleb following in his footsteps, showing interest in the family legacy. "Alright," he agreed, his tone final. "But only if you promise to focus on staying away from the press."

Caleb nodded, relief washing over him. He had said what he needed to say to stay in the Hamptons, to stay close to the few people who made him feel less alone. But the guilt gnawed at him, knowing he had manipulated his father's trust to get what he wanted.

Meanwhile, at Senator Morgan's campaign headquarters, the atmosphere buzzed with energy and anticipation. Elaine Ross, the campaign manager, had seized upon the recent events at Caleb's school with a sharp instinct. She saw an opportunity to turn the situation into a positive narrative for the senator's campaign, spinning the story with a deft touch.

Elaine sat in the conference room, her fingers tapping rhythmically on her laptop as she composed a press release. Her team surrounded her, a mix of strategists, media consultants, and assistants, all focused on the task at hand.

"We need to emphasize Caleb's resilience," Elaine said, her tone commanding. "He's a young man who's chosen to stay in public school, despite the challenges. It's a testament to Senator Morgan's values— commitment to family, integrity, and staying grounded in the face of adversity."

One of the media consultants, a woman named Sarah, nodded in agreement. "We can push the angle that this reflects the senator's belief in hard work and overcoming obstacles, just like his son."

Elaine glanced at the polling data projected on the wall. "If we play this right, we'll not only defuse any negative press but actually turn it into a strength. People love a story of triumph over adversity. We'll show them that the Morgans are just like any other American family— facing challenges, sticking together, and coming out stronger on the other side."

A young intern, raised his hand hesitantly. "Do you think Caleb's okay with all this? I mean, it must be tough for him."

Elaine paused, considering the question. "Caleb's stronger than he realizes. And this isn't just about the campaign; it's about showing him that he has the support of his family and the public. He'll see that in time."

As Elaine finished speaking, the team dispersed to carry out their tasks, preparing to release the story to the press. The plan was working—Senator Morgan's polling numbers were beginning to rise, the public admiring his commitment to keeping his family grounded and connected to everyday struggles. The narrative was perfect, and Elaine felt a sense of satisfaction knowing that she had once again steered the campaign in the right direction.

But not everyone was pleased with Caleb's newfound popularity.

Across town, Logan was fuming. He worked at his mother's car repair shop after school, the rhythmic sound of tools clanging against metal doing nothing to soothe his simmering anger. His thoughts kept drifting back to Caleb, the boy who seemed to be getting everything—attention, sympathy, and even Lila's affection.

Logan wiped the grease from his hands with a rag, his mind churning with resentment. Every time he thought about how Caleb's life was seemingly improving, it felt like a slap in the face. He couldn't stand it—the idea that Caleb was being hailed as some kind of hero while he, Logan, was stuck in the shadows, toiling away in the same old place with no recognition, no praise.

As he tightened the bolts on a tire, his mother, Martha, walked over, a warm smile on her face. She had noticed Logan's mood lately and was trying to figure out how to help.

"Hey, kiddo," she said softly, brushing a strand of hair out of her eyes. "You've been working hard. How about we take a break and grab something to eat?"

Logan didn't look up, his jaw clenched. "I'm fine, Mom," he muttered, his voice tinged with frustration.

Martha frowned, sensing the tension in her son's voice. "Logan, you can talk to me. I know something's been bothering you lately. Is it school? Or something else?"

Logan finally looked up, his eyes flashing with anger. "It's nothing, okay? Just leave it."

Taken aback by his tone, Martha stepped back, hurt evident in her eyes. "I'm just trying to help, Logan. I care about you."

Logan sighed, regretting his outburst almost immediately, but his anger was too raw to contain. "You don't understand, Mom. You wouldn't get it. Everyone's just—" He stopped himself, shaking his head. "Forget it."

Martha watched as Logan turned back to his work, his movements stiff and agitated. She wanted to reach out, to bridge the growing distance between them, but she didn't know how. All she could do was hope that whatever was troubling him would pass and that the son she knew—the kind, gentle boy who used to tell her everything—would come back to her.

As Logan tightened the final bolt on the car he'd been working on, his mind was far from the task at hand. The rhythmic tightening of the wrench was almost soothing, but it couldn't drown out the thoughts swirling in his head. The sting of jealousy and anger gnawed at him, growing stronger each day. It wasn't just about the car or the latest argument with his mother—it was about Caleb. Caleb, who seemed to have everything handed to him on a silver platter, while Logan had to fight for every scrap of respect, every bit of acknowledgment.

The unfairness of it all burned deep, a dark cloud that threatened to overshadow every part of Logan's life. He knew it was driving a wedge between him and those who cared about him, but he couldn't help it. The resentment festered, making it hard for him to see anything beyond his own pain. Every time he saw Caleb's face, it was a reminder of what he didn't have—what he would never have. And that bitterness was beginning to seep into everything he touched, including his relationship with his mother.

At school, the tide had turned dramatically in Caleb's favor. The same kids who once ignored or bullied him were now vying for his attention, inviting him to parties and trying to get close. It was as if overnight, Caleb had become the most sought-after person in the Hamptons. He was the golden boy, the one everyone wanted to be around. Invitations flowed his way—beach bonfires, exclusive gatherings at the local yacht club, and weekend parties.

But with this newfound popularity came an overwhelming sense of unease. Caleb could feel the weight of his choices bearing down on him, the consequences of actions that had propelled him into this spotlight. On the surface, it seemed like he had finally secured his place in the Hamptons, a world of privilege and status. Yet, beneath it all, he couldn't shake the feeling that something wasn't right.

The Hamptons community, with its picturesque streets and sun-kissed shores, had embraced Caleb like a long-lost son. Wherever he went, it seemed everyone knew his name. The local shop owners greeted him warmly, their familiarity with him growing with each passing day. But as much as the town welcomed him with open arms, the weight of his own thoughts often made him feel like an outsider.

Down the street, scent of fresh bread wafted from the bakery, drawing him in. As he approached the counter, Mrs. Thompson, the elderly widow who lived just down the street, looked up from behind a display of cookies. Her face lit up with a smile.

"Caleb, dear, you're just in time! I've got a fresh batch of chocolate chip cookies," she said, her voice warm and inviting as she held out a plate toward him.

Caleb forced a smile, accepting a cookie with a nod of thanks. "You're too kind, Mrs. Thompson," he replied, trying to muster some enthusiasm.

She looked at him with a gentle concern in her eyes, sensing the heaviness in his voice. "You know, these cookies have a way of chasing away the blues. And if they don't, my listening ear is always available."

Caleb chuckled softly, touched by her kindness. "I appreciate that," he said, taking a bite of the cookie. The familiar taste brought back memories of simpler times, but it also reminded him of how far he felt from those days.

As he left the bakery, he continued down the street, lost in thought. He barely noticed when Mr. Whitaker, the retired sailor with a thousand stories, called out to him from his porch.

"Hey there, Caleb!" Mr. Whitaker's voice boomed with the strength of a man who had spent a lifetime at sea. "How about joining me for some fishing this weekend? The fish are practically begging to be caught."

Caleb hesitated, knowing that the offer came from a place of genuine warmth. But the thought of sitting in a boat, surrounded by the stillness of the water, felt too introspective, too close to the emotions he was trying to avoid.

"Maybe next time, Mr. Whitaker," Caleb replied, trying to keep the disappointment from his voice. "I've got a lot on my plate right now."

Mr. Whitaker gave him a knowing look, the kind that only comes with age and experience. "Son, sometimes it's the quiet moments that help you find what you're looking for. But no pressure—just know the invitation's always open."

Caleb nodded, appreciating the man's wisdom, even if he wasn't ready to heed it. "Thanks, I'll keep that in mind," he said, offering a small smile before continuing on his way.

Despite the warmth and charm of the community— their smiles, their invitations, their stories—Caleb couldn't shake the feeling that he was walking through life with a shadow hanging over him. The kindness of the people around him was genuine, unwavering even, but it wasn't enough to lift the weight that pressed down on him, day after day.

He wandered aimlessly, the familiar faces and friendly greetings blending into the background as his thoughts drifted to Lila. She had become a beacon in his life, a light that cut through the darkness, yet even her presence couldn't entirely erase the emptiness he felt. The community had given him a place to belong, but he couldn't help but feel like an imposter—someone who was seen but never truly known.

Yet, even in this close-knit community, Caleb felt like an outsider. He saw the way people's eyes lit up when they spoke to him, but he couldn't help but wonder if it was all just a facade. Did they see him as he truly was, or was he simply a reflection of what they wanted to see?

That night, alone in his room, Caleb stared out the window at the darkening sky. The waves of the ocean crashed in the distance, a constant, rhythmic sound that usually brought him peace. But not tonight. Tonight, the ocean seemed more like a warning, its power and unpredictability mirroring the turmoil inside him.

He had gained everything he thought he wanted, but at what cost? The lines between right and wrong, truth and lies, had blurred so much that he could barely distinguish one from the other anymore. Was he really in control of his own destiny, or was he just a pawn in someone else's game? The choices he had made, the secrets he kept—were they guiding him toward the life he wanted, or leading him down a path of destruction?

CHAPTER 10: THE LAST BETRAYAL

The sudden rush of fame was like a tidal wave, sweeping Lila into a spotlight she never asked for. Overnight, her world shifted in ways she couldn't have imagined. It all started innocently enough—just a few pictures of her with Caleb Morgan, the senator's son. But in an instant, the whispers and speculations began. News outlets buzzed with stories about the "mystery girl," painting her as everything from a secret girlfriend to a social climber. The relentless gaze of the cameras followed her everywhere, always just around the corner, ready to capture the next moment that could feed the frenzy.

Lila tried to brush it off, telling herself it would pass, that people would eventually lose interest. But every morning, the headlines grew bolder, the pictures more invasive. At school, it felt like the walls were closing in on her. The stares from her classmates, the whispers behind her back—it all became too much.

But when she saw her school locker, Lila's heart sank. The word "CHEATER" was scrawled across it in thick, black letters, an accusation she didn't deserve. She stood there, frozen, as a wave of emotions crashed over her—anger, shame, and a deep sense of betrayal.

Just then, Caleb appeared at her side, his expression a mix of concern and guilt. "Lila, I'm so sorry," he said, his voice heavy with regret. "This is all my fault."

Lila shook her head, her eyes stinging with unshed tears. "It's not your fault, Caleb. You didn't ask for any of this either."

He desperately wanted to help her out, when he said, "Lila, I can talk to the press. I can set the record straight."

But Lila shook her head, trying to force a smile. "It's okay, Caleb. Just lay low. It'll blow over. These things always do."

Caleb clenched his fists, his jaw tightening. "I hate that you're being dragged into this mess because of me. If I could, I'd make it all go away."

"I'm exhausted," Lila sighed, leaning against the cool metal of the locker. "I just don't understand why people have to be so cruel. I didn't do anything wrong, but it feels like the whole world is against me."

Caleb placed a comforting hand on her shoulder, his touch warm and reassuring. "People can be awful, Lila. They see a story and they run with it, without caring about the truth or the people they hurt along the way."

She looked up at him, her eyes searching his. "Why does it have to be like this? Why can't we just be normal?"

"Because nothing about our lives is normal at the moment," Caleb replied, his voice tinged with bitterness. "Being my father's son means living under a microscope, and now you're caught in it too."

Lila felt a tear slip down her cheek, and she quickly wiped it away, not wanting to break down in front of him. "I just want it to stop, Caleb. I don't know how much more I can take."

Caleb's heart ached at her words. He wanted to protect her, to shield her from the ugliness of his world, but he didn't know how. "We'll get through this, Lila. I promise. We just have to stay strong and not let them win."

Lila nodded, trying to find strength in his words, but the weight of it all felt unbearable. "I don't know if I can be strong enough," she whispered.

Caleb pulled her into a gentle embrace, holding her close. "You're stronger than you think, Lila. And you're not alone in this. We'll face it together."

As they stood there, wrapped in each other's arms, the world outside seemed to blur. For a moment, it was just the two of them, sharing their pain, their fears, and their hope that maybe, just maybe, they could find a way out of the darkness.

But even as Caleb held her, his mind raced with guilt and anger. He couldn't help but feel responsible for the storm that had engulfed Lila's life. The thought of her suffering because of him gnawed at his conscience, making him vow silently to do whatever it took to protect her, even if it meant sacrificing his own happiness.

The bell rang, pulling them out of their moment of solace. Caleb stepped back, his hand lingering on her arm. "I'll walk you to class."

Lila nodded, grateful for his support. "Thank you, Caleb. For everything."

But deep down, Lila wasn't so sure. The fallout from being linked to Caleb was more than she had anticipated, and the weight of it all was beginning to press down on her in ways she hadn't expected. The whispers in the halls, the sidelong glances from classmates, and the subtle shifts in conversations whenever she entered a room were becoming unbearable.

She sat at the cottage kitchen table, absentmindedly

stirring her tea, her mind far from the comforting warmth of the cup in her hands. Her father, Mr. Hayes, watched her from across the room, his heart heavy with concern. He had seen the change in her, the way the light in her eyes had dimmed ever since the incident with Caleb.

"Lila," he began gently, breaking the silence. "You've been quiet lately. Is everything alright?"

She looked up, her eyes meeting his. For a moment, she considered brushing off his concern with a simple "I'm fine," but the truth was too heavy to carry alone.

"It's just... everything feels different now," she admitted, her voice barely above a whisper. "Ever since people found out about Caleb and me, it's like the whole world's turned upside down. The part-time jobs I relied on for college money—they're slipping away, Dad. Employers don't want anything to do with me anymore. They're making excuses, but I know it's because they don't want to be associated with the scandal."

Mr. Hayes frowned, his heart aching for his daughter. "I'm so sorry, Lila. I wish there was something I could do to make it easier for you."

She shook her head, trying to hold back the tears that threatened to spill over. "It's not your fault, Dad. I just didn't realize how hard it would be. I thought I could handle it, but now... I'm not so sure."

He moved to sit beside her, taking her hand in his. "You're strong, Lila. Stronger than you know. This situation, it's unfair, and it's painful, but you've got a good head on your shoulders. You'll get through this."

"But at what cost?" she asked, her voice trembling. "I used to blend into the background, you know? Now, I feel like I'm under a microscope, and it's ruining everything I've worked for."

Mr. Hayes sighed, wishing he could shield her from the harsh realities of the world. "Sometimes life throws challenges at us that we're not prepared for. But those challenges, as difficult as they are, they shape us. They make us stronger."

"I don't feel strong," she whispered, tears finally breaking free. "I feel lost. I don't know what to do, Dad."

He pulled her into a comforting embrace, letting her cry against his shoulder. "It's okay to feel that way, Lila. You don't have to have all the answers right now. Just take it one day at a time. And remember, you're not alone in this. I'm here for you, and so are your friends, the real ones who care about you, not what the rumors say."

Lila sniffled, nodding against his shoulder. "I know, but it's hard to see the light at the end of the tunnel."

"I know it is," he said softly. "But you'll find your way through this. And when you do, you'll be stronger for it. Just don't let the darkness make you forget who you are. You're Lila Hayes, my brave, intelligent daughter who's destined for great things."

She pulled back slightly, looking up at him with tear-stained cheeks. "I just wish things could go back to the way they were."

"Change is never easy," he said with a sad smile. "But sometimes it's necessary. And who knows? Maybe this change will lead you to something better, something you never expected."

Lila sighed, her heart heavy but a small spark of hope flickering within her. "I hope you're right, Dad. I really do."

He squeezed her hand gently. "I'm always right, aren't I?"

She managed a small laugh through her tears. "Yeah, most of the time."

They sat there in the quiet kitchen, the weight of the

world still heavy on Lila's shoulders but feeling just a little bit lighter with her father's support. Mr. Hayes noticed Lila's continued somber mood and decided to do something he knew would lift her spirits, if only a little. With a knowing smile, he disappeared and returned with a tub of mint chocolate chip ice cream, her all-time favorite.

Lila looked up and couldn't help but chuckle. "You always know just what I need," she said, her voice tinged with both amusement and affection.

Mr. Hayes grinned as he handed her the bowl. "You remember that time you made Caleb eat this? He looked like he was about to spit it out, but he didn't want to hurt your feelings."

She laughed, the sound brightening the room for a moment. "I do! He pretended to love it, but I could tell he was struggling with every bite. Poor guy."

Her dad chuckled along with her, the memory bringing warmth to both their hearts. "Well, I have a confession to make," he said, his tone light. "I didn't like it much either at first."

Lila looked at him, surprised. "Really? But you eat it all the time now!"

Mr. Hayes shrugged, a sheepish smile on his face.

"Yeah, I got used to it eating it with you. I guess it kind of grew on me. Now, I can't get enough of it. Funny how that happens, isn't it?"

Lila's laughter faded into a soft smile, the warmth in her eyes speaking volumes. "I guess it is. Thanks, Dad," she said, her voice brimming with heartfelt gratitude. "For everything."

Mr. Hayes reached out and squeezed her hand, his own roughened by years of work yet gentle with reassurance. "Always, Lila. I'll always be here for you."

Despite the comfort in her father's touch, Lila felt a gnawing emptiness inside her. Logan's silence was a constant ache in her chest. His avoidance was like a sharp wound that refused to heal, made worse by the cruel rumors circulating around school. The thought that he might actually believe those rumors about her stung deeply. It was as if her world was slowly falling apart, and Logan was a piece of that world slipping away.

Lila took a deep breath, her resolve firming. "Dad," she said, her voice trembling slightly, "I'm going to meet Logan at his shop. So don't wait up for me, okay?"

Mr. Hayes gave her a concerned look but nodded, understanding the gravity in her tone. "Alright, sweetheart. Just be careful. I'll keep the light on for you."

Lila left the house with a heavy heart and a determined spirit. The evening air was cool, and as she rode her bicycle through the familiar streets, she could almost feel the echoes of her past, filled with laughter and easy conversations. Yet tonight, it felt like everything was cast in a somber shade.

When she arrived at Logan's car shop, a place she had always considered a haven, she could sense the change in the atmosphere immediately. The usually welcoming space now seemed charged with an unspoken tension. The smell of grease and metal was a reminder of the countless afternoons she'd spent here, but today, it felt almost oppressive.

Logan was hunched over the workbench, his back to her. The rhythmic clinking of metal tools was the only sound that filled the room, a stark contrast to the silence that lay heavy between them. Lila's heart sank as she called out his name, her voice wavering. "Logan?"

He didn't turn around, and the lack of response sent a cold shiver down her spine. Each moment that passed in silence felt like a leaden weight, and Lila's anxiety twisted in her gut. She took a hesitant step forward, trying to steady her voice. "Logan, we need to talk."

The tension was palpable, almost suffocating. Lila's mind raced as she tried to piece together how they had ended up here, where the warmth of their relationship seemed to have evaporated. Every corner of the shop was now a painful reminder of what once was—a place of shared dreams and intimacy now marred by misunderstanding and hurt.

"Logan," she said softly, approaching him. "I've been trying to reach you. Why haven't you called me back?"

He finally turned, and the look in his eyes broke her heart. "Why do you think, Lila? I'm not blind. I see what's going on."

"What are you talking about?" she asked, confused. "Nothing's going on between Caleb and me."

"Wow," Logan's jaw clenched, his knuckles white as he gripped the edge of the workbench. "Everyone's talking, Lila. The whole school thinks you're with him. And now they're calling you a cheater. I didn't think you'd stoop that low."

"Stooping low?" Lila's voice shook, a mixture of disbelief and anger rising in her chest. "Logan, I've been trying to get a hold of you, to talk to you, but you've been shutting me out."

"Maybe I had a reason to," Logan shot back, his voice cold. "I don't need to hear it from you. I see the way he looks at you, the way you two are always together."

Lila's heart sank as she realized the depth of Logan's mistrust. "You really believe that, don't you?" she whispered, tears welling up in her eyes. "You think I would do that to you?"

Logan didn't answer, and that silence said everything. The boy she thought she knew, the one she had cared for, was now someone she barely recognized.

But her mind raced as she pieced together the fragments of the day's revelations. The bullying at school, the whispers, and the constant torment—it all pointed back to Logan. The truth struck her like a bolt of lightning, leaving her stunned and aching with betrayal.

She stared at Logan, her eyes searching for some sign of redemption, but his face betrayed him. "You started those rumors, didn't you?" Her voice trembled, a mix of hurt and anger. "You wanted to hurt me because you couldn't trust me."

Logan's gaze dropped, his shoulders slumping as if the weight of his actions was too much to bear. He looked up at her, his eyes flickering with guilt and shame. "I didn't know what else to do, Lila. I was angry."

"Angry?" Lila's voice cracked, her eyes filling with tears. "You went after Caleb. You made my life a living hell."

Logan's expression hardened, and he shrugged, a bitter edge creeping into his voice. "Maybe you deserved it. You're the one who decided to hang out with him in the first place."

Lila's heart shattered at his words. The pain was sharp and relentless, a physical ache that left her breathless. "You betrayed me, Logan. I thought you were different. I thought we were something real."

Logan's face contorted with a mix of frustration and regret. "It was supposed to be us against the world, remember? We were supposed to face everything together."

"Yeah," Lila's gaze was filled with steely resolve. "You're right. It was supposed to be us against the world. But you made sure that I was alone in that fight. You turned your back on me when I needed you most."

Without another word, she turned on her heel and walked out of the shop. The door slammed shut behind her, and the quiet that followed was heavy with the weight of her departure. Logan stood frozen, the reality of his actions crashing down on him like a relentless wave.

The shop, once a place of comfort and familiarity, now felt like a cage. Logan's heart was heavy with regret, each beat a painful reminder of the trust he had shattered. He watched as Lila disappeared down the street, her silhouette growing smaller until it was swallowed by the evening mist.

The realization that he had driven her away cut deeper than any insult or accusation. He was left alone in the dimly lit shop, the echoes of their argument lingering in the air. The emptiness was suffocating, a stark reminder of the love he had lost and the future he had ruined.

Logan sank into the floor, his head in his hands. The guilt and regret were unbearable, the knowledge that he had let his anger and jealousy destroy something precious gnawing at his soul. It was too late to undo the damage, too late to make things right. The only thing left was the crushing weight of his own remorse.

Lila wandered down to the beach, a place she had always turned to comfort in times of despair. The rhythmic crash of the waves against the shore was usually calming, but tonight it seemed to drown out the sound of her own heart breaking. The sky was a deep, inky blue, and the moon cast a silvery sheen across the sand. She sat down, pulling her knees to her chest, and let the tears fall freely. The world around her felt like it was slipping away, and no matter how tightly she held on, it was slipping through her fingers.

Her sobs mixed with the sound of the waves until a new noise interrupted the melancholic symphony: the rhythmic splash of someone swimming. Lila wiped her tears away and looked up to see Caleb cutting through the water with powerful strokes, his form a silhouette against the moonlight. He seemed to move with a grace that momentarily lifted her spirits, reminding her of the times she had taught him to swim. A small, teary-eyed smile broke through as she remembered those lessons, the way he had listened so earnestly and practiced with such determination.

Caleb swam to the shore after his night swim, his face a mask of concern as he approached her. Dripping wet and clad only in his swim trunks, he looked every bit the teenage boy struggling with his own troubles, but his presence was undeniably comforting. He settled down beside her in the sand, his concern evident in his eyes.

"Lila," he said softly, his voice barely above a whisper. "What happened?"

She shook her head, unable to put her emotions into

words. Caleb didn't press her, sensing that the silence was what she needed most. Instead, he sat beside her, allowing her to lean into him as she continued to cry. His wet skin against hers was cold, but it felt oddly reassuring, like a promise that someone was there, even when everything else felt uncertain.

Caleb, feeling awkward in his sodden state, tried to offer comfort. He moved his arm around her hesitantly, unsure of how to keep her warm without being too forward. His touch was tentative, but it was his way of showing that he was there for her, even if he didn't know exactly how to help.

In an attempt to lighten the mood, Caleb tried to bring a bit of humor into the situation. He took a deep breath and then, with a grin, attempted to make a silly face, scrunching up his nose and making exaggerated duck sounds. His clumsy attempt at cheerfulness earned a reluctant giggle from Lila, the first break in her tears. The sight of Caleb's ridiculous antics was endearing, a reminder of the boy she had taught to swim and the shared moments of laughter that had once brought them together.

"Not bad for an amateur," Caleb said, his smile widening as he saw Lila's mood lift. "Though I've got to admit, my duck impression needs some work."

Lila managed a genuine laugh, her tears slowing as the

weight of her sadness was momentarily lifted by Caleb's effort. In that shared moment of vulnerability and humor, they both took comfort in each other's company, a reminder that even amidst the darkest times, there was still a glimmer of light to be found.

CHAPTER 11: THE LAST DATE

Caleb and Lila met at the edge of the sprawling grounds of the Morgan's Hampton mansion, the morning sun casting long shadows over the manicured lawns. The air was filled with an uneasy tension, both of them feeling the weight of their unspoken agreement. They had decided to avoid each other at school to steer clear of gossip, especially with the news of Lila and Logan's recent breakup spreading like wildfire.

Caleb ran a hand through his hair, frustration etched on his face. "I hate this."

Lila sighed, her gaze on the rising sun. "I know. But if we're seen together, it'll just fuel the rumors even more. I don't want to be a part of that circus."

Despite their resolve, they both knew that the mansion was becoming their refuge. It was a sanctuary from the scrutiny that followed them at school. The truth was that everyone knew Lila was living here now, and it seemed like a twisted sort of break-up present from Logan, an attempt to assert control even after the relationship had ended.

The mansion's grandeur seemed to mock their

troubles, its opulence a stark contrast to the uncertainty they felt. As they walked along the gravel path, Lila finally broke the silence.

"You know what?" she said, determination in her voice. "I'm tired of playing it safe. I'm done with worrying about what everyone else thinks."

Caleb glanced at her, a mix of relief and concern in his eyes. "What are you saying?"

"I'm saying that if they want to talk, let them. I'm going to be with you, no matter what the rumors say."

Lila's defiant stance was a breath of fresh air, a spark of resistance against the tide that had been pushing her down. Her friends had made their position clear—they stood firmly with Logan, supporting him even as the rift between them widened. But Lila had reached her limit. The way they had turned against her stung more deeply than she'd expected, a betrayal she hadn't seen coming.

The afternoon sun beat down on the school's football field as Lila walked toward the bleachers. She could hear the roar of the crowd, the rhythmic chant of the school's supporters, and the sharp whistle of the referee calling the plays. Jacob was on the field, his jersey stained with sweat and dirt, but Lila barely noticed the game. She was there to show support, hoping that despite everything, she could find some sense of normalcy among her friends.

As she approached the bleachers, her steps slowed. Elara, Juno, and Kai were standing together, a solid wall blocking her way. Lila's heart sank as she realized they were deliberately keeping her from joining them.

Elara was the first to speak, her voice cold and unyielding. "Lila, you're not welcome here."

Lila blinked, stunned by the harshness of her words. "What do you mean?"

"You broke Logan's heart," Elara continued, her eyes narrowing with judgment. "We've chosen his side, and that means you're out. You can't sit with us anymore."

Lila glanced at Juno and Kai, hoping to find some flicker of sympathy in their faces, but they stood silently beside Elara, their expressions blank and unreadable. It was as if they had all made a pact, one that Lila wasn't a part of anymore.

She could see Logan sitting further down the bleachers, surrounded by the rest of their friends, laughing and cheering for Jacob on the field. He didn't even glance in her direction. The sight of him, so at ease while she felt so torn apart, fueled a surge of anger within her.

Lila straightened her spine, her voice steady despite the pain lacing her words. "Friendship isn't about picking sides in a breakup, Elara. It's about being there for each other, through the good and the bad. But if you think it's easier to turn your back on me because Logan's feelings are more important than mine, then fine. Don't worry about me. I'll find my way, just like I always have."

Without waiting for a response, Lila turned and walked away, her heart heavy but her resolve firm. She didn't need their approval or their pity. She had Caleb, and maybe that was enough.

Later that day, Lila made her way to Caleb's room, her mind still swirling with the events of the afternoon. She could feel the sting of rejection lingering, but there was also a sense of relief, a weight lifted from her shoulders now that she had finally confronted the situation head-on.

Caleb had invited her over to talk, to plan how they could put an end to the gossip that was swirling around them. He hadn't expected her to make a grand entrance with her own plans, but when she knocked on his door, he could see the sadness in her eyes.

"Lila," he began, sensing that something had happened, "are you okay?"

She gave him a small smile, one that didn't quite reach her eyes. "I'm fine, Caleb. I just... I had to stand up for myself today, and it wasn't easy."

He moved closer, concern etched on his face. "What happened?"

Lila sighed, running a hand through her hair as she leaned against the desk in his room. "I went to the football game, thinking maybe I could still be there for Jacob, even after everything. But Elara, Juno, and Kai made it pretty clear that I'm not welcome anymore. They've all chosen Logan's side."

Caleb's expression darkened, anger simmering beneath the surface. "That's not fair, Lila. You don't deserve to be treated like that."

"I know," she said quietly, "but I told them I don't need their friendship if it's so conditional. I'll be fine without them."

Caleb reached out, gently taking her hand. "You're stronger than you think, Lila."

She looked up at him, gratitude softening the hard edges of her emotions. "Thank you, Caleb." Lila moved around his room with a critical eye. "Okay, Caleb. We need to do something about your wardrobe.

If we're going to make a statement, we need to look the part."

Caleb raised an eyebrow, confused. "What are you talking about?"

Lila began rifling through his closet, pulling out various pieces of clothing and shaking her head. "The popular kids need to see that we're not just sitting around feeling sorry for ourselves. We need to get them talking. And for that, you need a wardrobe update."

Caleb sighed, leaning against the doorframe. "I don't know about this. It seems like a lot of effort for something that doesn't feel right."

Lila's eyes sparkled with determination. "I don't give you a choice. We're going shopping. It's not just about clothes; it's about showing them we're not broken."

Caleb couldn't help but smile at her fierce spirit. Despite the circumstances, her presence was a reminder that he wasn't alone in this. He knew she was right; sometimes you had to fight back against the tide, even if it meant stepping out of your comfort zone.

"Alright," he said, giving in with a reluctant grin. "Let's do it."

Lila's face lit up with satisfaction. "Great. Let's get

ready to turn some heads."

As they prepared for their impromptu shopping spree, Caleb felt a strange mixture of apprehension and excitement. The plan wasn't just about making Logan jealous; it was about reclaiming a sense of normalcy, even if it was under the guise of defiance. And for Caleb, Lila's willingness to stand by him, no matter the cost, was a reminder that sometimes, even in the darkest times, there was a spark of hope waiting to be ignited.

The walk to town was filled with an easy, almost giddy energy. Lila's enthusiasm was infectious, and Caleb found himself smiling despite the weight of his worries. They arrived at the shopping district, where bright storefronts and bustling crowds offered a vibrant contrast to the solitude Caleb had been enveloped in.

Inside the first boutique, the air was thick with the scent of new fabrics and fresh ideas. Lila's eyes sparkled as she led Caleb through racks of clothes, her laughter mingling with the upbeat music playing softly in the background. Caleb, initially skeptical, was soon caught up in the whirlwind of fashion. Lila's playful suggestions and keen eye for style had him trying on outfits he never would have considered before.

"Alright," Caleb said, giving in with a reluctant grin. "Let's do it."

Lila's face lit up with satisfaction. "Great. Let's get ready to turn some heads."

Their shopping spree was an adventure in itself. The boutique's mirror became a stage where Caleb transformed from the boy in plaid shirts to someone else entirely. They settled on a monochrome chic look—sleek black jeans, crisp white shirts, and a touch of edgy accessories. Caleb admired the final result, amazed at how different he looked and felt. The plaid shirts that had been his comfort zone were nowhere to be seen, replaced by a fresh, bold style.

As they walked through the mall, their laughter echoed off the walls, and Caleb felt a strange sense of freedom. It was as though the act of choosing something new for himself had become a form of liberation. The time spent together had brought them closer, their conversations peppered with laughter and moments of shared silence. They had stumbled upon a connection that neither had anticipated, and their accidental touches seemed to spark a new, unspoken understanding.

By evening, they were back at the mansion, the expansive lawn bathed in the soft, golden light of the setting sun. The gentle breeze rustled the leaves of the tall trees, and the distant sound of the ocean waves created a soothing backdrop to their quiet retreat. Caleb and Lila sprawled on a blanket, their earlier shopping adventure a shared memory that seemed to bind them together.

Caleb glanced over at Lila, his heart warmed by the day's unexpected turns. "You know, today was...fun. It was nice doing something together. It felt like a break from everything."

Lila nodded, a smile tugging at her lips. "I agree. It was really nice. It's been a while since I've had a day like this."

Caleb took a deep breath, feeling the weight of his internal struggles shift, if only slightly. He looked at Lila, the vulnerability he felt was tempered by the warmth of their shared experience. "Lila, I was thinking...maybe we could spend some time together outside the house. How about we go for a drive sometime?"

Lila's eyes widened slightly, her smile faltering for a moment. "A drive? I don't know, Caleb. I mean, with everything going on, it feels...complicated."

Caleb took a deep breath, trying to mask his disappointment. "Don't think of it as a date, Lila. Think of it as a chance to escape, even if just for a little while. We don't have to make it anything more than a moment for us."

Lila hesitated, her gaze drifting over the garden where shadows played under the setting sun. Caleb's words tugged at her heart, and she saw the sincerity in his eyes. After a pause, she nodded, her resolve softening. "Okay. I'm in."

The next morning, was a new day, and with it came a shift in the atmosphere—one that Caleb was not quite ready for. As he walked through the school's entrance, he couldn't shake the sense of unease that clung to him like a shadow.

Lila strolled beside him, her presence a stark contrast to the chaos of the school day. Her casual grace seemed to slow time itself, her footsteps light and confident. She wore a simple, yet stylish outfit that spoke of effortless charm, and Caleb found himself painfully aware of how out of place he felt beside her. His jeans and T-shirt, once his go-to comfort, now felt like a suit of armor that couldn't shield him from the prying eyes of his peers.

As they moved down the hallway, the clamor of students seemed to fade into the background, replaced by a sense of heavy silence. The typical hum of school chatter paused as heads turned to watch them walk by, the crowd's collective gaze fixating on the unlikely pair.

Caleb's face grew flushed under the intense scrutiny. He shifted uncomfortably, his hands jammed deep into his pockets as he tried to ignore the whispers that followed them. Every step felt like it was being watched, measured, and judged.

Lila, seemingly unaware of the effect her presence had, reached out and gently touched Caleb's arm. Her fingers brushed against his skin, a small, reassuring gesture meant to offer comfort. The touch was light, yet it carried an unexpected weight, a silent promise of solidarity.

Caleb flinched slightly at the contact but forced a smile in response. The touch seemed to ignite a spark of warmth, mingled with a tinge of embarrassment. He glanced over at Logan and his friends, who were grouped together nearby, their expressions a mixture of curiosity and amusement. Logan's smirk was particularly disconcerting, a reminder of the recent humiliations Caleb had endured.

"What's up, Morgan?" Logan called out, his tone dripping with false cheerfulness. "Did you finally make a friend, or is this just a new kind of public humiliation?"

Caleb's jaw tightened, but he said nothing. Instead, he

tried to focus on Lila's comforting presence beside him. Her calm demeanor was like a beacon in the storm of his emotions, though it did little to quell the unease swirling inside him.

Lila looked back at Caleb, her eyes full of understanding. "Ignore them," she said softly, her voice carrying an edge of defiance. "Let's just get to class."

Caleb nodded, grateful for her support but feeling a pang of guilt for the attention she was drawing. As they walked together, he couldn't help but think about how different this moment was from the one he had envisioned. The stark contrast between Lila's calm confidence and his own internal struggle only seemed to highlight how disconnected he felt from the world around him.

As they reached their classroom, the hallway noise resumed its normal level, but the earlier stares lingered in Caleb's mind. He took a deep breath, trying to steady his nerves. Lila's presence, though a comfort, also reminded him of the fragility of his own composure.

Lila turned to him as they entered the classroom, her smile gentle and encouraging. "You're doing great," she said, her eyes shining with sincerity.

Caleb trudged through the rest of the day with a sense

of weary detachment. Each class seemed to blur into the next, a relentless cycle of lectures and glances that only deepened his sense of isolation. But when he entered the classroom and saw Lila sitting there, it was as if the world had suddenly come into sharper focus.

Her presence was a beacon of calm in the storm that raged inside him. She was sitting near the window, the sunlight catching her hair and casting a warm glow around her. Her eyes were focused on the teacher, but every now and then, she would glance around with a soft, thoughtful expression. To Caleb, it felt like those fleeting moments were meant just for him. His heart pounded in his chest as he found himself lost in the rhythm of her breathing, the way she absently brushed a strand of hair from her face, and the gentle curve of her smile when she caught his eye.

The lesson began, but Caleb's thoughts were far from the history lecture being droned on by their teacher. Instead, they were wrapped up in the way Lila seemed so effortlessly at ease, a stark contrast to the turmoil he felt inside. The teacher's voice was a distant murmur as Caleb focused on Lila, unable to shake the sense of admiration and longing that welled up within him. It was as if, in that moment, she was the only thing that made sense in a world filled with chaos and uncertainty.

As he watched her, a flicker of resolve ignited in his

heart. Caleb realized that he had been letting his fears and insecurities dictate his life, keeping him trapped in a cycle of retreat and self-pity. But here was Lila, someone who seemed to embody strength and kindness without even trying. Her mere presence was enough to make him rethink his approach to the challenges he faced.

With a deep breath, Caleb made a silent vow to himself. He was going to stop letting his fears hold him back. He would confront the bullies, deal with the mounting pressures, and face his struggles head-on. No longer would he let the weight of his insecurities and the expectations of his parents dictate his life.

The bell rang, snapping him out of his reverie, and he realized he had missed most of the lesson. He looked over at Lila, who was now packing up her things with a serene smile on her face. Caleb felt a surge of gratitude for her unspoken support and for the newfound clarity she had brought him.

As they walked out of the classroom together, Caleb felt a newfound determination. Lila's presence had been the catalyst he needed to reclaim control over his life. It was time to stop being a passive observer in his own story and to start writing a new chapter—one where he faced his fears and embraced the strength that lay within him.

That evening, Caleb arrived at Lila's cottage with a mischievous grin, holding the keys to his family's Range Rover. The air was warm with the scent of summer, and a slight breeze ruffled his hair as he leaned against the sleek SUV, his heart racing with anticipation. He'd borrowed the car under the pretense of running errands, but his real plan was to surprise Lila with a driving lesson, something he knew would both thrill and challenge her.

Lila emerged from the house, dressed casually in a simple sundress that moved gracefully with her every step. There was an effortless elegance about her that always took Caleb's breath away. She noticed the Range Rover and raised an eyebrow, a mix of curiosity and amusement dancing in her eyes. "So, this is your idea of a grand adventure?" she teased, her voice light and playful.

Caleb chuckled, opening the passenger door for her with a flourish. "Just wait. I promise it'll be fun."

She slid into the seat, her fingers brushing against his hand briefly, sending a jolt of electricity through him. He closed the door and hurried around to the driver's side, trying to calm the fluttering in his chest.

As they drove through the winding roads of the Hamptons, the scenery shifted from lush greenery to open fields and finally to sandy shores that seemed to stretch endlessly. The ocean sparkled in the distance, a calming presence that contrasted with the excitement buzzing between them. Caleb guided Lila through the basics of driving, his instructions punctuated by laughter and the occasional playful jab.

"Ease into the brake, Lila, not like you're trying to stop a freight train," Caleb joked, grinning as Lila shot him a mock glare.

"Oh, like you were so perfect when you first started driving," she retorted, her hands gripping the steering wheel a little tighter.

"Hey, I only crashed into one mailbox, and it barely counts," he replied, unable to keep a straight face. "Besides, you're doing great. Look at you—already a pro."

Lila's initial nervousness began to melt away, replaced by a growing confidence. The sight of her smiling behind the wheel, her eyes bright with determination and pride, made Caleb's heart swell with something he couldn't quite name.

As they reached a secluded beach, Caleb gently guided Lila to pull over. She parked the car, and they both stepped out onto the sand, their shoes sinking slightly into the cool grains beneath their feet. The sun was dipping below the horizon and it was the kind of sunset that made everything feel possible, even the unspoken dreams they both carried.

"Wow," Lila whispered, her voice filled with awe as she took in the view.

Caleb watched her, captivated not just by the beauty of the scene, but by the way she seemed to become part of it, as if the sunset was made for her. "I thought you might like it here," he said softly.

They walked along the shore, hand in hand, the gentle roar of the ocean their only companion. The intimacy of the moment felt perfect, their connection growing stronger with each step. Caleb's hand felt warm and reassuring in Lila's, and for the first time in a long while, the weight on his heart seemed to lighten.

"This beach," Lila began, her voice carrying a hint of nostalgia, "this is where I caught my first wave. I was just a kid, but I felt like I could conquer the world that day."

Caleb smiled, imagining a younger version of Lila, full of energy and fearlessness. "You'll have to teach me," he joked, nudging her playfully. "You know, if I ever manage to stand up on a board without falling flat on my face."

Lila laughed, a sound that was pure and unguarded. "You can barely swim, Caleb! You'd probably need a life jacket just to paddle out."

"Hey, I'm not that bad," he protested, grinning. "Maybe you're just an overachiever."

She shook her head, still laughing. "Or maybe you're just a natural-born landlubber."

The banter flowed easily between them, but beneath the surface, something deeper was stirring. As the waves lapped gently at their feet, Lila found herself stealing glances at Caleb, noticing the way his eyes seemed to soften when he looked at her, the way his smile reached all the way up to his eyes.

Without thinking, Lila stopped walking and turned to face him. Her heart was pounding in her chest, louder than the waves crashing nearby. Before she could talk herself out of it, she reached up and pulled Caleb towards her, her lips meeting his in a soft, tentative kiss.

Caleb froze, shocked at first. He hadn't expected this—hadn't even dared to hope for it. But then, as the warmth of Lila's kiss spread through him, he realized that this was exactly what he'd been yearning for. When Lila began to pull back, her eyes wide with apology, Caleb gently cupped her face in his hands, stopping her.

"Don't apologize," he whispered, his voice husky with emotion. "I... I wanted this too."

And then he kissed her, this time with a tenderness that spoke of all the things he couldn't find the words to say. The world around them seemed to disappear, leaving only the two of them, wrapped up in the moment, feeling the spark that had always been there, just waiting for the right time to ignite.

As they pulled apart, both of them breathless, they stood there in silence, the night settling in around them. The moonlight cast a silver glow over the beach, and for the first time in what felt like forever, Caleb didn't feel alone. In Lila's eyes, he saw a reflection of his own longing, his own hope for something more, and it made him believe that maybe, just maybe, he was finally finding his way back to himself.

Caleb and Lila's connection had evolved into something deeper, more intimate, and undeniably real. The time they spent together at the mansion were filled with stolen moments and whispered conversations, each one a testament to their growing affection. Their secret meetings were their escape from the scrutiny and expectations that awaited them outside those walls.

One late afternoon, Caleb and Lila found themselves alone in the mansion's library. It was a haven of quiet, with shelves lined with books and large windows letting in the soft light. They had taken to meeting here frequently, finding comfort in the silence and the intimacy of their surroundings.

Lila sat on a plush armchair, her fingers tracing the worn leather of the book she held. Her gaze wandered around the room, occasionally settling on Caleb, who was sprawled on the sofa, lost in thought.

"Caleb," she said softly, her voice breaking the comfortable silence. "Do you ever think about what comes next? About the future?"

Caleb looked up, meeting her eyes with a mixture of surprise and vulnerability. "I used to," he admitted. "Before all this... before everything changed. I used to dream about a lot of things. But now, it's like I'm just trying to get through each day."

Lila shifted in her seat, her expression thoughtful. "I think about the future too, but sometimes it feels like a distant dream. Especially with everything that's going on with us, the way we have to keep our relationship a secret."

Caleb sighed, running a hand through his hair. "It's not fair. I wish we didn't have to hide like this, that we could just be… together without worrying about what people think."

"I know," Lila said, her eyes reflecting the sadness she felt. "But sometimes, the things we want most come with sacrifices. And maybe… maybe the sacrifices make them even more precious."

Caleb's gaze softened, and he reached out to take her hand. "I'm grateful for every moment we get to spend together. Even if it's hidden away from the world, it's still real. And it means everything to me."

They shared a quiet moment, their fingers intertwined, as if holding on to each other was enough to keep the world's harshness at bay.

Caleb turned to Lila, his voice earnest. "I know this summer's been tough. For both of us. But being with you, finding this… connection—it's given me something to hold on to. Something to hope for."

Lila's eyes sparkled with unshed tears. "I feel the same way. You've shown me a side of life I didn't know existed, a side that makes everything else seem a little bit brighter. Even if we have to keep this secret, I wouldn't trade it for anything."

Back in New York, Senator Thomas Morgan

lay in the quiet of Elaine's Manhattan apartment, reviewing his campaign materials on his tablet. The bright glow of the screen cast harsh shadows across his face, deepening the lines of worry etched into his brow. As he scrolled through the pages, his eyes fell on a series of photos that made his heart stop.

There they were—images of his son, Caleb, walking on the beach with a girl. Their faces were relaxed, their smiles genuine, captured in a moment of carefree happiness. But to Thomas, those pictures represented something far more troubling. They were not just innocent snapshots; they were potential fuel for a scandal that could unravel everything he had built.

His grip tightened on the tablet, and his expression darkened with concern and frustration. The photos had been snapped by a paparazzo, lurking in the shadows to catch a moment that should have remained private.

Elaine stirred beside him, the silk sheets rustling as she turned over in bed. They had spent the night together, as they often did, and the morning light filtered softly through the curtains, casting a gentle glow over her elegant features. But the tranquility of the moment was lost on Thomas, his thoughts consumed by the implications of what he had seen.

"Thomas?" Elaine's voice was soft, laced with the

intimacy of their long romantic affair and the burdens they had borne together. She reached out to touch his arm, sensing his tension. "What's wrong?"

He hesitated, the weight of his responsibilities pressing down on him. "It's Caleb," he finally said, his voice heavy with concern. "and there are photos... of him and a girl, on the beach. They're... they could be damaging if they got out."

Elaine propped herself up on one elbow, her gaze sharp. "But they won't get out. I handled it. We're safe."

Elaine, his campaign manager—and more than that, his lover—had managed to intercept the photos before they hit the press. She had negotiated with the photographer, leveraging her connections and using a hefty sum of money to ensure the images would never see the light of day. But as Thomas stared at those photos, safely hidden away, the damage had already been done in his mind.

"For now," Thomas muttered, running a hand through his graying hair. "But this—this is a sign, Elaine. Caleb is getting too comfortable out there in the Hamptons. He's distracted, and I can't afford any distractions right now. Not with the campaign at such a critical stage."

The thought of these images splashed across tabloids,

with headlines questioning the propriety of Caleb's relationship with the daughter of the estate's caretaker, filled Thomas with a sense of impending doom.

Elaine watched him carefully, reading the lines of stress on his face, the way his jaw tightened as he spoke. "Who is the girl?" he asked abruptly, his voice tinged with frustration. "I don't recognize her, and I've barely seen her around."

Elaine sighed, leaning back against the pillows as she considered how to respond. "She's the caretaker's daughter. The girl in the photos with Caleb. Her name is Lila Hayes."

Thomas frowned, his brow furrowing as he tried to recall the name. He had spent so little time at the Hamptons estate, always too busy with meetings, speeches, and the endless demands of his career. The caretakers and their families were part of the scenery, there but not really seen. "I don't remember her," he admitted, the confession laced with a hint of guilt. "I barely ever saw her."

Elaine nodded, understanding the subtle layers of his remorse. "She's grown up now," she said softly. "And from what I've heard, she's a good influence on Caleb. But I know how important this campaign is to you, to us. Maybe… maybe we should bring him back home. Rein him in a bit before things get out of hand."

Thomas sighed, the suggestion hanging heavily between them. He knew she was right, but the thought of pulling Caleb away from the one place where he seemed to find some peace made his chest tighten with a different kind of dread. "I don't want to lose him, Elaine," he confessed, his voice raw with emotion. "But I can't let him jeopardize everything we've worked for."

Elaine reached out again, this time taking his hand in hers, squeezing gently. "You won't lose him," she promised, her voice steady. "So, what do you plan to do?"

Thomas didn't answer immediately. Instead, he slipped out of bed and crossed the room to the small bar cart in the corner. He poured himself a glass of whiskey, the amber liquid swirling as he considered his next move. Elaine watched him, her expression unreadable, before she sighed and climbed out of bed, heading to the bathroom.

"I'll be in the shower," she said, leaving him alone with his thoughts.

As the sound of running water filled the room, Thomas took a long sip of his drink, letting the warmth of the alcohol momentarily ease his anxiety. But the respite was brief. His mind continued to churn with plans to bring Caleb back to New York. The idyllic Hamptons, with its serene beaches and summer flings, now seemed like a dangerous distraction for his son—a distraction that could jeopardize everything Thomas had worked for.

He knew he had to act quickly. The thought of Caleb entangled in a relationship with Lila—a relationship that could be easily twisted and exploited by the media—sent a chill down his spine. He couldn't let his son's happiness come at the cost of his career. But as he stood there, the glass of whiskey growing warm in his hand, Thomas felt a deep, unsettling conflict within himself.

He loved Caleb, of course he did. But that love was now tangled with fear and desperation—fear that his son's choices would derail his carefully crafted life, and desperation to keep everything under control.

And yet, as much as he wanted to protect his career, there was a part of him that wanted to protect Caleb from the harsh realities of the world he lived in. Thomas was torn, caught between his professional ambitions and his paternal instincts. He knew that whatever decision he made would have far-reaching consequences, not just for his campaign, but for his relationship with his son.

As he drained the last of his whiskey, Thomas made up

his mind. He would bring Caleb back to New York, away from the temptations of the Hamptons, away from Lila. It was the only way to keep everything from falling apart.

But deep down, as he placed the empty glass on the bar and listened to the distant hum of the shower, Thomas couldn't shake the nagging doubt that he was making a mistake—a mistake that might cost him more than he was willing to lose.

CHAPTER 12: THE LAST TIME

The sky over the Hamptons was painted with hues of soft pink and gold as Thomas and Evelyn Morgan pulled up to their summer estate. The vibrant sunset bathed the familiar landscape in a warm glow, but despite the picturesque scene, there was an unspoken tension between the couple. Thomas's hands gripped the steering wheel a little too tightly as they approached the grand entrance, the crunch of gravel beneath the tires bringing back memories of summers past, filled with laughter and family bonding. But those days felt distant now.

As the car rolled to a stop, Evelyn glanced over at her husband, her curiosity getting the better of her. "Thomas, why the sudden trip to the Hamptons?" she asked, her voice soft but laced with suspicion. "You haven't mentioned anything about coming here, and now, out of the blue, we're driving down?"

Thomas, always the composed senator, offered her a practiced smile. "I just missed Caleb, that's all. Thought it would be nice to spend some time with him before the he slips away to college next year."

Evelyn arched an eyebrow, not entirely convinced. Thomas was rarely the spontaneous type, especially when it came to something as significant as a visit to the Hamptons. But she decided not to press further, choosing instead to savor the idea that perhaps, just perhaps, her husband truly did miss their son. "Well, I'm glad," she said, a genuine smile softening her features. "It'll be good for all of us to be together."

Thomas nodded, but his mind was elsewhere, already contemplating the difficult conversation he needed to have with Caleb. He knew that simply "missing" his son wasn't the only reason for this trip, but admitting that to Evelyn would open up questions he wasn't ready to answer.

As they stepped out of the car, the grand estate loomed before them, a testament to the wealth and status they had built over the years. The sprawling gardens, meticulously maintained, framed the house with a sense of timeless elegance. Yet, as they crossed the threshold into the grand foyer, Thomas couldn't shake the feeling that something was off, as if the estate itself had sensed the underlying tension he carried with him.

Mr. Hayes, the estate's long-time caretaker, emerged from a side hallway, his weathered face lighting up with a surprised smile as he saw the Morgans. He wasn't expecting them—usually, they called ahead before arriving.

"Senator, Mrs. Morgan, what a surprise," Hayes

greeted them warmly, though there was a hint of curiosity in his eyes. "We weren't expecting you. Everything alright?"

"Good to see you, Mr. Hayes," Thomas replied, his voice carrying the authority of his position but with a touch of warmth that softened his usual stern demeanor. He handed his coat to Hayes, who took it with the ease of someone who had served this family for years. "How's Lila? Still helping out around the place?"

Mr. Hayes nodded, a hint of a smile playing on his lips at the mention of his daughter. "Yes, Senator. Lila's been a great help. Keeps the place running smooth. And thank you for letting us stay at the cottage all these years. It's meant the world to us."

Thomas waved off the thanks, though his gaze had already drifted toward the staircase leading up to the second floor where Caleb's room was. "You've earned it, Hayes. You've been loyal to this family for a long time."

Hayes nodded, though he couldn't shake the feeling that there was more to this visit than Thomas was letting on. It wasn't like the Morgans to drop by unannounced, especially not the senator. There was always a plan, always a schedule. This surprise visit made him uneasy. Something was different this time.

"Is Caleb upstairs?" Evelyn asked, her voice breaking through Hayes' thoughts.

"Yes, ma'am," Hayes responded, his tone respectful. "Lila has been keeping him company these days."

Thomas and Evelyn exchanged a glance, their unspoken concerns mirrored in each other's eyes. They both knew Caleb had been struggling, but hearing it from someone else made the reality harder to ignore.

"We'll go see him," Thomas said, his voice firm as he led the way up the stairs.

As they ascended, Hayes watched them go, his heart heavy with a sense of foreboding. He had known the Morgans for decades, had watched Caleb grow up in these very halls. But something about this visit felt different, as if a storm was brewing just beyond the horizon, and he couldn't shake the feeling that the family he cared for was on the brink of something that would change everything.

The Morgans reached the landing, the familiar creak of the wooden floor underfoot echoing through the quiet house. It was a sound that had always reminded them of home, of the life they had built together in this old estate. But tonight, it felt different—heavier somehow, as if even the house was holding its breath in anticipation of what was to come.

They approached Caleb's room, the door slightly ajar, and paused. Thomas took a deep breath, steeling himself for the conversation he knew was inevitable. His hand lingered on the doorknob, hesitant, as if he were searching for the right words in the silence. Evelyn, sensing his unease, placed a hand on his arm, offering silent support, though her own heart was racing. She knew how difficult this was for him, for both of them. But they had to try.

"Caleb?" Thomas called softly as he pushed the door open.

Inside, they found their son sitting by the window, gazing out at the garden. The fading light of the sunset cast long shadows across the room, highlighting the tension in his shoulders and the faraway look in his eyes. Caleb turned to face them, his expression guarded, as if he were bracing for whatever was to come.

"Mom, Dad," he greeted them, his voice devoid of the usual warmth.

For a moment, the room was filled with a heavy silence, each of them caught in the web of their own thoughts and fears. Then, to their surprise, Caleb stood up and walked toward them. Without a word, he wrapped his arms around Evelyn, pulling her into a hug. The gesture was unexpected, and Evelyn felt a lump form in her throat as she returned the embrace. She had missed this—missed him—more than she had allowed herself to admit. She exchanged a glance with Thomas, who stood nearby, equally surprised to see their son in better spirits than when they had left him.

Thomas, too, was taken aback by the sudden show of affection. He watched as his son held his wife close, and for the first time in a long while, he felt a flicker of hope. Maybe, just maybe, things weren't as broken as they seemed.

Caleb pulled back slightly, a faint smile playing on his lips. "I wasn't expecting you guys," he said, his voice softer now, the guardedness fading just a bit.

"We decided to come down for the weekend," Thomas explained, forcing a smile that didn't quite reach his eyes. "Thought it'd be nice to spend some time together."

Caleb nodded, though it was clear he wasn't entirely convinced by his father's reasoning. But for now, he was too tired to question it. Instead, he simply looked back out the window, the weight of his parents' unexpected visit pressing heavily on his chest.

The Morgan family stood in the quiet room, the

distance between them more palpable than ever. The walls of the estate had seen many things over the years—laughter, love, and loss—but the unspoken truths that hung in the air now felt heavier than anything that had come before.

Evelyn, who had been quietly observing the exchange, placed a gentle hand on Thomas's arm, signaling that it was time to go upstairs. "We should freshen up before dinner," she suggested, her tone smooth, almost practiced.

Thomas hesitated for a moment, his eyes lingering on Caleb. He wanted to say something more, to bridge the gap that had grown between them, but the words seemed to catch in his throat. Instead, he nodded and followed Evelyn out of the room, leaving Caleb alone with his thoughts once more.

As they ascended the staircase to their own room, Thomas's mind was already racing. In the privacy of the shower, with the hot water cascading over him, he allowed himself to think about what had brought them here. It wasn't just about a weekend visit; it was about something much bigger—about getting Caleb to come back home, to where he belonged. But the thought gnawed at him—how could he convince Caleb to come back, to reclaim the life that was slipping through their fingers?

Thomas had always been a man of action, someone who believed that problems could be solved if you just tried hard enough. But this...this was different. His son was slipping away from him, and no amount of planning or strategizing seemed to be enough. He knew Caleb was struggling, that there was something dark and painful festering inside him. But every time he tried to reach out, to offer help, Caleb only seemed to retreat further into himself.

As the water continued to pour down, Thomas racked his brain for a solution. He thought about the estate, the place that had been in their family for generations. Maybe if they spent more time here, away from the pressures of their everyday lives, Caleb might start to open up. Or perhaps if they planned a family trip, something they hadn't done in years, it could give them a chance to reconnect.

He wanted more than anything to fix things, to bring Caleb back to the way he was before. But deep down, he knew that it wasn't just about Caleb coming home. It was about healing the rift that had grown between them—a rift that no amount of parental authority or stern words could bridge.

He needed to find a way to reach his son, to remind him that he wasn't alone, no matter how distant they had become. But how? The question lingered as the steam filled the bathroom, clouding his thoughts as much as the mirror.

Dinner that evening was a quiet affair, the kind where words were left unsaid, hovering in the air like a storm cloud about to burst. The grand dining room, with its high ceilings and ornate chandeliers, felt almost too large for the three of them, amplifying the silence between them. The table, set with fine plates and gleaming silverware, was the very picture of formality. Crystal glasses caught the flickering light from the candles, casting delicate shadows across the room, but their beauty did little to ease the tension.

Caleb sat across from his parents, his posture stiff and uncomfortable, as if he were bracing himself for an inevitable blow. He pushed the food around on his plate, barely registering the taste. The warmth and comfort of the earlier conversation with Mr. Hayes had dissipated, replaced by a cold knot of anxiety in his stomach.

Evelyn, his mother, was the first to break the silence. Her voice was soft, but it carried the weight of concern. "How's school, Caleb?" she asked, her eyes searching his face for any sign of how he was really doing. "Have you made any new friends?"

Caleb hesitated, feeling the familiar pressure to give the right answer, the one that would ease his parents' worries. "School's...fine," he replied, avoiding their gazes. "Lila's still my only friend, though."

Evelyn's lips pressed together in a tight line. She exchanged a glance with Thomas, her husband, before turning back to Caleb. "Just Lila?" she repeated, a hint of disappointment in her tone. "She's a sweet girl, but don't you think it would be good to branch out a bit? Make more connections?"

Caleb shrugged, his shoulders tense. "It's not that easy, Mom. People at school...they're different."

Before Evelyn could press further, Thomas cleared his throat, his voice cutting through the conversation with the authority that came naturally to him. "Caleb, your mother and I have been talking," he began, setting down his fork and fixing his son with a stern look. "It's time you reconsider returning to private school. This...experiment with public school has gone on long enough. You need to focus on your future, on what's expected of you."

Caleb felt his heart sink. He had known this conversation was coming, but that didn't make it any easier to hear. "Dad, I don't want to go back to private school," he said, his voice barely above a whisper. "I don't fit in there. I don't fit in anywhere."

Thomas leaned back in his chair, his expression

unyielding. "You don't need to fit in, Caleb. You need to excel. You need to be prepared for the responsibilities that come with being a Morgan. That's what matters."

Evelyn nodded in agreement, her expression one of concern and expectation. "Your father's right, Caleb. You're a Morgan. There are standards to uphold, and we just want what's best for you."

Caleb looked up, meeting his father's gaze with a resolve that had been building for weeks. "I'm not going back to private school," he said, his voice steady despite the storm of emotions swirling inside him. "I'm staying where I am. I like it here, and I'm finally starting to figure out who I am, what I want to be."

Evelyn reached out, placing a hand on Caleb's. Her touch was gentle, but her grip was firm. "We're just trying to do what's best for you," she said, her eyes filled with concern. "We want you to have every opportunity, for your future."

Caleb pulled her hand away, the frustration and hurt bubbling up inside him. "I don't care about opportunities or the future," he snapped, his voice trembling with emotion. "I just want to be normal, to live my life without all this pressure."

Thomas's expression hardened, his jaw clenching as he

set down his fork. "You don't know what's best for you, Caleb. You're too young to understand the consequences of your decisions. You have a responsibility to this family, to the name you carry."

"But what about what I want?" Caleb's voice rose, frustration and anger lacing his words. "I'm tired of living up to everyone else's expectations. I want to live my own life, make my own choices."

Thomas's face darkened, the vein in his temple throbbing visibly. "You're making a mistake," he said coldly. "And I won't stand by and watch you throw your future away."

The room fell silent, the weight of Caleb's words hanging in the air. Thomas's jaw tightened, and Evelyn's eyes glistened with unshed tears. Caleb could see the disappointment in their faces, but for once, he didn't care. He was tired of living up to their expectations, of being the perfect son.

Finally, Thomas spoke, his voice low and controlled. "We'll discuss this further in the morning," he said, his tone leaving no room for argument. "For now, finish your dinner."

Evelyn reached out, trying to diffuse the situation, but Caleb pushed back his chair, the legs scraping loudly against the floor. "I'm done with this," he muttered, storming out of the dining room before either of his parents could stop him.

The echo of his footsteps faded down the hallway, leaving Thomas and Evelyn in the stifling silence of the grand room. Thomas's expression was unreadable, but his mind was racing, already deciding what had to be done.

Later that evening, as the night settled over the Hamptons estate, Mr. Hayes moved through the halls, performing his usual rounds. The comforting routine of checking the windows, securing the doors, and ensuring that everything was in its place gave him a sense of purpose, a way to close out the day with a sense of order. The mansion was quiet, its grand rooms dimly lit, and the only sound was the soft rustle of the wind outside.

As Mr. Hayes passed by the door to the library, he heard Thomas Morgan's voice call out, pulling him from his thoughts. He paused for a moment before stepping inside, the warmth of the firelight casting flickering shadows on the bookshelves. Thomas was sitting in a leather armchair, his expression serious, the weight of his thoughts evident in the lines on his face.

"Mr. Hayes," Thomas began, his tone curt, as if pleasantries were an unnecessary formality. "Come in."

"Is there something you need, Mr. Morgan?" Mr. Hayes asked, his voice steady, though he felt a slight unease creeping in. "I could bring you some tea or anything else before you retire for the night."

Thomas shook his head, dismissing the offer with a wave of his hand. "No, that won't be necessary. I've been thinking, Mr. Hayes, and I've come to a decision. It's time for you and Lila to find somewhere else to stay."

Mr. Hayes blinked, the words catching him off guard. "I see," he said slowly, trying to keep his voice neutral. "Have I done something to cause this? If there's anything—"

"No, it's not about that," Thomas interrupted, his tone sharp but lacking malice. "You've done good work here, and I appreciate that. But we need to make some changes around here. The estate… it needs to evolve, and that includes certain aspects of how it's run."

Mr. Hayes felt a heaviness settle in his chest, but he kept his composure. "I understand, Mr. Morgan. Lila and I will start making arrangements."

"You have until next week," Thomas added, his voice softening slightly, though the decision was clearly final.

Mr. Hayes nodded, a thousand thoughts running through his mind, but he chose his words carefully. "Lila will be disappointed. She's grown quite fond of this place."

Thomas looked away, his gaze distant as he stared into the fire. "It's for the best. We all have to move forward, don't we?"

The room fell into a heavy silence, the crackling of the fire the only sound. Mr. Hayes could see the weight of Thomas's own burdens, the pressures of his position, and the expectations he placed upon himself and his family. But there was little he could say that would change the situation.

"If there's anything else you need, Mr. Morgan, I'll be in my quarters," Mr. Hayes said finally, knowing that his presence was no longer required.

For a moment, the two men stood in silence. Thomas, with his back to Mr. Hayes, seemed to be struggling with something—perhaps guilt, perhaps regret. But whatever it was, he quickly buried it beneath his usual mask of authority. He gave a curt nod, signaling the end of the conversation, and turned back to his papers.

Mr. Hayes remained for a moment longer, searching for any trace of the man he had once known, the man who had trusted him with his family's care. But there was nothing left to say. With a slight bow, he excused himself and left the room, his heart heavy with the weight of the news he would have to share with Lila.

Morgan's estate had been more than just a place of employment; it had been a home, filled with memories of laughter, love, and life. The thought of leaving it behind, of uprooting Lila and starting anew, weighed heavily on him. But he knew he had to remain strong, for both of their sakes.

As he walked back to the small cottage they called home, each step felt like a leaden weight, dragging him down with the enormity of what had just happened. The thought of telling Lila, of seeing the look in her eyes when she heard they had to leave, was almost too much to bear.

When he reached the cottage, he paused outside, taking a deep breath before pushing the door open. Lila was sitting by the fireplace, a book in her lap, but she looked up as soon as he entered, sensing that something was wrong.

"Dad?" she asked, concern etched across her face. "What's going on?"

Mr. Hayes walked over to her, his steps slow and deliberate. He sat down beside her, his hands clasped together as he tried to find the right words. But there was no easy way to say it.

"We have to leave, Lila," he said finally, his voice thick with emotion. "The Senator wants us out by next week."

For a moment, Lila just stared at him, her eyes wide with disbelief. "Leave? But...why?"

Mr. Hayes shook his head, unable to explain what he didn't fully understand himself. "He says it's time for a change. I don't know what's really going on, but we have to start packing."

Lila's face crumpled, and for a moment, Mr. Hayes thought she might cry. But then, something else took over—a quiet determination that he had seen in her before, a strength that had always amazed him.

"We never really belonged here anyway, did we?" she said softly, her voice tinged with a bittersweet acceptance. "This was never our home, not really. We were just...passing through."

Mr. Hayes felt a lump form in his throat as he looked at his daughter, seeing the woman she had become. She was right, of course. They had always been outsiders, caretakers of someone else's life, never fully part of it. But that didn't make the pain of leaving any easier.

"You're right," he said, his voice barely above a whisper. "But that doesn't make this any less hard."

Lila reached out and took his hand, squeezing it gently. "We'll be okay, Dad. We've been through worse, and we'll get through this too."

Mr. Hayes nodded, grateful for her strength, even as his heart ached at the thought of leaving the place they had called home for so long. The memories they had made here, the life they had built, would soon be nothing more than a chapter in their past. But he knew, as Lila had said, that they would find a way to move forward.

Together, they sat in silence, the weight of the news settling over them like a heavy blanket. The cottage, once filled with warmth and comfort, now felt like a place of mourning, a reminder of the life they were about to leave behind.

The weekend slipped by like sand through Caleb's fingers, each moment with his parents a forced attempt at normalcy. The Morgans had left for New York early Monday morning, leaving the estate behind in its usual state of quiet grandeur. Caleb had spent the weekend maintaining his distance from Lila, a silent understanding that their worlds were too close for comfort while his parents were around.

But when the weekend ended, Lila seemed to have vanished. She wasn't at school, and Caleb felt a gnawing anxiety build up inside him. The halls that were once filled with the whispers of his classmates now felt like a maze of empty echoes. He couldn't focus, couldn't breathe, not without knowing where she was.

His resolve hardened. He didn't care about the rules or the consequences. He needed to find her.

So, Caleb made his way to the beach, his heart pounding with a mixture of worry and determination. The waves crashed against the shore with a kind of relentless fury that mirrored the storm brewing within him. And then, he saw her—Lila, a lone figure riding the waves, her surfboard cutting through the water like she was part of the ocean itself.

Without a second thought, Caleb stripped down to his shorts, feeling the cool sand beneath his feet as he sprinted toward the water. He dove into the waves, swimming with all his might, his eyes locked on Lila as she paddled out further, as if trying to escape him.

"Lila!" he called out, his voice strained with effort as he finally reached her.

She turned, her face a mix of anger and sadness. "Caleb, leave me alone," she said, her voice hard, but her eyes betraying the turmoil within. "I need space."

But Caleb didn't back down. "No," he said firmly, treading water beside her. "I need to know why you've been avoiding me. Why are you shutting me out?"

For a moment, the only sound between them was the crash of the waves. Then Lila sighed, her shoulders sagging as if the weight of the world had settled on them. "Caleb, I need to tell you something," she said softly, her tone laced with pain.

"What is it?" he asked, a sense of dread creeping into his chest.

"It's about my dad and me," she began, her voice barely above a whisper. "We...we have to leave. Your father told him to leave. We have until next week to move out."

Caleb's heart dropped, his breath catching in his throat. "What? Why would he do that?" His voice was a mix of disbelief and anger, the realization hitting him like a punch to the gut.

"I don't know," Lila admitted, her eyes glistening with unshed tears. "But it's happening, and there's nothing we can do about it."

The weight of his father's expectations, the looming loss of Mr. Hayes and Lila, and the growing sense of helplessness pressed down on Caleb like a tidal wave. The summer that was supposed to be his escape was quickly turning into a nightmare. Desperation clawed at him, the fear of losing Lila threatening to pull him under.

"I'm not letting this happen," Caleb said with a sudden burst of determination. "I'm going to talk to him. I'll make him change his mind."

"Caleb, please," Lila pleaded, her voice breaking as she reached out to stop him. "Don't make things worse. We'll figure something out. My dad will be okay. We'll be okay."

But Caleb wasn't listening. He was too far gone, too consumed by the need to fix things, to hold on to the one good thing in his life. The exhaustion from swimming, the emotions swirling inside him—it was all too much. His legs began to weaken, and before he knew it, he was struggling to stay afloat.

"Caleb!" Lila cried out as she jumped off her surfboard, wrapping her arms around him, keeping him above the water. "Caleb, stop! You're going to drown!"

Caleb clung to her, his breath ragged, his body

trembling. He looked into her eyes, the panic fading as he realized how close he had come to losing himself. "I'm sorry," he whispered, holding her tightly. "I just...I can't lose you, Lila. I'll do anything. If you want me to leave too? I will. I'll be there for you, no matter what."

Lila let out a soft laugh, the tension leaving her body as she shook her head. "You can't come with us," she said, her voice tinged with affection. "I can't have another mouth to feed."

They both laughed, the sound carrying over the waves, a moment of lightness in the midst of the storm. Caleb felt a small spark of hope flicker inside him, a glimmer of the carefree boy he used to be.

They swam back to shore together, the weight of their worries momentarily lifted. When they reached the beach, they stood there, catching their breath, the cool ocean breeze wrapping around them like a comforting embrace.

"Come on," Caleb said, taking her hand. "Let's get back to the mansion. We can figure things out from there."

Lila hesitated but nodded, allowing him to lead her back to the estate. Once inside, they both knew they had to avoid her father, who would be furious to find her cutting school. Caleb guided her up to his room, the familiarity of the space offering a brief sense of security.

As they sat on the edge of his bed, Caleb reached out, gently running his fingers through Lila's hair, trying to get the sand out. "You've got half the beach in here," he joked softly, his touch lingering longer than necessary.

Lila smiled, the tension between them shifting into something else, something softer, more intimate. "You're not much better," she teased, brushing a strand of wet hair from his forehead.

Their eyes met, the unspoken connection between them growing stronger with each passing second. Without thinking, Caleb leaned in, his heart pounding as he pressed his lips to hers.

Lila hesitated for a brief moment, then kissed him back, the world outside fading away. The kiss was sweet, tender, filled with all the emotions they had been holding back. It was a promise, a declaration of the bond they shared, a silent vow that no matter what happened, they would face it together.

When they finally pulled apart, both of them were breathless, their faces flushed. Caleb rested his forehead against hers, a small smile tugging at his lips. "We'll figure this out," he whispered. "I promise."

Lila nodded, her heart full of conflicting emotions, but for the first time in days, she felt a glimmer of hope. In Caleb's arms, she found the strength to believe that maybe, just maybe, they could make it through this storm together.

CHAPTER 13: THE LAST CONFESSION

Lila wiped the sweat from her brow as she stepped out of the stall at the horse farm where she worked the morning shift. The exhaustion clung to her, a constant reminder that she had no choice—she needed the money. With her father's arthritis worsening and the looming deadline to leave the Morgan estate in less than a week, she felt like she was drowning. The weight of her responsibilities pressed down on her, making each day feel like an insurmountable challenge.

As she made her way to the main barn, she couldn't shake the worry gnawing at her insides. Balancing school and work was already overwhelming, and the added burden of finding a new place to live felt like an impossible task. Every passing day only amplified her fears. The thought of failing her father, the one person who had always been there for her, filled her with dread. She couldn't bear the idea of letting him down, of not being able to provide for them both.

She reached the small office where her manager sat, buried in paperwork. Taking a deep breath, Lila stepped inside, her voice hesitant as she spoke. "Mr. John, I was wondering if I could talk to you about something."

The manager glanced up from his desk, his expression impatient. "Make it quick, girl. I've got a lot on my plate today."

Lila swallowed, her nerves getting the best of her. "I was hoping… maybe I could get a raise? I've been working extra shifts, and with everything going on, I just really need the money."

Mr. John leaned back in his chair, a smirk playing on his lips. "A raise? Girl, you're lucky to have this job. With all the new workers coming in, I could replace you in a heartbeat. You want a raise? You better work twice as hard and stop asking for favors."

The words stung, but Lila forced herself to nod. "Yes, sir. I'm sorry."

She left the office, her heart heavy with the realization that she was truly on her own. The fear of failure loomed larger than ever, but there was no time to dwell on it. She had to keep moving, keep working, keep pushing through the exhaustion. But as she walked away from the barn, she couldn't help but feel a pang of hopelessness. The clock was ticking down, and she was running out of options.

Lila pedaled furiously through the morning

mist, her bike tires crunching against the gravel road as she raced toward school. The scent of the horse stables still clung to her clothes, a pungent reminder of the hours she had spent mucking out stalls before dawn. She cringed at the thought, wishing she had more time to clean up, but there was nothing she could do about it now. She had done her best—wiped off the worst of it, pulled her hair into a tight ponytail, and hoped the cool morning air would mask any lingering smell. But doubt gnawed at her as she rode, her mind swirling with anxiety.

As she chained her bike to the rack and walked into the school building, her heart pounded in her chest, not from the exertion but from fear. She kept her head down, avoiding eye contact with the other students as she navigated the crowded hallways. The last thing she needed was to draw attention to herself, especially not today, when she felt so vulnerable.

But fate wasn't kind that morning. As she passed by a group of boys huddled near the lockers, she caught the unmistakable sound of Logan's voice. His tone was low, but the mocking edge was impossible to miss.

"Looks like someone's been rolling around in the mud again," Logan sneered, loud enough for his friends to hear but just quiet enough to avoid the teachers' ears. "What's the matter, Lila? Couldn't find time to shower this morning?"

His friends snickered, trading smirks and elbowing each other, clearly enjoying the show. Lila's heart sank, and she felt her cheeks flush with a mix of embarrassment and anger. She kept walking, pretending not to hear, but the words clung to her like a dark cloud.

But Logan was relentless as he continued mocking Lila, "Maybe she's just trying out a new look—horse stable chic."

Another round of laughter erupted, and Lila's grip tightened on the straps of her backpack. She wanted to turn around, to say something—anything—but the words lodged in her throat. Instead, she quickened her pace, desperate to reach the safety of her classroom.

Once inside, she slipped into her seat, her hands trembling as she pulled out her notebook. She could still hear their laughter echoing in her ears, each taunt a sharp jab at her already fragile self-esteem. She wished she could disappear, just melt into the floor and escape the cruel whispers and judgmental stares. But that wasn't an option, so she forced herself to focus on the lesson, pushing the hurt deep down where it couldn't reach her.

During lunch, Lila sat in the quietest corner of the school, her books spread out in front of her as she tried to focus on her homework. The silence was a welcome escape from the usual noise of the lunch period, but her mind kept wandering back to Caleb. His messages had been piling up on her phone, each one a reminder of the connection they had shared—one she wasn't sure she was ready to face again.

She shivered, the memory of their kiss lingering in her thoughts, a mix of warmth and confusion that she couldn't quite shake. It had been unexpected, stirring emotions she wasn't prepared to deal with. She knew Caleb was struggling, and a part of her wanted to be there for him, to help him through the darkness that seemed to envelop him. But another part of her was terrified—terrified of what that kiss had awakened in her, and of the complications it could bring.

Lila glanced at her phone again, the screen dark and still, as if waiting for her to make a decision. But she quickly forced her attention back to her homework. College applications were looming, and she needed to keep her grades up if she wanted to secure a spot at the school of her dreams. There was no room for distractions, no matter how much her heart ached to reach out to Caleb.

She took a deep breath, trying to steady her racing thoughts. This was important. Her future depended on it. And yet, as she tried to focus on the equations in front of her, the image of Caleb's haunted eyes kept intruding, a silent plea she couldn't ignore.

But she had to. At least for now.

Lila pushed the thoughts aside, forcing herself to concentrate as she chewed on some crackers. The numbers and formulas blurred together as she fought to stay focused, but deep down, she knew that Caleb's messages would still be waiting, just like the feelings she was trying so hard to suppress.

The school day dragged on, each minute feeling like an eternity. Every time she passed Logan in the hallway, she kept her gaze fixed straight ahead, determined not to let him see how much his words had affected her. But the knot of tension in her chest never loosened, not even when the final bell rang.

After school, Lila trudged to her next job, walking dogs for a few of the wealthy families in town. The weariness had settled into her bones, a deep, aching exhaustion that came from more than just physical labor. Each step felt heavier than the last, and every muscle in her body protested, screaming for rest. But rest wasn't an option—not for her. She needed the money, and there was no time to feel sorry for herself.

The sun was already beginning to set by the time she finished walking the dogs. They tugged at their leashes, eager to get home, while Lila's thoughts drifted to her father. She knew he'd be waiting for her, needing help with packing up the last of their things. The idea of moving out of the Morgan estate filled her with a sense of dread, but there was no avoiding it. Their time there was up, and they had to leave.

As she returned the dogs to their owners and collected her pay, Lila felt a pang of longing for the simplicity of her childhood, when life hadn't been so complicated, when she didn't have to worry about bills or moving or the harsh words of boys like Logan. But those days were long gone, replaced by the harsh realities of adulthood.

She mounted her bike once more, the ride home slower and more deliberate as the events of the day weighed heavily on her. The air was cooler now, carrying with it the promise of another long night ahead. All she could think about was getting home, helping her father, and maybe, just maybe, finding a moment to breathe amidst the chaos.

But even as she pedaled through the gathering twilight, the sting of Logan's words lingered, a painful reminder of how cruel the world could be. And though she tried to push it aside, to focus on the tasks ahead, a part of her couldn't shake the feeling that no matter how hard she worked, how much she gave, it would never be enough to escape the shadows that followed her.

Caleb sat on the edge of his bed, his phone clutched tightly in his hand, the screen glowing in the dim light of his room. The walls felt like they were closing in on him, the weight of the conversation he needed to have pressing down on his chest. He'd been putting it off for days, hoping somehow things would change on their own, but he knew better. His father was a man of decisions, not second thoughts.

With a deep breath, Caleb dialed his father's number, his heart pounding in his ears as the phone rang. Each second felt like an eternity, the sound of the ringing amplifying his dread. Finally, the line clicked, and his father's familiar voice came through, cool and businesslike.

"Caleb, what is it? I'm in a meeting," his father's tone was impatient, as if Caleb's call was just another interruption in his busy schedule.

"Dad, I wanted to talk to you about Mr. Hayes," Caleb began, trying to keep his voice steady despite the anxiety bubbling up inside him. "I don't think it's fair to let him go. He's been with us for so long, and he's like family."

There was a brief pause, and when his father spoke again, his tone was cold and detached, as if he were discussing a mere business transaction. "Caleb, we've already discussed this. The estate is changing, and Mr. Hayes is no longer needed. If you're so concerned about it, then maybe you should step up. If you want to stay in the Hamptons, you'll need to earn your keep by taking care of the house yourself."

Caleb felt a knot tighten in his chest, a mix of frustration and despair. "But Dad, this isn't right. He's done nothing wrong. He's been more than just a caretaker—he's been there for us, for me, through everything."

His father's voice grew sharp, cutting through Caleb's plea like a knife. "Enough, Caleb. I don't have time for this. If you don't like it, then you can come back home to New York. Otherwise, you'll do as you're told."

The line went dead before Caleb could respond, leaving him staring at his phone in disbelief. The silence that followed was deafening, echoing the finality of his father's words. He felt a deep sense of helplessness, as if a vital part of him had been crushed under the weight of his father's indifference.

For a long moment, Caleb sat there, struggling to process what had just happened. He had known his father was a hard man, driven by ambition and power, but this... this was different. This was cruelty, veiled in the guise of practicality. And Caleb didn't know how to fight it.

With a heavy heart, Caleb pushed himself up from the bed and made his way to the servant's quarters. His steps were slow, each one filled with the dread of what he would find. When he reached the door, he hesitated, his hand hovering over the knob. He could hear the quiet sounds of Mr. Hayes moving about inside, the rustle of boxes being filled, the muted thud of items being packed away.

Finally, Caleb pushed the door open and stepped inside. The room was small, but it had always been filled with warmth—a reflection of the man who lived there. Now, it felt empty, the life slowly being packed into cardboard boxes.

Mr. Hayes looked up as Caleb entered, his expression calm but tinged with a sadness that Caleb had never seen before. The older man offered a warm smile, though it didn't quite reach his eyes.

"I'm sorry about this," Caleb said quietly, his voice thick with guilt. "I tried talking to him, but..."

Mr. Hayes shook his head, his smile never wavering. "It's alright, Master Caleb. Maybe it's for the best. Sometimes change is necessary, even when it's hard to understand."

Caleb wanted to argue, to say that this change wasn't necessary, that it was wrong, but the words got caught in his throat. He could see the pain in Mr. Hayes' eyes, the quiet resignation of a man who had seen too much of life to fight against its unfairness.

"Mr. Hayes, you don't have to leave," Caleb said, his voice breaking slightly. "There has to be a way to fix this."

The old caretaker placed a gentle hand on Caleb's shoulder, his touch comforting in its familiarity. "Life has a way of working out, even when it seems like it's falling apart. You'll see. And I'm not going far away. You can visit anytime you like."

Caleb nodded, though it felt like a hollow gesture. He watched as Mr. Hayes continued packing, each item a piece of the life that was being dismantled before his eyes. The thought of losing him—of losing the only person who had always been there, unwavering and constant—was almost too much to bear.

As Mr. Hayes placed the last of his belongings in the box, he turned to Caleb, his smile returning, this time with a hint of mischief. "Besides, I think I deserve a bit of a break. Maybe even a vacation. I hear Florida's nice this time of year."

Caleb couldn't help but smile, the image of Mr. Hayes

lounging on a beach somehow lightening the heaviness in his chest. "You'd get bored in a week," Caleb replied, his voice soft but affectionate.

"Probably," Mr. Hayes admitted with a chuckle. "But it's the thought that counts."

As they stood there, sharing a quiet moment in the midst of the packing, Caleb realized that no matter what happened, Mr. Hayes would always be a part of his life. The bond they shared wasn't something that could be packed away or discarded—it was something that would endure, even in the face of change.

"Thank you," Caleb said, his voice barely above a whisper. "For everything."

Mr. Hayes gave him a warm smile, though Caleb could see the sadness in his eyes. "It's alright, Master Caleb. Maybe it's for the best. Sometimes change is necessary, even when it's hard to understand."

Caleb wanted to say more, to apologize for his father's sudden change of heart, but the words got caught in his throat. He simply nodded, feeling more lost than ever as he watched Mr. Hayes continue packing.

When Lila walked through the door of their small cottage, her eyes fell on the half-packed boxes scattered across the floor, each one a reminder of the uncertain future they faced. The room, once filled with warmth and the comfort of familiarity, now felt like a place of transition, a temporary stop before the next chapter of their lives.

Her father sat in his favorite chair, a worn-out blanket draped over his legs. Despite the heavy atmosphere, his face lit up when he saw her, a flicker of joy that momentarily eased the guilt gnawing at her insides. But the burden of their situation weighed heavily on her, and Lila struggled to keep her emotions in check.

"Long day, sweetheart?" he asked, his voice filled with concern that only deepened her internal conflict.

Forcing a smile, Lila tried to mask the turmoil raging inside her. "Yeah, but I'm okay, Dad. How are you?"

His sigh was soft, yet it spoke volumes, his eyes reflecting a mixture of pride and worry. "I'm doing alright, but you don't have to work so hard, Lila. We'll figure something out."

But Lila knew better. She couldn't afford to slow down, not when everything was on the line. She glanced around at the half-filled boxes, the weight of their situation pressing down on her. They had barely enough time to move out, but where would they go? The Hamptons was expensive, and her search for a decent rental place had come up empty.

"It's not fair," she muttered under her breath, her frustration finally bubbling to the surface. "The Morgans... they've made everything so difficult."

Mr. Hayes looked at her with the calm, steady gaze that had always been his strength. "It's no one's fault, Lila. We couldn't live here forever. This wasn't our home."

The words stung, but Lila knew he was right. Yet, that didn't make the reality any easier to swallow. The cottage, the estate, the life they had built—it was all slipping away, and there was nothing she could do to stop it.

They sat down to dinner in silence, the weight of unspoken thoughts hanging in the air. The simple meal felt like a last supper of sorts, a final moment of normalcy before the inevitable change. As they ate, Mr. Hayes broke the quiet with a gentle tone. "Caleb was here for a little while today."

Lila's fork paused mid-air. Caleb. The last person she wanted to think about right now. Their relationship— or whatever it was—had been pushed to the back of her mind, buried beneath the avalanche of responsibilities. They hadn't made anything official, hadn't even discussed what they were to each other. Yet, she knew she couldn't avoid him forever. Sooner or later, they'd have to face each other again, and the thought sent a pang of anxiety through her.

After dinner, Lila retreated to her room, the walls closing in as she continued to pack up her life into boxes. The familiar comfort of her space was being dismantled piece by piece, each item carefully wrapped, yet the act of packing felt like she was erasing herself from this place. Her hands trembled as she folded clothes, her mind racing with questions she had no answers to.

Where would they go? What would happen if she couldn't find a place in time? The fear of failure loomed large, and Lila fought back the tears threatening to spill over. She had to be strong—for her father, for herself. But deep down, she wondered how much longer she could keep it all together before everything came crashing down.

Later that night, Caleb found himself lingering in the dimly lit kitchen, the ticking of the old clock on the wall the only sound breaking the stillness. The mansion, usually buzzing with activity during the day, felt eerily quiet, its vastness amplifying his solitude. He absently licked a spoonful of mint chocolate chip ice cream, a flavor that was slowly growing on him, thanks to Lila. Each bite was a small reminder of her, a connection to something warm and familiar in a world that often felt cold and overwhelming.

He hadn't expected to see her tonight, but he couldn't help but hope. His heart was heavy with concern, both for himself and for her. The silence weighed on him, the unspoken words between them creating a tension he didn't know how to resolve.

The back door creaked open, and Caleb's heart leaped in his chest. He stood up, anticipation and worry swirling inside him. Lila walked into the kitchen, her shoulders slumped with exhaustion, her eyes dull with the weight of the day's burdens.

Lila froze when she saw Caleb, her expression shifting from surprise to something more guarded. She hadn't expected to run into him, especially not here, not now. There was an awkwardness in the air, a hesitation that neither knew how to break.

"You're home late," Caleb said softly, his voice tentative as he tried to gauge her mood.

"Yeah," Lila replied, rubbing her temples as if to ward off the headache that threatened to overwhelm her. "Work ran long. It's just...everything's piling up, you know?"

She glanced at the bowl of ice cream in front of him, a small smile tugging at her lips despite her exhaustion.

"Mind if I join you?" she asked, nodding towards the ice cream.

Caleb gestured to the seat beside him, a small, relieved smile on his face. "Of course. I saved some for you."

She sat down next to him, reaching for a spoon. For a moment, they simply ate in silence, the cool sweetness of the ice cream a small comfort in the midst of their worries.

"It's not just work," Lila said finally, her voice tinged with weariness. "It's my dad...his arthritis is getting worse. He's been in so much pain lately, and I can't stand seeing him like this. I don't know how I'm supposed to leave him when I go to college next year. But I want to see the world, Caleb. I want to have a life of my own, but I can't just abandon him. He'd be all alone here."

Caleb felt a deep pang of empathy for her. He knew all too well what it was like to feel trapped between the expectations of others and the desires of his own heart. "You're not abandoning him, Lila. You're just trying to live your life. It's okay to want that."

Lila gave him a small, tired smile, though the worry in her eyes remained. "I hope you're right. But it doesn't make it any easier."

The kitchen fell into a comfortable silence, the weight of their shared burdens hanging in the air. Caleb took a deep breath, knowing it was time to share his own pain, the secret that had been eating away at him for so long.

"Lila...there's something I need to tell you," he began, his voice trembling as the memories rushed back like a tidal wave. "About my dad...and Milo."

Lila's expression shifted, concern and confusion flickering across her face. "What is it, Caleb?"

He hesitated, the words catching in his throat as he thought back to that night—the night that had changed everything.

It was late, the kind of late where the world outside was quiet, and the only sounds were the low hum of the air conditioning and the occasional creak of the house settling. Caleb was in his room, trying to drown out the raised voices from the living room with music, but the argument between his parents was too loud, too fierce. He could hear his father's voice, thick with anger and something darker, a slur that only came when he'd had too much to drink.

Milo, sensing the tension, had stayed close to Caleb's side, his warm, reassuring presence a small comfort. But when the shouting escalated, the fear in Caleb's chest became unbearable, and he felt a desperate need to intervene.

He'd hurried out, finding his father in a rage, his mother pleading with him to calm down. Caleb had tried to step in, but his father's fury turned on him, the words cutting deep. Milo, always protective, growled low, his body tense as he tried to shield Caleb and his mother.

And then it happened. His father, in a blind rage, had grabbed the back door and flung it open. "Get that damn dog out of here!" he'd bellowed. Milo, confused and scared, had darted out the door, and in a panic, had run into the street. Caleb had screamed, his heart lurching in terror as he chased after him.

But it was too late. The screech of tires, the sickening thud—it all happened so fast. By the time Caleb reached him, Milo was lying motionless on the road, the light in his eyes fading as Caleb cradled him, sobbing uncontrollably.

Lila gasped, her hand flying to her mouth, her eyes wide with shock and sympathy. "Caleb, I'm so sorry...I had no idea."

"I've never told anyone," Caleb admitted, his voice breaking under the weight of the memory. "I just...I couldn't. And now my dad wants to get rid of Mr. Hayes too. It's like everything good in my life is slipping away."

Lila reached out and took his hand, her touch gentle and warm, a comforting anchor in the storm of his emotions. "You don't have to go through this alone, Caleb. I'm here for you. And we'll figure something out, okay?"

Caleb squeezed her hand, feeling a surge of gratitude for her understanding. "Thank you, Lila. That means more to me than you know."

They sat there, holding hands, the kitchen's dim light casting soft shadows on the walls. The silence between them was no longer heavy with awkwardness but filled with an unspoken connection, a shared understanding of the pain they both carried.

After a few moments, Lila looked up at Caleb, her cheeks tinged with a hint of color. "Caleb...what are we? I mean, are we...dating? Or are we just friends? I'm not sure where we stand."

Caleb's heart skipped a beat at her question. He had been avoiding this conversation, unsure of what to say or how to define what they had. But now, looking into her eyes, he knew he had to be honest.

"Lila," he began, his voice soft but filled with emotion, "You're the one person who makes me feel like everything might actually be okay. When I'm with you, the world feels a little less heavy. I don't know if that makes us something official. But I do know that I want to keep being with you, in whatever way that means."

Lila's heart fluttered at his words, a warmth spreading through her that chased away the lingering doubts. "I feel the same way, Caleb. Being with you...it just feels right."

He smiled at her, a smile that reached his eyes, something rare for him these days. "Then let's not worry about labels. Let's just...be us."

Lila returned his smile, a sense of peace settling over her. "Okay. Just us."

As they sat there, the ice cream melting in their bowls, the night seemed a little less daunting, the future a little more hopeful. In the quiet of the mansion, they found comfort in each other, a connection that transcended the words they spoke and the troubles they faced. And in that moment, amidst the uncertainty and the heartache, they knew they weren't alone. They had each other, and for now, that was enough.

CHAPTER 14: THE LAST DREAM

The next morning, Caleb found himself restless, his mind circling back to Lila and the uncertainty looming over her future. He knew he had to do something, anything, to help ease the burden she was carrying. The thought of Lila and her father being forced out of the only home they'd known weighed heavily on him. So, he took it upon himself to find them a new place, determined to make things right.

He started by reaching out to people in the community, asking for advice and assistance in finding a new place for Lila and her dad. But the search was anything but straightforward. Caleb's inexperience quickly became apparent as he scoured the internet for listings that seemed far too good to be true.

The same afternoon, he convinced Lila to join him for a round of house viewings. Armed with a list of addresses, they set off, the atmosphere between them light, filled with playful banter.

Their first stop was a quaint-looking cottage advertised as a "charming fixer-upper." But when they arrived, they were met with the sight of a decrepit shack that looked like it hadn't been lived in for decades. The windows were boarded up, the roof sagging, and the front yard was an overgrown jungle of weeds. Lila burst out laughing the moment she saw it, her giggles infectious as Caleb shook his head in disbelief.

"Okay, maybe that one's not exactly as advertised," Caleb said, scratching his head as they both struggled to catch their breath from laughing.

Lila wiped a tear from the corner of her eye, still chuckling. "Did the listing say anything about needing a bulldozer to get in?"

Caleb grinned, feeling a warmth spread through him at the sound of her laughter. "Hey, at least it's got character, right?"

Their next stop was even more bizarre. The directions had led them down a narrow dirt road that seemed to go on forever. Caleb glanced at Lila, who was trying to suppress another fit of laughter.

"Are you sure this is the right way?" Lila asked, her eyes wide with amusement.

"According to the GPS, we're almost there," Caleb replied, squinting at the screen.

As they pulled up to the final destination, they both stared in stunned silence. There was no house in sight—just a graveyard, old and eerie, with crooked tombstones scattered across a barren field.

"This can't be real," Caleb muttered, his face flushing with embarrassment.

Lila looked at him, her eyes sparkling with barely contained laughter. "Well, if you were looking for a place that's quiet, you definitely found it."

Caleb groaned, running a hand through his hair. "I'm never trusting the internet again."

They both laughed, the absurdity of the situation dissolving any remaining tension between them. Caleb glanced at Lila, her profile illuminated by the golden light of the setting sun, and felt a rush of affection for her. Despite the day's misadventures, she remained cheerful and kind, her spirit unbroken.

After more searching, Caleb finally found a small house on the outskirts of town. It wasn't much—a modest, single-story home with a tiny front yard and a few trees offering shade. But it was cozy, quiet, and had a sense of peace that Caleb thought Lila and her father might appreciate.

He arranged for Lila and Mr. Hayes to see the place, hoping it would be the fresh start they needed. As they pulled up to the house, Mr. Hayes couldn't help but chuckle, taking in the distance from the beach they had grown accustomed to.

"It's a bit far from the ocean, don't you think?" Mr. Hayes remarked, his tone light, though his eyes held a hint of concern.

Caleb grinned, trying to keep the mood upbeat. "Yeah, but it's peaceful. I think you'll like it."

As they walked through the house, the three of them took in the simple but welcoming interior. Caleb noticed how close he and Lila had become over the past few days. Their shared glances, small smiles, and even the inside jokes they had developed made him feel like they were slowly becoming more than just friends.

Mr. Hayes observed this too, his heart heavy with conflicting emotions. He couldn't deny that Caleb was a good kid, thoughtful and sincere in his efforts to help. But the worry in his heart remained—a father's instinct to protect his daughter from getting hurt. He had seen too many wealthy kids lose interest once the novelty wore off, and he feared Caleb might one day move on, leaving Lila behind with a broken heart.

Yet, as he watched Caleb and Lila together, he also saw something different in Caleb—an earnestness, a genuine care for Lila that made him question his own doubts. There was a quiet determination in Caleb's eyes, a resolve to be there for Lila in a way that went beyond simple gestures.

As they stood in the front yard, watching the sunset, Mr. Hayes sighed, the weight of his thoughts pressing down on him. He wanted to protect his daughter more than anything, to shield her from the pain he knew the world could bring. But he also knew that life had a way of surprising you, sometimes in the best ways. And maybe, just maybe, Caleb wasn't like the others. Maybe he was the one who could bring Lila the happiness she deserved.

Caleb turned to Lila, his voice soft and filled with a quiet curiosity. "So, what do you think? Could you see yourself living here?"

Lila's smile was warm, the light of the setting sun reflecting in her eyes, casting a gentle glow on her face. "It's not the beach, but it feels like home," she said, her voice carrying a note of acceptance that tugged at Caleb's heart.

In that moment, Caleb realized that home wasn't just a place—it was a feeling, a sense of belonging that he had been searching for all along. And as he stood there with Lila and Mr. Hayes, he knew that this small house on the outskirts of town might just be the beginning of something new, something that could heal the wounds of the past and bring them all closer together.

The day dawned with a softness in the air, the kind of light that made everything seem possible, even if only for a fleeting moment. The sky, a pale shade of blue, held the promise of a beautiful day ahead, though the undercurrent of change was palpable. As Caleb walked up the winding path to the small cottage on the Morgan estate, he couldn't shake the heaviness in his chest. The sight of the moving truck parked out front was a stark reminder that today was the end of an era.

When he arrived, the last of the boxes were being loaded into the truck. Lila and her father, Mr. Hayes, stood on the porch, their faces a mix of resignation and quiet determination. The porch, where they had shared countless moments of laughter and love, was now a place of goodbye. Caleb could see the weight of their departure hanging in the air, bittersweet and heavy with unspoken words.

"Morning, Lila. Mr. Hayes," Caleb greeted, his voice warm yet tinged with sadness. He walked up the steps and offered his hand to Mr. Hayes, who shook it firmly, the strength of his grip belying the exhaustion in his eyes.

"We couldn't have done it without you, Caleb," Mr. Hayes said, his voice thick with emotion. "You've been a good friend to us, more than you know."

Caleb's throat tightened at the sincerity in Mr. Hayes' words. This man had been more of a father figure to him than his own father ever was, and the thought of losing that daily connection hit harder than he had expected.

Lila turned to Caleb, her eyes glistening with unshed tears. "We're going to miss this place," she said softly, her voice trembling with the effort to hold back her emotions. "But I'm glad you're here today."

Caleb smiled gently, though it didn't quite reach his eyes. He knew how much this place meant to her, how it had been a sanctuary for both of them in different ways. "I wouldn't be anywhere else," he replied, his voice low and sincere.

After the last box was secured in the truck, Caleb turned to Lila with a grin, trying to lift the somber mood. "How about one last adventure before you go?"

Lila's eyes brightened at his suggestion, a spark of the carefree girl he remembered shining through. But the reality of the day wasn't lost on her. "Okay," she agreed, but then added, "But only after we've moved everything into the new house."

The warmth of the late afternoon sun bathed the small house in a golden glow as they arrived at Lila's new home. It was modest, a far cry from the grandeur of the Morgan estate, but there was something undeniably special about it. The house was old, with a charm that whispered of years gone by, of stories etched into its walls. The peeling paint on the shutters, the creak of the wooden steps, and the overgrown garden gave it a sense of history, of a place that had been loved and lived in.

When they arrived, Mr. Hayes immediately set to work, directing the movers with the kind of precision that came from years of managing the estate. But as the last of the boxes were carried inside, fatigue caught up with him.

Mr. Hayes sighed, wiping the sweat from his brow. "I think I need a nap," he admitted, chuckling softly. "You two can handle the rest, right?"

"Of course, Mr. Hayes," Caleb replied, nodding with understanding. "You've earned a break."

With Mr. Hayes resting, Caleb and Lila took charge, guiding the movers as they placed the boxes in the small living room. The house was beginning to feel homely, with each item finding its place, each room taking on a bit of their personality.

And as the last of the boxes were carried inside, Caleb took a moment to stand beside Lila, both of them gazing at the house that would soon become her new home. "It's not much, but it's ours," Lila said, a mixture of pride and apprehension in her voice.

Caleb turned to her, seeing the uncertainty in her eyes. "It's perfect," he said softly. "This place has character. It's like you—strong, beautiful, and a little rough around the edges."

Lila laughed, a small, genuine sound that seemed to ease some of the tension in her shoulders. "I guess I'll take that as a compliment."

They stood there for a moment, side by side, letting the warmth of the sun seep into their bones. Caleb couldn't help but feel a pang of sadness at the thought of leaving her here, in this new place, with so much uncertainty ahead. But he also knew that Lila was strong, stronger than she often gave herself credit for.

After everything was settled, Lila turned to Caleb, a determined look in her eyes. "Alright, let's go on that adventure you promised."

Caleb smiled, relief washing over him as he saw a glimmer of the girl he had always known. "Let's go," he said, offering his hand. "No plans, no worries—just us."

And so, they set out on their impromptu adventure, wandering through the familiar streets of the Hamptons as if seeing them for the first time. They visited the small beachside cafes, indulging in scoops of ice cream, the cool sweetness a balm for their souls. They reminisced about the summers they had spent together, their laughter echoing through the air like a melody from a simpler time.

As they wandered, the people of the community greeted them with warm smiles and friendly nods, their kindness wrapping around Caleb and Lila like a comforting blanket. It was as if the Hamptons itself was welcoming them into this new chapter of their lives, offering them a place to belong.

By the time the sun began to set, they found themselves at a quiet stretch of beach, their favorite spot. The waves lapped gently at the shore, the rhythmic sound soothing the tension that had been building within Caleb all day.

Lila sat down on the sand, pulling her knees to her chest as she gazed out at the horizon. Caleb joined her, the silence between them filled with a deep, unspoken understanding.

"This place," Lila began, her voice barely above a whisper, "it's always been special to me. It's where I come when I need to think, to just...be."

Caleb nodded, his heart swelling with a mix of emotions. "It's peaceful here. Like nothing else in the world matters."

They sat there for what felt like hours, watching as the sky darkened and the stars began to twinkle above them. In that moment, surrounded by the beauty of the world and the comfort of each other's presence, they both felt a sense of peace, of healing.

And as they finally rose to leave, their hands brushed against each other, a simple touch that spoke volumes. Caleb looked at Lila, his heart full of gratitude and something more—a quiet hope that this new beginning might just be the one they both needed.

"Do you ever think about the future, Lila?" Caleb asked, his gaze fixed on the horizon. "About what you really want in life?"

Lila looked thoughtful, her brows knitting together. "All the time," she admitted. "I want to do something meaningful, something that makes a difference. I don't want to be stuck in one place, following the path everyone expects me to. I want to live my life with passion, with purpose."

Caleb nodded, understanding her more than he could express. "I've been thinking about that a lot too. For the longest time, I thought I had to follow in my father's footsteps, that I didn't have a choice. But lately...I've been wondering if maybe there's another path for me. Something that's mine."

Lila looked up at him, her eyes filled with warmth. "There is, Caleb. You just have to find it. And when you do, don't be afraid to go after it, no matter what anyone else thinks."

When they walked back towards the car, with the sound of the waves growing faint behind them, Caleb felt something shift deep within him. Lila's words had settled over him like a soothing balm, easing the doubts that had weighed him down for so long. It was as if a heavy burden had been lifted, even if only for a moment. For the first time in a long while, he felt like he was exactly where he was meant to be.

But just as they reached the car, a soft, pitiful meow reached their ears. The sound was so faint that they almost missed it, but there it was again—an unmistakable cry for help. Lila's eyes widened as she turned toward the dunes.

"Did you hear that?" she asked, her voice tinged with concern.

Caleb nodded, his curiosity piqued. "Yeah, it's coming from over there."

They followed the sound, the beach now quiet except for the occasional crash of distant waves. As they neared a patch of dune grass, they found the source— a tiny, injured kitten curled up in the sand, its black fur matted and dirty, and its eyes wide with fear.

"Oh no," Lila whispered, her heart breaking at the sight. She knelt down, her voice soft and soothing as she reached out to the trembling creature. "Caleb, we have to help it."

Without hesitation, Caleb bent down and carefully scooped the kitten into his arms, cradling it against his chest. The kitten's small body shivered as it nestled into the warmth of his shirt, its meows growing quieter.

"There's a veterinary clinic not far from here," Lila said, his voice steady with determination. "Let's go."

They hurried to the car, the kitten still tucked securely in Caleb's arms. The drive to the clinic was filled with a shared sense of urgency, both of them silently praying that the tiny life in Caleb's hands would be okay.

When they arrived, the vet staff quickly took the kitten into the back room for examination. Caleb and Lila sat in the waiting area, the antiseptic smell of the clinic filling the air. Caleb couldn't take his eyes off the door where the kitten had disappeared, a sense of responsibility settling heavily on his shoulders.

After what felt like an eternity, the vet came out, a kind smile on her face. "The little one is going to be just fine," she reassured them. "She's a bit dehydrated and has a few minor injuries, but with some care and attention, she'll recover."

Relief washed over Caleb, his shoulders sagging as the tension left his body. "Thank you," he said, his voice thick with emotion.

The vet smiled, nodding toward the small carrier where the kitten was now resting comfortably. "She's going to need some basic care—a warm place to sleep, plenty of food and water, and lots of love. Do you have experience with cats?"

Caleb shook his head. "No, I've only ever had a dog before. But I'll learn."

The vet nodded approvingly. "Cats can be a bit different, but they're just as loving once you get to know them. If you have any questions, don't hesitate to call us."

As they approached the counter to settle the bill, Caleb pulled out the credit card his mother had given him for emergencies. He knew she'd probably have questions later, but this clearly qualified as an emergency. After paying for the vet services, he also picked up some kitten essentials—food, a small bed, and a few toys.

As they left the clinic, the kitten safely nestled in the carrier, Caleb turned to Lila with a smile that finally reached his eyes.

"I'm going to keep her," he said, a new sense of purpose evident in his voice. "I think Milo would have wanted me to."

Lila's face lit up with pride and admiration. "She's lucky to have you, Caleb. You're going to be a terrific cat dad."

Caleb chuckled, the warmth in his chest growing. "A cat dad, huh? I never thought I'd hear those words."

"Well, cats are pretty adorable," Lila teased, her eyes sparkling with humor. "Before you know it, you'll have a house full of them, and people will start calling you the crazy cat guy."

He laughed, the sound light and genuine. "Maybe I'll embrace it. Who knows? Maybe being a crazy cat guy isn't such a bad thing after all."

They drove back, and Caleb felt a moment of lightness that he hadn't experienced in what felt like forever. The tiny kitten, now dozing peacefully in the back seat, was more than just a new responsibility; it was a symbol of something deeper—hope. For the first time in a long while, Caleb felt the stirrings of a possibility that his life didn't have to be the way his parents had meticulously planned. Maybe, just maybe, he could forge his own path, one that brought him true happiness.

When they pulled up to Lila's new place, Caleb hesitated for a moment before turning to her. "I've got something for you," he said, his voice tinged with a mix of anticipation and vulnerability. "It's inside, in your bedroom."

Lila raised an eyebrow, curiosity piqued. "You didn't have to get me anything."

Caleb shrugged, a small, playful smile tugging at his lips. "Think of it as a birthday present or something. Just... go inside. It's in your bedroom." But there was something more behind his eyes, something deeper that he wasn't ready to put into words.

Lila leaned in, her gaze searching his, and for a brief moment, time seemed to stand still. The air between them crackled with unspoken feelings, years of friendship and unacknowledged emotions finally bubbling to the surface. Before she could second-guess herself, Lila closed the distance between them and pressed her lips to his, a soft, lingering kiss that spoke of everything they had been too afraid to say.

Caleb froze for a heartbeat, then melted into the kiss, his hand finding its way to the back of her neck. It was as if the world outside the car disappeared, leaving only the two of them in a bubble of warmth and tenderness. When they finally pulled away, both were breathless, their eyes reflecting the same mixture of surprise and certainty.

"Thank you," Lila whispered, her voice barely audible, but it was enough to send a shiver down Caleb's spine.

He gave her a soft smile, one that spoke of promises and possibilities. "Anytime," he replied, his voice warm and sincere.

Lila stepped out of the car, her heart fluttering with a mixture of emotions. She walked toward her new home, the warmth of the place offset by the clutter of unpacked boxes scattered around. As she entered, the familiar scent of home wrapped around her like a comforting embrace, but the sight of her father hunched over a box, trying to make sense of the chaos, brought a wave of reality crashing back.

"Hey, Dad," she greeted, setting her keys on the counter.

He looked up, weariness etched in the lines of his face, but his smile was genuine. "Hey, kiddo. You're back just in time for dinner."

"Yeah Dad," she replied, her thoughts still half with Caleb. "I'm going to order us some pizza. Sound good?"

Her father rubbed his temples, shaking his head. "I think I need something lighter tonight. Maybe some soup?"

"Soup it is," Lila said with a nod, pulling out her phone. "I'll get you something nice and warm."

After placing the food order on her phone, Lila made her way to her bedroom, her footsteps slowing as she reached the door. She pushed it open, her breath catching in her throat at the sight before her.

There, resting on her bed, was a surfboard, sleek and polished, with her name engraved delicately on its surface. It was beautiful, a perfect blend of craftsmanship and thoughtfulness. She ran her fingers over the engraving, her eyes welling up with tears.

Unable to hold back, she quickly dialed Caleb's number. When he picked up, she struggled to find the words.

"For you," Caleb's voice came through, soft and sincere. "To remind you of all the adventures we've had...and all the ones we still have ahead of us."

Lila's voice quivered as she spoke, the emotion thick in her throat. "It's perfect, Caleb. Thank you."

In that moment, as the connection between them hung in the air like a lifeline, Lila felt something shift. The surfboard wasn't just a gift; it was a promise. A promise of friendship, of memories yet to be made, and of a future where they both could find their own way— together.

CHAPTER 15: THE LAST REALITY

Caleb woke to the soft purring of his kitten, a tiny ball of fur nestled inside the carrier on the floor beside his bed. He smiled, feeling a warmth that had been absent for days. Carefully, he reached over and stroked the kitten's head, its delicate ears twitching under his touch. It had been less than a day since he'd brought the kitten home, but already, he was growing fond of her.

Sliding out of bed, Caleb tread softly across the cold floor, the mansion's vastness amplifying his solitude. The echo of his footsteps reminded him of just how empty the place felt, especially in the early morning light. As he dressed, pulling on a hoodie and jeans, he kept glancing back at the kitten, making sure she was still peacefully asleep.

He crouched down beside the carrier and whispered softly, "Hey there, little one. How about... Snowball? No? Maybe Whiskers? Luna?" But the kitten remained sound asleep, her tiny chest rising and falling with each breath.

Caleb chuckled quietly to himself. "I guess you're not ready for a name yet. We'll figure it out later. I've got to head to school for now, but I'll be back soon, okay?"

He filled her water bowl and set down some food inside the carrier, double-checking that everything was just right. This little creature had become his secret companion, someone to care for in a world that often felt too overwhelming. He was determined to protect her, to shield her from the darkness that seemed to creep into every corner of his life.

Satisfied that she was taken care of, Caleb made his way downstairs. The emptiness of the house weighed on him, each step a reminder of how isolated he truly was. As he reached the foyer, he was startled to see someone waiting for him.

The man stood with a stern expression, his presence imposing despite his unassuming height. Middle-aged and balding, he wore a crisp suit paired with dark sunglasses that obscured his eyes. He was a figure Caleb recognized all too well, though the sight of him here, in his home, sent a chill down his spine.

"Morning, Mr. Morgan," the man said, his tone formal and detached. "I'm Robert Smith. Your father has assigned me to provide you with round the clock security."

Caleb's heart sank. Smith was his father's go-to man for handling delicate matters—the kind that required a watchful eye and a heavy hand. But this? Why now?

Why would his father assign him a bodyguard at this moment?

"Why are you here?" Caleb asked, trying to keep his voice steady, though a sense of dread was already creeping in.

"Your father's orders," Smith replied, his face expressionless. "He wants to ensure your safety at all times."

The words hung in the air, heavy and final. Caleb clenched his fists at his sides, frustration boiling just beneath the surface. This was just another layer of control, another way his father kept him tethered, never allowing him to breathe freely.

"Do you have to follow me to school?" Caleb asked, his voice edged with desperation. He couldn't bear the thought of Smith shadowing him through the hallways, watching his every move. The idea made him feel even more suffocated, as though he were a prisoner in his own life.

Smith didn't budge, his stance unwavering. "If you have a problem with it, you should call the senator," he said, his tone as cold as the marble floors beneath their feet.

Caleb knew better than to argue. His father's decisions

were set in stone, and no amount of pleading would change that. But this felt like too much, like his father was tightening the noose around his neck, leaving him with no room to escape.

"Fine," Caleb muttered, his voice barely above a whisper. He turned away, the weight of the day pressing down on him like a dark cloud that refused to lift. The tension in his chest tightened as he pulled out his phone, his fingers trembling slightly as he scrolled through his contacts. He needed answers, and there was only one person who could give them. With a deep breath, he dialed his father's number, pacing the length of the grand foyer as he waited for the call to connect.

"Caleb," his father's voice came through the line, sharp and authoritative. It was a tone Caleb had grown accustomed to, one that always made him feel like he was under a microscope. "What is it?"

"Why did you send Smith?" Caleb asked, trying to keep the frustration out of his voice, though it was a losing battle. "I don't need a bodyguard."

There was a pause on the other end, followed by a sigh that Caleb knew all too well—the kind that signaled his father's growing impatience. "I saw the credit card notification, Caleb. Thousands of dollars at a vet clinic? What the hell were you doing there?"

Caleb's heart raced, panic seizing him. He'd never considered that his father would be notified—how could he have been so careless? "It was nothing," he stammered, the lie sticking in his throat like a bitter pill. "I was just helping out a friend."

"Helping a friend?" His father's tone was incredulous, laced with disbelief. "You think I'm stupid? Don't lie to me, Caleb. If I find out you're hiding something…"

"I'm not," Caleb interjected quickly, his voice shaky as fear gripped him. "I promise."

There was another long pause, the silence between them heavy with unspoken tension. When his father finally spoke again, his voice had softened, though the edge remained. "Smith is there for your protection, Caleb. Don't make this harder than it has to be."

Caleb swallowed hard, his mind racing for a way to break through the wall his father always seemed to put up. "Dad, I know you're worried, but it's not like before. The reporters have backed off, and there's no real threat right now. I'm just a normal kid at school, and having Smith around… it just makes things worse. I'm popular, sure, but that only makes me more of a target with him around. Can't we just let it go?"

His father's response was swift, cutting through Caleb's reasoning like a knife. "If you don't need security, then come back to New York. We'll discuss it here once you're back in private school."

The ultimatum hung in the air, and Caleb felt his chest tighten even more. Returning to New York meant stepping back into the life he desperately wanted to escape—the life that felt more like a gilded cage than anything else. He could already picture the high-rise apartment, the endless dinners with his father's business associates, and the constant scrutiny that came with being a Morgan. But the alternative—staying here, under Smith's watchful eye, with his father's looming presence even from miles away—felt equally suffocating.

"Dad, please…" Caleb started, but the line had already gone dead.

He stared at his phone, the silence around him suddenly deafening. His father's words echoed in his mind, leaving him feeling more trapped than ever. The walls of the mansion, once a place of comfort and memories, now felt like they were closing in on him. He couldn't risk his father finding out about the kitten he had saved—who knew what he might do, after what had happened with Milo. The thought sent a shiver down Caleb's spine, and he clenched his fists, trying to hold on to the small bit of control he still had over his life.

With a heavy sigh, Caleb adjusted his backpack and headed out the door, Smith's silent presence following close behind. The weight of his father's expectations, the fear of being discovered, and the pain of keeping secrets all pressed down on him, making each step feel heavier than the last. He glanced back at the mansion, a place that should have been his refuge, but now only reminded him of the life he was desperate to escape.

As he walked, Caleb couldn't shake the feeling that no matter how far he tried to run, he would never truly be free from his father's shadow. And in that moment, he wondered if he would ever find the courage to stand up to the man who had shaped his life in so many ways, both good and bad.

But for now, all he could do was keep moving forward, one step at a time, even as the darkness of his world threatened to swallow him whole.

The car ride to school felt like a prison sentence. Caleb stared out the window, trying to ignore the man sitting beside him. Smith's presence was like a dark cloud, heavy and oppressive, making the knot in Caleb's stomach tighten. He knew today was going to be rough—just like every day before it.

Smith was more than just a bodyguard; he was a reminder of everything Caleb wanted to forget. The secrets, the lies, the pressure to be perfect—all of it wrapped up in a crisp black suit. Caleb hated it. He hated being watched, controlled, and feeling like he couldn't even breathe without someone knowing about it.

When they pulled up to the school, Caleb took a deep breath, hoping for a moment of peace. But Smith was always there, hovering just a few steps behind, his silent presence impossible to escape. As Caleb walked through the school's entrance, he could feel the eyes of the other students on him, their whispers following him down the hall like a shadow.

By lunchtime, the tension had reached a breaking point. Caleb could hear the murmurs and see the curious glances thrown his way, but he tried to block it all out. He just wanted to get through the day unnoticed, but that was impossible with Smith tailing him.

Across the cafeteria, Logan and his friends—Elara, who was now dating Jacob, Juno, and Kai—sat at their usual table, joking and laughing. Elara was the first to notice Caleb and the man in the suit following him. She nudged Jacob, her eyes wide with curiosity.

"Who's the guy in the suit? He looks like Secret Service or something," she whispered, glancing over at Caleb.

Jacob snorted. "Secret Service? More like his personal stalker."

Juno rolled her eyes. "Maybe he's some kind of bodyguard. Or maybe Caleb's dad hired him to keep an eye on him. Rich people do that, right?"

Kai shrugged, smirking. "Or he's a predator. You know, those rich kids always have some weird stuff going on."

Logan, who had been silent until now, leaned back in his chair, his expression unreadable. "I don't care who he is," he said flatly. "It's none of our business."

Elara looked at him, concerned. "Logan, aren't you the least bit curious? It's Caleb Morgan, after all."

But Logan just shrugged. "I stopped caring a long time ago."

The table fell silent, the lighthearted conversation fading as Logan's words hung in the air. They all knew Logan had his reasons for not caring—reasons he never talked about. But the sight of Caleb, followed closely by the man in the suit, was enough to make them all uneasy.

Meanwhile, Caleb moved through the hallways, trying to keep his head down. But no matter where he went,

Smith right behind him, a constant reminder of the life he couldn't escape. The stares and whispers only made it worse, each one a dagger in his already fragile heart.

Then he saw her—Lila. She was a bright spot in an otherwise gray day, her smile like a ray of sunshine cutting through the clouds. For a moment, Caleb felt something close to relief. But as she walked toward him, her face bright with joy, the expression faded as she noticed Smith standing nearby.

"Hey," Lila said softly, glancing nervously at the man beside Caleb.

"Hey," Caleb replied, frustration bubbling under the surface. He wanted so badly to talk to her, to explain everything, but the ever-present shadow of Smith made it impossible.

"Can we talk later? After school?" Caleb asked, his voice tinged with desperation.

Lila nodded, her eyes filled with concern. "Sure."

As she walked away, Caleb felt a surge of anger. He couldn't live like this—being watched, controlled, unable to have a normal conversation with the one person who made him feel like everything might be okay. The life he was leading felt suffocating, the walls closing in with each passing day.

Smith's presence wasn't just physical; it was a constant reminder of the expectations he couldn't meet, the life he didn't want, and the person he was afraid he would never become. As Caleb turned away, his heart heavy, he knew something had to change. He just didn't know how.

Desperate for a solution, Caleb made his way to Principal Mrs. Cane's office, desperation driving him forward. Smith, his ever-present shadow, followed closely behind, not even bothering to take a bathroom break. The man was relentless, and Caleb could feel the weight of his presence pressing down on him, suffocating any sense of freedom he had left.

When Caleb reached Mrs. Cane's office, he paused for a moment before knocking. The door opened swiftly, revealing Mrs. Cane, a middle-aged woman with sharp eyes and an air of authority. She glanced at Caleb and then at Smith, her gaze lingering a bit too long on the latter.

"Principal Cane, this is Smith," Caleb introduced, trying to keep his tone neutral, though his frustration was barely concealed. "He's been assigned as my security, courtesy of my father."

Mrs. Cane's eyes brightened with a touch of interest as she extended her hand towards Smith. "Ah, Mr. Smith, it's a pleasure to meet you. I wasn't expecting such a...handsome addition to our school."

Smith, however, remained impassive. He shook her hand briefly, his expression unchanged. "Ma'am," he acknowledged curtly, his voice devoid of any warmth. He quickly released her hand and stepped back, his posture straight and professional.

Mrs. Cane's smile faltered slightly, but she quickly recovered, turning her attention back to Caleb. "What brings you here, Caleb?" she asked, though the lightness in her tone suggested she already knew.

Caleb took a deep breath, trying to steady his nerves. "Mrs. Cane, I came to ask if there's anything you can do about this." He gestured to Smith, who stood silently behind him like an immovable statue. "I get that this is for my safety, but this—this is too much. I need some space, some privacy."

Mrs. Cane sighed, her expression softening just a little. "Caleb, I understand your concerns, truly. But your father made it very clear that in return for his generous donation, that you would be coming to school with a security guy. He's concerned about your safety, and the school board can't go against his wishes. There's nothing I can do."

Her words hit Caleb like a punch to the gut. He had

hoped, against all odds, that she would side with him, that she would see the absurdity of the situation. But here he was, once again reminded of the gilded cage his father had constructed around him, one that no amount of pleading could dismantle.

"Thank you, Mrs. Cane," Caleb mumbled, barely able to look her in the eye. He turned on his heel and walked out of the office, his heart heavy with disappointment.

Smith followed close behind, his footsteps as steady as ever. Caleb could feel his frustration boiling over, but he bit his tongue, knowing it wouldn't do any good to lash out.

Meanwhile, Lila sat nervously in the guidance counselor's office, the familiar smell of old books and polished wood filling the air. The walls were lined with posters about college readiness, each one a reminder of what she was supposed to achieve. Her heart pounded as she watched the counselor flip through her file, her eyes scanning the pages with a look that Lila couldn't quite read.

Finally, the counselor looked up, her expression a mix of concern and disappointment. "Lila," she began, her voice soft but carrying an undeniable weight, "I'm worried about your grades. You're falling behind, and none of the colleges you applied to have accepted you for early admission."

The words hit Lila like a punch to the gut. She had known this conversation was coming, but that didn't make it any easier to hear. She swallowed hard, trying to keep her voice steady. "Is there any chance?" she asked, barely able to get the words out.

The counselor sighed, leaning back in her chair. "There's still hope," she said, but her tone was far from reassuring. "But you need to understand something, Lila. College admissions are highly competitive, especially with the scholarships you're aiming for. You can't afford to let anything distract you. If your grades don't improve, you might not have any options left."

Lila nodded, though her mind was racing. She had worked so hard, balancing school, her part-time jobs, and the responsibilities at home that seemed to grow heavier by the day. But now, it felt like all of that effort had been for nothing.

"I know you have a lot on your plate," the counselor continued, her voice softening slightly. "But if you want to make something of yourself, you have to prioritize your future. Whatever else is going on in your life—it's not worth sacrificing your dreams for."

Lila felt a lump in her throat, her eyes stinging with unshed tears. She knew the counselor was right, but the thought of giving up the few things that brought her happiness was almost unbearable. The long walks on the beach, the quiet moments with her father, even the fleeting smiles she exchanged with Caleb—they were all pieces of her life that made the hard times bearable.

But now, it seemed like she had to choose. And the choice felt impossible.

"Thank you," Lila managed to say, her voice barely above a whisper. The counselor nodded, giving her a look that was meant to be encouraging, but all Lila could see was the disappointment in her eyes.

As Lila left the office, the weight of her situation pressed down on her more than ever. The halls of the school seemed longer, the faces of her classmates blurrier. It was like she was walking in a dream, one where every step took her further away from the life she wanted.

She knew what the counselor was implying—she needed to let go of the things that made her happy, the things that distracted her from her studies. But as she walked through the crowded hallways, feeling more alone than ever, Lila wondered if that was even possible. Could she really sacrifice everything she loved for a future that seemed so uncertain?

For the first time, the dreams she had held onto for so

long felt like they were slipping through her fingers. And Lila wasn't sure how much longer she could hold on.

The rest of the school day passed in a blur. Caleb's mind was miles away, fixated on the suffocating reality he couldn't escape. When the final bell rang, he found himself standing by the school's entrance, dreading the thought of returning to the mansion, where the walls seemed to close in on him a little more each day.

"Smith," Caleb began, turning to the stoic man beside him, "I need to go visit a friend's house. We have some studying to do, and it's important."

Smith's expression remained unchanged. "I'm under strict instructions to take you straight home after school, Caleb. No detours."

Caleb's heart sank even further. "Please, Smith. It's just for a couple of hours. I'll be back before anyone even notices."

Smith shook his head firmly. "I'm sorry, but I can't allow that. Your father's orders were very clear."

Defeated, Caleb sighed deeply, the fight draining out of him. He knew there was no point in arguing; his father had thought of everything, leaving him with no room to breathe. As he climbed into the car, he felt the walls of his cage closing in once more. He needed to talk to Lila, to figure out what to do next. But even that seemed impossible now.

And as the car pulled away from the school, Caleb stared out the window, his thoughts swirling with frustration and longing. The day had been a relentless blur of humiliation and unspoken words. He wished, more than anything, for just a moment of freedom— an escape where he could be himself without the weight of his father's expectations crushing him. The landscape outside passed by in a haze, but inside, he felt trapped in a life that wasn't his own.

When they reached the estate, Caleb headed straight to his room, seeking refuge in its quiet familiarity. He collapsed onto his bed, pulling out his phone, fingers hovering over the screen. After a moment's hesitation, he texted Lila.

"Hey, can we talk?" he typed, his heart pounding with every word. But as he watched the message send, the silence on the other end felt like a gaping chasm. Minutes passed, stretching into what felt like hours, with no reply. The longer the silence persisted, the heavier the weight in his chest became.

In an attempt to distract himself, Caleb glanced over at

the small kitten curled up at the foot of his bed. The tiny creature had been a surprise gift, a rare moment of thoughtfulness from his father. Caleb had yet to settle on a name, and the kitten's inquisitive eyes seemed to be waiting for his decision.

"Lila," Caleb muttered to himself, trying out the name. The kitten's ears perked up at the sound, and she mewed softly, padding closer to him.

"Lila?" he repeated, this time with a hint of a smile. "Well, you seem to like it." But then, reality sank in, and he sighed. "It'll be confusing, though. I can't have my girlfriend and my cat sharing the same name. How about Millie instead?" The kitten blinked up at him, and Caleb chuckled, stroking her soft fur. "Millie it is then."

The evening stretched on, with the weight of Lila's silence still heavy on his mind. When Smith knocked on his door, Caleb barely acknowledged him.

"Dinner, Mr. Morgan," Smith announced, bringing in a tray with his usual calm demeanor. He set the meal on the small table by the window, adding, "You should eat something."

"I'm not hungry," Caleb replied, not turning away from the window.

Smith hesitated, his concern evident, but he didn't press further. "I'll leave it here. You need your strength."

But when the door closed behind him, Caleb's mind began to race. The quiet of the room became suffocating, and the idea of sitting alone with his thoughts felt unbearable. An idea began to form, one that grew more tempting by the minute.

He waited until the house was quiet, the lights dimmed, and the Smith retired for the night. Then, with a resolve that surprised even himself, Caleb quietly slipped out of bed. He dressed quickly, pulling on his workout clothes, lacing up his sneakers with a determination that felt foreign yet exhilarating. Grabbing a cap to pull low over his eyes, he crept to the door, every movement calculated and careful, like something out of a spy movie.

The corridors of the mansion were eerily silent, every creak of the floorboards sounding like an alarm in his ears. But Caleb kept going, his heart pounding with a mix of fear and excitement. He'd done this before in New York—snuck out when the weight of expectations became too much—but never with such a purpose.

As he slipped through the back entrance, he paused, listening for any sign that he'd been caught. But the night was still, and with a final deep breath, he took off running. The cool night air hit his face, refreshing and invigorating, as he made his way to the one place he knew he needed to be.

Lila's house wasn't far, but the distance felt longer under the weight of what he knew he had to say. His thoughts raced faster than his feet as he rehearsed the conversation in his head, searching for the right words to convince her that they could make this work.

When he finally reached her front door, he stood there for a moment, his breath catching in his throat. With a trembling hand, he knocked, the sound echoing in the quiet of the night. He could hear movement inside, and then the door opened, revealing Lila's familiar face. She stepped outside, closing the door gently behind her, and the two stood in the dim porch light, the tension between them almost tangible.

"Lila," Caleb began, his voice a mix of desperation and hope.

She looked at him, her eyes shadowed with worry. "Caleb, what are you doing here? It's late."

"I needed to see you," he confessed, the words spilling out before he could stop them. "I've been trying to reach you, but you didn't respond. I was worried."

Lila sighed, wrapping her arms around herself as if trying to protect herself from what was coming. "We need to talk," she said, her voice trembling slightly.

Caleb's heart sank at the words, a cold dread creeping into his chest. "Lila, please…" he began, but she shook her head.

"Caleb," she said, tears welling up in her eyes, making her words even more heartbreaking. "We're from different worlds. Everyone at school talks about how rich you are, how you have a bodyguard. And me… I'm just nobody."

"You're not nobody," Caleb insisted, his voice breaking with emotion. "You're everything to me. None of that other stuff matters anyway."

Lila shook her head, wiping away a tear. "I can't do this, Caleb. I have to focus on my grades, on my future. I can't afford to be distracted. We need to take a break."

Caleb felt his heart shatter, the pain of her words cutting deeper than he'd ever imagined. "But we can work through this. I'll talk to my dad, I'll figure something out—"

"No," Lila interrupted gently but firmly. "We can't keep doing this. It's tearing us apart. I love you, but we can't be together."

Caleb stared at her, the weight of her words sinking in like a leaden anchor pulling him down. He wanted to fight, to hold on to what they had, but deep down, he knew she was right. "I love you too," he whispered, his voice choked with emotion.

They stood there for a moment longer, the silence between them filled with everything they couldn't say. Caleb searched her eyes, hoping to find a spark of hope, something to cling to, but all he saw was the sadness of a decision already made.

Finally, without another word, Lila turned and went back inside, the door closing with a quiet finality that echoed in Caleb's heart. He stood there in the fading light, feeling the world shift beneath his feet, the night suddenly feeling colder and emptier than before.

Slowly, Caleb made his way back home, but his mind was a whirlwind of emotions—loss, regret, and the aching loneliness that came with realizing that sometimes love isn't enough. When he slipped back into his room, unnoticed by Smith, he felt like he had crossed a threshold, leaving behind the boy he had been and stepping into a world where nothing would ever be the same again.

CHAPTER 16: THE LAST HOMECOMING

The early morning sky over the Hamptons was awash with the soft, tender colors of dawn, as if the world itself was trying to offer Caleb Morgan a gentle farewell. Sitting in the backseat of the sleek black sedan, Caleb cradled Millie, the tiny kitten who had unexpectedly become his companion. She was curled up in his lap, her soft purring the only comfort in an otherwise bleak moment. Smith, his father's longtime security detail, glanced at him through the rearview mirror, his eyes filled with a quiet understanding that only years of service could bring. Though professional, Smith couldn't hide a small, secret smile—he was relieved, in his own way, to be returning to the city life he missed, with its familiar rhythms and lively nights spent bar-hopping with friends.

Caleb's gaze remained fixed outside the window as the familiar landscapes of the Hamptons slowly transformed into a blur of greens and blues, each passing mile pulling him further away from the life he had tried so hard to piece together over the summer. The fields, the beaches, the winding roads—each was a silent witness to the hopes and dreams he had dared to entertain, now fading like a memory.

His thoughts wandered back to the phone call he'd had with his mother the night before. He had tried to sound composed, but the decision to leave had felt like a surrender, a concession to forces far beyond his control.

"I'll come back to New York," he told his mother, his voice carrying the heavy burden of resignation.

There was a brief silence on the other end, and in that moment, Caleb was almost certain he could hear a quiet sigh of relief escape his mother's lips. She had always wanted him back home, where she could keep him close, away from the uncertainties and challenges that the Hamptons had presented.

"Are you sure, Caleb?" she finally asked, her tone cautious, as if she knew the weight of what he was giving up.

He swallowed hard, his heart aching with the truth he couldn't deny. "Yeah, I'm sure. There's nothing left for me here," he said, the sadness in his voice betraying the emptiness he felt inside. The Hamptons had promised so much—a fresh start, a chance to redefine himself—but in the end, it had all slipped through his fingers like sand.

Another pause followed, but this time it was gentler, more understanding. "You know we miss you, right?" Evelyn's voice softened, the motherly concern that Caleb had come to rely on making its way across the miles. "Home isn't the same without you."

And then, after he came clean about Millie, the kitten who had somehow wormed her way into his life and heart, his mother's tone softened even further, touched with a mix of amusement and concern that only she could balance so well.

"A kitten, Caleb?" Evelyn asked, her voice lightening with a hint of laughter. "You're bringing home a kitten?"

"Yeah," Caleb admitted, his fingers gently stroking Millie's fur as he looked down at her tiny, trusting face. "I found her, and I couldn't just leave her. Can you talk to Dad? Get him to let me keep her?"

His mother's laughter floated through the line, warm and soothing, like a balm to his weary soul. "Don't worry, sweetheart. I'll take care of everything. Just come back home."

Now, as the car rolled onto the highway that would lead him back to New York, Caleb felt a sense of finality creeping in, settling over him like a heavy blanket. He wasn't just leaving behind a summer filled with memories—he was leaving behind the person he had begun to discover, the person who had dared to hope for a life different from the one he had always known.

But as the familiar city skyline began to appear in the distance, a wave of conflicting emotions washed over him. He wasn't the same boy who had arrived in the

Hamptons months ago, full of expectations and uncertainty. He was stronger now, more determined, yet somehow more broken than ever. The summer had changed him in ways he hadn't anticipated, leaving him with a deeper understanding of himself—and a sense of loss that he couldn't quite shake.

He looked down at Millie, her small body curled trustingly against him, and he wondered what the future held. Would New York feel like home again? Or would it always be a place of shadows, a reminder of what could have been?

As the car sped on, carrying him back to the life he had left behind, Caleb knew that nothing would ever be the same. The Hamptons had given him something he hadn't expected—a glimpse of who he could be, who he wanted to be—and now, as he returned to the city, he was left to wonder if that person would ever truly find a place to belong.

New York greeted Caleb with its familiar rush of life, the towering buildings and bustling streets a stark contrast to the quiet serenity of the Hamptons. The city's noise and energy enveloped him, pulling him back into the world he had temporarily escaped. As the car pulled up to the building of his family's new penthouse, Caleb took a deep breath, bracing himself for what he knew was coming.

Smith expertly maneuvered the car into the underground parking garage. The dim lighting and the echo of their footsteps as they got out of the car only heightened Caleb's sense of foreboding. He opened the car door and gently lifted Millie, his small kitten. The little furball nuzzled into his chest, offering a comforting warmth that Caleb desperately needed.

Smith began unloading the bags from the trunk, his movements quick and practiced. Caleb watched him for a moment, a wave of sarcasm washing over him as he prepared to say goodbye.

"Thanks for the ride, Smith," Caleb said, his voice laced with irony. "I hope we never have to see each other again."

Smith looked up, his expression neutral, though there was a flicker of understanding in his eyes. "Take care, Mr. Morgan," he replied simply.

Caleb turned and walked toward the elevator, Millie nestled securely in his arms. The doors slid shut with a soft whoosh, and he felt the familiar jolt as the elevator began its ascent. He stared at the glowing numbers, each one bringing him closer to the inevitable confrontation with his father.

When the elevator doors opened, Caleb stepped out

into the grand foyer of the penthouse. The space was as intimidating as ever, with its marble floors, towering columns, and floor-to-ceiling windows offering a breathtaking view of the city skyline. But it wasn't the opulence that made Caleb uneasy; it was the man waiting for him.

Thomas Morgan stood in the center of the room, his presence as imposing as the penthouse itself. He was a tall, broad-shouldered man with a commanding air, his neatly tailored suit a reflection of the power and control he wielded in every aspect of his life.

"You're back," Thomas said, his tone flat, his expression unreadable.

"I am," Caleb replied, forcing his voice to remain steady.

Thomas's eyes flicked to the kitten in Caleb's arms, his brow furrowing slightly. For a moment, Caleb thought his father might say something, but instead, Thomas merely nodded, a rare gesture of approval that caught Caleb off guard.

"Where's Mom?" Caleb asked, trying to keep his tone casual.

"I sent her out to run some errands," Thomas replied, his voice clipped. "She'll be back soon."

Caleb felt a surge of disappointment. He had hoped to see his mother first, to find some comfort in her presence before facing his father's inevitable demands. But there was no escaping the confrontation now.

Thomas's gaze returned to Millie, a faint smirk playing on his lips. "You're carrying that kitten around, I see," he remarked, a hint of amusement in his voice.

Caleb squared his shoulders, feeling a spark of defiance. "Yes, and I'm keeping her," he said firmly. "She's mine."

Thomas raised an eyebrow, clearly surprised by Caleb's newfound courage. "You've grown up, Caleb," he said, his voice carrying a note of approval. "It's about time you started acting like a man."

Caleb swallowed the lump in his throat, resisting the urge to lash out. He knew his father mistook his determination for the kind of strength Thomas had always wanted to see in him. But Caleb wasn't stronger because he had conformed to his father's expectations. He was stronger because he had finally realized that he didn't need to.

"Come with me," Thomas said, turning on his heel and heading toward his study. Caleb followed, the familiar sense of dread settling in his stomach.

The study was as intimidating as ever, with its dark wood paneling, leather-bound books lining the shelves, and a massive desk that seemed to dominate the room. Thomas took a seat behind the desk, gesturing for Caleb to sit across from him.

"I've been thinking," Thomas began, his tone businesslike. "It's time you started getting more involved in the family's affairs. I want you to start working as an intern in my campaign after school. It's a good opportunity for you to learn the ropes and to start contributing."

Caleb felt his heart sink. He had been dreading this moment, knowing that his father would eventually pull him into the political world he had always despised. But as much as he wanted to refuse, he knew there was no point in arguing. In this house, his father's word was law.

"Okay," Caleb said quietly, his voice tinged with resignation.

Thomas leaned back in his chair, clearly satisfied. "Good. It's time you started taking your future seriously, Caleb. I expect you to show the same commitment and dedication that I have."

Caleb nodded, though inside he felt a deep sense of

loss. He had hoped that his time away in the Hamptons would give him the strength to stand up to his father, to carve out a path of his own. But now, sitting in this oppressive study, he realized just how hard that would be.

As Caleb left the study, he felt the weight of his father's expectations pressing down on him once again. He returned to his room, Millie still cradled in his arms, and sat down on his bed, the kitten curling up beside him.

Staring out at the city lights, Caleb couldn't help but wonder if he would ever truly be free from the life his father had planned for him. But as he stroked Millie's soft fur, he knew one thing for certain—he wasn't ready to give up just yet. The spark that Mr. Hayes had reminded him of still flickered inside him, and Caleb was determined to keep it alive, no matter how dim it might seem in the face of his father's towering expectations.

Returning to his private school in New York felt like stepping into a different world. The pristine hallways, lined with students in their neatly pressed uniforms, exuded an air of exclusivity. The corridors echoed with the sound of laughter and conversation, but it was a different kind of chatter—one filled with talk of exotic vacations, designer labels, and weekend getaways to private islands. It was a world Caleb had once belonged to, but now, it felt foreign, almost suffocating.

As he walked through the familiar halls, Caleb noticed that the months he had spent in the Hamptons had somehow erased him from the collective memory of his classmates. No one stopped to ask how his summer was, and there were no curious glances or welcoming smiles. He had become invisible, a ghost in a place where he had once been a fixture. And in a way, he was grateful for that. The detachment allowed him to move through the day without the burden of pretending to fit in.

"Hey, Caleb!" a voice called out from behind him, snapping him out of his thoughts. He turned to see Mark, one of the few people who had always been friendly with him, jogging to catch up.

"Mark," Caleb greeted with a nod, his voice neutral.

"Where have you been, man?" Mark asked, genuine curiosity in his tone. "How was your summer?"

"It was...different," Caleb replied, remembering that he hadn't talked to Mark in months. "Spent most of it in the Hamptons."

Mark raised an eyebrow. "The Hamptons? That's cool.

Did you hit any good parties?"

Caleb shook his head, a small smile tugging at his lips. "Not really. I kept to myself mostly."

Mark looked at him, sensing the change in Caleb's demeanor. "Well, if you ever want to hang out, let me know."

"Thanks, Mark," Caleb said, appreciating the offer but knowing he wouldn't take him up on it. "I'll see you around."

As Mark walked away, Caleb felt a pang of guilt for pushing him away, but the truth was, he no longer cared about the social hierarchy that once ruled his life. The parties, the popularity—it all seemed meaningless now. He was no longer the boy who craved their approval. He had something else now, something more important: a dream.

During lunch, Caleb found himself sitting alone in the cafeteria, a stark contrast to the previous year when he had been surrounded by friends and admirers. The large, noisy room only amplified his sense of isolation, but he didn't mind. It was a loneliness he had come to accept, even embrace. He had spent the summer learning to be alone, and now, it felt like a natural state of being.

He pulled out his phone and began researching veterinary schools, his fingers scrolling through the various programs and requirements. It was a secret he kept close to his heart, away from the prying eyes of his father and the expectations that came with the Morgan name. His father had always envisioned him following in his footsteps, perhaps pursuing a career in law or finance. But Caleb knew that wasn't the life he wanted. The summer had changed him, had opened his eyes to a different path, one that filled him with a sense of purpose he had never felt before.

In the quiet corners of his room, late at night when the rest of the house was asleep, Caleb began the process of applying to veterinary schools. He researched the best programs, the prerequisites, and the admission essays. Every detail mattered to him now because this was more than just a career choice—it was a dream born out of the summer, a dream that had given him hope when everything else had seemed to fall apart.

As he sat at his desk, the glow of his laptop screen illuminating his face, Caleb stared at the essay question on the application for one of the schools: *"What inspired you to pursue a career in veterinary medicine?"* The question was simple, but the answer was complex, rooted in a summer of self-discovery and loss.

Caleb took a deep breath and began to type:

"It wasn't until this past summer that I realized my true calling. The months I spent in the Hamptons were meant to be a time of relaxation, a break from the pressures of school and family expectations. But instead, they became a journey of self-discovery, one that led me to uncover a passion I never knew I had."

He paused, his thoughts drifting back to Milo, his loyal dog, who had been his companion through some of the darkest times. The memory of Milo's eyes, filled with trust and love, gave him the strength to continue.

"My dog, Milo, was more than just a pet; he was a friend, a source of comfort, and a reminder that unconditional love exists. When he died, I felt helpless, unable to do anything to save him. That feeling of powerlessness stayed with me, gnawing at me until I realized that I wanted to make a difference. I wanted to be there for animals the way Milo had been there for me."

Caleb's fingers flew across the keyboard, the words flowing easily now, each one carrying the weight of his emotions.

"The decision to become a veterinarian isn't just about caring for animals; it's about giving back to the creatures who give us so much without asking for anything in return. It's about being a voice for those who can't speak for themselves, about providing comfort and care in times of need. This is more than just a career for me; it's a calling, one that I'm ready to embrace with all my heart."

He sat back, reading over the words he had written. They were raw, honest, and filled with the hope that had been sparked during his time in the Hamptons. Caleb knew that this was the path he was meant to take, and no matter what obstacles lay ahead, he was determined to follow it.

As he clicked 'Save' on his essay, Caleb felt a sense of peace wash over him. For the first time in a long while, he knew exactly what he wanted, and it wasn't something that could be bought or handed to him because of his last name. It was something he had earned, something that came from deep within—a dream born from love, loss, and the desire to make a difference in the world.

Weeks turned into months, and life in New York settled into a familiar rhythm. Yet, even as the city's relentless pace kept him busy, Caleb couldn't shake the memories of the Hamptons, of Lila, and of the life he'd left behind. The shell necklace she had given him was tucked safely inside his desk drawer, a small but significant reminder of their time together. Sometimes, late at night, when the weight of his studies and the loneliness of his room grew too heavy, he would take it out, running his fingers over the smooth, delicate shells, each one holding a memory he couldn't forget.

To drown out the pain of losing his first love, Caleb threw himself into his studies with a determination that bordered on obsession. His days were consumed by textbooks and assignments, while his nights were spent in the company of Millie, the kitten who had quickly become the center of his world.

Millie, with her soft gray fur and wide, curious eyes, brought a kind of joy Caleb hadn't known he needed. The little kitten had a knack for getting into everything—her favorite pastime was batting pens off Caleb's desk, watching them roll away with a look of pure delight. She'd pounce on his feet when he was deep in thought, or curl up in his lap when he was trying to study, purring contentedly as if she knew she was exactly where she belonged.

When Caleb sat at his desk trying to concentrate on a particularly dense chapter of his economics textbook, Millie decided that his notes were the perfect place to nap. With a soft meow, she padded over to his desk, gracefully navigating the clutter, and settled down right in the middle of his open book. Caleb chuckled, unable to resist the kitten's charm.

"You've got impeccable timing, you know that?" he said, scratching her behind the ears. Millie responded by stretching luxuriously and rolling onto her back, exposing her tiny belly. Caleb couldn't help but smile, the tension of the day melting away as he played with her.

Despite his initial reservations, his mother had taken a surprising liking to the kitten. Caleb often found his mother in the living room, Millie curled up in her lap as Evelyn gently stroked her fur. It was the first time in years that Caleb had seen his mother so at peace, the shadows that had once haunted her eyes beginning to fade.

"It's like having a little piece of you with me all the time," Evelyn had confessed one evening, her voice soft as she watched Millie play with a ball of yarn. "She's brought some light back into this house."

Caleb smiled, feeling a warmth in his chest that he hadn't felt in a long time. The kitten had done more than just bring joy to his mother; she had also helped Caleb reconnect with the part of himself that had been lost in the chaos of his life. Millie was more than just a pet—she was a reminder that even in the midst of sorrow, there could be moments of pure, unfiltered happiness.

But not everything in the Morgan household was as peaceful as the moments shared with Millie. Thomas, Caleb's father, was hardly ever home, his absence a constant reminder of the pressures and responsibilities that came with his career. It was re-election time, and the demands of the campaign had taken over every aspect of his life. Dinner at the Morgan household had become a quiet affair, just Caleb and Evelyn sitting at the long dining table, the spaces around them echoing with the silence of what was left unsaid.

Evelyn Morgan had always been a master at masking her worries with a gentle smile and a soothing tone. She had spent years perfecting the art of making excuses for her husband, and tonight was no different.

"Your father's just so busy, Caleb," she said, her voice strained but tender, as she placed a delicate hand on his. "He's doing everything he can for this election. He wants to make sure everything's perfect."

Caleb nodded, swallowing the frustration that had been gnawing at him for months. He knew his mother meant well, and he didn't want to add to her burden. But the void left by his father's absence was impossible to ignore. There were nights when he would lie awake, longing for the days when they were a family—before the campaign, before his father's ambition had taken precedence over everything else. Now, it seemed like it was just him and Evelyn, trying to fill the emptiness that Thomas's constant absence had carved into their lives.

They sat together in the quiet dining room, the silence between them both comforting and heavy. Evelyn looked at Caleb with a softness that made his heart ache. She wanted so desperately to believe that everything was as it should be, that her husband's sacrifices were for the greater good.

"You know, Caleb," she said, her voice gentle, "your father loves you. He's just... trying to provide for us in the way he knows how."

Caleb forced a smile, understanding her need to protect the image of the man she loved. "I know, Mom."

Evelyn squeezed his hand, her eyes searching his as if trying to find the right words to comfort him. "But remember, this is the last big fundraiser before the election. After this, things might calm down a bit. Speaking of which, don't forget to get your tux fitted before the event. We need you looking your best."

Caleb nodded, though the thought of the fundraiser filled him with a sense of dread. These events were always the same—glittering spectacles of wealth and power, where people wore their success like armor and conversations were as polished as the crystal chandeliers above. He'd attended countless fundraisers as his father's campaign intern, spreading the word on the streets, shaking hands, and flashing a smile for the cameras. It had all felt so forced, so artificial. Over time, he had managed to pull back from his duties, his absence going unnoticed in the whirlwind of his father's campaign. After all, he was just the senator's son—a role that came with its own set of expectations, none of which felt like they truly belonged to him.

When the night of the fundraiser arrived, the Morgan estate was transformed. The grand ballroom was a sea of opulence, filled with New York's elite. The guests were dressed to perfection, their smiles as practiced as their handshakes. Caleb stood beside his mother, feeling more out of place than ever. He had never liked these events, the superficiality of it all grating against his nerves. But tonight, something felt different. He was different.

As they moved through the room, exchanging pleasantries with the guests, Evelyn introduced Caleb to Elaine, his father's campaign manager. Elaine was sharp, with a calculating smile and eyes that missed nothing. She was the kind of woman who could command a room with a single glance, and Caleb could see why his father trusted her so implicitly.

"It's a pleasure to finally meet you, Caleb," Elaine said, her tone smooth as silk.

"Likewise," Caleb replied, forcing a polite smile that didn't reach his eyes.

As they exchanged small talk, Elaine subtly pointed out his father, who was deep in conversation with a group of men in suits. "Those are the big donors," she said, her voice laced with admiration. "Your father's been working tirelessly to secure their support. They're the ones who can make or break this election."

Caleb glanced at his father, watching as he laughed and clinked glasses with the men. Thomas Morgan looked every bit the seasoned politician, confident and charming, but to Caleb, he seemed like a stranger. A man who had become so consumed by his ambition that he'd forgotten what truly mattered.

Elaine's voice pulled Caleb from his thoughts. "How's school going for you, Caleb? Must be tough balancing everything with the campaign."

"It's fine," Caleb replied, his tone dismissive. He wasn't in the mood for small talk, especially not with Elaine.

Sensing his reluctance, Elaine leaned in, her voice dropping to a conspiratorial whisper. "I'm sorry about what happened with Lila," she said, her words dripping with false sympathy. "I know it must have been hard, but your father only wanted what was best for you."

Caleb's heart skipped a beat as her words sank in. Lila. The one person who had brought light into his life when everything else seemed dark. And now, the realization hit him like a punch to the gut—his father had known about their relationship all along and had been pulling the strings behind the scenes.

"I see," Caleb said, his voice tight with anger, though he kept his expression neutral. "Thank you for letting me know."

He excused himself, needing to get away from the suffocating atmosphere of the party. As he stepped out into the cool night air, his mind raced, the anger and betrayal boiling under the surface. How could his father have done this? How could he have manipulated the one thing that made Caleb feel truly alive? The darkness around him seemed to mirror the turmoil in his heart, and for the first time, Caleb felt completely and utterly alone.

Without thinking, Caleb pulled out his phone, his fingers trembling as he dialed Lila's number. The party was in full swing around him, the laughter and clinking glasses a harsh contrast to the turmoil brewing inside him. He made his way to the staircase, seeking a quiet spot away from the crowd, a place where he could gather his thoughts and finally say what he needed to say.

As he reached the landing, the phone rang in his hand, each ring echoing louder, amplifying the pounding in his chest. He loosened his tuxedo tie, feeling suddenly constricted, as if the walls around him were closing in. Sweat beaded on his forehead, and he wiped it away with a shaky hand, praying that Lila would pick up, that he could somehow make things right.

Finally, the ringing stopped, and there was a click on the other end of the line. But instead of Lila's voice, he was met with one that was firm and unyielding.

"Hello?" It was Mr. Hayes.

Caleb's breath caught in his throat. "Mr. Hayes, it's Caleb. Is Lila there?" he asked, his voice barely masking the desperation that was clawing at his insides.

There was a heavy pause on the other end, one that seemed to stretch on for an eternity. Caleb could almost hear Mr. Hayes' mind working, considering the weight of his next words. When he finally spoke, his tone was measured, but there was an edge to it, a finality that cut through Caleb like a knife.

"Caleb, you need to let her go."

The words hit him with the force of a tidal wave, leaving him gasping for air. He leaned against the railing, his knuckles white as he gripped the phone. "But I need to explain—" Caleb started, his voice cracking under the strain of everything he was trying to hold back.

Mr. Hayes didn't let him finish. "You broke my daughter's heart, Caleb. As her father, I can't forgive that. And I don't think you should call her anymore. If it's meant to be, life will find a way, but right now, you need to move on."

The line went dead, the silence that followed more deafening than any noise. Caleb stared at his phone, his mind struggling to process the words that had just been spoken. He had lost Lila, and there was nothing he could do to change that.

For a moment, he stood there, his body numb, his thoughts a chaotic mess. The sounds of the party drifted up the staircase, distant and hollow. He felt like an outsider, watching his life unravel from a distance, powerless to stop it. The tightness in his chest intensified, a dull ache that spread through him, reminding him of the enormity of what he had lost.

Slowly, he lowered the phone, his hand dropping to his side. The realization settled in, cold and unyielding— he had hurt the one person who had seen past his wealth, past the facade he had built to protect himself. And now, because of his own mistakes, she was gone.

Caleb took a deep breath, trying to steady himself. He knew Mr. Hayes was right; he needed to let Lila go. But that didn't make it any easier. The memory of her smile, the way she had looked at him with such trust, was etched into his mind, a constant reminder of what he had thrown away.

As he descended the stairs, the noise of the party grew louder, but it all felt distant, like he was moving through a world that no longer belonged to him. The faces around him blurred, and he walked past them, his heart heavy with regret. He had to find a way to live with the choices he had made, to find a path forward, even if it meant doing so without Lila by his side.

But as he stepped back into the crowd, he couldn't shake the feeling that he had lost something irreplaceable, something that no amount of time or distance could ever truly heal.

The fundraiser was winding down, the once lively chatter and clinking of glasses now fading into a quiet hum. The evening had been a blur of forced smiles and polite conversations, but all Caleb could think about was finding his father. The frustration that had been simmering inside him all night was now boiling over. He needed answers—answers about why his father had interfered with his relationship with Lila, and why he insisted on controlling every aspect of his life.

As he wandered through the grand hallways of the event venue, his heart pounded with a mixture of anger and determination. He was tired of living in the shadow of Thomas Morgan's expectations, tired of being molded into something he was not. Lila's words from earlier that evening echoed in his mind, her gentle plea for him to stand up for what he truly wanted, for who he truly was.

He finally found himself near the entrance to a room marked "Private, Members Only." The door was slightly ajar, and from inside, Caleb heard the familiar low tone of his father's voice, smooth and authoritative, carrying just enough weight to ensure compliance without ever needing to raise it.

Caleb hesitated for a moment, standing just out of sight, his hand resting on the doorframe. He knew he shouldn't eavesdrop, but something compelled him to listen.

"Thank you for helping push my son's application through," Thomas was saying. There was a smugness in his voice that made Caleb's stomach churn. "It's good to know that we can still count on each other.

He'll be in law school by the fall—just as planned."

Caleb's breath caught in his throat, the blood draining from his face. The realization hit him like a punch to the gut—his father had bribed his way into securing Caleb's future, manipulating the outcome just as he had done with everything else in Caleb's life. Every decision, every path, had been laid out before him without his consent, without his input.

Anger surged through him, mixed with a profound sense of betrayal. This was not the life he wanted, not the future he had envisioned. Caleb's dream had always been to follow his own passions, not to walk the path his father had paved for him. And now, to know that even his admission into law school had been orchestrated behind the scenes—it was too much to bear.

He felt his chest tighten as he backed away from the door, his heart pounding in his ears. The idea of confronting his father had seemed daunting, but now it was a necessity. This charade, this life of lies and deceit, had to end.

For a moment, Caleb leaned against the wall, trying to steady his breathing. His mind raced, thinking of all the times he had tried to please his father, to live up to his impossible standards. And where had it gotten him? Trapped in a life that wasn't his own, torn away from the girl he cared about, and now, about to be forced into a career he didn't want.

He thought of Lila, her smile, her laughter, the way she made him feel like he could be himself—like he could be something more than just Thomas Morgan's son. And he realized, with startling clarity, that he couldn't continue living like this. He couldn't continue to be someone he wasn't just to make his father happy.

A sense of resolve washed over him. His high school graduation was only months away, and after that, everything would change. He would confront his father, tell him the truth about what he really wanted, and for the first time in his life, he would take control of his own destiny. He wouldn't let Thomas manipulate him any longer.

There would be no turning back after this. But Caleb knew, deep down, that he was ready.

Ready to face whatever consequences came his way, ready to choose his own path, even if it meant disappointing his father. Because for the first time, he was thinking about his own happiness, his own future.

And as he walked away from that door, Caleb knew that the man he was becoming was far stronger than the boy who had always sought his father's approval.

This was his life, and it was time he started living it on his own terms.

CHAPTER 17: THE LAST CONFLICT

The crisp autumn air brushed against Caleb's face as he walked through the familiar streets, cradling Millie in his arms. The leaves crunched beneath his feet, a symphony of reds, oranges, and yellows decorating the ground. There was something comforting about the change of seasons, the way the world seemed to shed its old skin and prepare for something new. It mirrored the changes within Caleb himself—subtle, but deeply felt.

As he made his way to the animal shelter, Millie nestled closer to his chest, her purring a steady rhythm against his heartbeat. Volunteering at the shelter had become his sanctuary, a place where he could escape the complexities of his life and find peace in the simple act of caring for those who needed love as much as he did. The shelter wasn't just a building; it was a refuge, a place where lost souls, both human and animal, found a second chance.

The moment Caleb stepped inside, the warmth of the shelter embraced him. The familiar scents of hay, fur, and antiseptic mingled in the air. The staff greeted him with genuine smiles, their faces lighting up as they saw Millie in his arms.

"Hey, Caleb! And hello, Miss Millie!" one of the volunteers called out, her voice filled with affection.

Caleb smiled back, feeling a sense of belonging that was often absent in other parts of his life. Here, he wasn't just the son of wealthy parents or the target of school bullies—he was simply Caleb, the boy who cared for animals with a tenderness that surprised even him.

He settled Millie into a cozy spot by the window, where she could watch the world go by, her bright eyes following every fluttering leaf and passing bird. Caleb knew she loved this spot, where the sunlight streamed in and warmed her fur. As he stroked her head, one of the volunteers, a woman named Jenna, approached him with an idea.

"You know, Caleb," Jenna began, her voice gentle yet filled with excitement, "Millie has such a calm and soothing presence. Have you ever considered training her to be a therapy cat?"

Caleb looked down at Millie, who blinked up at him with those knowing eyes, as if she was in on the conversation. The idea sparked something in him—an opportunity to give Millie a purpose beyond just being his companion. He nodded slowly, the thought of helping others with Millie's calming presence appealing to him.

"I hadn't thought about it," he admitted, a hint of a smile tugging at his lips, "but I'd love to give it a try."

Jenna grinned, clearly pleased with his response. "Great! We can start with some basic exercises, see how she responds."

Over the next few weeks, Caleb dedicated himself to training Millie, working closely with Jenna and the shelter staff to prepare her for certification. It was a new challenge, but one that filled him with a sense of fulfillment he hadn't felt in a long time. The training was no easy task, and Millie, like all cats, had her own mind about how things should be done.

On the first day of training, Millie was supposed to practice sitting still on command, a seemingly simple task. But as soon as Jenna gave the cue, Millie decided it was the perfect time to chase a stray beam of sunlight across the floor, her tail flicking in excitement as she pounced after it.

Caleb couldn't help but laugh. "Well, I guess she's more interested in solar therapy today."

Jenna chuckled too, shaking her head. "Cats will be cats. We'll get there."

As the days passed, they worked on more exercises—

teaching Millie to stay calm around loud noises, encouraging her to sit on strangers' laps, and rewarding her for being gentle with her paws. Each session was a mix of success and hilarity, with Millie often deciding that training time was better spent napping in the sun or demanding belly rubs from Caleb.

But despite everything, Caleb noticed something incredible happening. Millie began to understand what was expected of her, and she started responding to the commands with a newfound focus. She would look at Caleb with those big, trusting eyes, waiting for his signal before performing a task. And every time she succeeded, the bond between them deepened, becoming something more profound than just a boy and his cat.

One afternoon, as Caleb sat with Millie on his lap, he realized that the training wasn't just changing her—it was changing him too. For the first time in a long while, he felt like he was making a difference. Not just for Millie, but for himself and for the people she would one day comfort. The thought filled him with a quiet sense of pride, something he hadn't allowed himself to feel in a long time.

After a particularly successful session, Jenna patted Caleb on the back. "You're doing an amazing job with her, Caleb. She's going to make a fantastic therapy cat."

Caleb smiled, a genuine warmth spreading through him. "Thanks, Jenna. I think she's teaching me as much as I'm teaching her."

As they watched Millie settle down for a nap, her training done for the day, Caleb felt a flicker of hope. Maybe, just maybe, this was the start of something new—something that could help him find his own way in the world, just as Millie was finding hers. And for the first time in a long while, Caleb didn't feel so alone. He had Millie, the shelter, and a purpose that went beyond the walls of his home. It was a small, tender step toward healing, and Caleb was ready to take it, one day at a time.

When the clock struck midnight on a cold winter night, Caleb sat alone in the dimly lit kitchen, the soft hum of the refrigerator the only sound breaking the silence. It was his eighteenth birthday, and unlike other milestones in his life, this one passed without fanfare. Birthdays at the Morgans were seldom remembered, lost in the shadow of his father's political ambitions and his mother's social obligations. But tonight, Caleb decided to mark the occasion in his own quiet way.

He carefully mixed the ingredients for a single pancake, his movements deliberate as he measured out flour, sugar, and milk. The process was simple, almost meditative, a brief escape from the complexities of his life. As the pancake sizzled on the stove, Millie, his loyal cat, wound around his legs, purring softly.

"Guess it's just you and me, Millie," Caleb murmured, flipping the pancake with a small smile.

Once it was done, he sat down at the kitchen table, placing the pancake on a plate and adding a dollop of syrup. He cut a small piece, offering it to Millie, who sniffed it curiously before taking a tentative lick. Caleb chuckled, the sound echoing in the empty kitchen.

"Happy birthday to me," he whispered, the words tinged with both humor and melancholy. At least now he could vote, even if he wasn't old enough to drink. The thought brought a strange sense of empowerment, a small spark of independence in a life otherwise dictated by others.

Finally, the day of the Senate election dawned with a crisp chill in the air, the kind that heralds both change and uncertainty. New York was alive with the energy of democracy in action, the streets bustling with people heading to polling stations, their faces a mix of anticipation and anxiety.

Caleb and his mother, Evelyn, joined the line at their local polling place, a modest school gymnasium transformed into a hub of civic duty. The line snaked around the block, people of all ages waiting patiently, bundled up against the cold. Caleb noticed the diversity of the crowd—the elderly couple holding hands, the young mother balancing a toddler on her hip, the college students discussing their votes with a fervor born of newfound adulthood. It was a tapestry of lives, all woven together by the common thread of this election.

The Morgans stood silently in line, the weight of the day pressing down on them. For Evelyn, voting for Thomas Morgan was more than just supporting her husband; it was a reaffirmation of the life they had built around his political career. For Caleb, it was a complicated mix of duty and expectation, a role he had been born into but never fully embraced.

As they reached the front of the line, Evelyn took a deep breath, her hand trembling slightly as she was handed her ballot. Caleb watched her carefully mark her choices, her face a mask of concentration. When she finished, she turned to him, her eyes meeting his with a silent question—a moment of shared understanding. He nodded, then took his own ballot, his heart pounding in his chest.

Caleb's thoughts were a whirlwind as he chose to vote for his father's opponent, remembering his father's expectations, the unspoken pressure to carry on the

Morgan legacy. But as he fed the ballot into the machine, a quiet resolve settled in his heart. This was more than just his first election; it was a turning point, a moment where he began to take control of his own destiny, however small that control might seem.

Later that day, Caleb and Evelyn found themselves in a small, cozy café tucked away from the bustling streets. It had been years since they'd done something like this, just the two of them. The café was warm and inviting, with soft lighting and the comforting aroma of freshly brewed coffee. They chose a corner table by the window, the outside world feeling distant and unimportant.

Caleb sipped his coffee, the warmth spreading through him, easing some of the tension that had been building all day. Evelyn smiled at him over her cup, a rare moment of peace between mother and son.

"You know, I've missed this," she said softly, her eyes reflecting a mix of emotions. "Just spending time together, without all the noise and distractions."

Caleb nodded, understanding what she meant. "Yeah, me too. It's been a while."

They sat in comfortable silence for a moment, the clinking of cups and quiet chatter of other patrons creating a soothing background. But as their conversation turned to Lila, the atmosphere shifted.

"You still care about her, don't you?" Evelyn asked, her voice gentle, yet probing.

Caleb sighed, running a hand through his hair, a habit he had picked up whenever he was troubled. "I do, Mom. But it's over between us. Too much has happened, and I don't know how to fix it."

Evelyn reached across the table, placing a hand on his, her touch comforting yet firm. "Love isn't always easy, Caleb. Sometimes it's messy, and it hurts, but that doesn't mean you should give up. Maybe reaching out to her could bring some clarity, if not closure."

He shook his head, the memory of their last encounter too raw to revisit. "I can't, Mom. It's better this way."

Evelyn frowned, her heart aching for her son. She could see the pain he was trying to hide, the struggle between his head and his heart. But she knew when to give him space, to let him work through things in his own time.

"I understand," she said softly, withdrawing her hand but keeping her gaze steady on him.

Caleb looked out the window, the busy street outside a

stark contrast to the quiet turmoil within him. "It's not just about Lila," he admitted, his voice barely above a whisper. "It's Dad, too. He's barely home, and when he is, it's like he's not really here. I know he's doing important work, but..."

Evelyn's eyes softened, a sadness creeping into her expression. "I miss him, Caleb. More than I can say. But this election... if he wins, things might change. He'll be home more, maybe even take a step back from politics."

Caleb met her gaze, seeing the hope she was holding onto, fragile yet unwavering. "Do you really think that'll happen?"

"I have to believe it will," Evelyn said, her voice firm despite the uncertainty in her heart. "And so should you. Your father loves you, Caleb. He loves both of us. He's just... lost in his work right now. But he'll find his way back. We just have to be patient."

Caleb nodded, though he wasn't sure he fully believed her. Still, the comfort of her words, the warmth of this moment between them, was enough for now. As they finished their coffee, he realized how much he had missed this connection with his mother, the way she could ease his worries with just a few words.

And when the election results trickled in, Caleb and his mother, Evelyn, sat together in the living room, the tension between them thick and unspoken. The glow from the television flickered across their faces as they anxiously watched the news anchors dissect the latest polling predictions. Millie, Caleb's loyal tabby cat, was curled up in Evelyn's lap, purring softly, providing a small comfort amidst the uncertainty.

The reporters on the screen spoke with fervor, analyzing every number and statistic. "With 87% of the precincts reporting, it looks like Senator Thomas Morgan is holding onto his lead, but it's still too close to call," one of the anchors said, his voice filled with the kind of excitement that comes from a tight race.

Another anchor chimed in, "If Morgan pulls through, this will be his third consecutive term. A significant win, but let's not forget the controversies that have dogged his campaign in recent months."

Caleb shifted uneasily in his seat, the mention of controversies making his stomach tighten. Evelyn noticed and reached out, placing a comforting hand on his. "It'll be over soon," she whispered, though her own voice trembled with uncertainty.

As the final precincts reported, the room fell into a hushed silence. The only sound was the soft ticking of the clock on the wall, each second feeling like an eternity. Millie, sensing the tension, stirred in Evelyn's lap, her ears twitching as if she too was waiting for the inevitable.

Finally, the news anchor cleared his throat, the gravity of the moment reflected in his serious tone. "We can now project that Senator Thomas Morgan has won re-election, securing his third term in office."

A wave of relief washed over them, but it was tinged with a bittersweet aftertaste. Caleb glanced at his mother, who offered him a strained smile. They had won, but the victory felt hollow, tainted by the growing distance between them and Thomas. The man who had once been the center of their world now seemed like a stranger, a figure they only saw on television or read about in newspapers.

Millie, oblivious to the significance of the moment, suddenly lifted her head and snarled at the image of Thomas on the screen, her eyes narrowing in feline disdain. Evelyn and Caleb both burst into laughter, the tension breaking for a moment. "I guess Millie's not a fan," Caleb joked, scratching her behind the ears.

"No, I suppose she's not," Evelyn replied, her laughter fading into a sigh. She reached for the remote and turned off the TV, plunging the room into silence. They sat there for a moment, the weight of their thoughts pressing down on them.

Meanwhile, miles away in a dimly lit hotel room, Thomas Morgan stood in front of a large window, his reflection barely visible in the dark glass. The room was filled with the quiet hum of the city outside, but inside, the atmosphere was thick with tension. Elaine, his campaign aide, stood beside him, her expression unreadable.

When the election results rolled in, Thomas felt a surge of triumph, but it was quickly overshadowed by the reality of his situation. He had won the election, but at what cost? The distance between him and his family had never felt so vast.

Elaine, sensing his turmoil, stepped closer and placed a hand on his arm. "Congratulations, Senator," she said softly, her voice carrying an undertone of something more. Thomas turned to face her, and for a moment, their eyes locked in a shared understanding of the consequences of their actions.

In an attempt to break the tension, Thomas forced a smile and reached for the bottle of champagne on the table. He popped it open with a loud pop, the cork flying across the room. "To victory," he said, pouring two glasses and handing one to Elaine.

But she didn't take it. Instead, she pulled out a small

box from her purse and handed it to him. "I have something to give you," she whispered, her voice barely audible.

Thomas's smile faltered as he opened the box, revealing a pregnancy test with two glaring lines. His heart stopped, the room spinning around him. "I'm pregnant," Elaine said, her eyes searching his for a reaction.

For a moment, Thomas was frozen, his mind racing as he tried to process the gravity of the situation. The champagne glass in his hand trembled slightly, the liquid threatening to spill over. Anger, fear, and a deep, unshakable guilt churned within him. He had made a mistake, and now he was trapped in a situation that could destroy everything he had worked for.

"I want nothing to do with this," he said coldly, his voice devoid of emotion. His eyes, which had once been warm and charming, now hardened into steely resolve. "But if you decide to keep the child, I'll support it financially. In exchange, I expect your silence."

Elaine's eyes filled with tears, her heart breaking at the harshness of his words. She had known this was a possibility, but it didn't make it any easier to hear. She nodded slowly, knowing she had no other choice. "I understand," she whispered, her voice barely above a whisper.

Thomas reached into his pocket and pulled out a wad of cash, pressing it into her hand. "Take your time to think it over," he said, his tone more businesslike than caring. Without another word, he turned and walked out of the room, leaving Elaine alone with her thoughts and the weight of the decision she had to make.

As Thomas drove home, the victory that should have filled him with pride felt like a hollow achievement. The streets were empty, the city's lights casting long shadows that seemed to follow him, a reminder of the darkness he couldn't escape. When he finally arrived at his house, it was quiet, the only sound the soft rustle of the wind through the trees.

He slipped into the darkened bedroom where Evelyn lay sleeping, her breathing slow and steady. For a moment, he stood there, watching her, a pang of guilt tightening in his chest. She was his wife, the woman who had stood by him through everything, and yet he had betrayed her in the worst possible way.

Silently, he slipped into bed beside her, careful not to wake her. As he wrapped his arms around her from behind, pulling her close, he whispered, "I missed you." The words hung in the air, a fragile truth in a sea of lies.

Evelyn stirred slightly, her hand reaching back to rest on his arm. "I missed you too," she murmured, still half-asleep, her voice laced with the tenderness of a woman who had no idea how much her world was about to change.

Thomas held her close, closing his eyes against the tears that threatened to spill. For tonight, he could pretend that everything was okay, that the weight of his sins hadn't yet crushed him. But deep down, he knew that the storm was coming, and when it did, there would be no escaping the consequences of the choices he had made.

At school, Caleb focused on his studies, determined to finish his GED despite everything. It wasn't easy, but he poured himself into his work, finding solace in the routine of learning. The day of the exam came and went, and when the results were announced, Caleb felt a sense of accomplishment he hadn't felt in a long time. He had passed.

The private school held a small graduation ceremony for the students, and as Caleb walked across the stage to receive his diploma, he felt a surge of pride. It wasn't just about the piece of paper—it was about proving to himself that he could do this, that he could overcome the obstacles in his path.

Later that evening, Evelyn threw a small graduation party at their home, inviting a few close friends and family. It was a modest celebration, but it was filled with warmth and love. As the night wore on, Caleb found himself standing in the corner of the room, watching the people around him. The laughter, the smiles—they were all real, but there was an undercurrent of tension that he couldn't ignore.

Finally, after everyone had left, Caleb confronted his parents. He stood in the living room, facing them with a pounding heart.

"I need to talk to you both," he began, his voice steady despite the pounding of his heart. "I've decided what I want to do with my life. I want to become a veterinarian."

Thomas, who had been sipping a glass of scotch, set it down with a scowl. "A veterinarian? That's not a career, Caleb. That's a hobby."

"It's my passion," Caleb shot back, his anger rising. "I've thought about this for a long time, and it's what I want. I'm not asking for your approval—I'm telling you."

Thomas's face turned red with rage. "You're a Morgan! You have a responsibility to this family, to uphold our legacy. And you think playing with animals is going to do that?"

Evelyn looked between them, her expression one of shock and confusion. "Thomas, let's talk about this calmly—"

"There's nothing to talk about!" Thomas interrupted, his voice booming. He turned to Caleb, his eyes cold. "If you go through with this, you're on your own. No more money, no more support. You want to be a vet? Fine. But don't come crawling back when you realize what a mistake you've made."

Caleb felt a lump in his throat, but he stood his ground. "I don't need your money. I'll prove you wrong, Dad. I'll get into college myself, and I won't need you to bribe anyone to make it happen."

Evelyn gasped, her hand flying to her mouth. "Caleb, what are you talking about?"

But Caleb didn't answer. He turned and walked out of the room, leaving his parents in stunned silence. The path ahead was uncertain, but he knew one thing for sure—he was finally going to live his life on his own terms.

⎯⎯⎯⎯⎯•⪧•⬤•⪦•⎯⎯⎯⎯⎯

CHAPTER 18: THE LAST BEGINNING

Evelyn sat alone at the kitchen table, the morning light barely filtering through the heavy curtains, casting long shadows across the room. The penthouse was silent, an almost oppressive stillness hanging in the air, as if the walls themselves had absorbed the tension from the night before. She wrapped her hands around the coffee cup in front of her, seeking warmth, but the coffee had long since gone cold—just like her feelings for Thomas. The night had been a sleepless one, filled with tossing and turning, unable to escape the words that had been exchanged between them.

Caleb had stormed out after his confronting Thomas, his anger still echoing in the hallways. Evelyn stood frozen, her hands trembling slightly as she braced herself for what was to come. The weight of the truth she had long suspected but never dared to confirm hung between them, waiting to be unleashed.

Thomas sat slumped in his leather chair, a glass of whiskey in hand, the amber liquid swirling as he stared into it, lost in thought. The sharp scent of alcohol lingered in the air, mixing with the faint smell of cigar smoke that clung to his clothes. He was drunk, and the usual polished, composed demeanor he maintained had crumbled, leaving only the raw edges of a man who had long ago compromised his principles.

Evelyn took a deep breath, her voice steady but laced with pain. "How long were you going to keep this from me, Thomas?" she asked, her tone deceptively calm. "Or were you planning to take this secret to your grave?"

Thomas looked up at her, his eyes bleary but filled with a defiance she hadn't seen in years. He downed the rest of his drink in one gulp, then slammed the glass down on the table beside him. "What does it matter, Evelyn?" he slurred, his words heavy with bitterness. "It's done. Caleb got in law school, didn't he? Isn't that what you wanted?"

Evelyn felt her chest tighten, the hurt and betrayal slicing through her like a knife. "What I wanted?" she repeated, her voice rising. "You think this is what I wanted? For you to throw money around, bribing officials, so Caleb could live out your dream? What about his dream, Thomas? What about what he wants?"

Thomas scoffed, the sound harsh and dismissive. "Caleb doesn't know what he wants," he said, waving his hand as if to brush away the thought. "He's just a boy, Evelyn. He needs direction, guidance. I did what I had to do to ensure his future."

Evelyn shook her head, disbelief washing over her. "You did what you had to do? By betraying our son? By compromising his future before it even began? This isn't about guidance, Thomas. This is about control. You're trying to mold Caleb into something he's not, something he never wanted to be!"

"No!" Thomas stood up abruptly, his unsteady legs betraying his

inebriation. "I did it for him," he insisted, his voice loud and defensive. "He needs to be strong, to be successful. The world doesn't care about what you want, Evelyn. It cares about power, influence. I made sure Caleb has that."

Evelyn's eyes filled with tears, her heart breaking as she realized how far gone her husband was. The man she had married, the man she had once loved deeply, was buried beneath layers of ambition and greed. "You've lost your way, Thomas," she whispered, her voice trembling. "And in doing so, you've lost us."

Thomas looked at her, his expression hardening. "You don't understand," he said, his voice now cold and distant. "You never have. Everything I've done, I've done for this family. For Caleb. You can't see that because you're too blinded by your emotions."

Evelyn stepped back, the finality of his words hitting her like a physical blow. "You're right, Thomas," she said softly, wiping away a tear that had escaped down her cheek. "I am blinded by emotion. By love. For Caleb, for you...for the man I thought you were."

Thomas's gaze faltered for a moment, a flicker of doubt crossing his features, but it was quickly replaced by stubborn resolve. He turned away, pouring himself another drink, effectively ending the conversation.

Evelyn watched him, her heart heavy with the knowledge that the man standing before her was a stranger. The truth was out, and there was no turning back.

And as if that wasn't enough, there was Elaine.

Elaine. The name alone made Evelyn's stomach churn. She had known about her for some time now—the whispers, the late-night meetings, the lingering scent of another woman's perfume on Thomas's clothes. But until that night, she hadn't fully understood the extent of his infidelity. Thomas, her husband of twenty years, the father of her child, had betrayed her in the worst possible way. The lies, the deception, the sheer audacity of it all—it had been too much to bear.

Now, Thomas was holed up in his office, pretending to work, but Evelyn knew better. He was avoiding her, avoiding the mess he had made of their lives. She had already consulted a divorce lawyer, a meeting that had left her reeling with the cold, hard truths she hadn't been ready to face. The lawyer, a sharp-tongued man with little patience for sentimentality, had laid out the procedures, the prenup, the reality of what divorce would mean.

"You have to understand, Mrs. Morgan," the lawyer said, his voice devoid of emotion, "this isn't just about ending a marriage. This is about protecting yourself, your assets, your future. If you signed a prenup, you're entitled to very little, considering his wealth and influence. If you want to fight, it's going to be a long, ugly battle, and there's no guarantee you'll come out on top."

His words hit her like a cold splash of water, jolting her into the harsh reality of her situation. She sat there, numb, as he laid out the facts, his tone clinical and detached. He spoke of legal battles, custody arrangements, and financial settlements as if they were mere transactions, not the dismantling of a life she had spent two decades building.

Part of her wanted to fight, to claw back some semblance of the life she had once known. But another part of her—the part that was exhausted, broken, and betrayed—wondered if there was anything left worth saving. The marriage she had once cherished was gone, shattered by lies and deceit. What remained was a hollow shell, a mere shadow of what it had once been.

She had spent years supporting Thomas, standing by his side as he climbed the political ladder, sacrificed her dreams for his career, and raised their son almost single-handedly. And this was how he repaid her— with lies, betrayal, and an affair that everyone seemed to know about except her. The humiliation was almost too much to bear.

Evelyn stared down at her cold coffee, the liquid as dark and bitter as her thoughts. She had a decision to make—a choice that would determine the rest of her life. She could fight, drag Thomas through a bitter and public divorce, or she could walk away, start over, and try to find some semblance of peace in the ruins of her marriage.

But was there peace to be found in leaving? Or was she simply trading one kind of pain for another? The thought of a life without Thomas, without the stability they had built together, was terrifying. Yet the idea of staying, of continuing to live a lie, was equally unbearable.

As she sat there, lost in thought, Evelyn realized that no matter what choice she made, there would be no easy answers. The road ahead was fraught with uncertainty, with heartache, and with the painful process of letting go of the life she had once known. But one thing was clear—she couldn't continue like this. Something had to change, and it had to change soon.

Evelyn pushed her chair back, the sound echoing through the empty kitchen. She needed to talk to Thomas, to confront him once more, to make him understand the gravity of what he had done. But deep down, she knew that conversation would only confirm what she already feared—there was nothing left to save.

With a heavy heart, she stood up, her legs feeling weak beneath her. The divorce lawyer's words rang in her ears, a stark reminder of the battle that lay ahead. But for now, she needed to face Thomas, to look him in the eye and see if there was any trace of the man she had once loved. And if there wasn't, she would know what she had to do.

      Meanwhile, Elaine sat across from Thomas in his office, the dim light casting long shadows on the walls. The tension between them was palpable, hanging in the air like a storm waiting to break. She was calm, unnervingly so, as she handed him her resignation letter. Her hands were steady, but inside, she was unraveling.

"I'm not keeping the baby," she said, her voice betraying none of the turmoil she felt. "And I'll take the money you offered."

Thomas met her gaze, a flicker of emotions crossing his face—relief, regret, and something else, something she couldn't quite place. "Elaine, I—"

She had once loved him, perhaps more deeply than she cared to admit, even to herself. In the beginning, she had harbored secret hopes that this affair would blossom into something more, that a baby might finally make him leave his wife. She had envisioned a future where Thomas would choose her, where their love would be enough to build a new life together. But the man she had fallen in love with seemed to have disappeared, replaced by someone she barely recognized.

"Don't," she cut him off, her voice firm. "We both knew this was never going to work. I'm done, Thomas. I'm walking away, and so should you."

Thomas leaned back in his chair, his fingers drumming lightly on the desk. "My marriage is on the rocks anyway, Elaine," he said, his tone almost pleading. "If you could just stick around a little longer, maybe we could end up together. You know I care about you."

Elaine's heart tightened at his words, but she knew better than to believe him. She had seen the way he looked at his wife, the guilt and the confusion that clouded his eyes whenever her name was mentioned. This was a man who was lost, grasping at whatever pieces of his life he could salvage. But she couldn't be a part of that anymore.

She watched as he slid a document across the desk—a non-disclosure agreement. The final nail in the coffin of their ill-fated relationship. She knew what it meant. He wanted to erase her from his life, to make sure that nothing about their affair ever saw the light of day.

Elaine picked up the pen, but paused, meeting his eyes. "I'll need to let my lawyer review this," she said, her voice measured.

Thomas's expression hardened, and he leaned forward,

his tone laced with subtle pressure. "If you don't sign it now, Elaine, you won't be getting your settlement. You know how these things work."

For a moment, she considered walking away, letting her lawyer handle it. But then she thought about the long, exhausting fight that would follow, the public spectacle it would make of her life. She wasn't strong enough for that—not anymore.

With a heavy heart, she signed the document, sealing her silence and her fate. Thomas handed her the envelope, the money she had been promised. It felt cold in her hands, like a weight she would carry forever.

Elaine stood, her movements deliberate and final. She tucked the envelope into her purse, her resolve hardening with every step she took. As she turned to leave, she glanced back at him one last time, her eyes filled with a sadness that Thomas couldn't begin to fathom.

"This should have been over a long time ago," she said softly, her voice carrying the weight of all the things left unsaid. And then, without another word, she walked out the door, leaving Thomas alone with his thoughts, the silence of his office echoing with the consequences of choices made in the dark.

As Elaine stepped out into the evening air, she felt a

strange sense of relief, mingled with the sting of loss. She had loved him once, but that love had withered, suffocated by lies and half-truths. Now, all she had left was the hollow feeling that perhaps she had wasted too much of herself on a man who could never truly love her in return.

Back in the office, Thomas sat motionless, staring at the space where Elaine had stood. The door clicked shut behind her, the sound final, like a book closing on a chapter he wished he could rewrite. The regret gnawed at him, a bitter reminder that he was losing everything—his marriage, his affair, and most importantly, the pieces of himself that had once made him whole.

Caleb, unaware of the storm brewing in his parents' marriage, was caught up in his own battle—one that had nothing to do with the expectations his father had laid out for him. He had decided against pursuing law school, a choice that had taken more courage than he had expected. The weight of that decision lingered, but so did a newfound sense of freedom. Law school had never been his dream, but it had been the path laid out for him, the one everyone expected him to follow. Walking away from it had left him feeling both lost and liberated.

To make ends meet, Caleb had taken up odd jobs

around town—anything that would keep him busy and give him a sense of purpose. The work was humbling, but in a way, it grounded him. He was no longer the privileged son of Senator Morgan, but just another guy trying to get by. It wasn't easy, but it felt real, more authentic than the life he'd left behind.

It was after a long shift at a local diner, Caleb found himself in need of a vehicle. His parents' cars were out of the question, as was asking them for money. He needed something cheap, something that wouldn't remind him of the life he was trying to escape. After scouring the classifieds, he finally came across an ad for an old, beat-up truck. The price was right, and with no other options, he decided to check it out.

When Caleb arrived at the address listed, he found himself in a rundown neighborhood on the outskirts of town. The truck was parked in a gravel driveway, its faded red paint chipped and rusting in places. Standing beside it was a burly man with a thick mustache, wearing a sleeveless shirt that showed off his tattooed arms.

"Hey, you must be Caleb," the man said, his voice carrying a heavy Hispanic accent. "Name's Hector. This is the baby you called about."

Caleb raised an eyebrow as he took in the sight of the truck. "Baby, huh? She's seen better days."

Hector laughed, a deep, hearty sound. "Yeah, she's not much to look at, but she's got heart. Just like her owner. You take care of her, she'll take care of you."

Caleb walked around the truck, inspecting it. The tires were worn, the windshield had a crack running down the middle, and the interior smelled faintly of old leather and engine oil. But despite its rough appearance, there was something endearing about the old truck. It reminded Caleb of himself—rough around the edges, but still standing.

"How much are you asking for it again?" Caleb asked, trying to sound nonchalant.

"Five hundred bucks," Hector replied, leaning against the hood. "And I'll throw in a full tank of gas, just because you look like a nice guy."

Caleb chuckled, running a hand through his hair. "You're not in the mafia or something, are you? I don't want to find out this truck was used in some heist."

Hector grinned, showing a gold tooth. "Nah, man. I'm just a regular guy trying to make an honest living. I promise, no skeletons in this one. Maybe a few rusty bolts, but no skeletons."

Caleb laughed, feeling a weight lift from his shoulders.

"Alright, Hector. You've got yourself a deal."

They shook hands, and as Caleb counted out the cash, he couldn't help but feel a strange sense of satisfaction. The truck was far from perfect, but it was his— something he had bought with his own money, something that represented the life he was carving out for himself.

As Hector handed over the keys, he clapped Caleb on the back. "Take care of her, man. And if you ever need a mechanic, you know where to find me."

Caleb nodded, slipping into the driver's seat. The engine sputtered to life with a roar, and as he drove away, he couldn't help but smile. The truck wasn't just a way to get around the city; it was a symbol of his independence, a reminder that he was on a journey to find himself—one rusty mile at a time.

The next day, Caleb stood in the sweltering heat, the sun beating down on him as he finished mowing the last stretch of the lawn. His shirt clung to his back, soaked with sweat, and his muscles ached from the long hours of physical labor. Landscaping wasn't glamorous, but it was honest work, and it kept his mind busy. He'd taken up odd jobs around town— anything to keep himself afloat and to avoid the suffocating expectations that had once defined his life.

There were days he worked at the local hardware store, stocking shelves and helping customers find the right tools for their projects. On weekends, he did yard work for the wealthy families in the Hamptons, the same families who had once hosted him at their lavish parties. It was humbling work, and the irony wasn't lost on him—going from the golden boy expected to follow in his father's prestigious footsteps to a young man scraping by with manual labor. But it also gave him a sense of purpose, something he hadn't felt in a long time.

The money he made wasn't much, just enough to cover his basic needs and save a little on the side. He knew that if he wanted to pursue college, his only real options were a scholarship or a student loan. Both seemed like distant dreams, but at least he was doing something to move forward. The thought of law school, of becoming the next Senator Morgan, no longer held any appeal. Caleb had seen what that life did to people—the pressure, the sacrifices, the loss of self. He didn't want that, not anymore.

After a long day of landscaping, Caleb wiped the sweat from his brow and leaned against the mower, catching his breath. The smell of freshly cut grass filled the air, a scent that reminded him of simpler times, of childhood summers spent running barefoot through the fields with Milo at his side. But those days were gone, replaced by the harsh realities of adulthood.

As he packed up his tools, Caleb's thoughts drifted to Lila. It had been months since they last saw each other, but she was never far from his mind. There was something about her—something that made him feel alive, even in the darkest moments. She had a lightness, a freedom, that seemed to pierce through his own struggles, and he couldn't help but wonder what she was doing now, how she was spending her school year.

Curiosity got the better of him as he settled into his truck, the old vehicle creaking under his weight. He pulled out his phone, scrolling through Instagram until he found her profile. There she was, smiling brightly in every photo, the beach and the waves behind her. Her skin was kissed by the sun, her eyes sparkling with the joy that came from being in her element. Lila posted often about surfing, the ocean her constant companion, and in every picture, she looked so happy, so free.

Caleb couldn't help but smile as he scrolled through the photos, though a pang of longing tugged at his heart. She seemed to belong to a world that was far removed from his own—one filled with sunshine and laughter, where the only concerns were the tides and the surf. It was a world he had once been a part of, before life had gotten so complicated, before the weight of his family's expectations had crushed his spirit.

He paused on a photo of Lila standing on her surfboard, the waves curling behind her as she balanced effortlessly. Her smile was radiant, a beacon of light in a world that often felt too dark for Caleb to navigate. He wished he could be there with her, to feel that same sense of freedom and joy. But he knew that was impossible. His life was here, in the real world, where bills had to be paid and futures had to be planned.

Still, as he stared at the photo, a thought crossed his mind. What if he could find a way to bridge the gap between their worlds? What if he could rediscover that sense of adventure, of fearlessness, that he had once known? The idea was tempting, but it also scared him. It meant stepping out of his comfort zone, taking risks, and facing the unknown—things he hadn't done in a long time.

With a sigh, Caleb locked his phone and started the truck, the engine rumbling to life. He had a lot to figure out, but for now, he'd take things one day at a time. And maybe, just maybe, he'd find a way back to the person he used to be—the person who wasn't afraid to chase after what he wanted, even if it seemed out of reach. As he drove away, the image of Lila on her surfboard stayed with him, a reminder of the life that was still out there, waiting for him to seize it.

When Caleb returned home after his landscaping job, he found an envelope waiting for him on his bed. It stood out against the neatly made sheets, the university's logo in the corner catching his eye. His heart raced as he picked it up, the weight of the moment sinking in. This was it—the answer to the question that had been haunting him for weeks.

With trembling hands, he tore open the envelope and unfolded the letter. His eyes scanned the words, barely daring to believe it. He had been accepted into the zoology program at a university. No scholarship, but that didn't matter. He could apply for a student loan. The important thing was that he had made it.

For a moment, Caleb just stood there, the letter trembling in his hands. The news felt surreal, like a dream he hadn't fully woken up from. He had always loved animals, ever since he was a little boy chasing frogs in the backyard or watching birds from his bedroom window. There was something pure about them, something uncomplicated. They didn't judge, didn't expect anything from him other than kindness. The thought of dedicating his life to studying them felt like a piece of the puzzle finally falling into place.

But even as joy and relief washed over him, a familiar knot tightened in his chest. How would his parents react to this news? His father had always had big plans for him—law school, politics, carrying on the Morgan legacy. But zoology? That wasn't part of the plan. Would they see it as another disappointment, another way he had failed to live up to the Morgan name?

He could already hear his father's voice in his head, a mix of disappointment and frustration. "Zoology, Caleb? How is that going to secure your future? What about all the opportunities we've given you?"

And his mother, Evelyn—she would be more subtle, her disapproval wrapped in concern. "Are you sure this is what you want, Caleb? You know how much we've invested in your education. We just want what's best for you."

Caleb sat down on the edge of his bed, the letter still in his hand. The joy he had felt moments ago was now tainted by uncertainty. He wanted to share this moment with someone, to celebrate this victory, but the fear of his parents' reaction held him back. What if they didn't understand? What if they couldn't see how important this was to him?

He folded the letter carefully and placed it back in the envelope. The acceptance was a small victory, but it was his. For the first time in a long time, he felt a glimmer of hope, a sense of direction. Yet, the path ahead was still uncertain, and the weight of his parents' expectations lingered like a shadow over his joy.

Days later, Evelyn found herself wandering the aisles of the grocery store, her mind drifting as she absentmindedly placed items into her cart. The mundane task provided a brief escape from the turmoil brewing inside her. The weight of unspoken truths, of secrets she had long suspected but never confronted, bore down on her like a storm cloud.

As she reached for a jar of marinara sauce, a voice from behind jolted her back to reality.

"Evelyn."

She turned, her heart skipping a beat as she recognized the voice. Standing there, a few feet away, was Elaine, the woman who had unknowingly become a catalyst for Evelyn's unraveling. Elaine's expression was unreadable, her eyes searching Evelyn's face as if trying to gauge her reaction.

For a moment, the world around them seemed to fade, the chatter of other shoppers and the clinking of carts melting into a distant hum. Evelyn felt a wave of apprehension wash over her. She braced herself, unsure of what was to come.

"We need to talk," Elaine said, her voice calm but laced with a seriousness that sent a chill down Evelyn's spine.

Evelyn hesitated, her mind racing. Every fiber of her being wanted to walk away, to avoid whatever painful truths Elaine was about to reveal. But something in Elaine's demeanor stopped her. There was an urgency, a sense of finality in her tone that Evelyn couldn't ignore. Reluctantly, she nodded and followed Elaine to a quieter corner of the store, away from prying eyes.

The noise of the world faded into the background, leaving only the two of them in a bubble of tense silence. Evelyn's heart pounded in her chest as she waited for Elaine to speak, the anticipation gnawing at her insides.

"I'm sorry to do this here, but you deserve to know the truth," Elaine began, her eyes locking onto Evelyn's with an intensity that made it impossible to look away. "Thomas and I... we had an affair. It's been going on for a while, but it's over now. I'm leaving, and I won't be a part of his life anymore. I just thought you should know."

The words hung in the air like a heavy fog, each syllable striking Evelyn with the force of a sledgehammer. She had suspected, of course—how could she not? The late nights, the secretive phone calls, the way Thomas had grown distant, treating her like an afterthought. But hearing it confirmed, spoken aloud with such finality, was something else entirely. It was like a door slamming shut, a cold wind sweeping through her, leaving her exposed and vulnerable.

Elaine reached into her purse and pulled out a small, unmarked envelope. She held it out to Evelyn, her expression softening, a rare look of sympathy crossing her face.

Evelyn stared at the envelope, her hands trembling as she accepted it. "What is this?" she asked, her voice barely above a whisper.

Elaine took a deep breath, her gaze steady. "This is all you need to get a divorce settlement from Thomas. Inside, you'll find pictures of him with a much younger woman at a hotel. I know about the cheating clause in your prenup. With this, you can easily win your case."

Evelyn's breath caught in her throat as she peeked inside the envelope. The photos stared back at her, undeniable proof of Thomas's betrayal. Her heart sank, a mix of shock and disbelief washing over her. She had known there were cracks in their marriage, but this— this was a betrayal that cut deep, a wound that might never heal.

Elaine's voice softened, her tone almost apologetic. "I'm sorry, Evelyn. For everything."

But Evelyn shook her head, the tears she had been

holding back finally spilling over, tracing wet paths down her cheeks. "No, don't be. I should be thanking you. You've just confirmed what I've known for a long time—this marriage was over long before you came into the picture."

Elaine nodded, her eyes reflecting a mixture of regret and understanding. Without another word, she turned and walked away, leaving Evelyn standing alone in the aisle, her mind reeling with the gravity of what had just transpired.

As Evelyn clutched the envelope to her chest, a cold, hard truth settled over her like a shroud—her marriage to Thomas was dead. It had been for a long time, a hollow shell of what it once was. And now, with the evidence in her hands, she had to decide what came next.

But as the initial shock began to fade, Evelyn felt something unexpected—a flicker of hope. Maybe, just maybe, this was the beginning of something new. Something better. She wasn't sure what the future held, but for the first time in a long while, she felt a sense of agency, of control over her own destiny.

As she left the store, the weight of the envelope still heavy in her hand, Evelyn allowed herself a small, tentative smile.

The road ahead would be difficult, but she was ready to face it. After all, she had nothing left to lose, and perhaps, everything to gain.

CHAPTER 19: THE LAST REUNION

Sunday dinners at the Morgan household had always been a sacred tradition, a time when the family could come together, even if only for an hour, to share a meal and the facade of normalcy. But tonight, the atmosphere was different—thick with tension, like the calm before a storm. For the first time in months, Thomas Morgan sat at the dining table with his wife, Evelyn, and their son, Caleb. Yet, instead of the usual lively conversation, an uneasy silence filled the room.

Caleb could feel a knot tightening in his stomach as he prepared to speak. He knew that what he was about to say would change everything. His mother had gone out of her way to make his favorite meal—roast chicken with mashed potatoes and gravy—hoping to create a semblance of warmth in a household that had long since grown cold. She had noticed the change in him lately, the way his eyes seemed to carry the weight of the world, and she prayed that tonight, they might bridge the growing distance between them.

As Caleb looked down at his plate, the food tasted like ash in his mouth. He cleared his throat, breaking the silence. "I've been accepted into a zoology program," he began, his voice steady despite the anxiety gnawing at him. "I'm leaving for college in a few days."

His father, Thomas, looked up from his plate, his expression hardening into a mask of disdain. "Zoology?" he repeated, the word dripping with contempt. "And what exactly do you plan to do with that degree, Caleb? Waste your life chasing animals?"

Caleb's heart sank, but he held his ground. "It's what I'm passionate about, Dad. I want to work with animals, maybe in conservation or at a wildlife reserve. It's important to me."

Thomas scoffed, leaning back in his chair with an air of superiority. "Important to you? You've had every opportunity, every advantage, and you're going to throw it all away for some childish fantasy? Do you know how much time and money we've invested in your education, your future? And this is how you repay us?"

Evelyn shot her husband a warning glance, her patience with his arrogance wearing thin. "Thomas, this is Caleb's decision. He's passionate about this, and we should support him."

"Support him?" Thomas echoed, his voice rising. "In what? Throwing away every opportunity we've given him? I've had enough of this nonsense."

Evelyn's hand trembled slightly as she reached for her

glass of wine. The moment she had dreaded was here, but she knew it was time to stand up for herself—and for Caleb. She set her glass down and met Thomas's gaze, her eyes steely with resolve. "Thomas, I've had enough too. Enough of your condescension, enough of your bullying, and enough of your lies."

Before Thomas could react, Evelyn pulled out an envelope she'd been hiding under the table and placed it in front of him. "These are divorce papers. I'm done pretending everything is fine. I'm done letting you control our lives."

Thomas's face twisted with rage as he reached for the envelope, but Evelyn didn't flinch. Instead, she looked him squarely in the eyes, her voice calm but firm. "And before you remind me about the prenup," she continued, her tone icy, "let me remind you of the cheating clause in it. I have evidence, Thomas. Enough to win my settlement and more."

For a moment, there was nothing but stunned silence. Then, in a flash, Thomas's face turned a deep shade of red. He stood up abruptly, the chair scraping against the floor, and advanced toward Evelyn, his eyes blazing with fury. Caleb's heart raced as memories of that fateful night with Milo flooded back—the night his father's temper had spiraled out of control. He couldn't let that happen again.

"Mom, watch out!" Caleb shouted, moving between his parents just as Thomas raised his hand. The slap rang out in the dining room, the sound echoing in Caleb's ears as Evelyn fell out of her chair, clutching her cheek in shock.

Caleb's blood boiled. He stepped in front of his mother, his body trembling with a mix of fear and rage, but his voice remained firm. "No, Dad. Not this time."

Thomas's eyes narrowed, and he took a threatening step forward. "Get out of my way, boy!" he roared, his voice slurred from the alcohol he'd been consuming throughout the evening.

Caleb stood his ground, refusing to back down. "I'm not going anywhere," he said, his voice steady. "You can't keep doing this. I won't let you."

The tension in the room was electric, each word hanging in the air like a live wire. Thomas's hands clenched into fists, his face contorted with anger. "You think you can stand up to me?" he spat. "You're nothing without me. Nothing!"

Caleb felt the sting of his father's words, but he refused to let them break him. "I'm more than what you think I am," he replied, his voice trembling but determined. "I'm not afraid of you anymore."

Thomas sneered, his rage boiling over. He stormed to the liquor cabinet, grabbing a bottle of scotch and pouring himself a generous glass. He downed it in one gulp, then poured another, his hands shaking with fury. "You ungrateful little brat," he muttered, more to himself than to Caleb. "You think you can just walk away from everything I've given you?"

Evelyn struggled to her feet, her hand still on her cheek where Thomas had struck her. "Thomas, stop this," she pleaded, her voice thick with emotion. "This isn't the man I married. This isn't the man I loved."

Thomas's laughter was bitter and hollow. "The man you loved?" he echoed, his eyes glazed over with anger and alcohol. "That man is long gone, Evelyn. And so are you."

Caleb watched his father with a mix of pity and disgust. This was the man who had once been his hero, the man he had looked up to and admired. Now, all he saw was a broken shell, a man consumed by his own demons. He glanced at his mother, who was standing tall despite the tears in her eyes, and felt a surge of protectiveness wash over him.

"We're done, Thomas," Evelyn said softly but firmly. "We're done letting you control us with your anger, your money, your power. Caleb and I—we're going to be okay. Without you."

Thomas opened his mouth to retort, but the words seemed to die on his lips. He looked at Caleb, then back at Evelyn, a strange mix of emotions flickering across his face—anger, confusion, fear. For a moment, he looked like he might say something, anything, to make it right. But then, just as quickly, the moment passed, and he turned away, pouring himself another drink.

Without another word, Caleb pulled out his phone and dialed 911. His hand was steady, his voice surprisingly calm as he spoke. "I need help," he said, the weight of the situation bearing down on him, but his resolve unwavering.

Evelyn watched him, her eyes filled with a mixture of fear and relief. She didn't try to stop him, knowing that this moment had been a long time coming. The silence between them was heavy, each second stretching into an eternity as they waited for the police to arrive. Caleb stood close to her, a silent promise that he would protect her, no matter what.

Within minutes, police officers entered the house, their expressions growing serious as they took in the scene—the shattered glass on the floor, the bruise forming on Evelyn's face, and Thomas stumbling, his anger still simmering as he glared at his wife and son.

One of the officers stepped forward, his tone gentle yet authoritative. "Ma'am," he addressed Evelyn, "are you okay? Do you need medical attention?"

Evelyn shook her head, her voice steady despite the turmoil inside her. "I'm fine. But I want to press charges."

The officer nodded, his gaze shifting to Caleb, who stood protectively in front of his mother. "Son, can you tell us what happened?"

Caleb swallowed hard, his voice even as he recounted the events. "He hit her," he said, his eyes never leaving Thomas. "He's been drinking, and when we tried to talk to him, he got violent."

The officers exchanged glances before moving toward Thomas, who struggled as they restrained him. His curses filled the room, a stark contrast to the quiet strength Caleb and Evelyn displayed.

As the police led Thomas away, Caleb felt a strange mix of emotions—anger, sorrow, and a deep sense of loss. The man being taken away in handcuffs was once his hero, someone he had looked up to, admired, even feared. But now, that image was shattered, replaced by the harsh reality of who Thomas had become.

Evelyn reached out, placing a hand on Caleb's

shoulder. "You did the right thing," she whispered, her voice trembling but full of gratitude.

Caleb nodded, though his heart felt heavy. "I just wish it didn't have to be this way," he murmured, his eyes following the police car as it disappeared down the driveway.

Evelyn pulled him into a hug, holding him close. "We'll get through this," she promised, her voice soft yet determined.

Caleb closed his eyes, allowing himself to find comfort in her embrace, even as his mind wrestled with the reality of their new world—a world where the lines between love and pain, between forgiveness and justice, were more blurred than ever before.

Caleb had been keeping himself busy with packing for college, trying to distract himself from the tumultuous emotions swirling inside him. The once lively house had grown quieter in recent days, a somber stillness filling the air. He meticulously folded clothes, packed up books, and carefully placed mementos from his childhood into boxes. Yet, no matter how much he tried to focus on the task at hand, his thoughts kept drifting back to his mother and the storm that had shaken their family.

Once the chaos of packing had settled, Caleb found himself sitting with his mother in the living room, the weight of the past few days pressing down on them both. The room, usually filled with warmth and light, felt heavy with unspoken words and shared grief.

Evelyn's hand trembled as she reached for Caleb's, her fingers wrapping around his with a desperate need for connection. Her eyes, once so full of life, now brimmed with tears that she could no longer hold back.

"Caleb, I'm so sorry," she whispered, her voice breaking with the weight of her regret. "I never wanted it to come to this."

Caleb looked at her, his heart aching for the woman who had always been his rock, now crumbling under the strain of their shattered lives. He squeezed her hand, trying to offer her the comfort she so desperately needed.

"It's not your fault, Mom," he said softly, his voice steady despite the turmoil inside him. "You did what you had to do. We both did."

They sat in silence for a while, the only sound in the room the ticking of the old clock on the mantelpiece. The quiet moments stretched between them, filled with the shared understanding of a pain that words couldn't quite capture.

Finally, Caleb broke the silence, his thoughts turning to something that had been on his mind since he decided to leave for college. "Mom, I was wondering… Could you take care of Millie while I'm away at college? She loves you, and I don't want you to feel lonely."

At the sound of her name, Millie, the family's sleek black cat, came darting into the room from her usual perch by the window. Her green eyes sparkled with curiosity, and she leaped gracefully onto the couch, rubbing her head affectionately against Evelyn's arm.

Evelyn managed a small smile through her tears as she reached out to stroke Millie's soft fur. "Of course, sweetheart. I'd love to take care of Millie. She'll be good company," she said, her voice tinged with both sadness and gratitude.

Caleb watched the interaction between his mother and Millie, feeling a wave of relief wash over him. He knew how much his mother adored the cat, and the bond they shared was something that always brought a bit of light into the darkest of times. He was glad that Millie would be there for Evelyn during the difficult days ahead, offering her the companionship she would need once he was gone.

Millie purred softly, curling up beside Evelyn, as if sensing the comfort she was bringing to the woman who had always been there for her. Caleb couldn't help but smile at the sight, the bittersweet moment reminding him of the simple joys that still existed in their world, despite everything that had happened.

Evelyn looked up at Caleb, her eyes filled with a mix of sorrow and love. "Thank you, Caleb," she said, her voice barely above a whisper. "For everything. For being here, for being my son."

Caleb nodded, the lump in his throat making it hard to speak. "I'll miss you, Mom. But I know Millie will take good care of you."

As they sat together, the warmth of Millie's presence offering them both a small measure of peace, Caleb knew that leaving for college wouldn't be easy. But he also knew that his mother would be all right, with Millie by her side to remind her that she wasn't alone. And in that quiet moment, surrounded by the remnants of their once-happy home, Caleb found a glimmer of hope—a belief that, somehow, they would all find a way to heal.

The news of Senator Thomas Morgan's arrest spread like wildfire, igniting a media frenzy that quickly spiraled out of control. Within hours, every major news outlet was covering the scandal, the once-revered senator now at the center of a storm of public outrage.

The allegations of domestic violence had sent shockwaves through the political world, and public opinion polls reflected the fallout. Support for the senator was plummeting, with voters rapidly turning against him. The headlines were merciless, each one more damning than the last, painting a picture of a man who had betrayed the trust of his family and the nation.

Outside his office, a sea of reporters had gathered, their cameras flashing like lightning in a storm. Microphones were thrust into Thomas's face as he was escorted to his car, his expression dark and brooding. He felt the weight of the world pressing down on him, the burden of his actions now playing out in front of the entire country.

"Senator Morgan, are the allegations true? Did you assault your wife?"

"Are you getting a divorce, Senator?"

"How will this affect your career?"

The questions came at him in rapid succession, each one like a dagger to his already battered pride. Thomas said nothing, his jaw clenched tightly, his eyes narrowed with anger. Inside, he was seething—not just at the situation, but at the absence of Elaine, the woman who had always been so adept at making his problems disappear. She had promised him the world, had helped him rise to the top, and now, in his moment of need, she was nowhere to be found.

As he was driven away from the chaos, the reality of his situation began to sink in. His carefully constructed world was crumbling around him, the foundation of lies and deceit now exposed for all to see. He had spent his life cultivating an image of power and control, but now that image was shattered, and the man beneath was left vulnerable and alone.

Meanwhile, thousands of miles away, Elaine reclined on a sun lounger at a tropical beach resort, her phone in hand as she watched the news footage of Thomas's disgrace. The warm sun kissed her skin, and the gentle sound of the waves provided a soothing backdrop to the drama unfolding on her screen. A satisfied smile tugged at her lips as she sipped her pina colada, her eyes fixed on the image of Thomas being hounded by the press.

"He got exactly what he deserved," she murmured to herself, a sense of vindication washing over her. She had once thought Thomas invincible, a man who could weather any storm, but now she saw him for what he truly was—fragile, fallible, and, most of all, defeated.

As she watched the cameras capture the fall of a man who had once held her in his thrall, Elaine felt a strange sense of peace. She had been used and discarded by

Thomas, a pawn in his ruthless game of power, but now she was free. Free from his manipulation, free from his lies, and free to start anew.

A few weeks later, Caleb stood in the center of his new dorm room, surrounded by cardboard boxes and the faint smell of fresh paint. The room was modest, with just enough space for two beds, two desks, and a window that overlooked the bustling campus below. It wasn't much, but it was his—a place where he could begin again, away from the expectations and shadows that had followed him for so long.

He had made the decision not to ask either of his parents to accompany him on this new chapter of his life. After everything that had transpired, he needed to step into this new world on his own terms. This was his fresh start, and he intended to face it head-on, without the weight of their expectations pressing down on him.

Across the room, his new roommate, Henry, was already in the process of unpacking his belongings. He was a tall, lanky guy with a mop of curly hair and an easy grin that made Caleb feel instantly at ease. Henry looked up from his suitcase and smiled warmly. "Hey, Caleb," he greeted, extending a hand. "Welcome roomie."

Caleb returned the smile, though it was tinged with a mix of nerves and excitement. "Thanks, man. It's good to be here," he replied, shaking Henry's hand.

As Caleb began to unpack his own things, he couldn't help but notice the neatly arranged rows of books on Henry's desk and the assortment of posters he was carefully pinning to the wall. They ranged from classic movie posters to quotes from famous authors—each one reflecting a piece of who Henry was.

"So, Caleb," Henry began, a hint of curiosity in his voice as he hung up a poster of John Lennon. "Are you into parties? There's usually something happening around campus on the weekends. We could check it out if you're up for it."

Caleb hesitated, horror stories of wild parties and reckless behavior flashing through his mind. He shook his head with a slight smile. "Thanks, but I'm not really a party animal."

Henry raised an eyebrow, clearly impressed. "Well, I gotta say, I'm thanking my lucky stars. I was worried I'd get stuck with some crazy party guy who'd keep me up all night. Looks like I got a cool, responsible roommate instead."

Caleb chuckled, feeling a bit lighter. "I try," he said,

grateful for Henry's easygoing nature.

As they continued to settle into their new space, Caleb found his thoughts drifting back to the life he had left behind—the chaos and pain that had been his constant companions. He thought about his parents, the pressures they had placed on him, and the memories that still lingered like ghosts in the back of his mind. The hurt was still there, raw and undeniable, but there was also a sense of relief, like a weight had been lifted off his shoulders.

This dorm room, with its bare walls and simple furnishings, represented more than just a place to sleep. It was a symbol of the future he was determined to build for himself—a future where he could pursue his passion for animals and find the peace that had always eluded him. He could finally leave behind the shadows of his past and step into the light of his own making.

As he placed framed photos of Milo and Millie on his desk—Caleb felt a sense of hope stirring within him. It wasn't going to be easy, and he knew there would be challenges ahead, but for the first time in a long while, he felt like he was on the right path. A path that was truly his own.

The first day of university arrived with the

crispness of a new beginning, a sense of possibility lingering in the air. Caleb stood outside the large auditorium for freshman orientation, his heart pounding with a mix of anticipation and nerves. The campus around him was alive with the energy of hundreds of students, all eager to embark on this new chapter of their lives.

Beside him, Henry, his new roommate, adjusted the strap of his backpack, glancing around with wide-eyed excitement. "Man, can you believe we're actually here?" Henry grinned, his enthusiasm infectious. "I mean, we're officially college students now. No more curfews, no more parents breathing down our necks... Freedom!"

Caleb couldn't help but smile at Henry's exuberance. "Yeah, it's surreal," he replied, trying to match Henry's enthusiasm. "Feels like everything's changing so fast."

Henry laughed, giving Caleb a friendly nudge. "It's a good thing, though. I mean, think about all the new people we're gonna meet. New adventures, new experiences... And maybe, just maybe, some of those infamous college parties?"

Caleb chuckled, shaking his head. "Is that all you're thinking about? Parties?"

"Hey, I'm a simple guy," Henry said with a wink. "But

seriously, it's gonna be great. No more high school drama, no more cliques. Just a fresh start."

They made their way into the auditorium, the hum of chatter growing louder as they stepped inside. The room was massive, filled with rows upon rows of seats, all gradually filling with students. Caleb could feel the weight of the moment, the realization that this was the beginning of something completely new.

"Where should we sit?" Henry asked, scanning the room.

"Let's find something in the middle," Caleb suggested, leading the way.

As they found their seats, Caleb couldn't help but glance around the room, his eyes scanning the sea of faces. Strangers, every one of them. And yet, there was a comfort in the anonymity, a chance to reinvent himself in this new place. But as his gaze continued to sweep across the auditorium, he caught sight of something—no, someone—that made his heart skip a beat.

Lila Hayes.

She was sitting a few rows ahead, her attention focused on the stage where the university president was preparing to speak. Her hair fell in soft waves around her shoulders, and even from this distance, Caleb could see the serene expression on her face. It was as if she hadn't noticed the chaos around her, the excitement of the first day.

Henry noticed the sudden shift in Caleb's demeanor and followed his gaze. "Who's that?" he asked, curiosity piqued.

"Lila," Caleb murmured, more to himself than to Henry. "I didn't think I'd see her here."

"You know her?" Henry asked, his eyebrows raised.

Caleb nodded, his thoughts racing. "Yeah, we... we used to know each other. Back home."

Henry gave him a knowing look. "Used to, huh? You wanna go say hi?"

Caleb hesitated, a mix of emotions swirling inside him. Seeing Lila here, in this new and unfamiliar place, brought back a flood of memories. The summer they'd spent together, the laughter, the moments of connection that had once seemed so easy. But things were different now, and he wasn't sure if he was ready to face the past, especially when he was still trying to figure out his future.

"I don't know," Caleb admitted, his voice quiet. "It's

complicated."

Henry leaned back in his seat, crossing his arms. "Sounds like there's a story there. But hey, you don't have to do anything you're not ready for. Just... take it one step at a time, man. This is your chance to start over, remember?"

Caleb nodded, appreciating Henry's words. He glanced at Lila one more time before turning his attention back to the front of the room. The university president had begun speaking, welcoming the new students with an inspiring speech about the journey they were about to embark on. But Caleb's mind was elsewhere, caught between the promise of new beginnings and the inescapable pull of the past.

As the speech continued, Caleb felt a strange sense of calm settle over him. Maybe Henry was right—maybe this was his chance to start over, to let go of the things that had been weighing him down. But as much as he wanted to move forward, he couldn't deny the part of him that still longed for the connection he'd once had with Lila. The thought of her being here, of them possibly crossing paths again, filled him with both hope and uncertainty.

When the orientation finally ended, the students began to disperse, heading out into the bright sunlight of the campus. Caleb and Henry followed the crowd, stepping into the fresh air with a renewed sense of possibility.

"So, what's next?" Henry asked, pulling out a campus map. "Wanna check out the dorms or grab some food?"

Caleb took a deep breath, letting the warmth of the sun chase away the lingering shadows of doubt. "Let's get some food," he said, smiling at Henry. "We've got time to figure everything else out."

As they walked across the campus, Caleb couldn't shake the feeling that this was just the beginning. And though he didn't know what the future held, he was willing to face it, one step at a time. With Lila back in the picture, there was no telling what this new chapter would bring. But for the first time in a long while, Caleb felt a flicker of hope—a hope that maybe, just maybe, this was where he was meant to be.

CHAPTER 20: THE LAST MEMORY

For the next few days, Caleb found himself swept up in the chaos of a new semester. The campus felt vast, almost overwhelming, as he navigated between classes, trying to figure out where he belonged. The Zoology program was small, with only a handful of students, which made it both comforting and isolating. There was a certain familiarity among them, but Caleb couldn't shake the feeling that he was still on the outside looking in.

The program itself fascinated him. The intricate study of animals, their behaviors, and ecosystems offered Caleb a sense of purpose, something to focus on besides the weight of his past. Yet, in the quieter moments, when he allowed his mind to wander, thoughts of Lila would slip in, unbidden but persistent. He hadn't seen her since that fleeting glimpse, and it puzzled him. Was she even in the same program? Or had he imagined the whole thing?

The campus, despite its size, felt too small for her absence to go unnoticed. It gnawed at him, this lingering mystery of where she might be. He found himself searching the faces of students as he walked through the halls, hoping for just a glimpse of her, something to anchor the memory that felt too fleeting to be real.

In the Zoology lab, surrounded by students who shared his passion for wildlife, Caleb should have felt more at ease, but the questions about Lila kept tugging at the back of his mind. Each day that passed without seeing her made the memory of her seem more like a dream, something intangible and elusive. He found himself distracted, unable to fully immerse himself in the work that once brought him comfort.

As he stood in the lab, peering into a microscope, the image of Lila in the moonlit Morgan estate flashed in his mind. It was a moment that felt suspended in time, and he couldn't help but wonder if he'd ever see her again, or if she'd simply vanish from his life as quickly as she had appeared. The uncertainty gnawed at him, leaving him restless, and as much as he tried to focus on his studies, his thoughts kept drifting back to her, the mystery of her presence on campus becoming a puzzle he was determined to solve.

His answers came rushing in one afternoon, as Caleb was flipping through his notes in the library, the soft rustle of pages the only sound in the quiet room, Henry plopped down in the chair across from him with the kind of mischievous grin that immediately put Caleb on alert.

"Hey, guess what?" Henry started, not waiting for a response as usual. His eyes sparkled with a secret he could barely contain. "I finally found her. Your Lila's in my Econ class."

Caleb's head snapped up, his heart skipping a beat. "Seriously? Why didn't you tell me sooner?"

Henry shrugged, his grin widening as if he'd been holding onto the news just to see Caleb's reaction. "Didn't realize it until today. The professor asked her a question, and she nailed it. She's smart, Caleb. Really smart."

A surge of excitement bubbled up inside Caleb, momentarily easing the weight of everything else on his mind. "Henry, you've got to help me. I need to know if she's single. Can you, I don't know, find out for me? Maybe just talk to her?"

Henry leaned back in his chair, crossing his arms with a smirk. "Oh, so now you need my help, huh? What's in it for me?"

Caleb rolled his eyes but couldn't help the smile tugging at his lips. "Name your price, man."

Henry tapped his chin, pretending to think it over. "Well, for starters, you could do my laundry for the next week."

Caleb groaned but agreed without hesitation. "Done."

"And," Henry continued, his grin growing wider, "how about you take my next two shifts at the café?"

Caleb let out an exaggerated sigh, shaking his head in mock defeat. "Fine, fine. Just get me some info, will you?"

Henry chuckled, clearly enjoying the moment. "You got it, Caleb. Consider it done."

As they settled back into their usual banter, Henry's expression softened slightly, and he added, "By the way, she's beautiful, man. You weren't kidding."

Caleb couldn't resist a playful jab. "Hands off, mister."

Henry laughed, raising his hands in mock surrender. "Don't worry, she's not my type anyway. I'm into dark chocolate, remember?"

Caleb burst out laughing, the sound echoing through the otherwise quiet library. The tension he'd been carrying all day seemed to lighten just a bit in that moment, the warmth of their friendship reminding him that even in the midst of uncertainty, there were still things that could make him smile.

As Henry left to gather more intel, Caleb leaned back in his chair, a mixture of nerves and anticipation swirling inside him. He couldn't help but wonder what Lila was like in class, what her voice sounded like when she answered questions, and if she ever thought about him the way he was starting to think about her.

For the first time in a long while, Caleb felt a flicker of hope, the possibility of something good on the horizon. But with that hope came a familiar fear—the fear of what might happen if things didn't go the way he imagined.

A couple of days later, Henry was running late, as usual. The clock on the wall ticked louder with each passing second, and Caleb could feel his anxiety building with every minute that Henry wasn't there. When the door finally creaked open, Caleb was already on his feet, his nerves stretched thin.

"Where have you been, man?" Caleb demanded, the words tumbling out more desperate than he intended. He had been counting on tonight to distract him, to pull him out of the darkness that had been creeping into his thoughts. "I thought we were playing Dungeons and Dragons, whatever that is."

Henry, still catching his breath, paused at the door, his expression a mix of confusion and offense. "Whoa, hold up," he said, raising an eyebrow. "Whatever that is? Caleb, Dungeons and Dragons isn't just a game—it's an experience, a journey into epic storytelling, imagination, and...well, nerdy fun."

Caleb blinked, clearly unimpressed. "Yeah, okay, but I don't see how rolling dice and pretending to be wizards or whatever is supposed to be fun."

Henry put his hands on his hips, adopting a mock-serious tone. "You don't 'pretend' to be a wizard, Caleb. You 'become' the wizard. It's about strategy, creativity, and, most importantly, teamwork. Plus, it's not all wizards. There are also warriors, rogues, and—" He stopped himself, realizing he was about to launch into a full lecture. "Anyway, it's not just some game. It's a way of life for some of us."

Caleb couldn't help but chuckle at the intensity in Henry's eyes. "Okay, okay, I get it. I'll try to keep an open mind. So, what kept you? You're usually the first one here when it comes to nerd—uh, I mean, D&D."

Henry hesitated, scratching the back of his head, clearly debating how to phrase his next words. "Well, funny story... I accidentally went on a date with Lila."

Caleb's eyes widened in disbelief. "You what?"

Henry quickly raised his hands in defense, his face

turning a shade of red. "It wasn't intentional, I swear! We were supposed to be part of a group of students going out, but everyone else bailed. It ended up just being us."

Caleb felt a hot surge of anger, his chest tightening as he struggled to keep it in check. "And you didn't think to tell me?"

Henry shrugged sheepishly, looking genuinely apologetic. "I didn't think it would end up like that. We just talked, that's all."

Caleb ran a hand through his hair, trying to process this unexpected revelation. "Talked? About what?"

"Everything, really," Henry admitted, his voice softening as he remembered the evening. "She's actually really cool, Caleb. I didn't know she was into the same music as us, and she's got this whole thing about surfing. We just clicked, I guess."

Caleb's mind raced, trying to piece together what this meant. He couldn't shake the jealousy gnawing at him, though he knew it wasn't fair. Henry was his friend, after all, and it wasn't like he had any claim over Lila. Still, the thought of them together—laughing, talking—stirred something uncomfortable inside him.

Henry, noticing Caleb's silence, quickly added, "But,

hey, she's single, man. I didn't get any vibe that she's interested in me that way. We're just friends. Promise."

Caleb forced a smile, though it felt weak and uncertain. "Yeah, okay. Thanks for letting me know. I guess I was just...surprised."

Henry nodded, relief washing over his face. "Don't worry about it. And hey, if you want, we can skip D&D tonight and just hang out. Talk about whatever's on your mind."

Caleb considered the offer, the tension in his chest easing slightly. He appreciated Henry's gesture, even if the idea of talking about Lila felt like picking at an open wound. But maybe that's what he needed—a friend who would listen, who would help him navigate the complicated emotions swirling inside him.

"Yeah, that sounds good," Caleb finally agreed, his voice steadier now. "But you're still going to have to teach me this whole Dungeons and Dragons thing at some point. I guess I owe it to you after all the teasing."

Henry grinned, his eyes lighting up. "Deal. And who knows? Maybe you'll end up loving it."

Caleb was lost in thought when a soft knock on the door pulled him back to reality. Henry opened it, revealing Lila standing in the hallway.

"Hey, Henry, you left your jacket," Lila said, her voice gentle and her smile warm. She held out the jacket, her eyes briefly meeting Caleb's before she turned her attention back to Henry.

Caleb's heart skipped a beat. Seeing Lila there outside his room, was a shock he hadn't anticipated. She looked even more radiant than he remembered, her presence a sudden burst of light in his otherwise heavy day. For a moment, he was frozen, caught between the comfort of familiarity and the shock of surprise.

Lila's eyes widened as they landed on Caleb. The last person she expected to encounter on campus was Caleb Morgan. She blinked, her expression a mix of confusion and delight.

Henry, sensing the palpable tension between them, quickly took the jacket from Lila and offered a reassuring smile. "Thanks, Lila. I'll leave you two to catch up." With a quick nod to Caleb, he slipped out of the room, leaving them alone.

Caleb took a deep breath, trying to steady his racing heart. "Lila, it's… good to see you. I didn't expect to run into you like this."

Lila tilted her head slightly, her curiosity evident. "I wasn't sure I'd ever see you again, Caleb. It's been a while."

Caleb chuckled softly, his nerves still apparent. "I have to admit, I saw you at orientation but didn't approach you. I didn't want to intrude or make things awkward."

A smile tugged at the corners of Lila's lips. "That's really thoughtful of you. But I'm glad we're talking now."

Caleb's eyes met hers, and for the first time in a long while, he felt a genuine connection. "So, what are you studying?" he asked, trying to shift the conversation to safer ground.

Lila's face lit up with enthusiasm. "I'm majoring in environmental science. I want to make a difference, you know? How about you?"

"Zoology," Caleb replied, a hint of mischief in his voice. "I guess I'm following in my father's footsteps of sorts, but instead of law, it's animals."

Lila laughed softly. "Well, I'm glad you didn't end up as a lawyer. We need more people like you working with animals."

Caleb grinned, relieved to see Lila smiling. "Yeah,

lawyers have enough trouble as it is. I've heard they can be quite the handful."

They shared a laugh, the sound easing the tension that had lingered in the room. Caleb felt a lightness he hadn't experienced in weeks. A comfortable silence settled between them as they both took a moment to process this unexpected reunion.

Caleb finally broke the silence, his voice softer. "I've missed our talks, Lila.."

Lila looked down, her fingers brushing the wall she stood next to. "I've missed it too. Sometimes I think about that summer... it feels like a lifetime ago."

Caleb nodded, a bittersweet smile forming on his lips. "Yeah, it does. We had some good times, didn't we?"

Lila glanced up at him, her eyes filled with a mix of nostalgia and warmth. "We did. Those were some of the best days of my life."

They began to reminisce, sharing memories of the adventures they had during that last summer. The more they talked, the more those old feelings resurfaced— feelings that had never really gone away.

This was the Lila he remembered, the one who had always seen through his defenses, who understood him in a way no one else ever had. And here they were, older, perhaps a bit wiser, but still connected by something neither of them could fully explain.

Lila's smile grew as she looked at him, her voice soft but sure. "You know, Caleb, I've changed a lot since then. But one thing hasn't changed—I still care about you."

Caleb felt a warmth spread through his chest, a flicker of hope sparking within him. "I care about you too, Lila. More than you know."

They stood in the quiet of the dorm room, the weight of the past slowly giving way to the possibilities of the present. It wasn't just about rekindling a friendship; it was about rebuilding something even stronger, something that could withstand the challenges of their lives.

"Hey, would you mind if I walked you back to your dorm?" Caleb asked, his voice hopeful.

Lila's eyes sparkled with appreciation. "I'd like that. It's been a long day, and I could use some company."

CHAPTER 21: THE LAST CHOICE

The stark reality of financial strain had become a constant companion in Caleb's life, an ever-present shadow that followed him through each day. The weight of student loans felt like a shackle around his ankles, but it was the relentless tide of daily expenses that truly wore him down. No matter how carefully he budgeted, there was always an unexpected cost—a textbook he hadn't planned for, an emergency repair, or just the ever-rising cost of living.

In the dimly lit confines of his small dorm room, Caleb sat hunched over his desk, the only light coming from a desk lamp that cast long, flickering shadows. His face was etched with worry, the lines of stress deepening with each passing day. The small room, cluttered with textbooks and worn-out furniture, felt like a prison of his own making. Caleb had taken on every odd job he could find, from late-night shifts at the local diner to weekend gigs washing cars. Yet, despite his relentless efforts, the money never seemed to stretch far enough.

Every day felt like a precarious balancing act, trying to keep up with his academic responsibilities while juggling the mounting pressures of financial instability. Caleb refused to burden his mother with his troubles. She was already weighed down by her own heartache, navigating the painful process of divorcing his father and rebuilding her life from scratch. He couldn't bring himself to add to her burdens, so he kept his struggles to himself, putting on a brave face even as his resolve began to wane.

Defeated, Caleb sat in a lecture hall, as his professor, Dr. Reynolds, spoke passionately about the importance of hands-on experience in veterinary medicine. The lecture hall was dimly lit, with the late afternoon sun casting long shadows across the rows of seats. Caleb sat near the back, his posture slumped and his gaze distant. The room was filled with the murmur of students half-listening, their attention divided between Dr. Reynolds and their own thoughts.

Dr. Reynolds stood at the front, his voice animated and full of passion. "Veterinary medicine isn't just about diagnosing and treating; it's about understanding and connecting with the animals you're working with. Hands-on experience is crucial. It's what bridges the gap between theory and practice."

Caleb's mind wandered, his thoughts a swirl of frustration and uncertainty. The weight of his own struggles had made it hard for him to focus on anything but the growing distance between him and his dream of becoming a veterinarian. But then Dr. Reynolds said something that cut through his haze of despair.

"We have several local vet clinics looking for part-time assistants," Dr. Reynolds continued, his eyes scanning the room. "These positions are a fantastic opportunity for you to gain real-world experience, and they're also a chance to see if this is truly the path you want to pursue."

Caleb's heart skipped a beat. The idea of working directly with animals, of stepping closer to his dream, felt like a beacon of hope in his otherwise challenging life. He leaned forward, his attention sharply focused on Dr. Reynolds.

A student near the front raised her hand, her voice filled with curiosity. "How can we apply for these positions? Do we need special qualifications?"

Dr. Reynolds nodded, a smile tugging at his lips. "Most of these clinics are looking for enthusiastic individuals who are willing to learn. It's less about having a long list of qualifications and more about showing your passion and commitment. I'll share the contact information and details with you all after class."

Caleb's fingers fidgeted with the edge of his notebook, his mind racing with possibilities. Could this be his chance to break free from the endless cycle of disappointment? Could this be the way to prove to himself—and to his parents—that he was more than just a name on a list of failed expectations?

Another student spoke up, their voice tinged with skepticism. "But what if we're already swamped with coursework? How are we supposed to find time for this?"

Dr. Reynolds's expression grew serious. "It's all about balancing your priorities. If this is truly your passion, you'll find a way. It's about making choices and sometimes sacrifices to pursue what you love."

Caleb thought about his own struggles, the endless cycle of trying to meet expectations and feeling like he was falling short. The idea of working at a clinic seemed like a lifeline, a way to reconnect with the joy he once felt when he first dreamed of becoming a veterinarian.

After class, Caleb made his way to Dr. Reynolds' office, the excitement of a potential opportunity giving him a brief respite from his worries. He knocked lightly on the door and entered, finding the professor at his desk, surrounded by stacks of papers and veterinary journals.

"Dr. Reynolds, can I talk to you for a moment?" Caleb asked, his voice tinged with a mix of hope and nervousness.

Dr. Reynolds looked up from his papers, his expression warm and encouraging. "Of course, Caleb. What's on your mind?"

"I heard you mention that some local vet clinics are looking for part-time assistants," Caleb began, trying to keep his voice steady. "I'm really interested in applying. Do you have any advice on where I should start?"

The professor's eyes lit up with approval. "That's great to hear, Caleb. Gaining experience at a clinic is invaluable. I'd recommend starting with the clinics I mentioned. They're reputable and provide excellent training. Here's a list of a few that are currently hiring. I can also put in a good word for you if you'd like."

Caleb felt a wave of relief wash over him, grateful for the professor's support. "Thank you so much, Dr. Reynolds. I really appreciate it."

As Caleb left the professor's office, clutching the list of clinics, he felt a glimmer of hope for the first time in weeks. The prospect of working at a vet clinic not only offered a chance to earn some much-needed income but also brought him one step closer to his dream. It was a small light in the darkness, a reminder that even amid struggle, there were opportunities for growth and change.

Back in his dorm room, Caleb took a deep breath,

feeling the weight of his worries momentarily lift. He knew the road ahead would still be fraught with challenges, but for now, he allowed himself a moment of quiet optimism. The prospect of a new beginning was just what he needed to keep pushing forward, holding on to the hope that one day, his dreams would finally become his reality.

Despite the whirlwind of responsibilities that came with his new role as a veterinary assistant, Caleb found solace in the support he received from Lila. Their relationship, having rekindled, was now a beacon of genuine connection and understanding. Lila, juggling her own scholarship and part-time job on campus, navigated the challenges of university life with a resilience that resonated deeply with Caleb. Their shared experiences became the foundation of a bond that felt both comforting and transformative.

One afternoon, as Caleb hunched over his textbooks in the dimly lit library, Lila noticed the strain etched into his features. She slipped into the chair beside him, her presence a silent promise of solace amidst the chaos.

"Hey," she said softly, her hand gently resting on his shoulder. "You look like you're carrying the weight of the world."

Caleb looked up, his tired eyes meeting hers. A faint, weary smile tugged at his lips. "Just trying to keep up. It's hard to focus on studying when there's so much else going on."

Lila's eyes softened with empathy. "I get it. It's tough, but we'll get through it. You're not alone in this. We're a team, remember?"

Their support for each other extended far beyond the library walls. They became each other's anchors during late-night study sessions and emotional upheavals, sharing both the burdens and joys of their academic and personal lives. Lila's encouragement was a balm for Caleb's weary spirit, her unwavering belief in him lighting a path through his self-doubt.

As their relationship blossomed, they made a conscious decision to embrace their renewed romance openly. They walked hand-in-hand through campus, their affection evident to everyone around them. The whispers and sidelong glances that had once marked their love now seemed like distant echoes, overshadowed by their shared sense of joy and belonging.

Yet, with this newfound closeness came the necessity for balance. Lila, deeply committed to their relationship, was determined to ensure that their love did not eclipse their academic ambitions. She knew that they both needed to excel in their studies while nurturing their bond.

One evening, as they sat together in their favorite café, Lila laid out a plan to help them maintain that balance. Her tone was gentle but resolute, her eyes filled with both determination and affection.

"Caleb," she began, "I know how much we both care about each other and our goals. But we need to make sure we don't lose sight of what's important."

Caleb nodded, sensing the gravity in her voice. "What do you have in mind?"

Lila took a deep breath, her gaze steady. "Let's set some clear boundaries. We'll designate specific times, so we don't let our relationship overshadow our individual goals. We'll have dedicated study sessions, and we'll make sure to respect each other's time and space when we need to focus."

Caleb listened, his heart swelling with gratitude for her thoughtfulness. "That sounds fair. I'm really lucky to have you by my side, Lila."

She smiled, her hand reaching across the table to squeeze his. "And I'm lucky to have you. We're a team, remember? We just need to keep supporting each other and keep our priorities straight."

As they worked together to implement their plan, Caleb felt a renewed sense of purpose. Lila's commitment to their relationship, coupled with her unwavering dedication to their academic success, provided a steady rhythm to their lives. They balanced love and ambition with grace, finding strength in each other's presence and navigating the complexities of their journey with a shared resolve.

In the midst of their struggles and triumphs, Caleb and Lila discovered that love wasn't just about being together—it was about supporting each other through the highs and lows, and growing stronger together. Their relationship, once fragile and uncertain, had become a source of profound strength and inspiration, guiding them through the challenges of their lives.

Thanksgiving approached, and Lila extended an invitation to Caleb. "I'd love for you to come with me to the Hamptons," she said, her voice tinged with both excitement and warmth. "My dad would be thrilled to see you again."

Caleb's heart lifted at the thought of spending the holiday with Lila and Mr. Hayes. The idea of returning to a place where he had once felt a sense of belonging was comforting. He accepted with a grateful nod, looking forward to the opportunity to reconnect with

Lila's father.

After class, Caleb slumped into his dorm room chair and dialed his mother's number on his laptop. Evelyn answered almost immediately, her face appearing with a warm, reassuring smile that Caleb always found comforting.

"Hi, Mom," he said, trying to muster enthusiasm.

"Caleb!" Evelyn's voice was a soothing balm, despite the distance between them. "It's so good to see you."

Before Caleb could say more, Henry, his roommate, peeked over Caleb's shoulder. His eyes widened at the sight of Evelyn. "Is that your mom?" he whispered loudly, his eyes lingering on the screen.

Caleb rolled his eyes and gave Henry a light shove. "Yes, that's her. Why don't you give us a moment?"

Henry grinned, not deterred. "I just want to say hi. Hi, Mrs. Morgan! I'm Henry. Caleb's told me so much about you!"

Evelyn laughed softly, her gaze warm and welcoming. "Hello, Henry. Nice to meet you."

As Henry continued to fawn over Evelyn, Caleb kicked him out of the room with a playful but firm push.

"Okay, Henry, time to give us some privacy!"

Once Henry was out, Caleb focused on his mother's face. "Sorry about that. He's quite the character."

"It's alright," Evelyn said, chuckling. "It's nice to see you're making friends. How's everything?"

Caleb shrugged, trying to seem more upbeat than he felt. "I've been a bit busy. But I'm finding my footing."

Evelyn's eyes softened with concern. "I'm sorry to hear that. I wish I could be there to support you more. But listen, I've been working on myself. I've been seeing a psychic lately, and she said something old is going to come back into my life."

Caleb raised an eyebrow, skeptical but intrigued. "Really? That sounds... interesting. But I'm glad to hear you're doing well. Are you feeling better?"

"Much better," Evelyn said, her eyes bright with a new sense of purpose. "The divorce is finally settled. Your father had the good sense to settle out of court, so that's behind us now. I'm going on a cruise for Thanksgiving. I need some time to myself."

Caleb nodded, appreciating her honesty. "That sounds like it'll be good for you. I'll be spending Thanksgiving with Lila and her father at the Hamptons. It's a nice change of pace."

Evelyn's smile grew wider. "That's wonderful. I'm glad you're finding some peace and connection. And who knows? Maybe that psychic's prediction means something good is on the horizon for you too."

Caleb smiled faintly, the weight of his worries lifting slightly with his mother's words. "I hope so. Thanks for the encouragement, Mom."

"Anytime, sweetheart. Just remember, no matter what happens, you've got people who care about you. And I'm always just a call away."

As they finished their call, Caleb felt a strange mix of relief and melancholy. His mother's support was a beacon in his turbulent world, but he knew he had to navigate his own path, step by step, through the uncertainties that lay ahead.

The crisp autumn air of the Hamptons greeted Caleb and Lila as they drove up to the familiar streets, its white facade glowing warmly in the early evening light. Caleb felt a flicker of excitement, a rare spark in the midst of his ongoing struggle. Lila's invitation to spend Thanksgiving at Mr. Hayes' home had been a beacon of comfort, a chance to reconnect with the warmth and acceptance he had once known.

As they stepped out of the car, Mr. Hayes was already at the door, his face lighting up with a smile that seemed to erase years of Caleb's self-doubt. "Welcome back, Caleb!" Mr. Hayes said, his voice full of genuine warmth. He gave Caleb a hearty hug, a gesture that spoke volumes more than words ever could. "It's good to see you, son."

"Thank you for having me," Caleb said, his voice tinged with relief. "I've missed this place."

Mr. Hayes clapped him on the back. "We've missed you too. Come on in. Dinner's almost ready, and there's plenty of it."

Inside, the house was a flurry of activity. The scent of roasted turkey, cinnamon, and freshly baked pies filled the air, mingling with the crackling warmth from the fireplace. Caleb and Lila rolled up their sleeves and joined Mr. Hayes in the kitchen, where the old man was preparing the finishing touches.

As they sat down for dinner, the table was a spread of all the traditional Thanksgiving fare. Mr. Hayes raised his glass, his eyes twinkling with affection. "To old friends and new beginnings," he toasted, his voice thick with emotion.

Caleb's heart swelled with gratitude as he clinked his

glass against theirs. The warmth of the room, the kindness of the people around him, made him feel a sense of belonging he had been missing. He looked around at the people who had made him feel like family, and for the first time in a long while, he felt a genuine smile tugging at his lips.

Over dinner, they shared stories of past Thanksgivings, their voices blending with the clinking of silverware and the soft hum of the fireplace. Caleb found himself relaxing, the tension in his shoulders easing as he reveled in the simple joy of being with people who truly cared for him.

As the evening wound down, Caleb helped Mr. Hayes clear the table. They worked side by side, their conversation turning to more personal matters.

"Lila tells me you've been having a rough time lately," Mr. Hayes said quietly, his tone reflecting genuine concern. "Anything you want to talk about?"

Caleb hesitated, the weight of his unspoken troubles pressing down on him. He appreciated Mr. Hayes' concern but felt a pang of embarrassment. "It's just been... a lot. School's been tough, and I've been dealing with some family stuff."

Mr. Hayes nodded, his eyes filled with understanding. "You know, we all have our battles. It's okay to lean on the people who care about you. That's what family is for."

Caleb looked at Mr. Hayes, feeling a surge of appreciation for his kindness. "Thanks. It means a lot."

Later that night, Caleb and Lila wandered along the beach, their footsteps leaving fleeting impressions in the sand. The rhythmic murmur of the waves and the soft crunch of sand beneath their feet created a soothing rhythm, a gentle contrast to the turmoil that often roiled within Caleb's heart. The moonlight cast a silvery sheen across the water, illuminating their path as they moved in silence, each lost in their thoughts but comforted by the other's presence.

The cool night air wrapped around them, a crisp reminder of the season's change, yet it seemed to breathe life into their weary souls rather than chill them. The sea breeze carried with it the scent of salt and freedom, mingling with the whispers of their dreams and fears as they spoke of their futures and their pasts.

They eventually found a secluded spot on the sand, a place where the world seemed to disappear, leaving just the two of them under the expansive sky. They settled down, their bodies pressing close together as they lay on the soft blanket of sand.

The stars above shone brightly, like distant promises of hope, their twinkling lights casting a gentle glow on their faces. The waves' lullaby became a backdrop to their shared silence.

Lila nestled closer, her head resting against Caleb's shoulder. Her breath was warm against his skin, and for a moment, the weight of the world seemed to lift. "I'm really glad you're here," she whispered, her voice tender and sincere. The vulnerability in her words mirrored the openness of the night sky above them.

Caleb looked down at her, his heart swelling with a mix of gratitude and affection. "Me too," he said softly, his voice carrying the depth of his emotions. "Thank you for everything. For being here, for understanding."

Lila's eyes met his, and in that gaze, they found a shared understanding of their struggles and their hopes. The space between them seemed to dissolve as Caleb gently cupped her face in his hands.

He leaned in, and as their lips met in a kiss, it was as though the world outside their small bubble of intimacy ceased to exist. The kiss was slow and tender, an unspoken promise that even amid their troubles, they had each other.

When they finally broke apart, their faces were flushed,

and their breaths mingled in the cool night air. They lay back against the sand, their fingers intertwined, feeling the warmth and security of each other's presence. The vast expanse of the universe seemed to embrace them, offering a moment of peace amidst the chaos of their lives.

"I'm sorry," Caleb said, his voice heavy with emotion. "I hurt you back then."

"Caleb," Lila said, her eyes brimming with tears, "you have nothing to apologize for. I know I must have hurt you too."

"You mean so much to me," he murmured, his voice trembling. "I don't want to hurt you ever again."

"We would never," she whispered, her hands gently caressing his face. "I love you, Caleb."

He held her close, his heart racing. "I love you, too."

"Promise me you'll always be there for me," she said, her voice breaking.

"Always," he vowed, his eyes burning with intensity. "I'll never leave your side."

Under the sheltering sky, their hearts found solace in the shared comfort of their love. The darkness of the night was less intimidating with Lila by his side, her presence a guiding light that made the world seem a little brighter, even in the face of their fears.

CHAPTER 22: THE LAST SUMMER

Caleb sat on the edge of his bed, the shadows of the room playing across the walls. His phone buzzed softly on the nightstand, the screen illuminating his face with a cold, blue light. A missed call from his father, Senator Thomas Morgan, stared back at him like an unspoken challenge. Caleb had ignored it, unable to muster the courage to address the strained relationship that had grown between them. The unresolved tension felt like a heavy weight, one he wasn't ready to lift.

He tossed the phone aside and tried to focus on the distraction he had planned for the evening: a game of Dungeons & Dragons with Henry and two new recruits from across the hall. The game had always been a way for Caleb to escape his reality, to immerse himself in a world where he could be anyone but himself.

The door to his dorm room creaked open, and Henry, with his ever-present enthusiasm, burst in, holding a box of snacks. "Ready to slay some dragons, Caleb? I've got pretzels and soda to keep us fueled!"

"Absolutely," Caleb replied, forcing a smile as he grabbed a handful of pretzels.

The two new recruits, Jake and Riley, followed Henry in. Jake was tall and lanky, with a mop of curly hair that seemed perpetually in need of a trim. Riley was shorter, with a mischievous grin that suggested he was always up to something.

"Alright, everyone, gather around," Caleb said, spreading out the game board on his desk. "Tonight, we're taking on the dragon of Doomspire. This will be our greatest quest yet!"

Henry plopped down beside Caleb, adjusting his dice tray. "Just hope Doomspire's not as unforgiving as your last campaign. I'm still recovering from that trap we walked into."

"Oh, come on," Jake chimed in, grabbing a handful of chips. "That was your fault for trying to pick the lock with a spoon!"

Riley laughed, leaning back in his chair. "And let's not forget how you tried to convince us that the dragon was just a big lizard. We're lucky to be alive!"

Caleb couldn't help but chuckle at the banter. The laughter was a balm to his troubled mind, a brief escape from the heaviness of his life. The game unfolded with its usual mix of strategy and ridiculousness, the boys getting increasingly animated as they navigated their imaginary world.

"Okay, so you're standing in front of the dragon's lair," Caleb narrated, his voice taking on the dramatic flair of a seasoned Dungeon Master. "The air is thick with the smell of sulfur, and the ground trembles beneath your feet."

Henry's character, a burly warrior named Thorne, brandished his sword dramatically. "Thorne is ready! I'm going to charge in and confront the dragon head-on!"

Jake, playing a rogue with a knack for trouble, frowned. "Uh, can we maybe think this through first? You know, like, a plan or something?"

Riley's wizard, with a flair for the theatrical, threw his arms up. "No plans! We charge in and hope for the best! It's more fun that way!"

As the game continued, the boys' laughter filled the room, a welcome distraction from Caleb's internal struggle. Each roll of the dice brought new challenges, new victories, and new opportunities to bond over shared triumphs and failures.

The night wore on, and Caleb found himself sinking deeper into the fantasy world, the problems of his real life momentarily pushed to the periphery. The camaraderie with Henry, Jake, and Riley was a comforting reminder that, even in the midst of his personal turmoil, he still had moments of joy and connection.

When the game finally wound down, and the new recruits headed back to their rooms, Caleb and Henry sat together in the quiet aftermath. Caleb felt a pang of gratitude for the normalcy that Henry and the game provided.

"You know," Henry said, stretching his arms, "I didn't think we'd get anywhere near the dragon tonight. But we did pretty well."

"Yeah, we did," Caleb agreed, his voice softer. "Thanks for being here tonight, Henry. It means a lot."

Henry looked at him, his expression sincere. "Anytime, man. That's what friends are for, right?"

Caleb nodded, feeling a flicker of warmth in his chest. For now, he had managed to push aside the weight of his father's call and the unresolved issues that lingered between them. As he lay down to sleep, he was reminded of the simple pleasures of friendship and the small victories that made his burdens feel a little lighter.

But after days of tossing and turning, haunted

by restless nights and endless deliberation, Caleb decided it was time to pick up the phone. The ache in his chest was relentless, a constant reminder of the fractured relationship with his father. He hoped that perhaps a conversation might bridge the chasm that had grown between them. He dialed the number, his heart pounding with each ring, until Thomas's voice crackled through the receiver.

"Caleb, it's good to hear from you," Thomas began, his tone smooth but strangely detached. "I've been doing a lot of thinking about our family lately. Maybe it's time we talk about putting things right."

Caleb braced himself, trying to ignore the edge of rehearsed politeness in his father's voice. "Yeah, I guess we should. I've been dealing with a lot lately, and I think we need to clear the air."

Thomas's voice took on a casual, almost too relaxed tone. "I hear you. You know, I've been considering how important family is, especially in times like these. And with the media storm I'm about to face, it might be a good opportunity for you to get involved."

Caleb's stomach churned. "Involved in what exactly?"

"Well," Thomas said, a hint of strategic enthusiasm creeping into his voice, "I've got this big media interview coming up. It's a chance to rebuild my image, and having you there—studying to become an animal doctor, no less—could really show a different side of the Morgan family. It'd do you good too, to be part of something that might boost your future."

The words stung. Caleb could hear the thin veneer of concern covering his father's true motivation. "So, this is about the media? You're asking me to be part of your public relations effort?"

Thomas's voice faltered for a moment. "Caleb, it's not just about the media. It's about reconnecting, making things right. We haven't spoken in so long, and I want to make amends."

Caleb's disappointment grew, like a weight settling heavily on his shoulders. "I appreciate that you want to reconnect, but it sounds like you're more interested in how this will look for you rather than how I'm doing."

Thomas's silence spoke volumes. "That's not fair. I do care about you, Caleb."

"I think it's clear what this is really about," Caleb said, his voice gaining strength. "You've been more concerned with your image and your own problems than actually being there for me. You hurt Mom, you've shattered our family, and now you want to use me to fix your public image?"

Thomas's voice grew defensive. "I made mistakes, Caleb. I'm trying to make amends. This isn't easy for me either."

Caleb's heart ached with a mix of sadness and frustration. "I see now that nothing's changed. You're still manipulating situations to serve your own interests. I can't be part of that."

There was a heavy pause on the other end of the line before Thomas finally spoke. "Caleb, please—"

"I think it's best if we leave things as they are," Caleb said firmly as he ended the call with his father, feeling a curious blend of relief and sorrow.

The conversation had been brief, his father's words hollow and uninspiring. Caleb stared at the phone in his hand, the weight of his father's disappointment and manipulations heavy in the air. It was clear now that his father hadn't changed, nor did it seem likely that he ever would. The realization settled on Caleb like a heavy cloak. He knew he had to forge his own path, one far removed from the shadows of his father's expectations.

Seeking clarity, Caleb decided to visit his mother in New York for the weekend. The city's vibrant chaos was a stark contrast to the internal turmoil he had been wrestling with. As he stepped off the train and into the city's embrace, he felt a rush of relief. The familiar hum of New York was both overwhelming and soothing, a reminder that life continued, regardless of his personal struggles.

When he arrived at his mother's new apartment, the warm aroma of freshly brewed coffee welcomed him, mingling with the faint strains of classical music playing softly in the background. Evelyn opened the door, her eyes lighting up with a mix of surprise and joy. Her apartment, though modest, radiated a cozy charm that made Caleb feel instantly at home.

"Oh Caleb, it's so good to see you!" Evelyn exclaimed, pulling him into a warm hug. "I wasn't expecting you this weekend."

Caleb smiled, feeling the tension in his chest ease slightly. "I needed a change of scenery. And I wanted to see you."

As he settled in, he found comfort in Millie, his beloved cat, who immediately took to rubbing against his legs and purring contentedly. Caleb sank into the softness of the couch, his heart lightening with each playful swipe of Millie's paw and each soothing purr.

Evelyn joined him, pouring two cups of coffee. "I'm glad you came. You know, you always have a place here with me. No matter what's happening out there, this is your home too."

Caleb nodded, taking a deep breath as he sipped his coffee. The warmth of the drink mirrored the warmth of his mother's words. "Thanks, Mom. I needed to hear that."

As the evening progressed, Caleb and Evelyn sat in the cozy living room, bathed in the soft glow of lamps and the gentle hum of the city outside. Caleb took a deep breath and ventured into a more difficult subject. "Have you heard from Dad lately?"

Evelyn's face tightened for a moment before she spoke. "I haven't. I actually got a restraining order against him. He's not allowed to contact me anymore. It was the only way I could find some peace. I'm sorry, Caleb. I know it must be hard to deal with."

Caleb looked down at his coffee, feeling a pang of sympathy for his mother. "I understand. It's just... it's hard to reconcile who he was with who he is now. It's like there's no middle ground."

Evelyn reached over, placing a comforting hand on his arm. "It's okay to let go of him, Caleb. You don't have to carry that burden alone. You deserve to find your own happiness, just like I'm trying to."

Caleb felt a renewed sense of determination as he

absorbed his mother's words. He knew now that cutting ties with his father wasn't just necessary; it was liberating. It was a difficult decision, but one that gave him a sense of freedom he hadn't felt in years.

Changing the subject, Evelyn asked, "So, how are things going with Lila? I remember you mentioning her a while ago."

Caleb's face softened with a genuine smile. "She's... she's more than just a girlfriend to me. She's been amazing. Through everything, she's been there, helping me see the good and pushing me to be better. I can't imagine my life without her."

Evelyn's eyes sparkled with warmth and understanding. "It sounds like you've found someone truly special. And you deserve that. I'm glad to hear that she's been a source of strength for you."

That weekend in New York had been a source of clarity for Caleb's disturbed soul. For the first time in what felt like forever, Caleb found a fleeting sense of peace. The days passed in a soothing routine—long walks through Central Park, coffee at his favorite café, and evenings spent curled up with a book as the city hummed quietly outside. The noise, the chaos, the overwhelming pressures of his college life—they all seemed to fade into the background, replaced by the steady, familiar rhythm of home.

In those moments, Caleb began to see his life with fresh eyes. He realized that perhaps the future didn't have to be as bleak as it seemed. There was a glimmer of hope, a possibility that the shadows he had been navigating might one day give way to something brighter.

But even as he savored these moments of clarity, Caleb knew there was unfinished business to attend to before he could truly move forward.

On the day he was set to leave, Caleb made his way to his father's office. The towering building loomed above him, as imposing and cold as Thomas Morgan himself. The familiar dread settled in his stomach, but Caleb had made a decision. This would be the last time he let his father's presence cast a shadow over his life.

When he walked into the office, Caleb found his father seated behind his massive mahogany desk, papers scattered around him in a chaotic fashion that somehow still seemed meticulously organized. Thomas looked up, and for a brief moment, Caleb saw something in his father's eyes that he hadn't seen before—fatigue, maybe even a trace of regret. But the moment passed quickly, replaced by the same calculating gaze Caleb had known all his life.

"Caleb," Thomas greeted him with a nod, as if they were mere acquaintances rather than father and son. "What brings you here? Need some money?"

Caleb shook his head. "No, I don't need money."

Thomas leaned back in his chair, his expression unreadable. "You know, I was hoping we could do that interview together. It would be good for both of us."

"I'm not here for an interview," Caleb said, his voice steady. He took a deep breath, steadying himself for what he needed to say. "I'm here to tell you that I forgive you."

Thomas's brow furrowed slightly, a flicker of confusion crossing his face. "Forgive me? For what?"

"For what you did to Milo," Caleb replied, his tone firm but not unkind.

A sneer curled at the edge of Thomas's lips, his eyes narrowing in mockery. "I didn't do anything to that dog. He was your dog and he ran off into the street. He should have been on a leash. You were the one who messed up, Caleb."

There it was—the manipulation, the twisting of truth that had defined so much of their relationship. But

Caleb had come prepared this time. He wasn't the same boy who had once been crushed under the weight of his father's words. He was stronger now, more resolute.

"You can tell yourself that if it helps you sleep at night," Caleb said, his voice calm but resolute. "But we both know the truth. Milo ran off because you scared him. You were angry, and you didn't care who got hurt in the process. But I'm not here to argue with you about it."

Thomas opened his mouth to protest, but Caleb held up a hand, stopping him. "No, just listen. Milo is gone, and nothing can bring him back. And as much as it hurt, I've made my peace with that. I'm forgiving you, not because you deserve it, but because I need to move on. I need to let go of the anger, the pain… all of it."

For the first time, Thomas seemed to falter. His eyes flickered with something—uncertainty, perhaps even fear. But it was fleeting, gone as quickly as it had appeared. "Caleb, I—"

But Caleb wasn't finished. "I forgive you, Dad, but that doesn't mean things can go back to the way they were. I need to live my own life, without your shadow hanging over me. So, this is it. I don't want to see you again."

The words hung in the air, heavy with finality. Caleb could see the shock in his father's eyes, the disbelief that his son—his son—could be standing here, telling him this. But Caleb didn't waver. He had said what he needed to say, and now it was time to walk away.

Without another word, Caleb turned and walked out of the office, leaving his father behind. The door closed with a soft click, and with it, Caleb felt a weight lift off his shoulders. The past, with all its pain and anger, was behind him now. And as he stepped out into the bustling streets of New York, he felt something he hadn't felt in a long time—a sense of freedom, of possibility.

Returning to college, Caleb felt the weight of his past decisions and the burden of his hidden struggles pressing down on him. As he walked through the campus, the faces of his peers seemed to blur together, a reminder of how isolated he felt. The secret he had carried with him, the darkness he had fought alone, now loomed larger than ever. He knew he couldn't keep it hidden from Lila any longer.

In the hallway, Caleb's eyes met Lila's. He saw the concern etched on her face as she approached him. Her gaze, full of unspoken questions, made his heart ache.

"Caleb, you've been so distant lately," Lila said, her voice soft but firm. "What's going on? You can talk to me."

Caleb hesitated, his emotions swirling inside him. He took a deep breath, his resolve hardening. "I promise I'll tell you everything. Let's meet after class."

Later, in the quiet privacy of Caleb's dorm room, the air was thick with anticipation. The room, cluttered with textbooks and scattered notes, felt strangely intimate as they sat together. Caleb's gaze wandered around the room, finally settling on Lila.

"Lila, there's something I need to tell you," Caleb began, his voice trembling. "That summer... I planned to end my life. It was the darkest time for me, and I didn't know if I could keep going."

Lila's eyes widened, a mixture of shock and concern flooding her features. She reached out and took Caleb's hand, her touch both comforting and grounding. "Caleb, why didn't you tell me?"

Caleb looked down, the weight of his confession heavy on his shoulders. "I was afraid. But... you saved me from the ocean. Your presence, your kindness—it gave me a reason to keep going. Losing Milo took me to a place I didn't think I'd ever escape. I felt like I was drowning in my own darkness."

Lila's expression softened, her eyes full of empathy. "Caleb, deep down, I knew something wasn't right. I could see the pain in you, even if you tried to hide it. I wanted to be there for you, to offer whatever support I could. If I hadn't met you, I wouldn't have found the courage to leave the Hamptons, to follow my own path. You've been a part of my strength, too."

Caleb looked into Lila's eyes, feeling the depth of their connection. The vulnerability and raw honesty between them made his heart race. "I don't have a ring yet, but I want to ask you to marry me. I promise to give you the best of my future."

Lila's eyes filled with tears, her emotions spilling over. She nodded, her voice choked with emotion. "Yes, Caleb. Yes."

In the months that followed, Caleb and Lila began to weave their dreams together. The shared vision of their future became their guiding light. Lila's sharp mind for economics and Caleb's unwavering commitment to becoming a veterinarian formed the foundation of their plans.

After classes they would sit together in his dorm room, at a small table covered with plans and charts. Lila's enthusiasm was infectious as she explained her ideas.

"So, if we set up the clinic in this area, it'll be close to the university and accessible to the community. I've mapped out the costs and projected income, and with your skills, I'm confident it'll be a success."

Caleb listened, his heart swelling with admiration. "You've thought of everything. I'm so grateful for your support. I don't think I'd have had the courage to chase this dream without you."

Lila smiled, her eyes twinkling with excitement. "And I wouldn't have had the courage to leave my past behind without you. We're building something special together, Caleb. It's more than just a future; it's a new beginning."

Caleb and Lila had spent countless hours together, their lives becoming a beautiful tapestry woven with shared dreams and plans. They had navigated through the stormy seas of their past, weathering heartaches and misunderstandings that had only strengthened their bond. Now, their love was no longer just a fleeting emotion—it was a partnership built on hope, mutual aspirations, and the deep understanding that they were each other's safe harbor in a world filled with uncertainty.

One evening, they found themselves in Caleb's dorm room, the space dimly lit by the warm glow of a bedside lamp. It was their sanctuary, a place where they could escape the outside world and just be together. Lila was curled up beside him, her head resting on his chest, listening to the steady rhythm of his heartbeat. Caleb's hand gently traced circles on her back, the simple motion bringing them both comfort.

"You know," Lila murmured, her voice soft and full of affection, "I love nights like this. Just the two of us, no distractions. It's like the world fades away, and it's just you and me."

Caleb smiled, his fingers stilling for a moment as he took in her words. "Me too," he replied, his voice low and tender. "These moments are everything to me. Sometimes, I feel like we're the only real thing in a world that doesn't make sense."

Lila lifted her head slightly, looking up at him with those bright eyes that always seemed to see straight through him. "What do you mean?"

Caleb hesitated, searching for the right words. "I guess… I mean, when I'm with you, I feel like I'm exactly where I'm supposed to be. Everything else— school, my family, the expectations—it all just fades away. With you, I don't have to pretend. I can just be me."

A soft smile touched Lila's lips as she reached up to brush a strand of hair from his forehead. "And that's the person I fell in love with. The real you. Not the Caleb everyone else sees, but the one who's kind, thoughtful, and a little bit of a dork," she teased, her smile widening.

Caleb chuckled, the sound vibrating in his chest. "Only a little bit?"

Lila laughed, the sound like music to his ears. "Okay, maybe more than a little."

Their laughter faded into a comfortable silence, each of them lost in their thoughts. After a while, Caleb shifted slightly, his mind drifting back to memories of a simpler time. "You know," he began, a hint of nostalgia in his voice, "I miss my old truck."

Lila looked up at him, a curious smile on her face. "Your truck? The one you had back in New York?"

"Yeah," Caleb said, his eyes distant as he remembered. "It was this old beat-up thing, nothing fancy, but it had character, you know? I drove it everywhere. It was my escape when things got tough. I'd just get in, drive out of the city, and keep going until I felt like I could breathe again."

Lila nodded, understanding the sentiment. "I get that. There's something about the freedom of the open road, like you're leaving all your problems behind."

Caleb smiled, his eyes softening as he looked down at her. "Exactly. That truck saw me through a lot of stuff. It was my constant when everything else was changing."

Lila's smile turned playful. "So, what happened to it? Why'd you sell it?"

Caleb chuckled, a bit sheepishly. "Well, you won't believe this, but I sold the truck back to the same guy I bought it from."

Lila's eyes widened in surprise, and then she burst out laughing. "Wait, seriously? How does that even happen?"

Caleb grinned, his laughter mixing with hers. "I know, right? The guy couldn't believe it either. I guess he missed the old thing just as much as I did, so when I decided to sell, he jumped at the chance. It felt like I was closing a chapter, but… sometimes I wish I hadn't."

Lila's laughter softened into a gentle smile. "Maybe it was meant to be. Besides, now you've got me instead of that old truck."

Caleb's expression softened, and he leaned down to press a tender kiss to her forehead. "And I wouldn't trade you for a hundred trucks."

Lila raised an eyebrow, her curiosity piqued. "Really? Is that all you got for your truck?"

Caleb's grin was sheepish. "I bought it for five hundred bucks and sold it for two hundred."

Lila burst into laughter, her eyes sparkling with amusement. "You're seriously the worst negotiator I've ever met. I'm so glad I'm here to handle all the numbers."

Caleb joined in her laughter, the sound a balm for his troubled soul. He pulled her into a warm embrace, their faces inches apart. "Well, at least I'm lucky to have you to make up for my lack of bargaining skills."

Before she could respond, Caleb's playful side took over. With a sudden surge of energy, he tackled Lila onto the other side, their laughter mingling as they fell into a heap of tangled limbs and affection.

They stayed like that for a while, wrapped up in each other and the quiet peace that came from knowing they were exactly where they were meant to be. They talked about the future, their plans blending seamlessly with their love. Whether it was traveling the world, building a life together, or simply finding joy in the little things, every dream felt more real, more possible, because they were dreams they shared.

Years later, as their college life drew to a close, Caleb and Lila found themselves walking side by side along a bustling public beach near their campus. The vibrant energy of the place contrasted sharply with the quiet, reflective mood that had settled between them. The air was thick with the scent of saltwater and sunscreen, while the sounds of laughter and crashing waves wove into a familiar, comforting backdrop.

For both Caleb and Lila, this beach held none of the charm or memories that the Hamptons did, yet it had become their refuge in a time of change. It was here, amidst the noise and chaos of their final days of college, that they found themselves reminiscing about the summer that had changed everything.

"Remember that time I tried to teach you to surf?" Lila's voice was filled with a playful challenge, her eyes sparkling as she glanced at Caleb. "You were so convinced you could master it in a day."

Caleb chuckled, his laugh low and warm. "How could I forget? I spent more time falling into the water than actually standing on the board."

Lila grinned, her teasing smile a balm to the bittersweet emotions that lingered between them. "You were so stubborn. But hey, you did manage to ride one wave before wiping out."

"One wave," Caleb repeated with a mock-serious nod. "But that one wave was legendary."

They shared a quiet laugh, the kind that comes from years of shared experiences, the kind that holds within it the comfort of knowing someone deeply. Without a word, Lila suddenly darted ahead, grabbing her surfboard from where it lay in the sand. Caleb watched as she ran toward the water, her laughter floating back to him like music on the breeze.

He followed at a slower pace, savoring the sight of her as she paddled out to catch a wave. Lila had always been a natural in the water, her movements graceful and sure, as if she were born to dance on the waves. He admired the way she fit so perfectly into this world of surf and sea, a world that had once been so foreign to him.

As he reached the shoreline, Caleb sat down in the sand, letting the cool grains sift through his fingers. He watched as Lila caught a wave, standing effortlessly on her board, her hair whipping around her face like a wild halo. There was something freeing about seeing her like this, in her element, where she belonged.

After a few runs, Lila returned to shore, breathless and

exhilarated. She flopped down beside him, still dripping with saltwater, and they sat in comfortable silence for a moment, watching the horizon where the sun would soon begin its descent.

"Let's build a sandcastle," Lila said suddenly, her tone light but her eyes serious.

Caleb raised an eyebrow, a smirk playing on his lips. "A sandcastle? We're not kids anymore, Lila."

She nudged him playfully. "So what? It's our last summer before everything changes. Let's just... be kids for a little while longer."

He couldn't argue with that. Together, they began to scoop up handfuls of sand, shaping and molding it into a castle. It wasn't an impressive structure by any means, but it was theirs. Lila added intricate details—tiny windows, a moat filled with seawater, and even a flag made from a stray piece of seaweed. Caleb focused on the towers, making them as tall and strong as he could.

They worked in companionable silence, the sounds of the beach fading into the background as they lost themselves in the simple, pure joy of creating something together. For a brief moment, it felt like time had slowed, allowing them to hold on to this feeling just a little bit longer.

When the castle was finished, they sat back and admired their handiwork. It wasn't perfect—far from it. The towers leaned slightly, the moat was uneven, and the drawbridge was nothing more than a piece of driftwood they had found nearby.

It was imperfect, but it held a beauty that came from the love and care they had put into it. Just like their relationship, Caleb thought, it wasn't without its flaws, but it was theirs, and that made it perfect in its own way.

The sun began its slow descent toward the horizon, casting a warm, golden glow over the water. The sky was a canvas of oranges, pinks, and purples, blending together in a breathtaking display that only nature could create. Caleb sighed, his gaze fixed on the horizon as memories of summers past filled his mind.

"I miss the Hamptons," he murmured, his voice tinged with nostalgia. "There was something special about those sunsets and the peaceful moments by the water. It felt like time slowed down, just for us."

Lila nudged him playfully, a mischievous grin spreading across her face. "Oh, and don't forget how abysmal your swimming skills were before you met me. Remember when you almost drowned trying to show off?"

Caleb rolled his eyes, but the smile tugging at his lips betrayed his amusement. "Hey, I'm a lot better now, thanks to you," he said, squeezing her hand. He was grateful for how far they had come, for the lessons learned, and for the woman beside him who had taught him not just how to swim, but how to navigate the unpredictable tides of life.

Lila watched him, her eyes softening as she reflected on how much had changed since that summer. Caleb wasn't the same boy she had met all those years ago, and she wasn't the same girl. They had both grown, shaped by the experiences they had shared—their triumphs and their heartaches. Everything had worked out in the end, but not without struggles and sacrifices. Lila couldn't help but marvel at how far they had come, how they had managed to find their way back to each other despite the odds.

They settled under a beach umbrella, their hands still intertwined, as the waves lapped gently at the shore. The silence between them was comfortable, filled with the unspoken understanding that only two people who had been through everything together could share.

Caleb broke the silence, his voice thoughtful. "Now that we're engaged, have you thought about what kind of wedding you want? Big and extravagant, or something small and intimate?"

Lila shook her head, a small smile playing on her lips. "I never really had those kinds of dreams growing up," she admitted. "I wasn't the little girl who dreamed of a fairy tale wedding with a prince charming. I guess I just wanted something real, something meaningful. Honestly, I'd rather elope. Just the two of us, somewhere quiet and beautiful."

Caleb turned to her, his expression gentle. He could see the hesitation in her eyes, the way she was unsure of what the future held. He reached out, brushing a strand of hair behind her ear. "We don't have to decide anything now," he said softly. "We have time. And I'm a patient fella. Whatever you want, Lila, we'll figure it out together."

Lila's heart swelled with gratitude. Caleb had always been patient, always willing to let her take the lead when it came to their future. It was one of the many reasons she loved him. She leaned in, resting her head on his shoulder as they watched the sun dip lower in the sky.

As the golden glow of the sunset began to fade, replaced by the deepening shades of twilight, Caleb and Lila exchanged a glance of shared understanding. Without a word, they rose to their feet and ran toward the waves, the cool water rushing up to meet them as they jumped in, laughing like children. The ocean embraced them, its gentle current carrying them closer together.

In that moment, with the water surrounding them and the promise of a future together in their hearts, Caleb and Lila felt ready to face whatever came next. The journey ahead wouldn't be easy, but they had each other, and that was all they needed. Their love, tested and strengthened over time, would guide them as they followed their hearts and built a life full of possibility. And as the last rays of the sun disappeared beyond the horizon, they knew that whatever the future held, they would face it together.

ABOUT THE AUTHOR

Kathy Winslower is a gifted storyteller with a passion for weaving tales of love, resilience, and triumph. With her captivating narratives and richly drawn characters, she takes readers on unforgettable journeys that explore the depths of human emotions and the power of love to transform lives.

Born with an insatiable curiosity and a love for words, Kathy began her writing journey at a young age, filling countless notebooks with her imaginative stories. As she grew older, her passion for storytelling only deepened, leading her to pursue a career as a novelist.

Drawing inspiration from her own experiences and the world around her, Kathy's writing is characterized by its heartfelt authenticity and emotional depth. She skillfully delves into the complexities of relationships, capturing the raw and tender moments that shape her characters' lives.

When she's not immersed in her writing, Kathy can be found exploring nature, seeking inspiration from the beauty of the world around her. She believes that every moment holds the potential for a story, and it is her mission to capture those moments and share them with her readers.

www.ingramcontent.com/pod-product-compliance
Lightning Source LLC
Chambersburg PA
CBHW072036190726
48294CB00005B/1284